THE DEFIANT

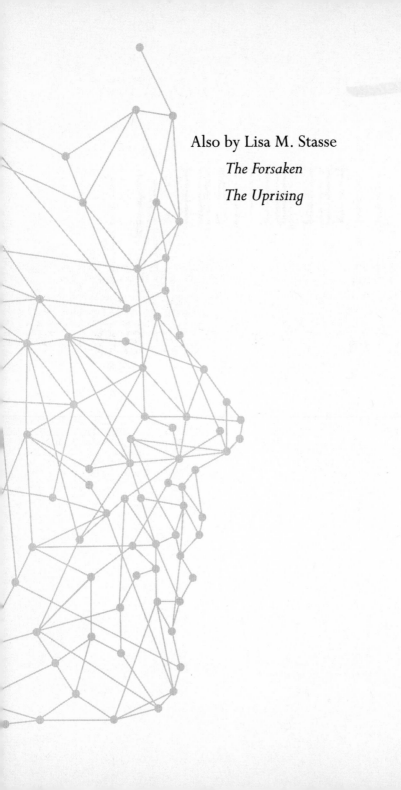

Also by Lisa M. Stasse

N TRILOGY

THE DEFIANT

Lisa M. Stasse

SIMON & SCHUSTER BFYR

NEW YORK   LONDON   TORONTO   SYDNEY   NEW DELHI

SIMON & SCHUSTER BFYR

An imprint of Simon & Schuster Children's Publishing Division
1230 Avenue of the Americas, New York, New York 10020

SIMON & SCHUSTER BFYR is a trademark of Simon & Schuster, Inc.
For information about special discounts for bulk purchases,
please contact Simon & Schuster Special Sales at 1-866-506-1949
or business@simonandschuster.com.
The Simon & Schuster Speakers Bureau can bring authors to your live event.
For more information or to book an event, contact the Simon & Schuster Speakers
Bureau at 1-866-248-3049 or visit our website at www.simonspeakers.com.
Jacket design by Lizzy Bromley
Interior design by Hilary Zarycky
The text for this book is set in Perpetua.
Manufactured in the United States of America
2 4 6 8 10 9 7 5 3 1
Library of Congress Cataloging-in-Publication Data
Stasse, Lisa M.
The defiant / Lisa Stasse. — First edition.
pages cm. — (Forsaken trilogy ; [3])
ISBN 978-1-4424-3271-0 (hardcover) — ISBN 978-1-4424-3273-4 (eBook)
[1. Revolutions—Fiction. 2. Fascism—Fiction. 3. Survival—Fiction.
4. Science fiction.] I. Title.
PZ7.S7987De 2014
[Fic]—dc23
2013031258

For Alex McAulay
for eternity

ACKNOWLEDGMENTS

THANK YOU TO MY brilliant agent, Mollie Glick, at Foundry Literary + Media. Without her advice and wisdom, the Forsaken Trilogy never would have come to life. I cannot thank her enough for all of her help and encouragement, and I am extremely grateful to her. Big thanks also to Rachel Hecht, Kathleen Hamblin, Hannah Brown Gordon, Stéphanie Abou, and the entire team at Foundry, as well as Shari Smiley at Resolution.

Gigantic thanks to my fantastic editor, Zareen Jaffery at Simon & Schuster. She helped shape this incredible journey, and gave me great notes and edits. Working with her is always a lot of fun. Thanks also to Julia Maguire, Lydia Finn, Lucille Rettino, Michelle Fadlalla, Venessa Carson, Dawn Ryan, Bernadette Cruz, Kelly Stidham, Sooji Kim, Mara Anastas, Brian Kelleher, Justin Chanda, Jon Anderson, and everyone else at Simon & Schuster. Thanks to Lizzy Bromley too, for the great cover designs!

I'd also like to thank the many librarians, booksellers, and readers that I've met along the way. Thank you for your dedication, passion, and friendship.

As always, much love and thanks to my family and friends—especially my husband, Alex McAulay, who has been with me every step of the way.

1 THE CRUCIBLE

A VOICE WHISPERS MY name: "Alenna."

I try to respond, but I can't. Besides, I don't even know if the voice is real. It's probably an auditory hallucination.

I have no senses. I can't see, hear, taste, or smell. I can't feel anything. And all around me is darkness. Blacker than any night you could imagine. I am totally disconnected from my flesh. My senses have been stripped away, like bark from a tree. My nerves are deadened, and I don't feel hunger or thirst.

I could have been like this for hours, or weeks, or months. Sometimes I sleep, and sometimes I'm awake. It's hard to tell the difference.

Often I want to scream. Other times, I want to break down and cry. But I am capable of neither.

I have no memory of how I ended up here, but I know that one of two things must have happened. Either I got captured somehow and placed in some sort of isolation pod, or else I died and now I'm stuck in limbo. It's worse than anything else I've ever experienced.

Over and over, I try to figure out the last memory I have before everything went black. It's a memory of a few weeks after we liberated everyone on Prison Island Alpha, the place also known as "the wheel." The specimen archive—where the captured kids were being held in stasis—was destroyed along with the flying machines known as "feelers," and we retook the island.

Most of the brainwashed drones converted to our side, once their minds were free of the government chemicals. Some didn't, and they formed guerilla groups in the forest that would attack us every night.

But even those attacks started dying down. Our plan was going well. Island Alpha was becoming our new home base, just like we intended. The different tribes on the island—the rebels, the scientists, and the travelers—were working together to turn the island into our staging ground for our assault on the continental United Northern Alliance, better known as the UNA.

But obviously something went wrong. *Was I captured and poisoned by rogue drones?* Maybe I hit my head, or was given some kind of drug along the way. My memory is so fuzzy. Trying to think about things too hard makes my head hurt, like looking through glasses with the wrong prescription.

The last thing I remember is helping build a cabin with my boyfriend, Liam, as we were working on a team constructing a new fortified village on the island. Liam and I were laughing and playing around. Things were good. I felt safe—for once.

My only lingering sadness was over David's death. David was the boy whom I'd woken up with the first day I'd gotten banished to Island Alpha by the UNA. He sacrificed himself by destroying the cooling core of the specimen archive, which halted the government machinery running the wheel. He did it so that the rest of us could live. And also so that the kids who were frozen in the specimen archive could survive. I still thought about him every night before I slept, and he appeared sometimes in my dreams. Often we were lost in the forest on Island Alpha together, on a dark hidden trail, and he was beckoning for me to follow him deeper into the darkness. Sometimes I would wake up crying.

I hid these dreams from Liam. I don't know why. Maybe I didn't want him to know how strong my feelings for David were. Maybe I didn't even realize how strong they were myself, until after David was gone. I was still sorting out my feelings, more than two months after his death. David and I shared a deep connection. When he died, it felt like I lost a piece of myself.

I will never know exactly how David felt about me. I suspect that he liked me more than he ever let on. His final words to me—"Keep me in your thoughts, Alenna"—linger in my mind. I keep wishing that we had done things differently, and that David was still alive.

Other than David, my other friends survived our massive battle with the army of drones. Liam, Gadya, Rika, and I found Cass and Emma alive but injured after the assault on the elevated highway. Both of them were still recovering but doing well.

I try to think past that final memory of me and Liam working in the village together, but there is only blackness. I'm suffering some form of amnesia.

I remember that our attack on the continental UNA was several months away. For once, I had felt so peaceful. It had seemed like we were free from worry—at least for a while. *Did someone attack us on that day?*

The final image in my head is that of Liam's smiling face gazing at me. After that there is nothing. No matter how hard I try, I can't bring any more memories to my mind.

Then, out of nowhere, I hear more voices crackling in my ear, saying my name. They are too loud and sharp to be imaginary.

"It's time to bring her up," a voice says.

"Alenna? Can you hear us?" another one asks.

"Say something if you're still sane in there!" the first voice commands.

The voices are familiar. Oddly reassuring. I realize that I must be wearing an earpiece. *Am I back in the UNA?* I try to touch my ear but I can't feel anything, not even my own hands.

Yes, I can hear you, I struggle to answer. But I can't speak. Then I try to say it again, and this time, I hear the words crackling back at me in my ear. My hearing is returning. "What happened? Where am I?"

"Hang on," another voice calls out. It's a girl. I recognize her voice at once. *Gadya.* She's one of my closest friends.

"Gadya?" I ask, confused. But as soon as I say her name, I feel a strong tugging sensation on my arms and legs. Other senses are returning. I'm floating in thick, warm liquid. And the substance around me is flowing and shifting, like a slow-moving river.

It startles me to feel any sensation. I must be in some kind of sensory deprivation chamber. I feel relieved to still be alive, but very confused about where I am—and why I got put here.

My sense of direction is skewed. I can't tell what is up, and what is down. Only that I'm finally moving.

My arms and legs start to throb, and my head begins pulsing. I'm being pulled up through the jelly-like liquid. It reminds me of the material that the barrier around the gray zone was built from. I struggle to kick and move my arms. I thrash and flail, and this time I can feel the motion. All my senses are returning at once, and they make my body ache. I see a circle of light appear directly above me. Shimmering and fluctuating. Growing larger as I'm pulled upward.

4

"Hey! What's going on?" I call out.

I feel wires tugging and pinching my flesh, like intravenous tubes. They feel like they're going to rip right out of my skin.

I cry out in pain.

"It's okay! Stay calm! You're doing great," I hear Gadya's voice say in my earpiece. "Don't mess up now!"

"Mess what up?" I ask, confused.

Air bubbles burst around me in the oily liquid. I realize there's a tube in my nose. I try to yank it out, but it hurts too much. I taste copper and realize that I'm bleeding.

I keep moving, wrestling with the tubes sticking into my body. I feel restraints and wires pulling away from me, setting me free.

And then I'm pulled out of the fluid and into harsh white sunlight. I yell in pain, as tubes whip out of my flesh one by one.

I'm in a bamboo hammock attached to a small metal crane. It's carrying my body up through a large metal hatch in the top of a giant isolation tank, and over to a stone walkway in a jungle clearing. *I must be on Island Alpha.* Rows of other isolation tanks sit next to the one that I was inside, monitored by scientists in white lab coats.

There is no sign of Gadya or my other friends. And my memory hasn't come back either.

The fresh air flays my skin. Every nerve feels like it's burning, as though I've been tossed onto a funeral pyre. The light is so bright, I can't even hold my eyes open. I clench them shut. Even with them closed, it's too bright for me. I see a burning red color on the inside of my eyelids.

"Gadya?" I call out, as I struggle to orient myself on the hammock. I put a hand to my ear and try to adjust the earpiece. "Where are you?"

"Right here."

"Where?"

"Watching you on a monitor."

I try to put the pieces together. I gasp for air. I feel like a fish from the river, thrown onto a rock and tortured by small children. I'm dressed only in my underwear.

"Stop flailing!" Gadya yells into my earpiece, her voice distorting. "Or else they'll fail you!"

"Quit helping her," another voice grouses faintly in my earpiece. "She has to do this on her own. If she fails, she fails."

"You mean like you did, Cass?" I hear Gadya retort.

Cass. Another friend. One whom I met at Destiny Station in Australia, when Liam and I first escaped from the wheel.

"I didn't fail the test!" Cass snaps back. "I was disqualified due to my injuries! There's a difference."

Their voices are loud and crackly in my earpiece. "Stop arguing!" I yell at them. "My head hurts!" *What test are they talking about?*

I finally manage to get my eyes to open again, into narrow slits. The crane is bringing my hammock to the ground. I keep shifting and writhing. It feels like my body has to keep moving, like I have insects under my skin, crawling around. I finally get deposited on cold stones. I curl up. Everything is throbbing.

"Surfacing is hard. But you need to stay calm," Gadya says. I adjust my earpiece to hear her voice better. "The scientists are judging you right now."

I take deep, shuddering breaths of air, lying on my side on the stone. I never realized how thin and cool fresh air felt before.

Suddenly a shadow falls over me. Startled, I try to get up, but my body feels too weak. Then I realize the shadow belongs to one of the scientists.

"How are you feeling, Alenna?" the scientist asks briskly. He's holding a gray T-shirt, jeans, and a pair of combat boots.

"Pissed off," I say. "Everything hurts!"

The scientist tosses the clothes and boots onto the ground in front of me. Then he checks my pupils with a small, piercing light. "Good," he says approvingly. "You're ready for the next phase of your test. Take out your earpiece and give it to me. Then get dressed."

"No," I tell him, as I struggle into the jeans and T-shirt. The earpiece is the lifeline to my friends.

"It's okay," Gadya says in my ear. She can hear our conversation. "Don't worry about it. You'll see us soon."

"Are you sure?" I'm scanning the jungle for them. There's no sign of anyone but the scientists.

"I'm certain of it."

"The next phase of the test involves physical combat," the scientist says with a sigh. "The earpiece might get broken, and we don't have many of them to spare. Give it to me."

Slowly, I raise a hand and pull out the earpiece. It's still glistening with fluid from the isolation tank. The scientist takes it from me. Then he closes the isolation tank and locks it.

I'm incredibly thirsty. My mouth and throat are burning and dry.

"How about some water?" I ask.

"Not yet."

"Why not?" I ask. "Where are my friends? And what's going on? What is this next phase exactly?"

He frowns. "You don't remember yet?"

"No. . . ." But as I say the word, memories start coming back to me in a rush. "This is some kind of test to figure out which ones of us can handle getting sent back to the UNA . . . which

7

ones of us can handle being tortured. I'm right, aren't I?"

The scientist nods. "We put a tiny dose of a natural neurotoxin in the IV tubes. It's meant to blank out your mind for a while, and affect your short-term and long-term memory, like a strong sedative. Don't worry. You'll get your memories back."

"Why did you do it?"

"To see how you handle the stress, mentally and physically. These isolation tanks were discovered on the island, and we reconditioned them. The UNA uses torture tactics like this to break any dissidents. They use drugs and isolation to get rebels to give up confidential information. Isolation can be a much more effective form of torture than pain." The scientist glances at the tanks. "You were in one of them for seventy-two hours."

"It felt longer."

He kneels down to spray with iodine the cuts where the tubes came out of me, and he gives me small bandages to put on them. "Just imagine being in one of those things for a month or two. The tubes keep your body running, but without any stimuli, the human brain can go crazy. We had to know if you could deal with it. Most kids can't. Not even seventy-two hours. We pull them out early." He stands up again.

I get to my feet too, legs shaking. I slowly put the boots on.

"You said that the next phase is physical. I have to fight someone, don't I?"

"In a sense." The scientist starts walking away from me. "I can't say too much, or it will interfere with the test results."

Memories are flooding back now in a vivid rush. Only a few kids will be getting sent back to the UNA. Only the ones who are strongest, mentally and physically. My stomach lurches. Liam and I helped design this test, along with the scientists and the travelers. *How could I forget such a thing?* We wanted to make sure the test was as harsh and brutal as possible. But I didn't think it would be this bad. I wipe residual slime out of my eyes.

"Hey!" I call out to the retreating scientist.

He pauses. "Yes?"

"How long is this going to take?"

"That part is up to you." He starts walking again, disappearing into the jungle. The trees close around him. I realize the other scientists have left too.

I am alone.

I stand there, checking myself for weapons. But I have nothing. Just my clothes and boots. I look around for something to use as a weapon. I don't want to get caught off guard. I also don't want to fight with my fists unless I have to. I know that whoever attacks me will probably be armed in some way.

My memories aren't perfect yet, but I remember that for this phase of the test, I will be expected to fight and disarm an opponent within a limited period of time.

I scan the jungle in every direction around the clearing. Everything is completely silent and still. I wonder if I can use the crane as a weapon somehow, but it's too high up. Then I see a thick tree branch, like a baseball bat, lying nearby. I rush over and grab it, spinning around in case someone comes up from behind. But nobody does. I stand there, clutching the branch.

"Come on then!" I yell into the forest. "What are you waiting for?"

I don't feel too afraid anymore. I know this is just a test now. My opponent will probably be someone I know, or maybe some other kid from the archives, stepping out of the trees to frighten me.

After the battles that I've been through, I'm pretty sure I can take whoever it is, or at least give them a good fight. *Besides, the worst that can happen is that I fail the test.*

But more memories keep coming back, including one of Liam and me talking about the test. I'm sure that he'll pass it, if he hasn't already, and will be headed back to the UNA. So if I fail, I might get separated from him again, and left behind on Island Alpha. I can't let that happen.

I look around more urgently. "Hurry up!" I yell. My voice is hoarse from my time in the isolation tank. "I'm ready for you now!"

The scientists must be watching me. I look for cameras in the trees, but I don't see them. I know that they are there. I have to do well and impress everyone, and show them that I'm capable of fighting hard, so that I can travel back to the UNA with Liam.

Initially, I had expected that everyone on the wheel would travel back to the UNA as a massive army and fight the government soldiers there. I thought that the scientists would create new weapons out of the feelers, or other materials on the island, and build ships to take us back to the UNA in an armada. But I was wrong about their plans.

The scientists only revealed their true strategy after the island was brought under control. According to them, sending everyone back at once would be too dangerous. We can't afford to lose any major battles. So instead, the scientists will only be sending back a select number of kids, a group at a time, who will be given safe haven by the rebel cells already existing in the UNA.

Our plan is to work with the rebel cells, and use our knowledge to help them bring down the UNA from the inside and jump-start a civil revolution. It turned out that the scientists have been in contact with the rebels inside the UNA for years. They believe the most effective way to destroy the UNA is to slowly dismantle it from within.

The power structure of the UNA is decentralized. We know that Minister Harka is just a figurehead. There is no prime person or location that we can find and easily attack. We must simply get the citizens to rise up against the soldiers and use their sheer numbers to overcome the government in every city and every town. That is our first and only order of business. Many lives will be lost, but the sacrifice will be worth it. Or so all the scientists and rebels hope.

After the citizens have stormed all the UNA headquarters and defeated the soldiers, a plan is in place for the European Coalition to swiftly move in and help us rebels rebuild, before chaos takes hold. The planet cannot bear the UNA's tyranny any longer, so the European Coalition is eager to give us aid. The UNA is fighting eight different countries at the moment, and they will never stop. The rest of the world can't tolerate its madness any longer.

This plan makes me nervous, especially the first part. I don't know if I'm cut out to be an enemy spy in a rebel cell. I was never in a resistance cell before being sent to the wheel, unlike David and Cass. I am used to battles and fighting, but not hiding and plotting. Those are different skills. Will I be able to urge the citizens to rise up? I'm not sure.

I also don't know if we can trust the European Coalition, although from what I've heard, they are a fair and relatively peaceful alliance of nations that do not subject their citizens to the violence and atrocities that the UNA does. They will supposedly help us reconstruct the nation, and help us put a new democratic form of government in place. Then, once the UNA is self-sufficient again, they will allow us to be a free and independent nation once more. Perhaps we will even be able to split back up into Canada, the United States, and Mexico, if the citizens so choose.

My thoughts are interrupted when I hear a noise from the trees. It's the sound of footsteps crackling on twigs in the forest. I spin toward the source of the sound. My fingers clench on my tree branch. I crouch low into a fighting stance.

I remember the shy, timid girl I once was. Before I got sent to Island Alpha, and before I met Liam and Gadya. Now I am no longer scared and weak. I am a warrior, tested by many battles.

"Let's do this!" I yell, banging my tree branch on the ground.

I expect whoever it is to yell something back, but instead I just hear a weird growling noise. Maybe the person is trying to scare me, but it's not going to work.

I keep hearing the branches crackle and the leaves rustle.

And then a figure steps into view.

I take a step back.

It is not some villager or rehabilitated drone here to fight me. Instead, it's a huge lumbering boy, his eyes glazed and his body rippled with muscles and weeping sores. He has a shaved head and homemade tattoos all over his chest.

He must be one of the drones that the scientists couldn't save. One of the crazy ones who lived down in the tunnels near the control center. Poisoned by UNA drugs. Banished there by Meira—the onetime leader of the drone army.

I feel a chill. I can't believe this is part of the scientists' test. Those kids were violent semi-mutants. Almost like wild animals. This boy could kill me. I'm shocked the scientists would do this to anyone. I definitely don't remember this element being part of the test. I even wonder if I've been set up, and this is some kind of attempt to murder me.

I watch the deranged boy, and I try to stay calm. My branch is tight in my hands.

He pivots his crazed eyes in my direction. He opens his mouth and growls again. His fingernails are like jagged, serrated knives. His teeth are filed into points. In the sunlight, his flesh looks gray and rotting. He takes a step toward me.

At least he doesn't have any weapons, I think. And although he's huge, he's clumsy and clearly demented. As long as I'm careful, I should be able to hit him on the head and knock him down and out. That should be enough to complete the test.

But then I hear another sound behind me. I turn around. A second mutant boy is stepping out from the trees. He's missing some fingers, and he has livid red scars on his face. But the edges of his mouth are turned up into a brutal sneer. His blue eyes, mottled with red around the edges, are fixed directly on me.

I hear more noises. I don't know how many of these crazed kids are out here with me, but I know that I'm going to get killed unless I do something. My heart starts pounding. I consider running away, but I imagine that then I would fail the test.

So I decide to fight.

I lunge forward at the first boy and strike him as hard as I can with my tree branch, right across the chest. He doesn't show any sign of pain.

He swings out one of his meaty fists. He's slow, and I duck.

Right then I hear the boy behind me approaching. I swing around with a yell, kicking outward, and catching him off guard. My right foot plows into his kneecap. He stumbles back, startled, nearly staggering to the ground. I rush forward and kick him in the knee again. He screams in agony.

My boot stamps down over and over, trying to dislocate his

kneecap. I have to disable him or he will kill me. I feel bone and cartilage crunching under my boot. Now he's sobbing and gripping his knee. I spin around.

Two more boys lumber out of the trees. They both have chiseled teeth and rabid looks in their eyes. *I can't believe the scientists are doing this to me.* Is this what the test was like for everyone? How did Gadya pass it? Or anyone else?

The first boy approaches again. I lash out with my tree branch, whipping it across his face this time. He cries out in pain and his hands press against his eyes. I turn around, prepared to fight the other two boys.

I pick the smallest one and run toward him with my branch upraised. I swing it as he tries to claw at me with his ragged fingernails. Suddenly, he grabs hold of the branch and whips it out of my hands, tearing the skin of my palms.

I leap back, raising my hands into fists.

And then I feel strong hands gripping me around the waist. I cry out in surprise. I can feel the hot breath of one of these awful drones on the back of my neck. I kick back with my foot, trying to hit him in the crotch, but missing.

"Get off me!" I yell.

Teeth gouge my shoulder, and I realize that he's trying to bite me. These drones are primitive animals. They use teeth and claws to fight. I feel his teeth pierce my skin like a row of knives.

Scared and horrified, I kick back again, finally slamming my heel into his crotch. He releases his teeth as he cries out. I slip out of his grasp.

But the drone who grabbed my tree branch is fast approaching, holding it in one hand. His eyes are blank, as though his mind has been fried.

I want to run again. The odds are against me. But I know that I can't.

So instead, I race toward the boy with a savage yell. He raises the branch, but I plow into his chest with my shoulder. He tumbles backward with me on top of him.

The branch crashes down across my back and I cry out. He arches his head back as he struggles to get up. I realize this is my one chance. I slam my right fist into his throat as hard as I can, connecting directly with his Adam's apple. He chokes and shudders. I can't relent even for a second.

I hit him again, savagely crushing his windpipe. He gasps for air. I roll sideways as the drone who bit me lashes out with his hand, his fingernails slicing my forearm.

I stagger to my feet. The second drone is still lying on the ground clutching his knee. The drone I hit in the throat continues to gasp for breath, flailing wildly on the grass. I stare at the two remaining drones. The one I hit in the face is bleeding from both eyes.

He opens his mouth and hisses at me, revealing a tongue that has been deliberately sliced in two. The drones do this to themselves, as part of a twisted ritual.

"You don't scare me!" I yell. I see a nearby rock, the size of my fist, and I rush forward and pick it up. The drones are both watching me. I can feel their desire for my flesh.

I stand there glaring back. I don't know when the test will end. Probably when I've defeated all the drones. Maybe even killed them. *But is that even possible?* It's four against one. The one I kicked in the knee is already trying to get up again.

I'm about to run forward and attack the two drones who are still standing, when the one I hit in the crotch suddenly pulls a large knife out from the back of his waistband.

I'm startled.

The blade glints in the sunlight.

He grins at me, his eyes burning with madness. His mouth tries to form words, but he can't speak. His mind has been affected by the UNA drugs. It's rotting from the inside out. But he can still kill. Those primitive impulses clearly remain intact.

He races forward with his blade outstretched. I can't get away in time. He crashes into me, swinging his arm back to stab me. The blade flies forward. I barely dodge the blow. The knife plunges deep into the grass as he grunts.

Without a second to spare, I slam my rock against his fingers as hard as I can. I hear bones breaking. He yelps and snatches his hand back. And for a second, the knife is left embedded in the earth.

I grab the handle and use my weight to pull it out of the ground as I roll sideways. I get to my feet, panting. The drone is clutching his hand. Blood is dripping from it. He and the other drone stare at the knife in my hand.

I begin advancing on them, holding the knife with the tip pointed downward, so I can slice up at them with my full strength if they approach. The drones don't look scared or worried. They look angry and demented.

I glance behind me and see the two other drones still on the ground. The one I punched in the throat is barely breathing. I doubt he's going to survive. The other drone can't stand up because his knee keeps giving out.

I turn back and continue toward the two remaining drones. They split up, moving sideways, one to my right and one to my left, so they will be harder to attack. I crouch low with my knife, ready to slice whichever one comes my way.

The boy with the injured hand makes the first move. He lunges toward me unexpectedly. I swing my knife up right before he hits me. The blade slides upward and over his chest and neck, cutting through his skin. He screams so loudly that it temporarily deafens me. Then his elbow crashes against my jaw. My vision sparkles for a moment. I kick against his clawing, bleeding body.

I scream as someone starts pulling my hair. It's the other drone. He has run forward, taken a fistful of my hair in his hand, and knotted it around his fingers.

I lash out with my knife and try to cut his hand, but he moves out of the way. I scream again as he pulls my hair. I can't find his hand anymore. So instead I use the knife to slash off part of my hair. I get free.

The boy staggers back, off balance, holding my hair in his hand. Then I slam the knife into the back of the drone who is bleeding on top of me.

He doesn't scream. He just slams my head again violently with his elbow. I stab him again and again in the back, as I kick against his body. He keeps forcing me against the ground. I don't feel any pain, just numbness and shock. *This can't be the test—something must have gone wrong.* I'm going to die here.

Then the boy is off me. I scrabble away across the grass. I glance back and see him convulsing there. The ground is soaked with his blood from multiple knife wounds.

Only one drone is standing. The one who pulled my hair. He looks uncertain, now that his fellow drones are dying or injured.

I feel exhausted and terrified. I grip my bloody knife. I just want this to be over.

"Come on!" I try to yell, but the words come out like a broken whisper. My whole body feels bruised and battered.

The drone keeps watching me. He is like a beast of prey. But even beasts of prey know when the odds are against them. I see his eyes pivot to take in the bloody bodies of his companions, writhing on the ground.

I raise my knife higher. My arm is shaking, and I try to keep it steady. I know that I cannot show any fear.

The drone bares his teeth at me. I prepare myself for the onslaught.

But then, startling me, he turns around and starts loping toward the jungle. It takes me a second to realize what is happening. He is running away.

Should I give chase? I can't believe the test has been allowed to go on for this long. Or be this brutal. I'm covered with wounds.

The drone is near the edge of the forest. Soon he'll be out of view.

I'm trying to decide what to do—when suddenly an arrow flies out of the trees and strikes him through the back. The drone keels over, dead. He didn't even have time to scream.

I just stand there, the knife in my hand.

A second passes. Then another. The injured drones around me are struggling on the ground, but none of them poses a threat.

I drop my knife. It tumbles to the grass. I refuse to kill them if they're no longer a danger to me. If killing is what the test requires, then I've done enough of it.

I glance around, looking for the hidden cameras again. "I'm done!" I yell. "The test is over."

"It sure is!" an excited voice calls out. A girl emerges from the trees nearby, clutching her bow and arrow.

"Gadya?" I ask, confused but relieved to see her. She looks the same as always: a tangled mess of blue hair, homemade piercings, tattoos, and haunted dark eyes.

She rushes over and hugs me hard, slinging the bow and arrow behind her.

"You made it!" she says into my ear. "I knew you would!"

"*I* didn't!"

I see Cass emerge from the trees behind her, lithe and poised, also holding a bow and arrow. Cass is frowning. She runs a hand over her short black hair. Her brown skin looks luminous in the sunlight.

"You got lucky," Cass mutters when she reaches us. "I had tougher mutants to fight." But she hugs me too.

Other kids step out from behind Gadya and Cass, and guard us from the injured drones.

I realize that I'm shaking. "I could have been killed," I tell Gadya. "I barely made it!"

"Naw," she says. "We had bows and guns trained on the drones the whole time. If any of 'em got close to killing you, we would have shot them first." She pauses. "But then you would have failed the test."

I take a deep breath.

"Nice job making that drone run away," Cass adds, somewhat grudgingly. "Impressive work."

I feel sick to my stomach. I wonder what will happen to the injured drones. Will they be killed, or will they be used to fight someone else? The one with the crushed larynx is unconscious. I can't believe the scientists are treating them this way. As though they aren't even human.

"Did you know it would be crazy drones?" I ask Gadya and Cass. They shake their heads.

"No," Gadya says. "That was a surprise from the scientists. To shake things up and make the test harder and less predictable for us."

I nod. I know that each of these insane drones was once normal. Just like me. But the UNA drugs affected them differently and turned them into monsters. It's only luck and genetics that prevented me from such awful mutations.

"Where's Liam?" I ask Gadya.

Gadya rolls her eyes. "You should be celebrating that you passed the test. You're going to the UNA with me! Quit worrying about Liam."

"I'm not worrying. I just want to know."

"He's in a mandatory strategy session with some hunters. He'll be out in a few minutes."

I nod. I see scientists now at the edges of the trees. They put shackles on the injured and dying drones and drag them away. The drones struggle, but the scientists keep them under control.

"I need some water," I tell Gadya, exhausted. "And I need to get cleaned up." I glance down at my clothes. They are covered with sweat and blood. I stink from the battle.

Gadya nods. "Come with me. I'll help you find something fresh to wear." We start heading away from the testing ground and back into the main camp, along with Cass.

I passed the test. I will be leaving this island and going back to the UNA with Liam and Gadya.

I look down at my hands. Today I killed someone, almost on instinct. My hands are shaking, so I jam them into my pockets. I must prepare myself to fight and win battles more intense than this one. My future depends on it. I can't afford to feel afraid.

2 RETURNING

Three Weeks Later

TODAY IS THE DAY when we begin the journey back to the UNA. Of all the kids and scientists, only a small number of us have managed to pass the brutal test. Some didn't even bother taking it because they knew they would fail, or they let their fear overwhelm them. But more than half of the entire population of the island volunteered to try, even if most of them never got past the isolation tanks.

I sit next to Liam and Gadya in a giant wooden meeting hall constructed from oak beams, with a thatched roof. It's just us and a group of fifty other kids. The ones who have passed the test. Dr. Vargas-Ruiz, the head scientist and one of the leaders of our colony, stands in front of us.

"I just want to review the strategy with you one last time, before you return to the UNA," she says.

"Boring," Gadya mutters, but I shush her. While we've heard the plan before, and gone over it in great detail, I want to hear what Dr. Vargas-Ruiz says.

"As you know, five small airplanes will be taking you back to the UNA today, each one covered with radar-resistant material," she says. "Each plane will be carrying ten to twelve people, along with two pilots."

I glance around at the kids. I wish more people were going with us.

"Once you arrive in the UNA, each of you will be sheltered by different rebel cells. They have already prepared for your arrival. You will share your knowledge with these rebels, and travel with them to different areas of the nation." She gazes around at us. "You are symbols that the UNA can be defeated. The rebels must grow their numbers. Your presence will encourage them to do that, and give them heroes to believe in. Many civilians want to fight the UNA, but they are afraid. You need to share your stories and information with them. You are pioneers. You must help the rebel cells find more recruits and coordinate the cells."

"Are you sure this will work?" Liam asks.

"Yes. We are laying the groundwork for a revolution. A civil revolt, where the people overthrow the government. The people outnumber the UNA guards a hundred to one. Most successful revolutions come from within. You know that."

"And after the revolution?" another rebel in our group asks. "Tell us the plan again. I want to know that risking my neck is worth it!"

"Once the citizens rise up and bring down the government, more scientists will come over and help set up a new provisional government, in conjunction with the European Coalition. The goal is to ultimately create a new democracy, and hold fair elections. We have no plans to hold on to power like dictators. The people need to choose their own leaders. We will help guide them onto that path, until the UNA is a free country once again. We will also work to distribute food and medical supplies, and to keep the infrastructure running as best we can." She pauses. We're all staring at her. "I'm not saying that any of this is going to be easy. There will be spies to root out, and pockets of government resistance to combat. But I believe that once the citizens know the truth, and hear your stories, and learn about the existence of the rebel cells, they will no longer be satisfied to live under the UNA's tyranny."

"I hope she's right," Gadya mutters.

"Me too," I reply. I feel a knot in my stomach. I reach for Liam's hand, and I squeeze it. He squeezes it back.

"Now let's go see everyone else," Dr. Vargas-Ruiz says. "It's time." We all stand up and follow her out of the meeting hall and up a wide dirt pathway. I glance around. The other kids look nervous, but also determined. We keep walking.

Our path leads to a huge cleared area in the forest where many of the other inhabitants of Island Alpha are waiting for us, along with the airplanes that will take us back to the continental UNA.

We walk onto a raised wooden platform, a foot off the ground. I stand between Liam and Gadya. The other kids who are going back to the UNA follow. To our left is a homemade dirt runway.

Many of our friends didn't pass the test, like Cass—mostly because they were hampered by old injuries. Alun was automatically disqualified because he only has one good eye. And Rika and Emma refused to take the test because they are avowed pacifists and don't want to fight anyone. I respect that stance. I used to be just like them until I was forced to become someone different.

But I wish they were traveling with us. I grew to depend on their various skills, and I trust them with my life. From our group of friends, it will only be me, Liam, and Gadya moving forward and being sent back to the UNA.

Of course, that's just in the first wave. There will be another wave after we have established ourselves within the rebel cells. Cass is going to train for the next round, and I hope that she makes the cut. She's already learning how to compensate for her injuries.

Nearly everyone is gathered here today to wish us good luck. It's a massive crowd.

My mother—who is one of the scientists running Island Alpha—will be staying here on the island. Not because she wants to stay, but because she is so recognizable to the UNA government. That makes her a high-value target for them. If she came back with us and got captured, the UNA soldiers would use any methods possible to extract information from her. She knows too much to take that risk.

The same is true of Dr. Vargas-Ruiz and the other head scientists. They must stay behind so they don't jeopardize our entire mission. That is one of the reasons they are sending kids like me, Liam, and Gadya back to the UNA first. We are not as recognizable to the UNA's facial recognition technologies, and we know far fewer secrets than the scientists do. All we know is the plan: work with the rebels and help them engineer a civil revolt from within the UNA. If we get caught and interrogated, we will have much less information to give away than some of these older scientists.

I know that many of the adults—such as the airplane pilots who will be flying us back to the UNA—have been given cyanide capsules to take, in case they are captured. When Liam and I asked Dr. Vargas-Ruiz a few days ago why they didn't tell us more information, and then just give us cyanide capsules to carry as well, she said she was afraid that some kids would get scared and not take them.

"But some of the adults might get scared and not take them too," I pointed out.

Dr. Vargas-Ruiz looked at me and said, "I agree. But there's no way we could authorize giving cyanide capsules to teenagers. That would make us just as bad as the UNA."

"But you're asking us to risk our lives for the cause anyway," Liam told her. "How is it any different?"

"It just is," she said, without further explanation. "Besides, you know everything you need to know to complete your mission successfully."

I'm still not fully satisfied. But I know that once I get integrated into a rebel cell, I will do my best to bring down the UNA.

The crowd in front of us suddenly starts quieting down. Dr. Vargas-Ruiz steps out from the throng. She adjusts her glasses and pushes back a wayward strand of frizzy gray hair. She's about to give an official speech. I have already said my good-byes to my mom in private, and to Rika and Cass, and all my other friends who are staying behind. I can't let myself think too much about what it means to leave them, or else I'm afraid I'll break down. I have to keep moving forward or else I will fall apart.

The relationship between me and my mom is still evolving. For years I thought I was an orphan, so I am still adjusting to her presence in my life again. Being together like this on Island Alpha has given us a chance to reconnect.

When I told my mom it was thoughts of her and my dad that had kept me going when I was sent to the wheel, she said that I'd served the same purpose for her.

"One of the reasons I fought so hard for everyone's freedom is so that you could know what it felt like to grow up in a free world, instead of in the UNA," she told me one day. "You deserve that. Everyone does."

I wish she were here right now. But she's hard at work

synthesizing DNA in a makeshift lab. Her absence would have upset me a few months ago, and made me feel like she didn't care about me. But now I know that sometimes she hides behind her work for a reason.

Strong emotions tend to make her feel vulnerable, so she walls off her heart. It was like that when I was younger—my dad was the one I was closest to. So I know that the real reason she isn't here to see me leave is because it would upset her too much. As one of the leaders of our rebel colony, she must keep her feelings in check.

Liam touches my arm. "Look."

"What?" I ask.

"It's about to start."

I see Dr. Vargas-Ruiz adjust the microphone.

"Today is the day!" she calls out, wasting no time on opening remarks. Her voice is loud through amplified speakers. "The revolution to reclaim our country begins here and now!" The crowd murmurs with excited anticipation. Liam takes my hand.

"We've been waiting years for this day," Dr. Vargas-Ruiz continues. She turns to look at us. "You are our only chance at establishing a new society in the UNA and stopping the government's tyranny. We will fly you there. And drop you down in the heart of the UNA behind enemy lines." She pauses, brushing away a drop of sweat. "But in the end, no matter what we do to help you, this journey is one that you must complete alone. Nobody else is going to help you. Your fate, and the fate of the UNA, is in your own hands. The rebel cells will take action. But they need your leadership and knowledge. You will give them strength. And after you, we will send a second wave, and a third and a fourth. Eventually this island will be abandoned and we will all be back home, setting up a new government."

She turns back to look at the crowd. I see Cass and Emma standing there watching us. Dr. Vargas-Ruiz starts talking again.

"These kids are your hope too," she tells the crowd. "While they are gone, we must keep order here, so that we're prepared to return to the UNA, and help rebuild it. I know that these chosen ones will succeed."

Some kids in the crowd cheer and applaud. Others just watch us calmly. I can't tell if they wish they were going too, or if they are glad that we're leaving instead of them.

"We will win, no matter what the cost," Dr. Vargas-Ruiz continues.

A few voices in the crowd rise up to support her, repeating her words: "No matter what the cost!" More voices pick up the cry. Some of the kids bang their spears and arrows against the rocks, creating a cacophony.

"If all goes well, we will ultimately liberate the UNA. Now is our time of victory!" she calls out. It's the first time I've heard her so emotional and intense. Usually she is cold and remote. But not today.

People are clapping and cheering, but I know that these are just empty gestures. We could fail just as easily as we could succeed. I have heard such speeches before, and they often preceded times of terrible chaos and war. I hope Dr. Vargas-Ruiz is right, but there is no guarantee.

The noise of the crowd is interrupted by a loud wailing noise. It's a keening, tortured sound. For a second I think it's a hoofer— one of those genetically engineered animals that roam the island and provide a source of food for us, like a cross between a boar and a hyena.

When I see the source of the sound, I flinch.

The wailing is coming from a man, not an animal. He's standing up high on a pile of jagged granite rocks, off to the side of our gathering. He's shirtless, covered in filth and mud, his white beard and hair making him look like a deranged prophet. His hands grip a long piece of copper electrical wiring that he's found somewhere.

This man is Dr. Barrett.

The crowd falls silent.

Dr. Barrett will not be coming back to the UNA with us. He may have recovered physically from the brutal injuries he sustained at the hands of Meira and the drones, but he has not recovered mentally. The scientists believe Meira gave him some kind of drug to permanently alter his mind. Most of what he says doesn't make any sense. He is a sad and shambling broken man who is no longer in control of his own thoughts.

At first, after we liberated the wheel and rescued him, he was violent, and his own guards from Southern Arc kept him confined in a wooden shack. They took turns watching him. Eventually he calmed down, and they released him. But his sanity didn't return. Now he roams the island freely, often talking to himself. His face bears the circular scars of the metal torture mask that Meira forced him to wear. He is like a ghost of himself.

At times I've caught glimpses of him through the trees, his sagging, scarred white flesh visible through the verdant foliage. I usually look away, not wanting his eyes to catch mine. He is proof of what the UNA can do to a person. He was once a charismatic leader, but now he has lost his mind.

Dr. Barrett wails again, tilting his head back to cry out at the blue sky. Flecks of foam hang on his beard at the corners of his mouth.

"Not him again," Gadya mutters.

Two of Dr. Barrett's former guards from Southern Arc start heading in his direction, to restrain him.

"Someone take care of Dr. Barrett, please," Dr. Vargas-Ruiz says softly. We keep watching. "Help him."

Usually Dr. Barrett is in his own world, and doesn't respond to what people say or do. At least not in a normal way. But today is different. He has heard Dr. Vargas-Ruiz's words, and he pivots his head in her direction.

"I don't need your help!" he cries out, in a tortured wail.

"Sure you do," Gadya says next to me. "Why can't someone shut that freak up?"

"Shhh," I tell her. "C'mon."

Dr. Barrett sees his former guards approaching, and he scampers up higher on the rocks as we watch.

"You don't know what's going to happen to you!" Dr. Barrett calls out to us in his hoarse voice. He holds up the piece of stripped electrical cable in one hand, like a whip. "You don't know what's waiting for you!" His eyes gleam with total madness. The circular scars on his face look weird and plastic-like under the glare of the sun.

"Please," Dr. Vargas-Ruiz cautions him.

The silent crowd parts so that his guards can reach him, and take him away. But as the guards get closer, he moves even farther up the rocks. His feet are bare, and his toenails are like crusted yellow talons.

Dr. Barrett raises the electrical cable high above his head. "You're all going to die!" he cries out. "I've seen it! I know what's going to happen to you next!" His hand is trembling.

"Stop it, Doctor—" one of his guards begins.

Dr. Barrett holds out his bony arm, swinging the cable around.

29

I think he's going to try to whip the guards to keep them away from him. But then he brings his arm up, and lashes the wire down hard against his own back.

I realize that he's flagellating himself. He cries out in agony. But then he whips himself again. Bits of skin and blood spray off his back, where the wire has torn into his flesh.

"Someone needs to stop this," Liam says, stepping forward.

I step forward with him. "He's really hurting himself this time." But we are too far away to intervene.

"Let his guards help him," Gadya says. "They know him best. He won't struggle as much."

Dr. Barrett whips himself again, and follows it with yet another anguished cry.

"Stop! Stop!" a guard cries out. People nearby in the crowd are trying to reach Dr. Barrett, but he staggers away, up to another rock, kicking at them with his feet. I see Alun in the crowd, trying to help the guards reach him.

"The Monk showed the future to me! In a vision! In a dream! When I was in his camp!" Dr. Barrett screams.

Unable to stop myself, I yell out, "That wasn't the Monk! That was just a girl from our village wearing his mask. A spy named Meira!"

"There is no Monk!" Liam seconds. "It's a myth!"

Dr. Barrett hears us over the noise of the crowd, and his eyes meet mine. His eyes are no longer bluish gray, but now slightly white and clouded as though he is getting cataracts. He glares at me.

I glance away for a second, feeling sick to my stomach.

"Yeah, there is no Monk and there never has been!" Gadya yells out in support of me and Liam. "Stop trying to scare everyone!"

Other kids start calling out in agreement. Dr. Vargas-Ruiz

tries to restore order but no one listens to her.

One of Dr. Barrett's guards finally reaches him, but Dr. Barrett lashes at the guard's face with his whip, making the guard quickly retreat.

"The Monk is real!" Dr. Barrett screams at all of us. "I saw him. I know him. You are the ones who don't know the truth about what the government is creating. You will die back in the United Northern Alliance! Don't get on those airplanes!" He whips his own back again, writhing in pain. "I cry for each of you! You are already dead. You just don't know it!"

One of the guards appears from behind him on the rocks, and yanks him sideways. The two of them tumble off the rocks together. Dr. Barrett is screaming as he claws at the guard's bare skin. The guard starts screaming too, as Dr. Barrett bites down on his wrist and blood sprays into the crowd.

"There's more than one Monk!" Dr. Barrett wails. "More than one of them! They are infinite! And their offspring will decimate the entire earth!"

Other guards and scientists pile onto him, trying to stop the violence. All of us watch from the stage, somewhat shocked. Alun is in the fray, now joined by Cass. Alun is trying to use his bulk to keep Dr. Barrett pinned to the ground. But Dr. Barrett is struggling, like he has the energy of ten men.

"This is pretty messed-up," Gadya remarks. But she can't tear her eyes away from the scene. Neither can I.

"What does he mean by 'their offspring'?" I ask.

Gadya shakes her head. "No clue."

"I don't think he has long to live," I tell Gadya. "I mean, despite how strong he seems right now. It's like his mind has melted. He's just one step above those drones we fought for the test."

"Agreed."

I watch as the guards wrestle the electric cable from Dr. Barrett's thrashing hands and hustle him away from us, down a dirt trail and into the forest. He struggles hard against them, whipping his head back and forth. I see the tendons in his neck straining underneath his sagging, mottled skin.

He finally moves out of view, but we can still hear his deranged cries and screams. They quickly grow fainter.

"Now settle down, everyone," Dr. Vargas-Ruiz says loudly, trying to restore order.

It's obvious that Dr. Barrett is completely insane, and I should put him out of my mind. But despite myself, Dr. Barrett's words have filled me with dread. Not at the thought of being killed when we get to the UNA. That doesn't scare me at all. But at the thought of ending up like him.

I know that if the UNA could somehow turn Dr. Barrett into this shambling madman, then I have no doubt they can break absolutely anyone. *The right drug. The right threats. The right torture.* Everyone has something that they are afraid of, or susceptible to.

I wish I knew exactly what Meira and the drones did to him. Maybe some of the spikes on the metal mask damaged his brain when they forced it on him. Or maybe he was slightly crazy from the start, after being trapped in Southern Arc for so many years.

"Don't think about him," Liam says softly into my ear, sensing my distress. "Just ignore everything he says. He's lost it. He's broken."

I nod. "But everyone has a breaking point, Liam." I turn and look up at him. "Aren't you afraid that could happen to one of us?"

"No." Liam squeezes my hand again. "Not to you or me, because we have each other. Besides, we need to look forward, not backward. We need to focus on our mission."

In the distance, I catch a final unexpected glimpse through the trees of the guards, half-dragging Dr. Barrett up the trail. He continues to struggle and rave.

I glance away.

"Who knows, maybe he'll get better one day," Liam says. "We don't know how this stuff works."

"Doubtful," Gadya adds.

"You can't be sure of anything on Island Alpha," I point out, although secretly I don't think Dr. Barrett has any chance of getting better.

"Come back to order!" Dr. Vargas-Ruiz calls out.

The crowd starts quieting down.

"The planes leave today in roughly two hours, as you already know," Dr. Vargas-Ruiz continues loudly. "You should say any final good-byes while you have the time."

"And while we're still alive," Gadya adds.

She means it as a joke, but a few people shoot her dirty looks and hiss at her to be quiet.

I look out at the crowd. So many lives depend on us.

"You are dismissed until launch time," Dr. Vargas-Ruiz intones. "We will reassemble then."

I look from Liam to Gadya and back again. My boyfriend and my best friend. "I'm ready to leave the wheel behind forever, and go back home," I say to them. "How about you guys?"

"Definitely," Liam replies.

Gadya nods. "Sounds like a plan I can get behind."

I feel nervous. The pressure and stress is hitting me, but I work hard to hide it. I take a deep breath. Soon we will be in the air, and heading back into the dark heart of the UNA.

3 FROM THE SKY

TEN HOURS LATER, I'M leaning back against the rattling hull of an airplane. We are gliding high in the night sky above the continental UNA. Somewhere above New Texas. I gaze out the window at the earth beneath me. I can see the lighted dots of cities and towns. They look so small. Spectral and multicolored. I should feel tired, but nervous energy and adrenaline keep me awake.

The airplane is one of the old UNA aircraft that transported pods off the island. The scientists have reconfigured it and coated it with radar-resistant material. There are no seats inside. It's just a large, loud canister.

The journey across the ocean has been uneventful, just as the scientists predicted that it would be. We took off from the bumpy dirt runway on Island Alpha and were soon cutting a path through the cloudless sky. Compared to the journey on the submarine to Southern Arc, and then the voyage on the airships back to the island, this is oddly peaceful.

It's hard to conceive that by airplane, we were only half a day away from the UNA. Island Alpha felt much farther away—like an entirely separate world. I glance out the window again and see nothing but stars in the darkness.

Soon the peacefulness will come to an end. I wish we were landing on a runway at a real airport, but of course we aren't.

We will be jumping out of this airplane, and skydiving straight down into the UNA. Our landing site will be a field on the outskirts of New Dallas. It's one of the few safe places to land, according to the rebels and the scientists. The planes will be returning to Island Alpha—assuming they don't get shot down.

I remember how afraid I was of heights when I had to climb up and down those ropes back at the travelers' camp with Gadya. I thought I'd gotten over that particular fear, until now.

"How high up are we?" I hear Gadya ask.

"Too high?" I murmur, gazing down.

"Three thousand feet!" someone else shouts back.

"I need to double-check your pack," Liam says to me.

"I'm fine," I tell him. "I already checked three times." But secretly I don't mind. "I'll check yours."

"Deal."

I turn so he can inspect my parachute.

My heart is in my throat. I felt eager to get into the air, but now I almost wish I could go back to the island for a little longer. I try not to think about Dr. Barrett's words—that we're doomed for returning to the UNA. *Does he know something that we don't?* I wish we were taking guns with us, but it's too dangerous. If we get spotted with guns, the UNA police will instantly know that we're rebels and will kill us—or torture us for information. So instead, we must make do with knives, hidden in our belts.

"We're almost above our destination," a scientist says, consulting a digital display screen. We will be landing in a deserted field. From there, we will travel north to meet up with a rebel convoy that will take us in and give us shelter temporarily. We will then be split up, and sent to different rebel cells.

The scientist unexpectedly throws open the door of the aircraft. A blast of freezing air gushes into the airplane. I shudder against the cold. "Who wants to go first?" he yells over the noise.

"Me!" Gadya says, stepping toward the doorway and then pausing. "I think."

Liam and I stand there next to her, the wind whipping through our hair. The noise is deafening up here. My skin feels like ice. I hold on to Liam for stability. The wind is stronger than I imagined, and there's nothing else to hold on to. I'm afraid I'll get sucked out of the plane before I'm ready.

"You scared?" Liam asks me, yelling over the noise.

I shake my head. "No."

"Good. We'll be fine."

I nod. "I know. We'll find each other as soon as we get to the ground."

"Definitely."

A surge of fear courses through my veins as I look down, out of the plane. I just see blackness. At any moment, the UNA might spot us somehow and send an airship to gun us down.

I keep staring down at the ground, out the open door. It's so dark, but I can faintly make out a huge field surrounded by forests. This is our landing site.

"Better get moving," the scientist says impatiently. "Someone's gotta go first!"

To our left I see another airplane in the distance, with seven people already tumbling out of it in a row. Heading down toward a field in the UNA to help begin the rebellion.

"I'll go first," I say loudly. Gadya looks surprised.

"You sure?" Liam asks. "I was going to wait for you on the ground and—"

"No. It's my turn. I'll wait for you guys."

The scientist puts a hand on my pack. "You ready?"

I nod.

I lean back to kiss Liam quickly. His lips are warm against mine. I hug him one last time.

Then I turn back around, shut my eyes, and step out of the plane.

The wind instantly slams into me and knocks me sideways. I scream, despite myself, out of shock and fear.

And then I'm falling through the freezing night air, tumbling head over heels. The wind whips at me so fiercely, it feels like it's going to tear off my clothes, and skin me alive.

The wind is so loud now that it sounds like a hurricane. I can't hear anything else. I didn't know that skydiving would feel like this. My body is getting battered by currents of air. I'm in danger of losing my bearings. My eyes keep clouding over and watering from the cold and the wind. I try to wipe them clear with the back of my hand.

"Liam!" I yell, but I know he can't hear me anymore. I contort my body and get a glimpse of the plane above me. I keep tumbling over and over.

I'm starting to panic. I trained for this, by jumping off rocks on the wheel, but reality is completely different from any kind of simulation.

I keep plunging downward. I finally get into a steady position and hold out my arms and legs. This slows me down, but I'm still moving faster than I thought possible. Below me is darkness spotted with tiny dots of light.

I hear an alarm start beeping next to my head. This means it's time to open my parachute. I pull the cord, expecting to have the parachute explode out, and snap me back up into the sky.

But nothing happens.

I yank on the cord again.

Still nothing.

My mind goes numb.

This cannot be happening to me.

The ground looks like it's expanding and contracting beneath me in a vertiginous frenzy.

My freezing fingers fumble for the cord that leads to the safety chute. I can't find it.

The alarm is beeping faster next to my ear. I flail as I try to find the emergency rip cord. If I can't locate it soon, then I'm going to die. I will hit the earth at approximately 120 miles per hour.

I look down at the ground again. It's getting even closer.

A strange, almost peaceful feeling starts to come over me. It's like a feeling of comfort and warmth. *I'm probably not going to survive this free fall.* Somehow my parachute has malfunctioned.

I shut my eyes. Maybe it won't be so bad. To hit the ground that fast will mean that everything is over quickly. No more stress. No more pain. No more fear. No more battles. Just an end to everything.

But then I push the feeling away and lunge my hand behind my back again, desperately searching for the cord. Death is no answer. It's the easy way out. And it would separate me from Liam. It would also mean that I'd play no role in bringing down the UNA. If I die in battle, then that's different. That's how I want to die if I have to. *Fighting.* But to die here would mean nothing.

I yell out as the tips of my fingers feel something hard and plastic. It's the orange ball at the end of the emergency cord. I struggle for it as I continue falling. The noise of the alarm and the wind keeps blaring in my ears.

Then I finally manage to grab the cord. I have no idea if it will work, but I pull it with my full strength as I let out a savage yell.

Instantly, I'm thrown upward as though by a giant, invisible hand. The force is so violent that it rattles my whole body, jarring my jaw and snapping my head back. The emergency chute has worked. I'm now drifting in the sky, peacefully.

I exhale shakily. My body is cold. I look at the ground. I'm still going much faster than I thought I would be. But I'm high enough that I'm going to survive the impact. I gaze around. I see a shadow passing a few hundred feet away from me. Is it Liam? Gadya? I call out to them but get no reply.

I can't see anyone else in the freezing darkness around me, but I know that they must be in the sky somewhere. I stare down at the few lights beneath me. I can't see the field too clearly. It's just an area of blackness waiting to swallow me up.

I keep drifting downward. The parachute straps are biting into my underarms. A gust of wind drifts me sideways.

I continue moving lower. Now I can finally see the ground beneath me a little better. It's a grassy field. But it's so dark, I can't see if anyone else has landed yet.

Now I'm only a hundred feet above the ground. Now fifty. I'm drifting in silently. The noise of the wind has become just a peaceful whisper. It's hard to imagine that a minute ago, I almost died.

Now I'm just ten feet above the surface.

Finally, my feet touch the ground and I start running, trying to keep my balance.

But I trip over my feet and tumble onto the ground, landing

with a bone-shaking crash in the grass. The emergency parachute falls down heavily behind me, making a rustling noise. I lie there for a moment, the wind knocked out of me, until I manage to stagger back up to my feet.

I take off the parachute straps and immediately start gathering up the parachute. I can't let any trace of it remain. Working quickly, my heart in my throat, I manage to get it stuffed into the backpack. I button it up and sling it over one arm.

Later, I will inspect my pack and try to find out why my main chute didn't deploy. I need to know whether it was an accident, or whether it was some sort of sabotage attempt. Although all of us are supposedly fighting for the same goal, I know that it's possible there are spies among us.

Around me is only silence. I don't see anyone else. I feel alone, scared, and cold. I look up in the sky, searching for Gadya, Liam, or any of the other kids from my plane. I don't see anyone. Clouds are passing across the moon, making it hard to see.

Then I hear a nearby rustle. I freeze. My hand goes to the knife on my waistband.

"It's me," I hear a voice hiss in the darkness. My eyes are adjusting to the dim light, and now I see Gadya approaching from about twenty feet away. "Back in the good ol' UNA," she whispers. I can hear excitement in her voice. But also some fear.

"Did you see what happened?" I ask, moving toward her.

"No. What?"

"My parachute didn't open! I had to use my emergency one."

"Really?" She sounds startled.

"Was yours okay?" I ask.

She nods. "Yeah. I'm glad you're safe."

"Me too," I say. "So where's Liam?"

"I don't know. I was just looking for him. He went out right before I did."

"He's probably landed by now."

"I'm sure he has. Maybe the wind drifted him away from us."

We both stare around in the darkness. "I'm worried that someone did something to our parachutes," I say.

Gadya thinks it over. "Sabotage? But who would do that?"

"I know it's doubtful, but maybe there's someone who doesn't want us to succeed. Like someone with old allegiances to the UNA."

"Anything's possible on the wheel." She stares around for Liam. "If he's not here soon, we have to get going."

I nod. "Maybe he's already headed for the rebel convoy. Maybe he'll meet us there." I look around at the trees.

"Liam will be okay," Gadya says, trying to comfort me. "He's a hunter and tracker. He knows where to find us."

I nod. I have to accept her logic. If I don't, I'll give in to despair.

I pull out a paper-thin digital screen. It's a map of the area. The scientists gave them to us, along with fake government papers, forged back on Island Alpha. The screen glows dimly green in the darkness. I hold it close so that the light doesn't give us away. "Look. We're not far from where we're supposed to meet the rebels. We just head north into the forest, find a large river and follow it, and then meet them on a dirt road on the other side. They'll be waiting for us."

Gadya glances at the map. "Only two miles or so."

"We better start walking."

I take a final glance at the map, and then shut it off, putting the folding screen back into my pocket. I wish I could communicate with the scientists, or anyone else, but it's too dangerous now to transmit any signals. They would be picked up by the government's monitoring systems.

Gadya and I start heading toward the trees at the edge of the field. I'm thinking about Liam and hoping that we'll find him out here. If not, I plan to wait for him when we reach the convoy, even if Gadya doesn't want to.

The sudden snap of gunshots in the distance triggers my reflexes, and I instantly crouch down to the ground. The shots are too soft and far away to be aimed at us, but we need to be cautious. I can hear Gadya cursing.

"They're onto us!" she hisses. "They must have spotted someone."

"It could be a police drill," I say. "It could have nothing to do with us. They could be doing target practice, for all we know—"

More sharp cracks interrupt my words. I don't hear any screaming in response. If they are shooting at something or someone, it sounds like they're missing their target.

"We have to go faster," Gadya says. "If there are government soldiers or police out here, then we need to reach the rebels as soon as we can."

The two of us begin racing toward the edge of the trees. The trees are so tall in front of us that they blot out the moonlight. They stand like an impenetrable mountain of foliage, their branches and leaves forming a thick canopy. We make it into the forest just as more gunshots ring out.

We quickly find the river, using our ears to locate it. It's wide, and its rushing water sparkles in the few slivers of moonlight that penetrate the cover of trees. My mind churns. Our landing was supposed to be secret. If there are soldiers out here in the trees, already looking for us, then we're in trouble.

Gadya and I travel rapidly alongside the river. Tree branches lash our arms and faces, and I feel the underbrush crunch beneath my feet. The rushing sound of the river next to us is our sole companion, hiding the noise of our footsteps. We keep low to the ground, running in a half crouch. Trying to stay hidden from view in case anyone is watching.

I can scarcely believe what we're doing. It feels like we're still back on Island Alpha instead of in the continental UNA, close to a big city. Soon we will be rescued by the rebel convoy and then taken right into the heart of New Dallas.

As we continue racing forward, my folding screen nearly falls out of my pocket. I cram it back in and keep running. I can't afford to lose it.

A few more minutes pass. Our breath is ragged in our chests as we run. We're making good progress. By now we are probably just a mile away from our destination, and I haven't heard any more gunshots. But just as I start thinking that we've escaped, I hear a voice scream out.

"*Stop!*"

I freeze. So does Gadya. I sink down to the ground. She does the same. We crouch in the brush, trying to hide. The smell of dank earth is thick in my nose. I can feel my heart pounding against my ribs.

Gadya's eyes lock on to mine. There's no need for us to say anything to each other. The slightest noise could give us away.

I can't believe we've been spotted. Are these the rebels that we've been expecting, or someone else? I'm going over a cover story in my mind, in case we've stumbled upon government soldiers. But there's no good reason to explain why we're out here in the forest, even with the fake government papers that we carry.

Our presence is far too suspicious. We're going to have to fight if we get cornered by anyone other than rebels.

I also know that we're going to have to cross the river soon in order to rendezvous with the rebel convoy. We don't have any time to waste.

I hear footsteps crunching through the underbrush. A figure appears in the darkness, stepping out into a shaft of moonlight.

"You there! You girls!" it yells, seeing us instantly. But the voice is high-pitched and oddly unsteady.

As the figure gets closer, I stare down the source of the voice. It's a chubby boy, about twelve years old at the most. His face is dirty with mud, and his blond hair is long and ragged. He's clutching an old bolt-action shotgun.

"Who are you?" I call out.

"Jonah. I'm a rebel." He keeps the shotgun pointed at us, his cherubic face marred by the suspicious look in his blue eyes. "Names?" he asks us. "Real ones."

I stare back at him. "Alenna," I say.

Gadya gives him her first name too.

The boy nods. "You're late."

"There are soldiers out here—haven't you heard the gunshots?" Gadya asks.

The boy nods. "That's why they sent me. To find you." He pauses. "There's supposed to be more of you."

"They got lost on the way down," I say. "They'll be here soon. One of them is named Liam."

The boy nods again. "I know. The head of my resistance cell gave me the manifest for the flights." Gadya and I exchange wary glances. We expected to meet rebels when we landed, but we did not expect that one of them would be a child.

Jonah takes a primitive-looking walkie-talkie from his belt. "Short-range encoded signal. No one can intercept it," he explains. Then he presses a button and talks into the device. "Two of them are here. Alenna and Gadya. I'm sending them to meet you. I'll wait for the others and take them to the next convoy. Over."

A voice on the other end crackles back to us: "Tell them to get here fast. Over."

"Will do. Over and out." Jonah looks back at us, finally lowering his gun. "Better start walking."

"Are you safe out here on your own?" I ask him, suddenly worried.

"I've been on my own since I was ten. I'm an orphan. The rebels are my family. I'm safer than you out here. I'm smaller, faster, and I can hide better." He looks at me intensely.

"You heard the kid," Gadya mutters, sounding almost amused. "We better move."

We hustle past Jonah as he watches us closely. Soon he is behind us. We hike for another five minutes. I consult the map again. We're at the point where we need to cross the river.

I tug Gadya's sleeve. "Stop. We're here."

I gaze up ahead. Here, the river makes a bend before it widens. This is its narrowest point before it grows to about forty feet in width and runs off as far as I can see, winding into the darkness of the forest. We just have to make it across without drowning.

"Ready to swim?" Gadya asks.

"I'm ready for anything."

I walk forward and kneel down at the edge.

Gadya joins me, plunging her hand into the water. "It's cold. Figures."

I start unlacing my boots. Gadya kicks off her boots and snatches them up in her hand.

We quickly step into the water, clutching our boots. I shiver. Gadya is right. The water is freezing. It comes up to my thighs and to her waist. I realize now that it's too deep to walk quickly in, but too shallow and rocky to swim.

I take a step forward. The water pulls at our clothes, making foamy wakes around our bodies. We start wading across the river as fast as we can.

We don't talk much. We just keep pushing ahead. Our clothes are soaked.

The river starts to get deeper and moves even faster. I'm worried for a moment that if I slip, the water might carry me away.

I stare out at the bank. We're only fifteen feet away now. I just keep trying to move forward.

I hear a sudden yelp.

It's Gadya.

"You okay?" I whisper loudly to her, over the sound of the water.

"Almost lost my balance. Watch out—the rocks are slippery here."

I move closer to her. We help each other along.

When we reach the muddy bank, we crawl out of the river. We both stand there, dripping with water and shivering.

I don't hear any more gunshots. The whole area seems deserted.

We pause for a moment on the riverbank, getting our boots back on. I hope that Jonah will be able to find Liam and guide him to our convoy. If not, I suppose Liam will find the next one. I know how resourceful he can be.

"We're going to die if we just keep standing here," Gadya grouses. "Someone will find us. C'mon."

We begin walking. The forest on this side of the river seems even thicker, like it's closing in around us. I glance back and see the river receding into the distance.

Soon, we reach a path that's been cleared in the forest. It's a narrow dirt roadway through the trees, wide enough for a car.

"Is this it?" Gadya asks.

"I think so," I tell her. I take out the digital map and glance at it. "Yes, we're in the right place."

"Where is everyone? Didn't that rebel kid say they were waiting for us?"

I stare around at the darkness. I feel like we're the last two people alive on earth. There's only silence and the noises of the forest. "Maybe the kid was wrong."

We look in both directions. There's no sign of a car.

"Could be a trap," Gadya says.

We exchange worried glances. This is not a good start to our return to liberate the UNA.

"We should hide—" Gadya begins.

But the faint noise of vehicles approaching us on the dirt road stops her short.

"Cars. Two of 'em. Heading our way," I whisper.

I can't see them. Their headlights must be dimmed. I crouch down next to Gadya in the darkness, in the underbrush at the side of the road. We make sure to hide ourselves well, peeking out through the foliage.

The noise of tires on the dirt road gets louder and then stops, just out of view. I hear car doors opening, followed by someone's footsteps.

"Can you see anything?" Gadya whispers into my ear.

"Not yet," I say back, straining to look.

"Alenna?" I hear a voice call out from the road. "Gadya?" The voice is female, and it has a slight Southern twang.

I don't know if I can trust this person, although I assume she is a rebel. I get into a defensive posture, ready to run or fight if she does anything suspicious.

Neither Gadya nor I respond.

The silhouette of a person grows closer. I can see her now through the trees, walking down the road. She is illuminated by the faint glow of yellow headlights.

"Alenna?" the woman calls again. "Gadya? Where are you? Jonah said you were on your way!"

She's going to find us in the underbrush anyway, so I decide to make myself visible.

"I'm getting up," I murmur to Gadya.

"I'll cover you," she whispers back. "I'll throw my knife at her heart and kill her if she threatens us." I know that she means it.

I stand up from the underbrush, with my blade in my hand. I still don't say a word. I know that this woman is probably a rebel who is on our side, but I've also learned not to trust anyone in the UNA.

The woman doesn't look surprised to see me, or my knife. In fact, she's carrying a rifle. It's hanging loosely by her side. Behind her are two vehicles—a pickup truck and a sedan. Drivers sit in both of them, barely visible beyond the dim headlights.

The woman staring back at me has red hair, tied back in a bun. She looks like she's in her late thirties. Her face is pretty, but her eyes glint hard in the moonlight.

"You're Alenna," the woman says to me. "I recognize your photo."

I nod. "Yes."

"You can lower that weapon. I'm here to help you. We don't have much time." She pauses. "I assume Gadya is with you? Probably hiding with a weapon aimed at me, in case I turn out to be a spy or something?"

"Correct," Gadya's voice says from the underbrush.

The woman smiles. "I'd expect nothing less." Then her smile fades. "Come with me. Alenna, you'll be riding in my vehicle. Gadya will be in the one behind us."

Gadya stands up loudly from the brush, her arm cocked to throw the knife if she has to. "We don't want to be separated yet."

"I agree," I say. "We're supposed to stay together for now."

"There's no other way to get past the government checkpoints on the highway. They're worse than we thought they would be today. We're going to smuggle you through as family members. Two teenage girls will look more suspicious than one." She eyes Gadya's blue hair and tattoos. "Especially someone who looks like you. So c'mon. Alenna, follow me. Gadya, to the truck. We have fresh, dry clothes for both of you in the cars. You need to change right away."

"Are we going to the same destination?" I ask. "I mean, me and Gadya?"

She shakes her head. "Not right away. We're taking you to different safe houses. I'll explain in the car."

She's about to turn away, when I call out, "What about the others? We lost some on the way down. Liam—" My voice catches when I say his name. I have to be strong.

"I know. I heard Jonah's dispatch. We'll send scouts to find them if they don't turn up soon. Other vehicles will then come and pick them up." She pauses. "You need to worry about yourself right now, not your friends. They were trained just like you, right? If they survived the jump, then they know what to do." She turns back around again, and starts heading away from me. "Now hurry up. Get out of those wet clothes."

Gadya and I look at each other.

Gadya steps forward and hugs me hard. "I know we'll see each other again. And Liam too. Soon."

"Definitely. I'll contact you the first chance I get."

"I'll do the same."

"This is the start of everything," I whisper. "We're going to get our country back."

"Or die trying," Gadya replies.

"Come on!" the woman yells at us. Her voice now has an edge of frustration. "We have to go. Other convoys will be coming soon."

I part with Gadya.

I never expected to be alone like this so quickly. That wasn't part of the plan. I thought we would have more time together with the rebels before going our separate ways. I am now isolated from Liam and Gadya. *I hope this woman is the ally that she seems to be.* I cling to that thought as I follow the woman and climb inside her waiting car.

4 THE NIGHT DRIVE

I HAVEN'T BEEN INSIDE a UNA vehicle in months. I'd
forgotten how small and utilitarian they are, compared to that
tram on the wheel. All new cars look pretty much the same now,
mandated by the government. Gray metal sedans with curved
hoods. They're mass-produced cheaply by giant factories located
in the place that used to be called Mexico. Older cars are on the
road too, but they are clearly being phased out.

I slide into the back of the car, and close the door behind me.

A man is sitting behind the wheel. He doesn't turn back to
look at me. The woman sits in the passenger seat.

As promised, there's a pile of clothes and a new pair of shoes
waiting there for me on the backseat. They are simple and utilitarian. A green blouse, a gray jacket, and jeans. Designed not to
attract any attention. I start stripping off my wet shirt and pants.

"Don't watch," I say, although there's really no room for mod-
esty. I awkwardly get my wet clothes off and the dry ones on.

"Slip your old clothes into this bag," the woman says, handing
me a plastic bag. Then she takes the bag from me and tosses it out
the window and into the forest. It disappears from view into the
brush.

"Won't that leave a clue if someone's looking for us?" I ask, startled.

"The bag is coated with chemicals. It will disintegrate itself and the clothes within fifteen minutes."

I nod. "Good."

The woman hands me a passport and some documents. "Additional fake papers. Things they couldn't forge on the wheel. Keep them safe."

I glance down at them. One of them is a very official-looking government ID card. It has my photo on it. *A photo of me from before I got sent to the wheel.* I look younger and more innocent in it than I ever remember feeling. It has the name "Elyssa Jones" on it, instead of my own. I put the documents into my jacket pocket and button it.

"Take this too." The woman hands me a government earpiece. "It's disabled so you won't hear anything through it, but it looks official."

I slip it into my ear.

The middle-aged man sitting behind the wheel finally glances back at me without warning. He's wearing thick glasses, and he's balding slightly. His wide face does not look friendly. Unlike the woman, he doesn't even look confident. Just pale and sweaty.

"What's the code?" I ask him, suddenly nervous about his identity. I need to check that he's a rebel. I'd forgotten until now, but Dr. Vargas-Ruiz gave me and the other kids numbers to remember—codes we could use to confirm a person's identity and make sure that they were on our side. We're not supposed to use them except in emergencies, but without Liam and Gadya around, I feel vulnerable.

"Seven-eight-one-four," the man replies. "But you should save that for emergencies, remember?"

I nod, relieved. "I know." It's the right number.

"Let's go," the woman says.

I think about Gadya, who is probably watching me right now from the truck. I glance back, looking for her out the windows, but it's too dark. I know that both of us are worried about Liam.

I want to ask this man and woman in the car with me a million questions. They are the first continental UNA rebels I've met, other than Jonah. The man pulls the vehicle back onto the road, the tires sending up a sudden spray of dirt and gravel.

"Careful," the woman cautions.

The man nods. "Sorry."

We start driving down the bumpy dirt road. The headlights are completely off now. The man is navigating by a small LED screen mounted behind the steering wheel. It makes everything look surreal and green.

"What do I call you?" I ask. "What are your names?"

"I go by Kelley," the woman says. "You can call me that."

"Call me Shawn," the man says.

"I'll never know your real names, will I?" I ask. "Doesn't seem fair."

"You'll know our real names when we defeat the UNA," the woman replies.

We keep driving.

We pull out of the forest, and suddenly I see wide roads and a city sprawling before us in the distance. We're on the edge of a construction site near the forest. The man slows down, driving the car down another gravel road, mostly hidden from moonlight in the shadows of trees.

"Are you sure people aren't watching this place?" I ask. I glance behind us to see Gadya's vehicle, but it's not there. "Where's the truck?" I ask.

"Waiting for three minutes. We've timed everything perfectly so that we won't both get caught if there are any roadblocks."

We continue driving. It doesn't take us long to reach a two-lane road. We pull out of the construction area and stop in front of a chain-link fence. It's a gate. Two figures rush out and open it for us. Both of them are dressed in black and wearing stocking masks, obscuring their faces. Our car starts moving again, through the opening.

"They're with us," Kelley says, in response to the masked men.

"I figured as much," I tell her.

I stare back out the window and see the men racing to close the gate again and lock it. They disappear into the shadows.

"You have to relax," Kelley says, sensing my nerves.

"Would you be relaxed if you were me?" I snap back.

"Probably not, but I'm not you, am I? If you're nervous and tense, and we get stopped, then that will cause a problem for all of us."

We reach another larger road, this one with four lanes. Shawn pulls onto it. I look past the reflections through the curved windows of the car. There aren't many cars on the road at this time of night. Yet I see a few headlights behind us, and a few up front. This is not a Megaway, or even a large highway. It's just a regular road, winding its way around the city.

"Maintain a constant, steady speed," the woman cautions Shawn. "Not too fast and not too slow."

"That's what I'm doing."

I wonder if this is a married couple. She seems to be the one in charge. I realize they are risking their lives to do this for me, and to help the revolution. I'd almost forgotten what a huge risk they're taking. If they get caught, they'll probably get tortured right along with me.

54

"Thank you," I suddenly say.

"For what?" Kelley asks.

"For taking this chance on me, and on the others."

"Thank us when we get to the safe house," the woman replies, without turning around. "We're not out of danger yet."

We keep driving. On the side of the road are trees and then, set farther back from the road, monolithic gray towers. Government housing, like the kind I grew up in with my parents, before they got taken away. It will be the people living in these buildings, the everyday inhabitants of the UNA, who will be the ones to help us reclaim the country. *Or at least that's what I hope.*

I still can't believe that I've returned here. It's been six months since I set foot on the continental UNA. In a weird way, Island Alpha feels more like my home now.

"Look up ahead," Kelley says to Shawn.

I peer between their heads to get a view out the windshield. I see a row of cars slowing. Some have already stopped in a line far ahead of us. "What is it?" I ask nervously.

"It's a roadblock," Shawn says. I can hear the fear in his voice. He turns to Kelley. "Maybe they know."

"They don't know," Kelley replies, her voice calm and firm. "Keep driving. Don't slow down."

"But—"

"Do what I say." Her voice is unflinching.

"It's not too late to turn around," Shawn says softly. "We could find another road. Try to avoid detection."

Kelley looks straight ahead. "Anything we do now will draw attention to us. We don't have a choice. We must keep going."

Shawn doesn't say anything. He just keeps driving.

I clutch my knife, ready to fight if I have to. If this car is overtaken by UNA troops, then I'm going to take some of them out with me.

I remember what Gadya once told me—that she refuses to be taken alive. That she would turn her weapon on herself if she had to. I know I have the strength to fight. I also hope I have the strength to end my own life like that.

We approach the line of cars. I glance back and see more cars slowing behind us. My heart is beating faster.

I turn to look out the front windshield again. I see government soldiers and police officers standing at the front of the line, checking IDs. A few cars have been pulled over to the shoulder of the road. The cars are being thoroughly searched as the occupants stand there, being guarded by uniformed men with assault rifles.

I see a family of five—three young kids and two parents—being herded over to the side of the road to be publicly strip-searched.

My mind is racing. This is the worst-case scenario. I knew getting stopped at a roadblock was possible, but I didn't think it would happen. Not so soon. I was hoping we'd be able to make it to the safe house before the roads got shut down.

Our car comes to a halt. There are six cars ahead of us. Soldiers are walking down the line. I see an officer near us, eyeing our vehicle. But he doesn't do anything, at least not yet.

The officer just stands there. Every traffic lane is being stopped, in both directions. Other officers stand around under glaring portable spotlights. They wear full uniforms and visors. My heart sinks. *They must know.* I've never seen a roadblock this large, not even on the Megaway, and this road is much smaller.

Kelley turns back to me, as if sensing my thoughts. "Don't panic, Alenna. I told you the roads were rough tonight. Remember your cover story and we'll be fine. These things happen. It might have nothing to do with any of us. It could be routine. The guards will check our papers, but they are perfect forgeries. We can get through this roadblock without any problems as long as you act calm and don't say or do anything suspicious."

I nod.

"Can you handle that? I need to hear you answer me."

"Yes, I can handle it," I tell her. "Don't worry."

"Good."

Shawn doesn't say anything. He's just gripping the wheel tightly, his knuckles white.

"I'm not going to panic," I add, partly to reassure the woman, and partly to reassure myself.

In my head, I rehearse my cover story. That I am their daughter. That my name is Elyssa Jones, and that I'm sixteen years old, and live in New Dallas. The scientists made us rehearse these stories as part of our training.

I unbutton my jacket pocket so that I can access my fake ID documents easily. I know that these papers might not hold up under extreme scrutiny, but they should be more than enough to get us through a roadblock. Unless the police already know about us, and are on the lookout for me and the others.

"It'll be our turn soon," Shawn says, staring straight ahead. His voice is tense. "What if we get caught?"

"Relax," the woman tells him. "You're more liable to give us away than Alenna. Calm down."

"You've done this before?" I ask softly. "Right?"

Kelley nods. "I have, many times. He hasn't. I only met him a month ago. This is his first time."

"Seriously?"

"Yes. And you should be grateful that he's here. There weren't many volunteers for this assignment. It's considered the most dangerous one." She pauses. "To be caught aiding someone like you carries a mandatory death sentence, without a trial, for both the culprit and his or her entire family."

"I didn't know that," I say softly, feeling sick.

"Now you do." We move forward again.

"So you're not really a couple?" I ask.

"Of course not," Kelley says, sounding almost annoyed. "My husband was killed by government soldiers three years ago." She doesn't say anything more, but she doesn't need to. I understand why she is helping us.

"What about you?" I ask the man softly. I need to know that these are people I can trust in a crisis.

"My brother was taken six months ago," he replies. "He was at home with his wife and their little boy. Soldiers came and grabbed him. We never saw him again. I vowed that I wouldn't sit around and let bad things keep happening to people who didn't deserve it. I started asking around, and then I was contacted by a rebel cell—"

"We're almost here," the woman says. "Stop talking."

But the man's words make me feel better. We have each suffered losses. That will bind us together against the violence and horror of the UNA.

The guard starts ambling over to the passenger side of our car. I try to look as calm and normal as possible.

"Hello, Officer," Kelley says as she rolls down the window, her voice fake and pert. She sounds nothing like she did just a moment ago. "What's all this fuss about?"

"Pull over, put it in park, and step out of the vehicle," the guard says brusquely to Shawn. He nods.

I know there's no point asking why, or we might just be beaten for the hell of it.

But Kelley laughs. "Oh, Officer. Really? Is there a need for that? We're just headed home."

"Do as I say. Now." He turns away from the car and waves another officer over to join him.

With a sigh, Shawn starts pulling the car over to the side of the road. "This really isn't necessary," Kelley calls out to the officer through the open window.

"I'll decide what's necessary."

The officer follows us over to the side of the road. The other officer joins him, ready to search our car. Shawn turns the engine off.

"Get out," the officer says. "The three of you. You first, driver."

Shawn opens his door and steps into the night. Kelley and I follow suit, moving slowly and cautiously.

Soon, we are standing there on the edge of the road. I can feel the weight of the knife in my waistband. If they try to strip-search me, then I will be forced to use it, because there's no way I can explain a weapon away. Then I realize that Kelley's gun must still be in the car. That's going to be a lot harder to explain than a knife.

Kelley puts a hand on my shoulder. Maybe it's a way to appear motherly. Or maybe she's trying to signal something to me. I can't tell.

"Papers," the officer commands us.

We reach into our pockets and extract our government ID cards. Then we hand them over to him.

He scrutinizes them one by one with his flashlight. On the road, I see other cars going through the roadblock without any problems.

"Where are you headed?" he asks, without looking up at us.

"We're on our way home from New Lakeport," Kelley says.

"From a camping trip," Shawn adds. "Up near Lake Nedra." His voice cracks nervously, but luckily the officer doesn't seem to notice. He keeps looking at our ID cards.

I remain completely silent. I'm worried that the officer will notice my wet hair, and think that it's suspicious, but maybe that's why Shawn said we were coming home from a camping trip at a lake.

I'm watching the officer. He's holding Kelley's and Shawn's ID cards in one hand, and mine in the other. He raises mine closer to his face, bringing it up to the light.

"Date of birth?" he asks me.

I tell him the fake birth date on the ID card, without hesitation.

He squints at me, turning the bright flashlight to my face. "You look old for sixteen."

"Life will do that to you," I snap, before I can stop myself.

Time seems to stand still for a moment.

I don't know why I said it. It just came out.

For a moment I see something pass across his eyes. I shouldn't have said anything. I wish I could take the words back, but it's too late. I'm overcome by sudden fear. I'm about to say something else to try to make it better. If this officer gets angry at me, or thinks I'm mouthing off to him, then our entire cover might get blown.

Then the officer nods. "Life does that to everyone, I guess," he says, as he hands my card back to me.

"What's going on out here tonight?" Kelley asks, sounding perky and fake again. At first I'm worried because I don't want her bringing more attention to us. But then I realize that she's trying to figure out how much the government knows.

The officer shrugs. He seems more at ease with us now. "Escaped convicts," he says. "A couple guys broke out of the maximum-security prison in New Fort Worth. At least that's what they're telling us."

Kelley nods.

"It's a good night to stay off the roads. They've got roadblocks set up from here all the way to New Austin."

"I'll keep that in mind, Officer."

He nods. "And remember, it's your duty as a citizen of the UNA to report any suspicious activities that you might observe."

"Doing my part for the UNA is a real pleasure," Kelley chirps happily. "So we can go now?"

"Yeah," the officer says, lowering his flashlight. "Sure."

We get back into the car.

I'm shaking a little bit. I can see the tip of Kelley's rifle poking out from under the seat. If they'd searched the car, they would have found it.

Shawn starts the car and begins driving again, slowly pulling back onto the road. I see beads of sweat running down his cheek, even though the night is cool.

"See? I told you it would be okay," Kelley says. Her voice is no longer chipper. It's firm and as cold as steel.

"Barely," Shawn mutters.

"Barely is good enough for me," I tell him.

I gaze out the window. The road ahead is clear. We've passed the roadblock. I should feel relieved, but instead I feel more anxious than ever. The officer mentioned other roadblocks. We might not get so lucky next time.

"Faster," Kelley says to Shawn.

He speeds up.

"How far are we now?" I ask Kelley, as the trees rush by at the side of the road. "I mean, from the safe house."

"Twenty minutes. Unless we hit another checkpoint."

"You think that's possible?"

"I hope not," Shawn mutters. "But there's a chance."

I sit back in my seat, gazing out the windows. "I'm ready for whatever happens."

"I know you are," Kelley says, glancing back at me. "You handled yourself well back there. But this is only the start of your journey. Don't be too cocky and overconfident. That can get a person killed." She pauses. "Remember, this isn't Island Alpha. You can't go around fighting and killing people with impunity—at least not until the revolution starts. This is New Dallas. The rules are different here. And we must play by them, until we get the chance to rewrite them."

"You think I don't know that?"

She turns back around. "Just checking. Remember, a lot is riding on bringing you and the other kids to the rebel cells. You're meant to be a catalyst to help us start the revolution. But if you get caught, then we've wasted a lot of time and energy, and you've jeopardized a lot of lives."

"I'm not planning on getting caught."

"Neither am I," Shawn says.

"Nobody ever does, right?" Kelley asks. "Yet people get caught every day. Shawn, you acted too nervous back there. You were too quiet."

There's a moment of silence.

"I'll do better," he finally says.

Kelley nods. "Just keep driving. If everything goes well, we'll be there soon."

I gaze out the windows at the cityscape now passing on either side of the road. I'm looking forward to arriving at the safe house. But more than that, I'm looking forward to meeting the rebel cells and starting the process of tearing the UNA to pieces.

5 THE SAFE HOUSE

Twenty minutes later, after driving down several winding roads, we reach the safe house. We were lucky and did not encounter any other roadblocks or military checkpoints along the way.

We are now in a suburban development of old, large tract homes. Built before the UNA took power. They are run-down and ramshackle. Some look abandoned, with caved-in roofs and broken-down walls. But others look no worse than the tower blocks of New Providence, or even the orphanage where I grew up.

"That's it," Kelley says, pointing to a huge house up ahead, with two massive dead oak trees in the front yard. "The safe house. It's empty right now. We're the only ones using it. There are twenty other safe houses spread around New Dallas in a radius of thirty miles."

A couple of the safe house's windows are broken, and the shutters hang awkwardly off their frames. The house is black and imposing, as though its exterior was scorched by flames at some point.

"Thank god we made it," Shawn says, finally exhaling in a big rush of air, like he's been holding his breath for a long time.

"Park over there. To the left," Kelley instructs. Shawn does as she says, pulling up the driveway and shutting off the car. He flicks the headlights off.

I stare out the windows at the darkness. Inside the house, I can see faint light, as though candles are flickering somewhere in there. I feel a chill run over my body, and not just from my wet hair and the cool night air.

"Let's go," Kelley says.

Then I catch a glimpse of movement inside the house.

I freeze.

"Stop!" I hiss. "I thought you said the house was empty?"

"I did," Kelley replies, pausing. "Why?"

Sensing that something is wrong, my hand creeps back to my knife. "Someone is in there! I just saw their shadow. The house is definitely not empty."

Kelley doesn't respond. Shawn doesn't either. The two of them exchange a glance. My fingers find the knife's grip, and slowly and silently, I begin to draw it out of its leather sheath. *Have I been led into a trap?*

"Who's inside that house?" I ask, keeping my voice very calm and low.

"You'll understand when you get inside, Alenna," Kelley says.

"You've been lying to me," I say. "Why?" I pull the knife up higher, clasping my fingers around it. "Tell me what's going on right now. Before we get out of the car. How do I know this isn't an ambush?"

"It's not what you think," Kelley says.

In the darkness of the back of the car, I begin raising the knife. *This is it.* I wonder if this is how we passed through the roadblock so easily. Maybe the policeman knew who we were the whole time and let us through. *But why?* If it's a trap, why go to these lengths? Kelley could have shot me and Gadya at the side of the dirt road and left our bodies there in the forest. Or she could have shot me once I was inside their car.

"Just stay calm," Kelley cautions, but I sense rising tension in her voice.

"I knew I never should have been separated from Gadya," I tell her, my fingers tightening more on the knife handle. "That seemed suspicious at the time. But it didn't seem like there were any other options."

"This doesn't involve Gadya," Kelley says. "It involves you. Gadya isn't part of it."

I wonder if Gadya is even still alive. *Have we been double-crossed?* I don't have time to think about any of that now. I just need to survive this moment or else there won't be any mission.

I whip out my knife.

At the same moment, Shawn pivots in his seat to face me.

He is holding a sawed-off shotgun. "Easy, Alenna," he says. "If you stab me or Kelley with that knife, then I fire."

I'm frozen.

"Why are you betraying me like this?" I ask. "Why are you betraying the rebels? I thought you were on our side!"

I'm not going to put my knife down yet, even if it means I get shot.

"We're not betraying anyone," Kelley says. She turns around to stare at me. Even in the darkness of the car, I can see her eyes glinting with anger and frustration. "You don't understand yet. But you will soon." She turns back to the imposing house. "Once you get inside."

I look at the house, at those dark mysterious windows, and I see the shadow moving again on the second floor, behind shabby, torn curtains. I swallow hard. There has to be a reason why these people aren't telling me who is inside there.

"Lower your knife," Shawn says tiredly. Slowly, I do what he says. Then he swings his shotgun away from me. "We're on the same team, whether you know it or not."

"Prove it to me," I snap.

Kelley sighs. "We're wasting time." She opens her door and steps out. "Stay in the car if you want, Alenna." She shuts her door.

Shawn turns and opens his door. "It's safe, I promise you," he says. Then he gets out of the car too.

I sit there for a moment, in the silent darkness. I don't know who is inside the house. And I don't know why Kelley and Shawn are being so strange about it. Obviously there's more going on here than I was led to believe. I miss Gadya and Liam right now. I hope that they're both okay. And I hope that Kelley and Shawn can be trusted.

I get out of the car, clutching my knife. If anything unexpected happens, then I'm ready to fight back. And Kelley and Shawn will be my first targets, for daring to betray everything that we've worked toward.

The two of them are waiting for me, just a few paces away.

"This way, Alenna," Kelley says, walking up the stone steps to the front door of the house. I follow her cautiously, my senses on alert for any signs of danger.

She reaches the front door, takes out a set of keys, and unlocks it. The door creaks open on rusty hinges. She disappears into the darkness within, followed by Shawn.

I take a deep breath and step into the house after the two of them. I was right about the candles. They burn in large candelabras and in lamps mounted on the walls. Wax drips onto the warped wooden floor and forms little pools.

Kelley sees me notice the candles. "We don't use electricity. We don't show up on any UNA power grid."

I'm staring around at the shadows. I feel like someone is watching us. The sensation makes the tiny hairs stand up on the back of my neck.

"This house has been condemned," Kelley continues. "By the government. Most of this neighborhood is."

"Why?" I'm looking around, aware of every creak in the floorboards. There is some simple, functional wooden furniture in the corner and a couple of old dusty couches in the main room. Nothing else.

"There was a chemical spill here two years ago. Petroleum chloride. Everyone was evacuated within a ten-mile radius, and the area was declared unsafe for the next two decades. It got quarantined. But people crept back in here to live. People who didn't have any other place to go. The government thinks it's an empty wasteland. A no-man's-land. But us rebels also sneaked in and have been using it as a base."

"Is it safe here? I mean, if there was a chemical spill?"

"Safe enough. Short-term exposure shouldn't do us much harm." She pauses. "We have more immediate threats to worry about."

"Such as?"

"I might not be the best person to answer that question."

"Then who is?"

"Follow me," Shawn says, motioning me up a flight of stairs. It's huge, wrapping itself around the edge of the massive main room. This must have once been a pretty nice house to live in. But no longer. I see a chandelier hanging lopsided from the ceiling, most of its glass smashed. And there are rat droppings beneath my feet.

I pause for a moment, staring upward at the staircase. The top level of the house is pitch dark. I can't see anyone there.

"I'll lead the way," Kelley says, stepping in front of me and Shawn.

"Why all this secrecy?"

"You'll understand soon enough."

She strides up the staircase. I follow, with Shawn bringing up the rear.

"You keep saying that, but I'm getting sick of hearing it," I tell her. "I didn't come all the way from Island Alpha to get jerked around. Tell me what's going on. This is not the plan I agreed to."

"You're right," Kelley says, sounding very matter-of-fact. "We've gone off the plan a little bit."

"Tell me more." I pause on the stairs, my fingers tightening on my knife handle again. "What happened? Why aren't I with Gadya and the others right now? Why did you deviate from the plan?"

Kelley glances back at me. "Because someone asked us to. Someone that we trust more than anyone else. More than the scientists, even."

She keeps walking. I follow again because I don't know what else to do. I'm conscious of Shawn behind me, still armed with his shotgun. I think about trying to turn on him and get back down the staircase, but there's nowhere for me to go once I get outside the house. And also, an awful curiosity keeps pulling me forward.

We reach the top of the stairs, where a closed door awaits us. Kelley knocks softly on it.

"She's here," Kelley says to the closed door.

There's no response from behind it.

Just silence.

"I said, she's here." Kelley raps on the door again.

Still nothing.

Then I hear a faint tapping sound in response.

I glance back to see Shawn watching me closely. I turn toward Kelley again.

"Go ahead," Kelley tells me. "Open the door. Shawn and I will wait for you downstairs."

"What if I don't want to open the door?" I ask.

For the first time, Kelley smiles. "I know that you do."

Then she moves out of my way and begins heading downstairs. Shawn follows a few paces after her. I wait until they reach the bottom of the staircase.

Then I slowly reach out my hand and touch the bronze doorknob.

For a second, I wonder if I should run for it. I could rush down the stairs, slash Kelley's and Shawn's throats, and get out of the house and into the car. Make a break for it. But Kelley is right. I want to know who is behind that door.

Before I can think too much, I turn the doorknob and fling the door wide open.

The large room is dark, except for a thin white candle sitting on an empty oak desk. I can't see anyone inside. Faint moonlight comes in from two large windows opposite the door, shrouded with thin white curtains.

"Hello?" I call out. I keep my voice flat and calm, despite the tension that I'm feeling. There is no answer. I take a slow deep breath and then I step inside the room.

It seems like I'm alone in here with the desk and the candle.

Then a husky, ravaged voice says from the darkness, "Close the door."

70

I'm startled. I can't see the source of the voice. I have my knife positioned to lash out if anyone tries to touch me.

"Where are you?"

"Shut the door," the voice says again.

"Why?" I ask, straining to see into the darkness.

"It's safer that way. For both of us."

I reach back and slowly swing the door shut. It latches behind me.

Then I look around the room again. "Where are you? Who are you? Tell me what's going on."

I see a shadow pass behind the desk, in front of the windows. It's too dark to make out any of the details. I lower my body into a fighting stance and raise my knife. "If you touch me or try to surprise me, I will stab you, whoever you are."

"You don't need that weapon here," the voice says.

"I'll be the judge of that."

I hear the voice chuckle softly.

"Quit hiding!" I command. "Show yourself."

"Sure. If you really want," the voice responds.

There's a spluttering whoosh as an oil lantern comes to life, bathing the center of the large room in a dim orange-yellow glow.

I take a step back, startled.

There is a grinning figure sitting behind the desk now, holding the lantern.

The figure is barely human. Pairs of vertical tubes and wires run down the sides of his neck. One of his eyes has been replaced with some kind of electronic sensor that whirs and tracks my every move. Wires run out of a metal plate in his chest, visible through his white shirt, and directly into a nearby computer terminal on a moveable pole, attached to a car battery. He has scars running down his forehead like vertical gashes.

But I recognize this person just the same.

"*David . . . ,*" I breathe.

I'm stunned to the core.

And also completely horrified.

"Alenna," he says back to me, sounding faintly amused. His voice is nothing like it once was. It sounds like his larynx has been crushed and then reconstructed. He grins at me. Some of his teeth have been replaced with metal ones. "It's been way too long."

"I thought you were dead," I say, still feeling unable to move.

I stand there like I'm paralyzed. My whole body is numb. I want to run over and hug him, but I'm also confused and scared.

How is it possible that David is alive? And how is it possible that he's here in the UNA with me, in this house?

Slowly, David begins to stand up. I see metal braces on his legs, supporting his limbs, controlled by the electrical device across his chest. His body looks ravaged. I can't believe that he survived his injuries.

"How did you . . ." My words trail off.

I feel like I'm going to cry.

I want to touch him, but I'm too afraid.

He takes a step toward me, around the side of his desk. I see that one of his hands is missing two fingers. They have been replaced by some strange sort of electric tendrils, made of thin metal filaments. He sees me staring and then, surprising me, he wiggles them at me.

Somehow, that breaks the spell.

"What the hell happened to you?" I ask, finding my voice again.

"You don't like it?" he asks, smiling a little. "I think it's an improvement over being a corpse."

I walk across the room and around the desk, arms outstretched to hug him.

"Careful," he says. "You don't want to get an electric shock."

I pause for a split second until I realize that he's joking.

We hug, and I hold him tight. I shut my eyes. I've been dreaming about him for so long. But I thought he was dead. Or if he was alive, I never imaged that he'd look like this.

I pull back from him. "What did they do to you?"

"Sit down with me," he says. "I can't stand up for too long. It hurts."

I help him back down into his chair.

Then we sit across from each other at the desk. I can't believe what has become of him. I'm trying to act normal. His electronic eye, which seems to stare blindly ahead at me, is profoundly disturbing. I try to keep the sadness from my face, but I know that it must show.

I turn my attention to the spacious room, lit by the orange glow of the oil lamp. The curtains are rotting. The furniture looks like old wooden antiques. The walls are covered with peeling yellow wallpaper. The carpet is worn away in some places, revealing old floorboards. There's a mattress and multiple computer terminals shrouded in shadows in the right-hand corner opposite the door. The electronic devices are connected to giant batteries. There's also another small door, probably leading to a closet or a bathroom.

"You live in here?" I ask.

"Yes. I mostly stay in this one room."

"Why?"

"So other people who take refuge in the safe house don't know that I'm here. And because I can't risk anyone tracking me."

"I saw you from the windows. It wasn't hard."

"I wanted you to see me. I knew you were coming, so I made an exception."

"So what's going on, David? Why did you bring me here? How long have you been here?" My mind spins with questions. "How did you even get here?"

"I made it out of the specimen archive in time. Once I smashed the cooling core, the fumes overwhelmed me, and burned me. But I didn't lose consciousness. I found another exit tunnel for emergency workers and I tumbled down it. Then I passed out. I was pretty sure I wasn't going to wake up again. When I did, it was a huge surprise."

"Who found you?"

"The scientists."

"And they didn't tell me!" I practically yell.

"I told them not to. We knew I could be a big advantage if nobody knew I was still alive. They patched me up and sent me here on a secret rebel submarine a few days later. I got here about two months ago. That's when the surgeries began and they made me what I am today."

I feel stunned. "Did my mom know about this?"

He nods. "Of course."

I shut my eyes for a second, feeling like I've been punched in the gut. *How could she keep such a huge secret from me?* I feel betrayed.

"I made her promise not to tell," David says. "Don't be mad at her. It was a question of safety. Secrets save lives. She thought you might tell Liam. Besides, she wanted to protect you."

I open my eyes and stare at him. "I understand why she did it, but I can still be mad. At both of you."

"Look. I've made more sacrifices than most people. I even

spent my recovery time learning as much as I could about how to gain power, and how to win this fight. I had a lot of time to think, just lying there in bed as I recuperated. New possibilities and new strategies occurred to me. I shared them with the rebels."

I nod. "So tell me why I'm here. That's what I need to know."

"I can't tell you everything, or it will endanger your life."

"Do your best. What's my role in all of this? I thought I was going to get assigned to a rebel cell."

"You are."

"Then why am I here? David, none of this makes any sense."

"You're going to join a rebel cell. You're going to advocate for them to expand and form a local army to rebel, just like all the other kids who parachuted down to the ground tonight. We are going to strike against the UNA eventually, just like we planned." He pauses. "But there's one extra wrinkle. You're going to have to let yourself get captured first."

His words hang in the air. He stares at me, a mix of flesh and machinery.

"Captured?" I say.

"Yes."

"Why?"

"Because you, out of everyone I know, have the greatest chance of bringing down the UNA."

"I don't understand. Why me?"

"Because I was studying the kids on the island. That was part of my job for the rebels. I was looking for the one who had the most even temperament, but who could learn how to kill and fight without losing their humanity. I also needed someone who could blend in—who could be invisible and quiet when they needed to be."

"But Liam's much better at that! Why not someone like him?"

"We need a girl. You'll understand when you get there."

"Get where? What's going to happen to me?"

"When you're captured, you will be taken to an isolated rural area in New Iowa. The local rebels call it the Hellgrounds. It's a farming community—but with a horrible twist. There are farms there, but also scientific labs. It's where they do experiments on kids."

I feel sick. "What kind of experiments?"

"Mind control. They don't just want armies of drones now. They want to be able to control people and keep them functioning at a higher level. They also want to reeducate citizens there. Some of the people who have been recruited to live and work in the Hellgrounds have a religious sort of fervor for Minister Harka. They're obsessed with him, like a cult, and they think he has divine powers."

"That's insane."

"Obviously. But they've noticed some of the same things we have. The way he never ages, for example. They've started to look toward him as a god. The government obviously encourages this."

"So it's like the Monk all over again."

"Worse. Because they also have the power of technology behind them. They can do whatever they want. It's up to you to get sent there."

"And do what?"

He hesitates. "I can't say until you arrive."

"David, you can't do this to me! I'm risking my life, but you don't trust me to know the full plan of action? That's not fair! You have to tell me everything."

He smiles. "This is the way it has to be. For your own good. For everyone's good."

"I know you're trying to protect me," I tell him. "That's why you're not telling me what I need to know. You're acting just like Liam, and like the scientists, and like my mom. Trying to shield me. I don't need that. I'm sick of it! I just need honesty."

David looks at me. "I'm telling you exactly what you need to know, but nothing more. And it's not just to protect you. If you get caught along the way and tortured, and you know all the secrets, then you might jeopardize our entire mission."

"I would never do that."

"Everyone has a breaking point. Trust me. I'll give you updates when you need them. We'll work together. You'll be on the ground, fighting and strategizing. I'll be here, giving you guidance and advice."

I sigh, frustrated. "You have to tell me something more. What will happen to me in the Hellgrounds? How will we communicate once I get there? What is my purpose for being sent there?"

"You'll wake up in a farmhouse. I'll make sure there's a communication device hidden nearby. I'll get one of the rebels to sneak in there and plant it. I'll make sure you find it." He sighs. "And your purpose is going to involve detonating a unique device in an unusual location—I can't say more than that."

"A bomb?"

"Of sorts." He just stares at me.

"What if I say no to all of this?"

David stares at me. "That's your choice." He pauses. "But there's something you should know. I didn't want to tell you, because I thought it might force your hand, or make you feel like I'm trying to manipulate you." He pauses again for a second. "But Liam is already en route to a work farm in the Hellgrounds, as a captive. It's the near the farmhouse where you will be sent."

My blood runs cold. "What? How do you know that?"

"After he landed tonight, he was captured by a group of soldiers on the lookout for rebel activity. Right now he's on a truck bound for the Hellgrounds. They'll make him do hard labor there, until they break him. That's what they do with every rebel boy that they catch. Then the experiments begin."

"How do I know you're telling the truth?" I challenge him. "You've lied to me so many times before that I don't know if I can believe you."

He smiles. "I knew you'd say that, Alenna. I'd be disappointed if you didn't." Then his smile fades. "I wish I were lying, but I'm not. In fact, I can show you." He turns to the wall. I'm confused for a moment, until he says, "Watch."

Suddenly a light springs forth and shines on the wall, like some kind of small movie projector. It takes me a second to realize where it's coming from. *His eye.* A beam of light is pouring out of it, painting an image on the wall. It must be powered by the same large batteries that power the computers.

I stare at what I see projected in front of me. It's images of Liam being taken by armed soldiers. He's struggling against them, veins throbbing and muscles straining. It takes six men to hold him. They beat him with nightsticks as they drag him toward a waiting vehicle.

I'm glad that he's alive. But all my hopes that he had escaped and would soon meet me are dashed. I have to face the truth. Liam is a hostage, and supposedly he's headed straight to one of the most dangerous places in the UNA.

"Do you want to see more?" David asks.

"No," I tell him. My mouth is dry. Then I add, "Yes. Keep going."

More images unspool on the wall. I see Liam being thrown

into the van. He lunges, swinging hard at the soldiers. He knocks one out cold. He kicks with both feet, and he almost makes it back out. But finally he's just overwhelmed by their numbers. He's forced inside the van and the doors are slammed shut and locked. The van quickly speeds away into the night.

The light emanating from David's mechanical eye clicks off. He turns back to face me.

"How did you get that footage?" I ask.

"A rebel filmed it, hiding in the trees. He uploaded it into his computer system and I downloaded it directly into my eye." He pauses. "So there are some advantages to getting 'messed up' like I did." He smiles again, but he looks tortured to me.

"Is there a way to fix you?" I ask him. "I mean to make you normal again? Like, can't they do transplants or something?"

He nods. "Yes. They could have made me almost back to normal. With a few scars, and a lot of stitches. But I wanted this done to me."

"That's crazy," I tell him, shocked. "Why would you do that?"

"Because this is my second life. I feel like I died once already." He places his metallic fingertip on the table. "But I lived, despite my injuries. Remember that I took a vow once to do everything possible to fight the UNA. When the scientists told me that having computers embedded directly inside me was an option, I immediately saw the potential."

"The scientists suggested this? Was my mom involved in your surgeries?"

"No. In fact, she tried to talk me out of it. But the others were."

I want to cry again. The sudden feeling just overwhelms me. "David, they tried to make you into some kind of monster. Have you looked in a mirror lately?"

"I don't care what I look like in a mirror, Alenna. None of that stuff matters to me. I'm better than I was before. I have more power." He smiles again. "Besides, it's going to take monsters to fight the UNA."

"So what happens now?" I gaze at him. "I'll let myself get captured. I need to find Liam and rescue him."

He nods. "You spend the night here. Then in the morning you'll be taken into the city, under cover, to meet with a rebel group. The group will be raided by police—because I will tip them off—and you will be arrested and sent to the house in the Hellgrounds. From there, you will receive further instructions on what to do, and how to reach Liam."

"You really won't tell me more?"

"I can't. It's easier this way."

"Easier for who?"

"Both of us. They might give you truth serum. I can't risk your knowing things before you need to." He blinks. "Just trust me that when you get out of the Hellgrounds, you will have a very tight deadline—and the entire success of our takeover of the UNA depends on you."

"You're sure you won't tell me more about this detonation, whatever it is?"

"If they give you truth serum, you won't be able to keep any secrets. I know that you received torture training on the wheel, and learned how to endure isolation, but the UNA truth serum can break anyone. You already know more than you should."

"It doesn't feel that way."

"I know. Just try to get some sleep while you still can," David says.

"Yeah, as if that's likely," I retort.

He smiles.

"You need sleep more than I do," I tell him. "And I know you're going to stay up the whole night, working."

"We can sleep peacefully only when the UNA has been turned into ashes, right?" he says.

"Right," I agree.

We hug one more time. He feels so fragile. I am both afraid of him and drawn to him.

I finally turn to leave the room. I glance back once, as he extinguishes the lantern, fading back into darkness. *Have I dreamed this encounter?* It seems so surreal and confusing.

I exit the room and carefully shut the door behind me. I walk down the long, curving flight of stairs, to where Kelley is waiting for me.

"So now you understand," she says.

"Some of it."

"Let me take you to your bedroom for the night."

I nod and follow her. This will be my last night of freedom before I am captured.

But I'm not really thinking about myself. I'm thinking about the fact that David is still alive. He looks so different, but there are flashes of the old David that I remember.

I vow to talk to him more in the morning before I get sent to the rebel cell, and then on to the Hellgrounds. I only now realize how much I've missed David, and I'm grateful for the chance to spend more time with him before I get sent away.

6 THE REBELS

THE NEXT MORNING I wake up in my shabby bedroom. My back hurts from the sagging mattress. It takes me a second to remember that I really am back in the UNA. I stare up at the stained ceiling. Then I shake off the strange feeling, get dressed, and leave the room.

I don't search for Kelley and Shawn. I just go straight upstairs to the door of David's room. I need to talk to him before I leave the safe house. I know he probably won't answer any questions about my journey, but I want to make sure that he's doing okay.

I knock softly on the door. There's no answer. I turn the doorknob, expecting it to be locked, but it turns easily in my hand.

"David?" I ask, surprised.

I push against the door, opening it and stepping inside.

The blinds are open, and gray light floods the room from the large windows. The curtains have been pulled back. The desk is still there, along with the mattress and the computers on the dusty wooden floor. But there is no sign of David. It's like he was never there in the first place.

"David?" I ask hesitantly.

"He's already gone," a voice says from behind my shoulder.

I turn around. Kelley is watching me.

"When did he leave?" I ask her.

"Last night. When you finally went to sleep."

"Is he somewhere else in the house?"

"No. He couldn't risk it."

I nod. I don't need to ask any questions about why. I know why he left. So that if I'm caught and interrogated, I can't give away his location.

"Is he safe?" I ask Kelley.

She nods. "David will be fine. He's a survivor. And he's a key figure in our plans for a revolution."

"How did he get so much power?" I ask her. "It almost seems like he's running things."

"He's not, but he's vitally important. Since he was twelve, he was groomed to revolt against the UNA—" She breaks off suddenly. "I shouldn't say more. Ask him yourself if you see him again. You two were close on Island Alpha, right?"

I nod. "Yes."

She looks at me. "Was there something between the two of you? On the wheel? More than friendship?"

The question comes out of nowhere. I can't believe she just asked me something so personal. "No," I tell her awkwardly. "Why would you think that?"

"Intuition." She shrugs. "Guess I was wrong."

"Did David say something about me?"

She shakes her head. "No. But he left you a note downstairs on the kitchen table."

I move past her quickly, immediately heading down the stairs to get it.

"I didn't read it," she calls out behind me. "It's still sealed."

I get downstairs and head into the kitchen. Shawn is sitting there in a wooden seat, his eyes glued to a digital display.

"They're looking for us already," he says glumly.

"Of course they are," I tell him. "What did you expect?"

I see the letter on the table and I snatch it up. As Kelley promised, the seal is unopened.

"You don't have long until men come for you and take you to meet the rebels," Shawn says.

"I know."

I get the feeling that David didn't tell Shawn or Kelley that I'm going to be captured on purpose. *That's David's way.* Everyone only knows one piece of the puzzle.

I walk out of the room, holding the letter, and go into the dingy bathroom. I know this is the one place I won't be bothered by anyone for a moment. I sit on the closed toilet and tear open the envelope.

I'm not sure what I'm expecting exactly, but my heart is racing. I slide out a sheet of paper folded in threes.

As I do this, an object falls out of the paper and onto the ratty carpet. I lean over and pick it up. It's a thin metal key on a chain, like the kind that might open a safe-deposit box. I hold it in one hand, as I unfold the piece of paper.

It's blank.

I turn it over. Nothing. I feel disappointed, and a bit insulted. I don't know what I expected. Some kind of message, at the least. But there's only the key. David didn't even leave me a note.

Sighing, I stand up and put the chain around my neck to keep the key safe. I fold up the paper and the envelope and put them in my back pocket.

Typical David, I think. But then I realize that maybe he didn't know what to say. I assume the key has something to do with the bomb—or whatever it is—that I have to detonate. I must keep the key safe and make sure it doesn't get taken from me by anyone.

I'm about to leave the room, when I catch a glimpse of myself in the mirror. My hair is messy and I pull it back, trying to smooth it down. I see circles under my eyes from tiredness and worry. I look like a stranger. I try not to think about Liam and what he's going through right now. Soon enough I will be joining him in the Hellgrounds.

I hear a voice call my name. It's Kelley.

"They're here!" she says, from outside the bathroom.

"I'll be right there," I tell her, looking at myself for a final time.

Then I leave the bathroom and step into the hall.

Kelley is standing there. "Someone is waiting for you."

"Already?"

She nods. "Come this way."

I follow her through the house and out a side door. I step into the cool air. The sky is gray, but rays of sunlight occasionally poke through the cloud cover.

A flatbed truck is parked in the driveway, carrying a load of large square boxes and straw. Shawn is standing outside talking to the driver, a burly man in a thick jacket and a cap.

"Alenna?" the driver calls out.

"That's me."

I walk over to him. He sticks out his hand. "It's best if you don't know my name," he tells me, "but it's an honor to meet you."

I shake his hand.

"You can call me Tomas if you want, but it's not my real name. Let me show you how we're taking you to meet the other rebels," he says. He moves around to the back of the truck. "Look. Right in here."

I peer into the back. He shoves aside a few boxes to reveal a narrow hiding place beneath the cargo.

"It's an old-fashioned method, but it works," he says. "We'll never get stopped by the police, even though technically, we're an illegal vehicle."

"I don't understand."

"The UNA elite like to get unprocessed foods from farms in the country. Not for the citizens, just for themselves. That's where my truck comes in. It's meant to take fresh goods from the country to the lavish homes and apartments in the city where the local leaders of the UNA live. Fresh fruit, fresh vegetables. Everything they deprive the regular citizens of. So I bring them their fresh produce, but I've also used this truck to transport about fifty rebels, right under their noses." He smiles, like he's laughing at a joke. "Not all at once, I mean. But one by one."

I nod. I can tell he has no idea that I'm going to be captured today. He just seems happy to meet me and help me reach the rebels. I wonder what he would think of David's plan. *What will happen to the other rebels at the meeting once I get captured? Will they be exposed? Will they be killed?*

"Let me help you on board," Tomas says. "We don't have much time."

As Kelley and Shawn watch, I clamber into the hiding space and lie flat. The man puts some boxes back, so that I'm completely hidden from view.

"You good?" he calls out.

"Yep," I call back.

"It'll take about half an hour to get there. Hang tight, Alenna."

He starts walking around to the driver's side of the truck. I hear him open the door.

Then pale fingers suddenly poke through the slats on the side of the truck. It's Kelley.

"Good luck, Alenna," she says. Surprising me, her voice is warm with emotion. "I want you to know that I'm rooting for you. I know you can do this—whatever it is that the scientists or David have told you to do."

I grab on to her fingers and squeeze. "Thank you for everything," I tell her, glad for a moment of human warmth.

Then the noise of the engine starts up with a clatter. Kelley pulls her hand back. I feel the truck slowly start to move. I just lie there, as though I'm in a coffin. The vehicle backs out of the driveway and onto the road. Soon we are picking up speed.

I remain flat in the back of the pickup truck, covered with a layer of boxes. The smell of wood and hay is strong in my nose. I fight the urge to sneeze. It's hot and uncomfortable. The air is stale, and exhaust fumes from the truck keep seeping into my space. Even though the driver said that we wouldn't be stopped, I know that anything is possible. Memories of the roadblock from last night are fresh in my mind.

After thirty minutes of winding through streets, we reach our destination. My body is sore from being jounced around. The truck slows and comes to a complete stop. I have no idea where we are.

I try to see outside, but I only get little snatches of light through the metal slats in the side of the truck. I can't really see anything.

I hear voices above me and I look up. The boxes shake, and I realize that the truck is being unloaded. For an instant, I'm afraid that maybe I've ended up in the wrong place.

Then I hear the driver's voice. "We're here, Alenna," he says.

I start pushing boxes aside, as more get unloaded from the truck. I burst into the daylight. It's bright, and it takes a moment for my eyes to adjust.

"Where are we?" I ask, looking around.

Tomas doesn't answer.

We're near a handful of abandoned brick buildings, some bearing battle scars from old gunfire. Scars that were probably made in those years before my parents got taken, when I was a little girl. The scars remain on the rocks, impervious to the passage of time.

I grab the edge of the truck and then climb down onto the dirt.

"Is it just us?" I ask.

Tomas shakes his head. "The others are nearby. They're probably watching us right now. We're at the outskirts of the city."

"Why are they watching us instead of helping us?"

He shrugs. "Maybe they don't trust you yet."

"They don't trust me? We're taking the bigger risk by coming here."

"It's going to be okay," Tomas says quietly. "You understand why they're suspicious. If they're discovered, then they'll be arrested and killed, and their families will be in danger as well."

"I understand," I tell him, thinking that I'm glad they don't know that I'm setting them up. *I hope David knows what he's doing.* I don't want to get innocent people hurt. "Let's go inside. I'm ready."

"Follow me."

I walk after him toward the building closest to us. A flash catches my eye and I look up at a smashed-out window. I see the metallic glint of a gun muzzle. I glance around at some of the other windows. These buildings are not as abandoned as I thought. Guns are trained on us from five separate windows. The rebels are not taking any chances.

We step inside the brick building and pause at the doorway. It takes my eyes a second to adjust to the dim light.

I'm startled to see a group of about eighty people gathered there in a large room with a low ceiling, watching me walk in. None of them says anything or makes any sound.

I walk a little farther into the building, with Tomas at my side. I see rebels with guns pointed in my direction, at the edges of the crowd.

I scan the assembled throng. These people range in age from about twelve to seventy—an equal mix of men and women, and all different races. They are also dressed differently from one another. Some of them look like businessmen. Others look like farmers. But all of them have the same serious look in their eyes. Many of them openly display guns or knives.

The last time I was in front of a crowd watching me so intensely, I was playing guitar and giving a performance at Destiny Station. But there will be no guitars or music today. That is in the past.

The people keep staring back at me. They don't look friendly, but at least they look prepared to listen.

"My name is Alenna Shawcross," I begin. "I've come here from Island Alpha, to help your rebel cell, and—"

"We know who you are," a woman calls out loudly.

I falter, falling silent for a second.

"You escaped from the wheel. My son is there. Eric Vendoza. Do you know him?"

I shake my head. "No, I—"

"What about my brother?" a teenage girl cries out. "Jason Goldsmith. Do you know him? Did you see him on the wheel?"

"No—" I begin again, trying to explain to them how huge Island Alpha is. The chance of me knowing any of their relatives is slim.

Voices overwhelm me, calling out more names.

I look at Tomas, confused. I had no idea this was what today would be like. I realize now that most of these people probably became rebels because their loved ones got banished to the wheel.

The names keep coming faster and faster. *This is why they're here.* They don't want to know what it's like to escape the wheel. They want to find out if I have any information about their kidnapped family members.

"Quiet!" a man calls out, cutting through the noise of the crowd. "Stop tossing names at her!" The man steps out from the mob of people, gesturing for their silence. He's heavyset, wearing overalls. His face is ruddy.

At first I think he has intervened to help me. But he's staring at me angrily. "You could be a spy from the UNA, sent here to deceive us—and expose this cell! You could be here to betray us to the government." He looks out at the crowd. "By giving her the names of your relatives, you're giving her data. And she will use it against you and your families if she's a spy."

The crowd falls silent, eyeing me suspiciously again. I know that I have to do something to turn things around. While it's true I'm here on false pretenses, I am not a spy.

"I don't work for the UNA," I declare firmly, shooting the man a fierce gaze. "And I'm sure the government already knows about this cell." I didn't expect this kind of response from the rebels. "You don't understand. The UNA knows almost everything. They just don't always choose to act on it, because they don't have unlimited resources."

The man looks at me.

"The government just thinks you don't pose any real threat to them," I continue. "The government knows that some rebel cells exist. They know about the rebellion on Island Alpha. But they don't know that we're all working together to bring them down. They think we're just isolated rebels who will never have enough power to destroy them. They're spending their time and money fighting other countries like the Asian Alliance and European Coalition. They're not worried about us yet."

"And what if they're right?" a woman calls out from the crowd. "We can't take to the streets and fight. We'll be killed. Some of us have young kids."

"Most likely, you're going to be killed anyway," I say. "You don't understand what I saw. On Island Alpha, life was cheaper than dirt. You mean nothing to the UNA." I stare around at them. "To them, we're disposable. Lives don't matter. Only power and control does."

Tomas steps up next to me. "You should listen to Alenna. Her experiences on the wheel will be extremely valuable to you. She and her friends managed to turn the UNA's technology against itself, and they destroyed the UNA's main prison colony. If that's possible, then anything is. You need to be quiet and let her speak."

I look around. I'm waiting to get captured but it hasn't happened yet. Maybe David was wrong and it's not going to happen today. Or maybe it will happen after I leave the building. I might as well take this opportunity to try to help the rebels.

In the ensuing silence, I say, "You can't worry about your own lives. Or your families. I know that sounds cold, but our struggle is bigger than that. It's a fight for the whole nation, and maybe the whole planet. The UNA needs to be taken down. Remember that whatever happens, you are the only ones who are going to do it. Most citizens are too afraid to fight back right now. But when they see us, and the rebel cells united as an army, more will join our ranks. We will start a civil war in this country and overturn the government."

"That's what you hope for," a man's voice calls out. "We do too. But is that reality?"

"It is if we want it to be. We can make it a reality."

"What if——" a woman's voice begins, but it gets interrupted.

"Stop!" someone hisses. "Did you hear that?"

There's a moment of silence.

I hear the creaking of floorboards. Then, before I can say more, there's a loud disruption outside. I hear the sharp pops of gunfire and the noise of a helicopter in the sky.

Everyone starts rushing around and yelling at once. I hear people screaming for more guns. Everyone scatters.

So this is it. I'm going to get taken.

Government soldiers burst into the building and crash through the crowd. They beat people with their nightsticks and with the butts of their assault rifles. Gunshots go off. The soldiers and the rebels are exchanging gunfire as other rebels try to run. I hear more clashes from outside.

I'm not sure why my capture is so violent and sudden. The soldiers could have just driven up with guns and taken me before I even met with the rebels.

"I knew she was a spy!" a voice yells.

I hear the sharp retort of a gunshot. I duck, thinking that it's coming from a soldier firing at the crowd.

Then I realize it's coming from the heavyset man with the ruddy face. He's firing at me. "I could tell this was a setup!" He's clutching an illegal homemade pipe gun, and it's aimed at my face. He should be running for his life, but he's too furious at me to flee. "Traitor!" he yells, firing the weapon again. I manage to dive out of the way at the last second, dodging the projectile, which explodes against the brick wall.

Uniformed soldiers in riot gear keep flooding the building.

My instinct is to run, but I know that's not the plan. Not if I want to see Liam again. I just stand there in the middle of the room.

The soldiers find me and their hands grab me roughly. "Alenna Shawcross!" one of them yells. "You have been remanded into state custody for treason and murder. You are coming with us!"

Their hands start punching and clawing at me. I don't fight back. But they keep coming. I know that I'm supposed to let myself get taken, just like David said, but it's hard to breathe. There are so many of them that I feel like I'm being smothered. I struggle for air, but their numbers are endless and brutal.

A fist knocks me in the side of my head and my vision goes dark for a moment. I don't want to lose consciousness. I let my body go limp. The blows let up a bit. The soldiers force me outside and start dragging me along the street.

A rebel runs at a policeman nearby, gun raised. The policeman shoots him right in the chest without any hesitation. The rebel fires back and misses. The policeman shoots him again and again. I shut my eyes against the senseless violence.

David better be right, I think. Or else I've just essentially committed suicide by getting captured—and endangered all these other lives as well. I can't believe that David would be so careless with other people's lives. It didn't have to happen this way. But I have to keep my faith in him. I think about the sacrifices that he's made, from the very start of our journey together. Only someone truly driven to destroy the UNA would risk their mind and body in such a way.

I see a gray metal van with massive bulletproof tires ahead of me. The soldiers are going to put me inside it and take me away. *Just like they did to Liam.* I arch my body backward.

One of the soldiers jams a black hood over my head and pulls it tight. I can't see anything.

I cry out in surprise because I can't help it, and when I breathe back in, fabric gets sucked into my mouth, smothering me. I choke and gag. The soldiers continue to carry my body.

Suddenly I crash against something. I realize that we've reached the van. Handcuffs are slipped around my wrists, trapping my arms behind my back. The soldiers push me inside the vehicle. I fall down onto the metal floor, yelping in pain. I hear the van doors slam shut behind me. The engine starts up and we begin moving rapidly down the street.

I gasp for air. The hood makes me feel like I'm suffocating again. I force myself to calm down and relax. I focus on Liam. I focus on David. I force myself to take slower breaths. My pounding heart finally starts to calm down. Eventually the panicked feeling subsides and I just lie there, as we go over bumps at rapid speed.

The journey lasts for many hours. I just lie there on the floor of the van, trapped, with my vision obscured by the hood. I know that this is part of David's plan, but I'm nervous about letting myself get captured. It goes against everything that I learned on Island Alpha, and it feels unnatural. I want to escape and fight the guards. But I know I need to suppress that urge, at least for now.

I have no clue where I am headed. I just have to trust David. I remember what Kelley said, that helping someone like me means a mandatory death sentence. *Is that what's going to happen to the members of the rebel cell?* Is that what's going to happen to me?

I don't know how David ended up with so much influence, and with such an understanding of how everything works. Since the start he has been that way. I think of Kelley's words, that he was groomed since he was a little boy to play this role. There is something unique about him. I don't yet understand what it is.

The van eventually comes to a stop. My body aches all over. I have no idea what part of New Texas we're in anymore. It could be anywhere. Maybe we've even left the state. I try to suppress my fear.

I hear noises outside the van. People yelling and screaming. I also hear the guards cursing.

The back door suddenly opens up. Arms grab me and yank me forward. "Get out!" a voice yells. "Hurry!"

7 THE CHAMBER

A HAND GRABS ME by the arm and pulls me out of the van.
I fall onto the pavement, scraping my shoulders and knees. The
black hood is yanked off my head. Around me is an angry crowd
of citizens, screaming and yelling at the guards in the van. There
are also more guards standing at the sides with guns, trying to
keep order.

The sight of people openly rebelling against the government
gives me a surge of hope. Such a thing would never have happened just a few months ago, before I got sent to Island Alpha.

"I can't believe you've caused us this much trouble!" one of the
guards screams at me. He yanks me to my feet. A rock hurtles by,
nearly hitting his helmet.

I try to push him off me using my shoulder, but he shoves me
in the stomach with his assault rifle. The air goes out of my lungs.
I bend over, gasping.

"Do you know where you're headed?" another soldier asks me.
The agitated crowd is screaming. I realize that they're screaming
for me to be released, and hurling insults at the soldiers.

I shake my head. It hurts too much to speak. My hands are
locked behind my back by the handcuffs.

Soldiers on either side of me start dragging me through the mob, heading toward a large silver skyscraper. I've never seen this place before. We must have driven to another city. Probably New Austin. The soldiers look exhausted from dragging me through the crowd.

"There's been a request to see you in private," one of them yells, putting his hand under my chin and pulling my face up to his. "Before you get shipped off to the Hellgrounds." I'm still struggling to catch my breath.

"A request from the local minister himself," another soldier proclaims, taking off his helmet and rubbing his sweaty brow. "He wants to see you in his office."

"The local minister?" I ask, confused. "Who the hell is that?"

"Our boss. He's in charge of this city now."

This is not what I expected. "Why does he want to see me?"

"You'll find out soon enough." He pushes me forward roughly.

I walk, but I keep an eye on him. I'm worried that he and the other soldiers are just going to beat me up when we get inside the building. David didn't warn me about any of this. I thought I'd be headed straight to the Hellgrounds.

We keep walking, heading up a short flight of concrete stairs, until we reach the revolving door that leads into the skyscraper. It's heavily guarded by officers with guns drawn. I glance back and see the angry crowd. In some ways, I feel elated. A public demonstration like this would have been met with swift gunfire not long ago. But now, for some reason, the soldiers aren't firing.

I'm pushed through the revolving door and into the huge atrium of the skyscraper.

"Move!" the guard says, prodding me. I walk across the marble floor, beneath high arching stairways. The soldiers stop when we reach a bank of elevators.

"Where are we going?" I ask. "I really don't understand what—"

"Shut up!" he interrupts me.

"We're going to the very top," another soldiers adds. The tone of his voice suggests that I'm in serious trouble.

I want to ask more questions, but I'm forced into the elevator along with two soldiers. One of them places his finger against an electronic reader and says, "Penthouse level." The elevator doors shut and we begin gliding upward.

As the elevator ascends, one of the soldiers turns to me. "Remember, do not speak unless spoken to. Do not look directly at the minister unless he requests it of you. Keep your eyes on the floor." His tone is brusque. "Do you understand what I've just told you?"

"Yes," I tell him, my mind flashing back to the drones and the Monk. They too were afraid to gaze at the Monk's face. *What is going on here?*

The elevator comes to a halt. Its doors open, and I find myself staring down a long, bright tunnel. There is only one door in sight—a massive circular steel one, like the door to a bank vault—right at the end of the hall. I keep walking, sandwiched between the two soldiers.

I have no idea what this building is. Or who this local minister is. I've never heard of such a thing. I don't even know where I am. Was David lying to me about being sent to the Hellgrounds? Or did something unexpected take place along the way? Something that even he couldn't predict?

"Move!" snaps one of the soldiers. I pick up the pace.

We reach the steel door. Both soldiers place their right thumbs against electronic readers. One of them taps a code into a nearby panel with his left hand.

A voice crackles back through a loudspeaker, "You've brought the girl?"

"Yes," the soldier says. He removes his thumb. So does the other guard.

My heart is beating wildly despite my efforts to stay calm. I don't know who—or what—is waiting for me behind this door.

The door begins to open inward, under its own power, much like the giant hatches back in the specimen archive.

Beyond it is darkness. I'm surprised. I thought it would be bright up here in the penthouse of this skyscraper. But it's nearly as dim as the rock tunnels back in Destiny Station.

"Enter the chamber of Minister Hiram!" one of the soldiers declares, as he shoves me forward into the massive space. I feel the other soldier behind me, unlocking my handcuffs. I swing my hands forward, relieved to finally have my freedom.

I turn around to ask, *Minister who?* But the guards are already stepping back into the hallway. The circular door swings shut behind them with an ominous clank.

I stand there for a moment, unnerved, staring into the gloom. I'm in a huge circular room, two hundred feet in diameter, right at the top of this building. It probably takes up the entire penthouse level.

All of the windows are covered with thick metal folding sheets, locked at the bottom with huge bolts. The walls are made of exposed concrete. It's like a bunker up here. The space is cavernous and cool. At first, nobody else seems to be inside.

But as my eyes adjust to the light, I realize that I'm not alone. Lining the curved walls is a row of guards, clutching rifles. Probably twenty of them.

For a moment, I think they're surreal statues. But they are real people, merely standing, silent and stationary. An entire army on pause. I don't understand why a minister I've never heard of—not from the rebels or scientists, or from anyone else—would be guarded as heavily as this.

The guards said that this minister runs the city. I wonder how much power he actually has, if any. Perhaps this is some sort of bureaucratic show meant to scare me before I get sent to the Hellgrounds.

A spotlight is turned on, illuminating the center of the room. Directly underneath the light sit two chairs facing each other at a marble table. The table is embossed with the UNA emblem in gold. But when I look closer, I see that this emblem has been modified. Instead of an eye hovering over a globe, it shows five eyes surrounding the globe. Its golden contours gleam in the bright light.

Confused, I take a few steps toward the table. Then a few more.

I glance back and see the guards lining the walls watching me. I consider saying something to them, or trying to fight them, but there doesn't seem to be a point. I don't want to jeopardize getting sent to the Hellgrounds and finding Liam, let alone whatever mission awaits us there.

I keep walking cautiously toward the chairs and the table. I imagine this is what I am supposed to do.

Other than the silent soldiers who stand guard, I am alone. None of them acknowledge my presence here.

"Hello?" I finally dare to ask, my voice cracking.

I feel a hand on my shoulder.

I yelp, spinning around in surprise. I slip on the slick marble floor and go crashing down to one knee. A second ago, there had been no one behind me. But now a man is standing there. He's smiling, wearing an expensive-looking suit, with slicked-back hair.

I get to my feet, wary. I'm still trying to figure out what's going on.

"Alenna," the man says, fixing me with an unblinking gaze. His face is impossible to read. Inscrutable. He is curiously ageless, with few wrinkles at the corners of his eyes, although I know he must be in his late forties. His strong nose and wide mouth make his face look swollen and masklike. He has a diamond-shaped scar on his left temple. I recognize this face because I've seen it up close before. "Do you know who I am?"

"You're one of Minister Harka's body doubles," I say, feeling sick.

He chuckles. "It's true. I was. But that was several years ago." He pauses, a thin smile playing over his lips. "Since then, I've been promoted."

"To what?"

"To someone in charge." He looks closely into my eyes. "See, just like the wheel, the UNA is now divided into certain sectors controlled by different ministers."

"Why?"

"For economic and social reasons." He pauses again. "Do you know where I take my name from?"

"No." I shake my head, completely confused. "Why are you asking me?"

"I like to teach the uninitiated." He smiles. "I take my name from Hiram Abiff. Also known as Hiram Abi. He's a mythological figure in the world of Freemasonry. A master builder and crafts-man who constructed great temples. His tools were gold and silver, bronze and iron, stone and wood." He pauses contemplatively. "He's an inspiration to me."

I nod, pretending that I understand what he's talking about. I suppose I should be glad that he's talking to me instead of torturing me. But maybe that part is coming next. I try to ignore the armed soldiers who stand, completely still and silent, around the edges of the room.

"Once I was promoted, I was free to name myself. I could become my own man, so to speak." He shrugs. "Well, actually, given my resemblance to Minister Harka—thanks to the plastic surgery—I usually claim that I am his brother. So nobody gets suspicious." He winks at me.

I nod. This man is giving me the creeps. I wonder who he was before he became a body double. There is something unhinged about him. Even more so than Minister Harka himself. I remember that Minister Harka mentioned being pushed out of his own government and sent to the wheel by men who were even more corrupt than he was. *Is this one of those men?*

"Would you like to see something interesting, Alenna? Something few citizens of the UNA ever get to see?"

"Depends on what it is."

A flicker of annoyance passes across his features, but it quickly passes. "Follow me." He steps over to the chairs. "Have a seat."

I take a seat across from him at the table. Here, under the lights, his face looks even more waxen and synthetic.

"So this is what happens to Minister Harka's body doubles," I say. "You end up advancing your careers."

"Some of us do. Others just get shot or poisoned. It depends." He glances away from me for a moment. "Now take a look at this."

Without any obvious signal, a red curtain is automatically drawn away from one of the walls. Six of the guards move forward and start rolling an object toward us. It's a glass box on wheels, about ten feet high and four feet wide. Inside it is a huge person—stuck in there, like a trapped insect. It's too shadowy for me to see any details.

"Observe this creature," Minister Hiram says to me, as the box draws close. He turns in his seat to look at it. "Do you know what you're staring at?"

I swallow hard. "Somebody that you're torturing?"

He shakes his head. "No. You're staring at the future of the UNA Army. We are reinventing not just the UNA, but the entire world, and how warfare is conducted." He glances back at me. I see the fervor in his eyes. I can't believe that he is revealing this to me. "Come, come," he continues as the glass box stops moving. "Up to the glass. Have a look for yourself. It can't hurt you." He gets up from his seat and I follow him.

I walk cautiously up to the glass box. The figure inside slowly pivots toward us. It raises an arm, and places one hand on the inside of the glass, fingers splayed. As I move closer, the figure coalesces into view.

It only takes me a second to realize that it's some sort of mutant.

The mutant's skin is dark, almost purple, and the mutant is massive—about seven feet tall. Its eyes burn red beneath hooded brows. They look oddly human and I can see the intelligence behind them, but I'm not certain this creature is sane. It's rippled with muscles and covered in a light dusting of fur. I see strange gills on its neck. I'm not sure what it is—a person or an animal. Or maybe some demented hybrid between the two.

"How can it breathe?" I ask, swallowing my horror. There are no airholes in the glass.

"They don't breathe. Not like you and me." Minister Hiram presses his gloved hand against the glass, matching his fingers to those of the mutant. "The perfect warrior. He can survive for hundreds of years. Fight thousands of battles. We found a way to turn off the aging sequences in his DNA, so he will live forever and never get a day older."

I lean in closer. The figure's red eyes are watching Minister Hiram. It doesn't even notice me.

"Would you trade your soul for eternal life?" Hiram asks me, his voice barely above a whisper now.

I'm silent. *How did this mutant get created? Government drugs?*

"Tell me your thoughts," Minister Hiram prompts. "I want to know."

"No," I finally say. Then add, "I don't think I'd trade my soul for anything. Eternal life means nothing without freedom, or love, or a million other things."

Minister Hiram chuckles again. "Yes. True. What does a teenager care for eternal life?" He turns away from the trapped mutant, breaking the spell for a moment. "Most teenagers feel like life is eternal. I did too, when I was young."

"I don't. I saw too many friends die on Island Alpha."

The mutant takes its hand off the glass and retreats to the other side of the box, curling up away from us. The soldiers wheel it back to the wall.

The red curtain starts moving again, slowly shrouding the giant glass box from view.

"Why did you show me the mutant? Why are you telling me all this?"

He pauses for a beat. "Because I am proud of our work," he finally says. "And I want you to see what you are up against. Any weapons you muster will be no use against these mutants." He pauses for a moment. "These mutants are what broke Dr. Barrett."

I'm surprised at the mention of his name. "What do you mean?"

"Meira showed videos of them to him. She explained that there was no way he could win against them. That he would always be many steps behind us. He was already in so much pain that seeing the mutants took his last shred of hope away. That, along with all the beatings and drugs that he received. Meira picked his brains for us and left him shattered."

"You're evil," I spit at him.

In response, Minister Hiram places a black-gloved hand on my shoulder. I instantly feel a weird sensation. A mild electric shock. Like he's pinching one of my nerves. The feeling shivers and trickles down my arm. I squirm away from his painful grasp.

"Now we must talk about other things, Alenna. Much less pleasant things than eternal life, the future of warfare, and Dr. Barrett's destruction."

He strides back over to the table and chairs. I follow, aware of all the soldiers watching us. I'm nervous again, afraid of what's coming next. I sit down across from him.

"You broke the rules that the UNA lives by," he tells me calmly.

"I know," I reply.

"And you survived. You even managed to make it off Island Alpha, and back to our soil."

I nod, unrepentant. He keeps looking at me with his piercing eyes. "I showed you my secret captive. My mutant inside the glass. But now you must share some secrets of your own."

"I don't have any secrets to share."

"None?"

I shrug. "Not today."

Hiram smiles, but his eyes remain cold and glassy. "So you had no plans, then. No plans to exhort the rebel cells hiding in the UNA to rise up? No plans to move around from cell to cell? No plans to take down our government?" He takes a piece of electronic paper out of his pocket, as I struggle to stay calm. I can't believe what I'm hearing.

How can he know about all our plans?

He holds the paper up, making sure I get a good look at it.

A series of geographic coordinates and names scroll across the paper endlessly.

"I don't know what that is," I tell him. But it's a lie. I have seen these coordinates before. They represent the rebel cells scattered throughout the UNA.

Minister Hiram smiles at me. "I can read it on your face. This is a list of every rebel cell in the UNA, isn't it?" He pushes the piece of electronic paper across the table to me. "I've already committed all the numbers to memory." He sighs. "The rebels are such hapless souls. Disorganized and paranoid."

I pick up the sheet of electronic paper. My fingers are trembling slightly. I try to conceal it from Minister Hiram, but I'm sure he can tell. I stuff it into my pocket. I can't tell yet if he knows about David's plans, or that I got captured on purpose.

"Why do you think the UNA has laws?" Minister Hiram continues, sounding almost philosophical.

"To make our lives hell."

"No. It's to uphold a system of belief. A perfect circle. Life as it should be. There doesn't need to be so many countries on this planet. Only one."

"That's fascism. The UNA has destroyed too many lives and way too many countries."

Hiram ignores me. "Tell me what I should do with you," he continues, his unblinking eyes fixed on mine. "You are a rebel. And a killer. And you've destroyed millions of dollars of government property. You should be put to death."

"Then kill me," I tell him. "Just do it already." I feel defiant.

Then something completely unexpected starts to occur. At first I think I'm imagining things. But then I realize that it's actually happening.

Minister Hiram is crying.

His eyes well up, and a tear breaks free. It rolls down his oddly smooth cheek. It's followed by another. He doesn't try to conceal the tears. He just stares at me through them, as they run from the corners of his eyes, down his face, and drip onto the marble floor.

I don't know what to do. If the tears are genuine, then he is insane.

Minister Hiram reaches out with his gloved hand and takes hold of my forearm. Again, I get a weird, prickling electrical feeling from him. I try to pull away, but he won't let me go. His fingers encircle my arm.

"You need to understand the pain that you've caused me," Hiram says. A few more tears spatter onto the marble tabletop like raindrops and run down the ridges of the mutated UNA logo. He dabs at his eyes with his free hand. "Do you understand it?"

Before I can answer, his hand suddenly tightens with a pressure unlike anything I've felt before.

It's like a bench vise—so tight that I'm afraid he is going to break a bone in my arm. I cry out in pain and tumble off the chair, falling onto my knees on the marble floor. "Stop!" I gasp.

"There is no escape from the UNA. Don't you know that by now?"

I try to pull away from his grasp, but the pain is incredible. I'm gasping for air. Afraid I'm going to pass out.

"We were aware of your plans. We will dismantle you rebels before you even begin to pose a threat to us."

"Please . . . let me go . . . ," I say, fighting against the pain.

He releases me abruptly and I slip, stumbling backward and knocking my head against the marble floor. My ears ring for a moment. I scramble away from him, trying to keep my distance. Even if I tried to fight him, I know that the armed soldiers surrounding his chamber would intervene. And besides, I have no idea of his strength. I get back up to my feet, rubbing my skin where he grabbed me.

Minister Hiram walks over. The friendly man who showed me the mutant in the giant glass box is gone. He's been replaced by someone terrifying.

"I see everything here. I know everything," he intones. "And I wish I could have you put to death for your crimes. I wanted to meet you so I could stare into the face of an unrepentant rebel and a scourge to our great nation. Now I know what it looks like. And what I have in store for you is far more fascinating and useful than death. You're going to become part of a scientific study." He turns his gaze from me and toward the soldiers lining the walls. "It's time now!" he declares, clapping his hands. "Come and get her!"

"Where are you taking me?" I ask. "What kind of scientific study?"

This must be the part where I get sent to the Hellgrounds.

"We have big plans for you, Alenna," Minister Hiram continues. "The other ministers think you will be useful to us if we keep you alive. Not to torture you, but to help you see things our way. To help you work on our side. You have strength, courage, and perseverance. Those are traits we need to cultivate in such difficult times. We want you to work with us, and fight on our side."

"I'll never fight on your side!" I hiss at him. "What makes you think I would? My dad is dead because of the UNA, and my mom lives in exile. You ruined my family, and my life. I'd rather die than help you."

"Dying takes free will. What if we take free will away from you, Alenna? What if you have no choice in the matter?"

"I don't understand what you mean."

He smiles again. "You will soon enough."

Soldiers begin walking forward from the walls, heading over to surround me. Minister Hiram steps backward, out of the way.

There are so many soldiers that I'm instantly overrun. They start hitting and kicking at me. There's no way to evade all their blows. I curl up into a ball. The beating doesn't cease, even though I don't fight back.

"Your pain is my pain!" I hear Minister Hiram call out over the noise. "I feel every blow, Alenna. I will bear every scar. Soldiers, take her to the white chamber! And then onward, to the Hellgrounds!"

Hands start lifting me up, even as they pinch and smack me. I struggle, yelling for help, as I'm borne out of the chamber and through a secret passageway behind a curtain, and into a dark tunnel.

We finally reach a door, and one of the guards shoves it open. I'm dragged into a cavernous space gleaming with sunlight. The roof is made of glass. It's the antithesis of Minister Hiram's dark lair. This must be the white chamber, whatever that is.

Its walls and floor gleam with fresh white paint. A gallery of plastic chairs, all white, sits on both sides. They are empty, except for a few clusters of old women in nurses' outfits.

The soldiers force me down onto an empty gurney, and then they buckle leather straps across my chest, hands, and feet, restraining me completely. I try to kick and fight back, to lash and bite them. But they dodge my blows. Their faces are completely blank, like the drones on the island after Meira took control.

I stop struggling, trying to conserve my strength. I refuse to do anything for these soldiers but stare at them angrily, trying to burn my fury into their souls. But they seem unfazed by my glare. Maybe they've seen such looks from kids like me before.

Two old women step forward as the guards move out of the way. I have no idea who they are, or what they're doing here. Each one clutches a side of my gurney. They begin wheeling my body along a narrow hall, the gurney painfully jouncing my body.

"Who are you?" I ask them.

"Attendants of Minister Hiram," one says.

"Servants of the UNA," another adds.

"Where am I going?" I ask them.

"Isolation," one of them says cryptically.

I remember the sensory deprivation tank back on the wheel. *Is this what that training was for?* Did the scientists know that this would happen to me? I feel like a pawn in some larger game, and I hate it.

"How long will I be in isolation for?" I ask, hoping against the odds that these women will give me information. I need to find out everything I can while I have the chance.

"Hush now, Alenna," one of them says.

"Please. You have to tell me."

"No one knows, child," the other woman says. She speaks with a dazed, drugged voice, like she's only partly there. "It's up to the minister. It could be for a month, or it could be for a year or two. Or longer than that."

I start struggling against my restraints. "A year? You have to help me! Let me out of here!"

Instead of a response, I see the flash of a white handkerchief in the corner of my eye. One of the old women has taken the handkerchief out of an old brown satchel, along with a black medical flask. I try to turn my head to find out what she's doing, but leather straps bite hard into my neck.

"What's going on?" I ask, as I see her pouring the contents of the bottle into the handkerchief. "What is that?"

"It's time to sleep now," the other old woman says. "Don't struggle anymore. You have a long journey ahead of you, and you need to be well rested for it."

Before I know what's happening, the first woman presses the soaked handkerchief tightly against my nose and mouth.

I instantly feel like I'm suffocating. I start trying to get her hand off my face, clawing and kicking. But the straps prevent me from escaping. I scream, but the sound is muffled.

A sweet, rotten scent fills my nostrils. My hearing begins to get muffled, like I'm about pass out. I feel woozy.

"No!" I try to yell, but the word comes out as a whisper. My arms and legs are growing heavy. My vision starts constricting into a tunnel. I fight against the restraints, but it feels like I'm partially underwater. About to drown.

"David . . . ," I whisper, barely able to move my lips. The total, absolute blackness of synthetic slumber overwhelms me as the world fades into a circle of nothingness.

8 THE HELLGROUNDS

MY SENSES RETURN IN a violent rush of color and sound. It seems like only one second has passed since I got drugged, but it must have been far longer.

I am not inside some scary isolation tank.

Instead, I'm lying on a soft mattress, looking up at a wood beam ceiling.

I check my senses quickly, doing a rapid inventory of my body and my mind. I can still see. I can still hear. All my other senses are intact as well.

I run my hands over my body, looking for wounds.

At first, I find nothing. But then, as I bring my hands up to my neck, I discover something absolutely terrifying.

My hands stop moving. I feel like I'm going to throw up.

On the back of my neck, two vertical plastic tubes have been implanted in my flesh, bulging out of the skin. Each of them is about two inches long.

I yank my hands away, shocked and sickened. The tubes don't hurt much. They just feel weird and heavy. I don't know what these tubes do, or why they're in me. It makes me think of what happened to David's body.

Panic rises inside me. *What has been done to me? How long was I unconscious?* Obviously some kind of torture device has been implanted in me.

There are no soldiers anywhere in sight. And I'm not held down by restraints anymore.

I struggle out of the bed. My legs are shaky, but they support my weight. I glance down and see that I'm wearing a simple gray, handwoven T-shirt and jeans.

I'm standing on the second floor of a large farmhouse.

There is no doubt that I'm in the Hellgrounds now. *Just like David said I would be.*

I must have been transported here while I was unconscious. I stare through a huge picture window at a field of corn. And at the dark forest beyond that. This must be New Iowa. I wonder how far I am from the place where Liam is being held. At least Liam and I are both in the Hellgrounds together.

I touch the back of my neck again and feel the plastic tubes. Both tubes run in vertical lines, soft and rubbery, like external veins made of plastic. They don't hurt as much as they probably should, but they make me feel sick.

I'm not even sure what these tubes will do to me. Maybe they're meant to poison me. I just know that I've been altered in some revolting way. And by people that I despise.

I think about Minister Hiram saying that free will would be taken away from me. *Are the tubes in my neck somehow going to do that to me? Are they going to affect my brain?*

I turn and gaze at myself in a large, gilded mirror that hangs on the wall across from the window. It's sandwiched between framed photographs of Minister Harka.

From the front, I look totally normal. So I turn sideways to get a better view. From this angle I can actually see the tubes in my neck. They come out at the base of my skull and then reenter my body above my shoulders. The tubes are made of yellow plastic. They look a lot smaller than they feel.

"Alenna Shawcross?" a voice suddenly asks.

I spin around to the doorway, feeling vulnerable and groggy.

A middle-aged woman in a simple gray frock stands there watching me. Her freckled face is creased with lines, from too many years of sun exposure. Her skin looks like a crumpled sheet of paper. She's tall and thin, and wears metal-frame glasses that are slightly too large for her face. Her brown hair, just beginning to turn gray, is held back in a tight bun.

"That's your name, isn't it?" she asks. "Alenna."

"Yeah," I tell her.

"You may call me Miss Caroldean."

"Who the hell are you?"

She stares at me for a long time. Her black eyes are as hard and cold as glass. "You're quite pretty for an agitator. I'll give you that," she finally says.

An agitator. It's a strange choice of words. I expected to be called a rebel. I don't say anything in response. I just nod. I can feel the tubes in my neck tugging at my flesh, so I stop nodding.

"Do you know how many agitators like you our family has hosted?"

I shake my head. "No. How could I?"

"Seventeen. All girls your age. All girls who slipped through the Government Personality Profile Test, but then turned out to be troublemakers." She waits for me to be impressed. I try to fake it. "And each one of them went on to become productive citizens for the highest echelon of the UNA. They are the pride of my life."

"Really," I say.

"You probably have a lot of questions for me. And I'm sure you've noticed those vessels in your neck. Do you know why they've been placed there?"

My hand goes up to them again. "No clue."

"The tubes are there in case you get it into your head to run away," Miss Caroldean replies. I don't like the sound of this, and she can see it in my eyes. "That's right. Agitators often try to run. Surgeons implanted those tubes before you were delivered to me."

She slips her hand into her pocket, and extracts a metal UNA emblem painted black. Again, it's different from the one I'm familiar with. *Five eyes hover around a globe.* In the center of it is a blinking red switch.

"This switch is wired to those tubes in your neck," she continues. "If you try to run, I will throw the switch, and the electrical signals that power your body will instantly bypass your spinal cord. You will be paralyzed, and lose your senses. Not for good, but until I decide to throw the switch again and open up your electrical pathways. Understand? Then you will recover. Of course, sometimes there are lingering complications. Nerve injuries and such." She pauses. "You are under my command from now on. Do you understand?"

I swallow my feeling of dismay. Could she be telling the truth, or is it a bluff? I feel too shaky and new here to test her yet.

"This switch stays with me at all times," she continues. "I am never to be challenged. You must obey my every command. Or I will not hesitate to punish you—and I have the full authority of the UNA in such matters."

I nod again. Her bony hand slips the metal device back into her pocket.

"Now, I was told that you are an exceptional girl. Of high intelligence, who can learn easily, and has proven herself to be very brave. Is that true?"

"I don't know."

"There's no need to be humble. You wouldn't have been sent here unless the UNA saw great potential in you. And I know that you made it off Island Alpha, and survived when others would not have. That means you're made of strong stuff, and you're not afraid of hard work. And there's lots of hard work to be done on a farm."

I look down at the floor, feigning sheepishness because I don't want her to see the look of sudden rage in my own eyes. I'm reminded that every second I'm imprisoned here, terrible things could be happening to Liam.

But somehow I don't fool her.

"You're worried about your boyfriend," she says. "You know that he's out here somewhere too, don't you?"

I can't disguise my surprise at her words. She smiles when she sees the look on my face.

"I know everything, Alenna. You cannot hide a grain of rice from me. Not in this house. Not on my own farm. So you best behave, and learn what you can from my example. That is why you were sent here—to stay with me and my children, and learn how moral citizens of the UNA behave. And to learn how to overcome your own hasty emotions. To learn the value of sacrifice." She stares past me, out the window and across the fields baking under the sun. "Do you know what happened to my husband?"

I shake my head.

"Three years ago, an agitator ran away from a city. A girl, not much older than you are now. Soldiers were sent in search of her, of course. Foolish rebels gave her help along the way, and she made it all the way here. My husband volunteered to help guide the soldiers through this region when they were looking for her." She brushes back a strand of her graying hair. "He led them up to the edge of the forest. There, they were ambushed and attacked by rebels. My husband disappeared. They never found his body. He was presumed dead."

Her eyes turn back to me. She clears her throat and continues speaking, "But the soldiers managed to defeat the rebels. Their leader was hung in public, and the others were sent to work camps in New Alaska, where they eventually died of exposure. I continue to run the farm in memory of my husband. I raise our children in his name. And now I take in agitators so that I can train them to be good leaders for the UNA. I can take an unanchored soul and turn her into the most effective citizen."

She's staring at me hard. Unblinking. I don't know what to say. "I'm sorry about your husband," I finally offer, even though it's a lie.

She blinks. "What happened to your own parents no doubt taught you about suffering. Which is why you must learn to cease agitating, and begin to serve your country." She pauses. "Do you love Liam Bernal?"

I don't reply. There's no way I'm going to talk about my feelings for Liam with someone like her.

"Answer me."

I stare back at her defiantly. My lips remain sealed.

She sighs. "If you do love him, then you must put him out of your head forever. It will only cause you heartache to pine for someone whom you can never have. Romantic love has no place in the UNA. The only love I wish to see from you is love of your nation and love of Minister Harka." She pauses. "I know what you agitators call our community."

I stare back at her. "The Hellgrounds," I say.

She nods. "Exactly. But if you open yourself up to Minister Harka and submit to the will of the UNA, it can become heaven on earth." She turns away from me. "Now come this way. I will show you around the house, where you'll be living for the next three months, while I train you."

Three months. I don't plan on being here for more than three days. David said I would have a tight deadline. I need to figure out what my next step is as soon as possible.

Miss Caroldean leads me out into the hallway. The walls are painted light yellow, with lime-green trim, and the floor is made of creaky wood planks. Photos and drawings of Minister Harka line the walls. Everything looks old, like it comes from the previous century. Or maybe even the one before that. I wonder how long this massive farmhouse has been here.

I follow Miss Caroldean down a wide flight of stairs, and into a huge, airy living room. It's sparsely furnished, with handwoven white rugs strewn over the wood floor, and rough-hewn oak furniture.

A large homemade portrait of Minister Harka done in oils hangs above a massive fireplace. To the left is an open kitchen and dining area. This house is by far the largest I've ever seen—perhaps its size is one of the few perks of living in the Hellgrounds. Miss Caroldean and I walk to the center of the room.

We're not alone in here. There's an older boy sitting on a stool in an antechamber near the front door. Sharpening a knife on a piece of whetstone. A hand-rolled cigarette dangles unlit from one corner of his mouth.

"This is Mikal. My youngest son," Miss Caroldean says. "Nearly eighteen. My other sons are grown and have left the farm."

Mikal slowly turns toward me. His black hair is slicked back with grease, and he has a white scar running from his nose to his lip. His features are severe—a thin nose, thin lips, and sharp cheekbones. His blue eyes are narrow with hooded lids. He's dressed all in black—jacket, shirt, jeans, and boots. He smiles warmly, but his eyes remain as cold as his mother's. "Hey there," he says to me.

"Hey," I say in response. I can already tell I'm going to have to watch my back around him. I feel his eyes roam over my body, checking me out. It gives me the shivers.

"Mikal is going to enter the UNA Military Training Academy in two months," Miss Caroldean says proudly. "You can learn a lot from him."

I nod. Mikal just keeps staring at me creepily, wearing that odd, thin smile, made slightly crooked by his scar.

Then he takes out a cigarette lighter and flicks the flint. He brings the flame up to his cigarette and lights it.

"Yes, you will learn a lot of things from Mikal," his mother reiterates, her voice rising slightly in irritation. "But smoking is *not* one of them!"

Mikal slides off the stool, unfazed. "Sorry," he says insolently. He stands up, uncoiling his lithe body.

"Take your cigarette outside," she instructs, coughing. "You know I have asthma."

Mikal does as he's told, stepping outside onto a large front porch. Through the window I see him settle down into a wooden porch swing, lounging back as he sucks on the cigarette.

"He's so eager to be a soldier," Miss Caroldean says. "And of course a lot of them smoke. He's following their example, I suppose." She sighs. "Mikal is a tender soul. He takes after his father in that way."

I just stand there. He looks more like a delinquent than anything else, but obviously I'm not going to point that out.

"Now come this way," Miss Caroldean says. "There's so much to see!"

Miss Caroldean continues her tour of the farmhouse and its grounds. The house itself is huge, but it's dwarfed by the massive barn and stables behind it, as well as a grain silo and a large dog kennel.

Few people work this land other than her, Mikal, and six farmhands—mostly older men. They don't look interested in me. Only in their work. There are also a number of mangy dogs roaming the property. I take everything in, studying my environment. Planning potential escape routes. I have no clue how David is going to give me instructions, but I hope that he somehow contacts me soon.

Here, at the Hellgrounds, I have a much better chance of finding Liam and continuing on my mission than at any other point in my journey. *And I don't plan on wasting the opportunity.* I must reconnect with David and learn what it is that I have to detonate.

Once the tour is over, we return to the main house through the back door. Miss Caroldean has explained that she expects me to work—to help out the farmhands and Mikal. She's also mentioned that she has two other children: twin eight-year-old girls, currently at a neighbor's farm for a birthday party. I will be expected to help watch them when she needs me to, but only after I've proven myself to be reliable and honest, and not some dangerous crazy person.

We stand in the kitchen. Miss Caroldean pours a glass of water and squeezes half a fresh lemon into it, followed by a dash of sugar. I'm so hot and thirsty, I assume it's for me. But it's not.

"Take this to Mikal," Miss Caroldean says. "He should be out front, chopping firewood. And remember, if you feel like running, think again." She puts her hand in her pocket and brings up the black UNA emblem again, fingering the switch. "Some girls try running the very first chance they get, as soon as they arrive here and their strength comes back. They always regret it."

I pick up the glass of lemonade and stare at her. "I won't run."

She nods. "Then you're one of the smarter ones."

I feel her eyes heating my back as I walk through the house, and step outside onto the porch. I see Mikal standing at a tree stump in the grass, about a hundred yards away from me, his shirt off. He's holding an ax, cursing. Around him are splintered chunks of firewood. He tosses the ax down and rummages for something else at his feet.

I walk across the grass toward him. The sun is hot, and my skin still feels tender. I can feel the sun warming the tubes in the back of my neck. Around me I hear insects buzzing. I try not to think about Miss Caroldean and her awful device.

Mikal doesn't hear me coming. By the time I reach him, he has traded the ax for a large metal saw. He's bent over an old window frame, sawing it into pieces of wood. He finally sees me and stops working, the saw still in his hand.

"That for me?" he asks, eyeing the lemonade.

I nod.

He wipes sweat out of his eyes. "Hot enough for you today?"

"I guess."

"How old are you, anyway?" He squints at me.

"Sixteen."

"That's young for an agitator. Usually they're seventeen. Guess you started early?"

"I guess so."

"So you really made it off that island. You and your boyfriend, and those other rebels." He stares at me. "I'm betting the men did the work. Not a pretty girl like you."

"You're wrong," I say.

"Oh yeah?" He takes a step closer. "Why don't you tell me more?"

I don't want to explain anything to Mikal. I feel like the less I interact with him, the better. I hold out the glass filled with lemonade, expecting him to grab it. "Here, just take it, Mikal."

Suddenly he lashes out with the tip of the saw.

He catches my wrist and hand, instantly shattering the glass and splattering me with lemonade. I'm left holding the jagged, broken bottom of the glass.

On instinct, I lunge forward with a yell, using the broken glass bottom as a blade. Without thinking, I slice the air where his neck was a second earlier.

He only barely manages to stumble out of the way. I see a flash of fear cross his eyes. I know that I could cut his throat. I grip the broken glass, desperate to leap forward and slash his neck.

But if I attack Mikal now, Miss Caroldean will have her revenge on me. So I force myself to step back. I clutch my hand to my chest. It's stinging as drops of blood bead on it. I pretend that it hurts more than it does.

The look of fear is now gone from Mikal's face. He advances on me, clutching the saw like a weapon.

"Why the hell did you do that to me?" I yell at him, trying to sound hurt.

"'Sir!'" he barks. "That's what you will call me—'sir.' You don't get to say my name. You're not my equal. It's 'sir' when my mom's not around. Got it?"

I stare back at him. I want to fling myself at him and cram the saw right down his throat. It wouldn't be hard. But I don't do anything. I can't risk it.

Mikal senses my anger. He pokes my shoulder with the tip of the saw. "Is there something you want to say to me?"

"No."

He sighs. "You forgot to add 'sir.'"

"I didn't forget."

His eyes narrow. "We'll keep working on it. There'll be plenty of time to practice. At the end of three months, you'll be licking my feet."

He takes a step forward. I stand my ground.

"You're gonna have to go back inside now," he says, "and explain to my mom how you broke that glass. Just say you dropped it 'cause you're clumsy. Don't mention that we had an interaction, or things will just get worse for you. What my mom doesn't know won't hurt her."

He takes another step toward me. We're just two paces away from each other now. I don't back down.

"I've seen a lot of girls like you, Alenna. You think you're so smart. And so strong. But it's luck and a smart boyfriend that's kept you alive this long."

"Liam is smart, but I don't feel lucky," I murmur.

"Well, you are. And luck has a nasty habit of running out at the worst possible moment." Mikal turns away from me, getting back to work. "Go fetch me another lemonade, girl. Be quick about it." He starts whistling jauntily as he returns to sawing at the window frame.

123

Careful not to take my eyes away from him, I back up a few steps, and then walk back toward the house with the broken glass in my hand. When I glance behind me once, I see that he's watching me. His eyes are fixed on my body. He grins. I get inside the house and shut the door.

Later that day, alone in my room upstairs, I sit down on the mattress for a moment. I've been granted a brief rest from the heat, and a chance to have some water and use the bathroom.

Seventeen girls have been here before me. There is no trace of any of them. I wish they had left notes, scrawled or scribbled on the walls. But of course Miss Caroldean would have found them and erased any traces.

I don't want any more girls to get sent here after I have left this place. I plan on being the last in the line. I gaze out the window at the endless fields. From here, there is no sign of a city. No sign of Liam. It's just me. I don't even see Mikal or Miss Caroldean anywhere. Just a few laborers hauling bales of hay into the barn.

I reach my hand up and feel the tubes in my neck again. I tug at them gently. Then harder. The more pressure I put on them, the more they hurt and make me feel nauseous. There's no way for me to pull them out.

I try to lie down on the bed, but the tubes push uncomfortably against the back of my skull. So I get up and walk over to the window. I don't know what to do with myself. I'm stuck here in the farmhouse with this family. And there's no way to get to Liam.

David promised me he'd tell me what to do once I got to the Hellgrounds. But so far, there's no indication of how to reach Liam, or what the next step in my plan is.

"David?" I murmur. "Can you hear me somehow?"

There's no answer. I feel foolish for even trying.

The only response is the chirping of cicadas outside in the fields, and the trilling of sparrows and longspurs in the trees.

I was hoping there was a hidden microphone somewhere, hidden by a rebel at David's behest. But obviously there isn't.

The only answer I get to my plea is Miss Caroldean's voice. She's calling for me to come downstairs and help her with some laundry. I force my tired limbs to obey her.

That night before supper, I finally meet her twin eight-year-old daughters—Loretta and Lorene. Both of them have long, straight blond hair, halfway down their backs in braids.

Oddly, they look nothing like Mikal. Their eyes are blue and guileless, but they have a familiar glazed look. One that I saw many times back in New Providence, the look of true believers in the UNA. These kinds of kids would never dream of questioning a single one of Minister Harka's laws.

They introduce themselves to me with overly formal gestures, like they're trying to mimic their mother.

"So, you're an agitator," Loretta says matter-of-factly. Or at least I think it's Loretta. They look so similar, it's hard to tell them apart.

"Don't use that word," snaps Miss Caroldean. "You're too young to know about all that. Her name is Alenna."

"I'm sorry for calling you an agitator, Alenna," Loretta tells me.

"Me too," Lorene adds softly. "For thinking it."

They both keep staring at me weirdly, their heads tilted slightly. I wonder if they're trying to catch a glimpse of the tubes in my neck.

Miss Caroldean seats her family around the table, but I get

seated back away from them, against the wall, watching. I am not allowed to share in any of their delicious-smelling food: a roasted ham, potatoes, carrots, spinach, and eggs. I have a small ceramic plate of corn bread in my lap, along with one hard-boiled egg. An elderly farmhand, silent and grizzled, helps tend to the food in the kitchen.

"Now let us give thanks to Minister Harka," Miss Caroldean says. Everyone around the table holds hands. But they don't hold hands with me. I notice that Mikal has already sneaked some bites of ham into his mouth, without anyone noticing. It's like they're about to pray to Minister Harka. Like he's become some sort of god in their mind. *Just like David said.*

The twins glance over at me, their blue eyes sparkling in their pale faces. "Watch us and learn," Loretta says somberly.

I nod, thinking about how creepy this family is.

Miss Caroldean shuts her eyes. "The glory of the UNA is founded on three things," she declares. "Our military might, our technology, and us pioneers out here in the Hellgrounds."

"Hear, hear!" Mikal adds at the mention of the Hellgrounds, but his mother shushes him.

"And those three things depend on the mercy and greatness of Minister Harka. Without him nothing would be possible. We owe him our lives, and our every waking breath. And we owe him for this meal we are about to partake of." Her voice takes on a trance-like quality: "Minister Harka, you are the fields that sustain us. You are the sun that brings us light. You are the earth that we live on. You will set *everything* right."

Mikal, Lorene, and Loretta recite the words along with her. At the end, they bow their heads for a moment. But not in silent contemplation. Their lips chatter wildly, like they're continuing to pray, just much faster and more quietly. Or maybe they're speaking in tongues.

Of course, I know that none of them has met Minister Harka personally, let alone any of his body doubles. *What would the twins think of Minister Harka if they'd seen him as I have, dying on the shore of the frozen lake? Or if they'd seen his power-mad former body double, Minister Hiram, inside that vast chamber with his mutant?* They'd probably be terrified.

But of course they will never see him that way. They only know the smiling, powerful man as he is depicted in all the photographs and paintings hanging throughout their house, and through the entire UNA.

After dinner, I do some more chores—including cleaning the dishes—and then I am sent to my bedroom, to "think about what you've learned," according to Miss Caroldean. It's an early bedtime on the farm. Everyone must rise at five a.m., before the sun, to get to work.

Having some time alone again is a welcome relief. I lie down on the bed thinking about my own mother. Being here on the farm with Miss Caroldean and her children brings back memories of my family.

I'm grateful that my mom is nothing like Miss Caroldean. In fact, I can't think of anyone more opposite. I wish I were with my mom right now. In fact, I wish I'd never been separated from her to begin with. Not when I was little, and not again when I left Island Alpha.

I wonder what's going to happen to me out here in the Hellgrounds. I feel like I could disappear and nobody would even notice or care. This place is nearly as desolate as the wheel.

Am I just supposed to wait here until I get some sign from David to start moving again? Not knowing what awaits me makes me nervous. I hope that the tubes in my neck are the only form of biological experimentation that is going to be performed on me in the Hellgrounds.

I turn over onto my side in the bed, trying to get the dark thoughts out of my mind. I need to focus on saving Liam and continuing my mission.

9 THE SOUND OF HIS VOICE

A WEEK GOES BY. I spend the days working hard, doing chores and running errands for Miss Caroldean, waiting for a clue from David about what to do next. But the more time passes, the more I worry that I'll never find one. I think about running away, but I know that I'd probably be caught—and my senses would be cut off by Miss Caroldean's awful switch.

I'm haunted by bad dreams each night at the farmhouse. I dream of my time on Island Alpha before we freed it, and of the drones with painted faces and pointed teeth. I dream that I'm facing down drones by myself. Stabbing and hacking at them with knives. But the stream of drones is endless. I often wake up gasping and sweaty, slightly sick and disoriented. I don't know what these dreams mean. Maybe it's an indication that I'm cracking under the stress.

I also worry about Mikal, and I struggle to keep my distance from him. But he continues to bait me into a fight, no matter what I do or say.

"I know you're making plans to run," he hisses into my ear, on my seventh day at the farm. I've been ordered to help him gather some firewood. "I've been watching you. You're too good to be true, Alenna. You're putting on an act for my mom. You think I can't tell? I can read girls like nobody else can."

I just ignore him. The alternative would be to fight him. I know that I would probably win, but in the process I would give away my strength and get punished. Besides, he's not worth my time.

He shoves me against the wall of the barn. Startled, I drop the logs I'm carrying. They tumble everywhere. Mikal laughs. "When your act slips, I'll be there, agitator. To teach you a lesson you'll never forget. I'll be sure that everyone sees who you really are."

I bend down and start picking up the logs. Mikal walks away, chuckling to himself.

On my tenth day at the farm, Miss Caroldean summons me into the dining room. It's late afternoon, and the yellow rays of the sun shine through the stained-glass windows, making everything glow.

Miss Caroldean is sitting at the long dark dining table. For once, her placid demeanor looks frayed. Her brow is creased.

Mikal lounges in a barrel chair in the corner, watching me. I immediately get suspicious. *Something's going on here.* The look in Mikal's eyes gives it away—smug, knowing, and cruel.

"Alenna?" Miss Caroldean begins primly. "I'd like to ask you a question."

I stand there clutching a pile of wet laundry that I was about to hang outside to dry. "Yes?"

"Are you enjoying your stay with us?"

"I don't really have a choice," I mutter.

She sighs. "What I mean is, do you feel like you're gaining anything from the experience? That you're learning things? About how to live a moral life in the UNA."

"Sure. I guess," I lie.

Mikal keeps staring at me from the chair, like he's expecting his mom to start yelling at me.

"Then I have another question for you, Alenna," Miss Caroldean continues. "Why—if you are enjoying your time here—would you steal from me?"

"Steal?" I ask, confused.

"You know what I'm talking about."

"No, I actually don't."

My eyes flit to Mikal. His knife is out and he's whittling a piece of wood. Smiling that thin, crooked smile of his. *Has he set me up somehow?*

"Now isn't the time for more lies," Miss Caroldean presses. "Now it's time for the truth."

"I'm telling you the truth," I protest, still clutching the laundry, even though I want to fling it in her face. "I haven't stolen anything. Nothing at all."

Miss Caroldean gets up and takes a step toward me. "Lying about a sin is often worse than committing the sin itself. To lie is to align oneself with the devil."

I'm not sure what she's ranting about, so I just say, "I'm really not lying. Honest. Why would I steal anything? I don't have anywhere to put it."

Miss Caroldean takes another slow, deliberate step in my direction. Mikal increases the pace of his whittling. I put the laundry down on top of a china cabinet next to me. I feel my heart beating faster.

"I'm surprised your mother didn't teach you better than to lie and steal," Miss Caroldean snaps. "But then again, I suppose she was a useless rebel."

131

The mention of my mom unexpectedly makes me flinch. I just look Miss Caroldean straight in the eyes and say, "What is it that you think I've stolen?"

She seems surprised by my directness. "My rouge amulet, of course!" she retorts. "The one I always wear around my neck. I only remove it when I bathe, and I always put it in the same place near the sink. But it's missing." She touches the bare space on her neck, above her breasts, as if to emphasize its absence. "It's one of my most important possessions. I know that someone snatched it. And that person can only be you."

"That's completely illogical," I tell her, still looking calmly into her eyes. Mikal has stopped whittling. He's listening closely now. "I didn't take your amulet. I didn't even notice that you wore an amulet."

She acts like she doesn't hear me. "I knew you tried to run from your fate when you fled the island, but I didn't think you were a thief," Miss Caroldean continues. "I thought you were better than that. Or why else would you be sent here?"

"I didn't take your amulet."

Miss Caroldean folds her hands together, like a praying mantis. She shuts her eyes for a moment and then opens them again, like she's trying to control her temper. "Do you know the history of the amulet, Alenna?"

"No."

Mikal is curled forward now, in a state of eager expectation. Openly smirking at me.

"The amulet was given to me by Minister Harka himself," Miss Caroldean continues. "Three years, nine months, three weeks, and two days ago. On the very same day he told me to continue working this farm and this land. It was right after the death of my husband. I have worn it every day since then." Her voice starts rising in pitch, verging toward hysteria. "Minister Harka is a living prophet, Alenna. The closest we can get to god." Her hands are trembling. "And you have taken this amulet from me! You have stolen what is rightfully mine—the one object that links me to Minister Harka forever. Give it back right now."

"Look, I understand that you're upset," I say. "But I really didn't take it. I'm not a thief."

"Then who is?"

Mikal's eyes narrow. Maybe he's worried that I'll accuse him. But I doubt it. He'd probably be pleased if I did that. Maybe he's even expecting it. I know he'll just deny it. Then I'll be accused of lying again, and Miss Caroldean will have yet another reason to condemn me. So I simply say, "There are other people who live in this house. Maybe you should talk to them."

Miss Caroldean faces me, trembling with anger. "It could only have been you! Who else would dare to do such a thing? Confess it now, or face the consequences. No other agitator has stolen such a precious item from me—not in all these years."

I feel sick to my stomach. This is not going well. "I can't confess to something I didn't do."

"Fine," Miss Caroldean says, walking another step forward. She's so close now that I can feel her hot breath on my cheek. "So you're just a filthy, lying thief. Right here in my own house. You've probably honed your thieving skills for years. In a rebel cell, no doubt, and then on the island, and then back in the UNA. A traitor hiding in plain sight. You were probably planning to steal my amulet so you could run away again, weren't you? Planning to sell it for money to fund some rebel cause."

"No, I—"

"Do you know what I do to thieves?" she asks, her voice suddenly much quieter, but dripping with venom. She leans forward, her lips almost brushing against my ear. "I give them some time alone to think about their crimes." One of her hands slips down into the pocket of her frock. Her fingers pull out the black UNA emblem. "It's time to dwell upon your sins, Alenna."

She draws back from me then, standing there in the living room, clutching the emblem. Her trembling index finger wavers above the red switch. I can hear Mikal whittling again in the corner, feigning nonchalance.

I realize that Miss Caroldean is going to flip the switch and plunge me into darkness. I reach out and try to grab her hand. I want to swat it away and plead my innocence some more. But suddenly, I feel an icy sensation flooding the plastic tubes in the back of my neck.

Time grinds to a halt, like in a bad dream.

The world starts spinning.

What is happening to me?

I cry out and put my hands behind my neck, grabbing at the tubes. I try to yank them out, but it's too painful. The tubes are part of me now, like actual veins. They feel different from before. They are rigid and cold to the touch, as though some strange icy chemical is being released inside them.

"No!" I try to yell, but it comes out as a whisper. "Don't do this to me!" My vision constricts down to a tunnel. I hear the whooshing sound of blood in both my ears. I fall down to one knee, gazing up, trying to catch my balance.

I get a final glimpse of Mikal's face. He's standing up now, a few feet behind his mom. His knife is dangling down from his hand. He's smiling at me sadistically.

Then I fall forward, sucked down into a vortex of whirling nothingness. Only blackness rushes up to greet me as I topple over.

But I don't lose consciousness. Not exactly.

It's just like the entire world has disappeared from under my feet. I feel like I'm floating again, just like I did in the isolation tank back on Island Alpha. I can't even feel the hard, wooden floor that I know is beneath my body. With her switch, Miss Caroldean has disabled everything except my thoughts.

I try to call out, but I have no voice. I am trapped.

I know I must still be lying on the floor, probably with Miss Caroldean and Mikal standing over me.

I wonder how long they're going to keep me paralyzed. Whether it'll be a few minutes, or hours, or longer than that. I'm angry at myself. I suspected that Mikal was dangerous. I should have predicted that he'd try to get me in trouble. Now it will be harder to find Liam.

I'm inwardly cursing this awful place when my thoughts are jarringly interrupted:

"I knew I'd be talking to you again," a raspy voice suddenly blares in my ear. "I just didn't know it'd take this long!"

"*David!*" I gasp.

"Who else?"

"How are you talking to me right now? Is this some kind of telepathy?"

"Yes. I'm using the metal filaments in the plastic cables in your neck as a radio receiver and transmitter, to broadcast my words directly into your skull and receive your thoughts. I can only come during these sorts of times. The in-between times. Times when they shut you down. Otherwise they'll find us out. They have sensors that monitor the electrical activity in your brain. The sensors are hidden behind those crappy paintings of Minister Harka. But when they put you to sleep, they stop monitoring your brain activity. Whatever you did to get that crazy woman to block off your senses was actually a really smart move. In fact, I thought you'd get in trouble sooner."

"I didn't even do anything," I say. I realize I am not really speaking—David is hearing my thoughts—but it feels like I'm speaking even if no one can hear me and my lips are not moving. "Her son set me up. Now she thinks I'm a thief."

"Figures. Listen, we don't have long. She can't risk causing permanent harm to your nervous system, so she'll flip that switch again pretty soon. If you get messed up, then the government won't send her other rebels to look after—and she'll lose the stipend of money and food that she gets for hosting kids like you on her farm. There are some really important things I need to tell you."

"Start by telling me how to escape, where to go to find Liam, and what I have to detonate!"

"Don't worry. I have a plan for you to accomplish all those things. But you're going to have to follow it to the letter. If you screw up, then I can't help you anymore."

"Deal." I stop for a moment, because an awful thought has just come into my mind. "How do I know this is really you, David? Maybe it's someone using a voice simulator tapping into my brain. This could be a trap."

David laughs.

"Maybe I'm just being paranoid," I mutter.

"No. You're being smart." He pauses. "But it is me. I can prove it."

"Then do it."

"Remember that first day on the island? I had those matches with me. I made us torches, and you climbed up into the tree to scope out the land. We talked about spending the night up there, until drones showed up. No one else would know that."

"And back in New Dallas?" I challenge. "What were the last words you said to me on the morning when I left? I remember them. Do you?"

He laughs. "That's a trick question. I'd already left the safe house by the time the sun rose. So I didn't say anything. I just left you a key and a piece of paper."

"Okay," I tell him, appeased. "It really is you. So what happens now?"

"My main priority is to make sure you get out of the farmhouse and continue the mission."

"Keep talking."

"When they wake you back up, look out your bedroom window the next chance you get, facing south. Imagine the face of a clock in front of you. At about two o'clock, on your right, you'll see a large, black oak tree in the forest. Slightly larger and much darker than the others around it. Large enough to hide behind. You have to get to that specific tree."

"If I run, someone will see me."

"That's why it has to be at night. Tonight—the sooner the better. We're running out of time. Do it at nine fifteen p.m., after they've sent you and the twins to bed tonight, when Miss Caroldean is taking her bath. And Mikal is feeding the dogs. That's your best shot."

"How do you know their routines?"

"The house was surveilled by a group of traveling rebels who passed through this area several weeks ago, before you got here.

So at nine fifteen, go downstairs, grab a knife from the kitchen, a towel, and some alcohol too, and then run directly from the front porch to that tree. You'll find something hidden behind it. Something that one of the rebels left there for you, based on my instructions. It will help guide you on your journey."

"What? A weapon? A map? And what's up with the knife, towel, and alcohol?"

"The less you know, the safer you'll be. You have to trust me."

"David, at some point you have to start leveling with me. I do trust you. But stop making it so much work."

"I'll consider it." I can hear the faint smile in his voice.

"Fine. I'll run to the tree. But if I don't find anything, then—"

I'm about to add, *Then I'm going to be really mad at you, David!*

But halfway through my sentence, I feel a strange, vertiginous, heaving sensation, like I'm being dragged up out of syrup. The world spins around, and my senses are flooded with noise and light, drowning out my words.

I try to curl into a ball, choking and gasping, even though I can barely feel my body.

Then my senses return to me all at once, as rapidly and violently as a car crash.

I open my eyes, but bright light makes them flare with pain. My head is throbbing, and the tubes in the back of my neck feel like they're on fire.

I push myself up off the wood floor, onto my knees. I move as quickly as I can, in battle mode. I don't know what's coming next.

I'm still in Miss Caroldean's dining room. I see scuffed leather boots walk past me. They belong to Mikal. I get a head rush and remain kneeling for a second.

Then Mikal leans down, his face in front of mine.

Before I can stop him, he kisses me quickly on the lips.

Then he dances out of the way as I lash out at him.

I want to vomit.

"Hey now," he murmurs, as I get to my feet, hands balled into fists. "Nothing wrong with stealing a little sugar when you can."

"Keep away from me." My voice is like steel. I wipe my lips on my arm.

He laughs. "Don't worry. I'm not gonna touch you. I could have done anything to you when you were unconscious, but I left you alone. It wouldn't have been gentlemanly otherwise." His thin grin curdles into a wide sarcastic smile.

"How long was I out?" I ask.

"Half an hour. You writhed and moaned like a baby the whole time. You kept muttering stuff that didn't make any sense. I just thought you should know that."

"Where's your mom?"

"In the garden. She wanted me to personally supervise your waking." He's smirking at me. "I told her it would be my pleasure."

I put out a hand to steady myself on an oak cabinet. My head is spinning. I shake the dizziness off.

"Hurts, doesn't it?" Mikal asks.

"What would you know?"

He chuckles again.

My neck flares with pain. I wince, reaching back to feel the tubes. The place where they meet my flesh is painful and swollen, tender like a bruise.

"Now that my mom has flipped the switch once, she'll just do it again and again," Mikal explains matter-of-factly. "Next time you'll be out for a couple hours. After that, maybe for a whole afternoon." He laughs. "She's trigger-happy."

I push myself off from the cabinet and stand shakily on my feet as I recover my balance. "I'm not scared of you, Mikal."

His smile vanishes in an instant. "You will be."

I look him dead in the eyes. "I fought and killed people tougher than you on the island—boys and girls alike. I'm not afraid of you, or your threats." I stare him down. "You stole your mom's amulet, didn't you? To frame me."

"Prove it."

"You know I can't." I don't want to get into a fight with him right now, but I can't let it drop. *Or else he might set me up again before nighttime, before I can get to that black oak tree and the secret that awaits me there.* "Why?" I ask.

He smiles again, even broader. "Because you're a scummy rebel that no one cares about. You might have been a big shot on Island Alpha, but you're nobody here. I can do whatever I want with you." He turns away. "You better go clean yourself up. You drooled on your blouse, and on the floor too." He strides out the door, leaving me standing there.

I stare after him. Then I glance at the grandfather clock standing against the wall across from the front door. It's just past five in the afternoon. I only have four hours left until I will try to make my escape. I must act as normally as possible until then, so that no one suspects me.

"Alenna?" I suddenly hear a voice ask.

Startled, I turn around and see Lorene standing there. I'm not sure where she's come from. She's watching me with her intense blue eyes.

"Yes?" I ask warily.

"I brought you this." She holds her hand out. A red apple rests in her palm.

140

Tentatively, I reach out and take the apple from her. I'm surprised by her gesture of kindness. She keeps watching me, unblinking. I'm not sure why she brought me the apple. *Maybe to make up for her mom and her brother's cruelty?*

"I thought you might be hungry," she tells me somberly. "I waited until Mikal left."

"Thank you," I say.

She nods. "Eat it fast, before my mother sees." She pauses for a moment, like she wants to say something more. But then she turns quickly and is about to walk away into the hallway.

"Wait—" I call out.

She hesitates. "Yes?"

"Were you going to tell me something else?"

She looks back at me balefully. "You should know something about the other girls who came here. . . ." Her words trail off into a whisper.

"What?" I whisper back.

"Not all of them survived. . . ."

Then, before she can say any more, she turns and rushes out of the room.

I stand there for a moment, contemplating her words. I feel scared. But at least her honesty makes me feel like there's some hope for people in the Hellgrounds after all. For her to tell me the truth about the other girls means she can't be deluded and evil like her mom and brother.

I look for her in the hallway, but there's no sign of her. If she had stayed, I would have told her that I'm not afraid to die. And I would have thanked her for telling me about the other girls. It means I need to be more cautious than I thought.

I bring the apple to my lips and take a bite. I'm starving. I quickly devour the entire apple, eating the seeds and core. Then I wipe my hands on my jeans.

Slowly, I walk over to the front door. I'm still recovering from being knocked unconscious. My head feels heavy and my vision is a bit blurry.

I head outside to find Miss Caroldean and get a list of chores for the rest of the day. I'm worried that I don't have the second part of David's message. But I tell myself that if things go well, tonight will be my very last night in the farmhouse—and the start of my journey back to Liam and the destruction of the UNA. But if things go wrong, then I might never leave this place alive.

10 ESCAPE

THAT NIGHT, I SIT on my mattress, watching the hands of the clock in the bedroom click inexorably forward. The clock face is dotted with tiny glass stars. It's handmade. Maybe even built right here on this farm. Or maybe it predates the UNA and the Hellgrounds. Maybe it's from a simpler time.

I only have forty minutes left before nine fifteen comes around. It's already dark outside. I'm nervous about leaving the safety of the farm, although I'll be relieved to escape from Miss Caroldean and Mikal. I just hope that I can make it to the black oak tree before I'm spotted.

I'm so exhausted from working on the farm that I'm on the verge of falling asleep. I pinch my leg, forcing myself to stay awake, and glance at the clock. Now it's almost nine. I sit up on my mattress.

I wait and listen. The farmhouse has gone silent. The twins are probably sleeping already.

I soon hear the faint creak of a faucet being turned on, and old iron pipes clattering in the walls underneath me. Then I hear tuneless singing, and I know Miss Caroldean is taking her nightly bath.

The time has come.

I swing my legs over the edge of the bed and quickly put my shoes on softly. Then I gently rest my feet on the floor.

I glance out the bedroom window. I can't see or hear Mikal from here. He might not be outside yet, but I suspect that he probably is. He usually goes from the barn directly to feed the dogs, and then inside for a late snack and a jug of cider.

I turn to the clock again.

It's precisely nine fifteen.

I risk standing up. The floorboards groan. I wince and pause. I think about taking off my shoes, but if I get caught outside and have to run, I'll need them on my feet.

I stand still for a moment, waiting. But no one seems to have heard anything. All Miss Caroldean can probably hear is her own voice, still singing off-key.

A few seconds later I hear the distant sounds of dogs yipping and barking in the kennels. I'm flooded with relief. Mikal is feeding the dogs their nightly supper of rinds and other leftovers. It's time for me to get moving.

I walk quickly and quietly across the wood floor, over to the door. I grasp the knob and turn it slowly. *I cannot get caught.*

I take a deep breath and swing open the bedroom door. I step onto the landing. Farther down the long hall is the closed door of the twins' bedroom. I walk carefully and silently down the hall, over to the wide flight of wood stairs. I step on the outside of the beams, so the floor doesn't creak too much.

Slowly, I descend the staircase, as the sound of Miss Caroldean's singing grows louder. I'm going to have to walk right past the downstairs bathroom that she's bathing herself in—there's no other way out of the house. Of course, the door to the bathroom is closed, so it's doubtful she'll even know that I'm there.

I reach the bottom of the stairs, and exhale. *Not much farther.* I look around the living room. I can hear the dogs barking out back, and Mikal's voice taunting them. If I go out the front door right now, I'll be safe. But there's still Miss Caroldean to get past, and I also need to gather the items from the kitchen.

Miss Caroldean's voice is loud, even through the bathroom door. She's switched songs, and is now singing a hymn about the greatness of Minister Harka.

I ignore her off-key warbling and start my journey toward the kitchen. I walk slowly, keeping to the rugs, so my feet don't make noise.

I reach the spacious kitchen and dart over to grab a knife from the wooden knife block. I take the largest, sharpest one I can find. The whole time I stay out of view from the windows, just in case Mikal walks around the house and decides to peer inside.

I snatch up a white cotton dishtowel from the countertop, along with a half-filled bottle of spirits sitting on a shelf above a cupboard. Then I leave the kitchen, turning to head past the bathroom again, on my way out the front door.

I consider trying to find Miss Caroldean's switch, to destroy it. But I know that it must be with her in the bathroom. She would never part with such an important tool of control.

Then, I suddenly realize that the singing has stopped. And so has the running water.

My heart lurches. *Did I lose track of time?* Miss Caroldean usually bathes for at least twenty minutes. Today, it's been less than ten.

I take a step forward, not sure what to do.

The floor creaks in the silence.

"Mikal?" I hear her voice call out. "Is that you, honey?"

I freeze.

The knife is in one hand. The towel and the alcohol are in the other. *David didn't say what to do if this happened.* He was trusting me not to get caught. My fingers tighten on the knife handle.

"Mikal?" Miss Caroldean calls out again.

I look down at the blade. Fighting drones in the forest is different from stabbing an old lady in her own house. But I can't let her get to that device again. If I have to kill her, then I will.

Then I hear the water turn back on. And a second later, Miss Caroldean's voice rings out, fervently singing the second verse of her hymn to Minister Harka.

I take a breath. Trying not to think about it, I walk through the living room. Right past the bathroom door. I just keep moving.

Within seconds, I reach the vestibule. My feet are louder here on the tiles. I reach the front door and take hold of the doorknob. I swing the door open. The hinges creak. In front of me stretches the cornfields under a full moon, and then beyond that, the pitch-black forest.

I step out into the hot night, gently closing the door behind me. I stare in the direction that David instructed, the one I've already memorized from my window upstairs. I can see the black oak tree he told me about. It looks far away from here.

Once I get into the fields, I'll be visible from the windows of the house. I'll also be alone outside with Mikal. If he deviates from his usual routine with the dogs, then I might get caught.

I need to start moving right away. I rush down the porch steps and straight into the fields.

I move quickly and silently. In places, the corn comes up to my waist. I keep hustling through it rapidly, toward the black oak, about a quarter of a mile away. The full moon allows me to see where I'm going, but it also puts me at risk of being spotted.

Still, if I planned everything right, then Miss Caroldean and Mikal should be occupied for several more minutes. I should have enough time to reach the tree.

I risk a glance behind me at the farmhouse as I run. All is quiet and still. From here, the house looks peaceful and nice.

Just as I turn back around, I hear a loud barking sound. For a terrifying moment, I think that Mikal knows I'm out here. That he's unleashed his dogs on me. I crouch down, clutching my knife, dropping the towel and the bottle of alcohol.

But then, slowly, I realize it's just the barking of a lone dog. And I can hear Mikal cursing faintly in the distance. A dog must have escaped from the kennels and gotten loose into the corn-fields behind the house. Hopefully, this distraction will buy me even more time.

I stand up and continue moving swiftly toward the black oak.

But, to my dismay, the barking starts getting louder. The dog is heading in my direction. He must have caught my scent.

I start running faster, telling myself that I have to get to the oak tree. I hear the dog getting even closer. I can hear it growling now, as well as barking. I look behind me as I run, and I see its dark silhouette moving through the corn, making the fields ripple.

There's no way to outrun this dog. I'm forced to stop and turn around, so it doesn't leap on me from behind.

I spin around just in time to see it standing there, about fifteen paces away in the corn. The dog is a black Doberman. It has stopped chasing me, but it's walking back and forth, barking madly. Growling and showing its white fangs in the moonlight.

"Shhh," I say to it softly. "Stay!" My words don't do any good. These dogs are trained to corner any intruders—human or animal—and attack upon Miss Caroldean's or Mikal's command.

I can hear Mikal trampling through the corn in the direction of the barking. I back away from the dog. "Good boy," I say warily. "Now just stop barking, and everything will be fine!"

But the dog moves forward, keeping pace with me.

And then it barks again. The sound is loud in the peaceful night.

This dog is not going to let me out of its sight. It's going to lead Mikal right to me.

I wish I'd brought some food from the kitchen to throw at it. A big chunk of ham from the ice chest would occupy it. But it's too late now.

I see Mikal's lantern moving toward me over the corn. I crouch down even farther, although that makes me more of a target for the dog. Luckily, the dog keeps its distance.

"Sammy!" Mikal is yelling in the distance. "Get back here!"

So now I know the dog's name. *Sammy.* I look at it. Its fangs are still bared, revealing sharp incisors and mottled pink-and-brown gums.

"Sammy," I whisper. "You don't want to hurt me. I'm just trying to get away from this place." I show my knife to the dog. "I have a weapon, but I don't want to use it on you, or anyone else. I just want to leave."

The tone of my voice doesn't calm Sammy down. In fact, the sight of the knife just incites him into a frenzy. Other dogs far away in the kennels begin barking and wailing as well.

Mikal is getting closer now, thrashing his way through the corn. It's too late to run. *Too late to do much of anything.* This one encounter with the dog has destroyed the careful plan I made with David.

So I just stand up, clutching my knife.

As Mikal gets closer to Sammy, he sees me.

For a split second, he recoils, startled. Then his lanky body relaxes.

"Alenna," he calls out, almost conversationally. "Hey."

I hold up the knife. It glints in the moonlight. "Keep away from me or I'll cut your face off."

Mikal glances at Sammy. Then back at me. He doesn't seem afraid of the knife. "What are you doing out here?"

"You know what I'm doing."

"Running away, as predicted." He swaggers forward, leashing the dog. Sammy tries to get away but Mikal cuffs him hard on the top of his head. Sammy whimpers. Mikal attaches the other end of the leash to a metal tent stake, and uses his foot to push it into the earth. Sammy is trapped. "That's what you're doing, isn't it? Running?"

There's no point in lying. "Absolutely. You'd do the same."

He cocks his head to one side. "Isn't running part of the same antisocial behavior that got you classified as an unanchored soul?" He glances at my knife and grins. "Running from your responsibilities to the UNA. Running from your friends and enemies on Island Alpha. Even running away from your own mom to come back here." He pauses. "You agitators never really change, do you? Were you planning on using that knife on Sammy?"

I shake my head. "I just want to go free. I'll take my chances in the forest." I grip the knife tighter.

"I can't let you go. I mean, maybe if you had something to offer me in return, we could make a deal." I feel his eyes moving up and down my body.

"You're disgusting," I tell him. "Keep your distance."

"Or what?" He grins. "Fine, if you don't want to make a deal, I guess we have to fight. I've never lost to a girl before. I don't plan to start now."

He walks forward. Now that he has inexplicably tied up his dog, I guess I could run. But he could probably outrun me. This is where he lives. Where he grew up. He must know the terrain, the fields, and the edges of the forest much better than I do.

He starts rolling back his sleeves. "Keep your knife. I'll get it off you in under thirty seconds." He laughs. "And if you're wondering about Sammy, I could have sicced him on you, and he would have torn out your throat. Just like I trained him to do. But I don't need to hide behind a dog. I got three older brothers who are all UNA soldiers. You think I don't know how to fight?"

I hold up my knife, gesturing to his prominent scar. "Looks like you aren't too good at it."

He scowls. "You think you're so smart, don't you?"

I shrug. "I grew up in an orphanage. Then I got sent to Island Alpha. You think that didn't make me tough?"

"Sounds like a challenge," he says, and leers. "I like a tough girl. It makes me happy when I break them. Girls are like horses that way."

Repulsed, I start backing away. The last thing I want to do is halt everything to fight Mikal. I have more important things to do. But as I back up, he follows me. Sammy keeps barking relentlessly.

"So, I'm gonna tell my mom that I caught you trying to cut up little Sammy here. That he got in the way of your escape, so you tried to stab him." He flexes his muscles. "Mom likes her dogs, so she won't take pity on you. I can turn your pretty face into jelly, and I'll have every justification in the world." He cocks his head to one side thoughtfully. "Maybe catching you will even help my application to the UNA soldier academy."

"I'm sure it will," I tell him sarcastically. "They need more thugs like you."

He steps forward. "Better a thug on the winning team than a rebel on the losing one."

I'm debating whether I should attack him with the knife or run, when he suddenly leaps forward. His long arms give him reach, and before I can turn, he slams a fist into my face.

I slip and fall sideways, and he's on top of me in an instant, clawing at me, as his dog goes crazy with barking. In those terrified, frenzied moments I'm not sure whether he's trying to kill me or worse—trying to get my clothes off.

He uses his weight to pin me against the ground. His left hand holds my wrist down, so that I can't stab him. I yell and struggle, but he keeps me pressed down on the ground.

"Stop, stop," he says. "I don't want to hurt you. Just listen!"

"I'm going to kill you!" I yell. I finally manage to twist away from him and escape from his grasp. I still have my knife. I get to my feet and back away from him. He stands up too, brushing dirt off his knees.

"Listen!" he says. "Hear me out! It's not what you think!" He pauses for a moment. We're both breathing hard. "You think I like it here?" he yells. "At this stupid farm?"

I stare back at him. "What? I don't care!"

"Well, I hate it here! My mom is crazy! And I don't want to go and get killed fighting for the UNA."

I'm startled. "Then don't become a soldier."

"Maybe I won't." He lowers his voice. His dog has stopped barking. "I could come with you. Wherever you're going. I know you must have a plan. You're not like the other agitators who stayed at the farm. I can tell. Let me come with you."

I'm so surprised that I stand there for a moment. Is he serious? His words are a desperate plea. "I can't let you come with me," I tell him cautiously. Whether he's serious or not, there's no way I can trust him, not after how he acted toward me. In fact, this might all be a misguided attempt on his part to spy for the UNA. "Just let me go. I promise you I won't cause you any harm. You can just tell your mom you never saw me out here."

His face hardens. I've angered him. "So you're telling me no?" he asks. "You're telling me I'm not good enough to join the rebels."

"I'm not saying that."

He shakes his head. "And I opened up to you and everything."

"You should have said something sooner. You shouldn't have acted so mean."

"I don't know why I did that. It's just how I am. I'm moody. I don't fit in here. I never did. I don't know what to do."

I watch him closely. "If you're being sincere about wanting to help, then just stay here. Try to help the next girl who gets sent to the farm—if there ever is a next girl. And when the time comes, fight for freedom and against the UNA."

"I don't want to help the next girl. I want to help you. And if you won't let me, I gotta take you back to my mom." He steps forward, reaching out to grab me again. I can see the anger at being rejected in his eyes. But this time I'm prepared for his assault.

I lean back and kick him hard in the chest with my boot. He yelps in surprise. He rushes forward to attack. He manages to grab my right hand, trying to pry the knife out of it.

"I'm gonna cut off your ears," he hisses furiously. "Forget everything I just said! I'm gonna mark you as an agitator for the rest of your life! You're never getting off this farm. You don't know what I've done to some of the other girls. Maybe I'll make a baby inside you the next time my mom presses that switch and—"

I punch him with my left hand in his mouth as hard as I can. I feel the satisfying crunch of teeth breaking as he howls in pain. Then I punch him again, before he can stop me. I yank my other hand back, still clutching the knife.

My left hand flares with pain where his broken teeth sliced my knuckles. Mikal goes down to one knee, his hands pressed to his mouth.

This is my chance. I kick him again, my boot connecting directly with his upper lip. He makes a wet choking sound as more teeth are knocked from his gums.

Then I turn around and start running.

I race in the direction of the black oak tree as fast as I can. For a second, I think I've gotten away. But then I hear footsteps and realize that Mikal is giving chase after all, even though he's wounded. I hear him rushing through the corn after me, cursing and shrieking.

"Alenna!" he yells, through a mouthful of blood and broken teeth. "I'm never gonna let you go!" His voice is a tortured wail. "I'm gonna make you pay for what you did to me! You'll see me again!"

I just put my head down and keep running.

11 SANCTUARY

I RUN FASTER THAN I thought possible, my chest burning, and my legs plunging forward. Fortunately, I've got a head start on Mikal. He might not be able to make up the distance before I reach the forest. And at least if he's chasing me, then he won't be able to run back to the house and tell his mother to flip the switch on her UNA emblem.

I keep running, my sides aching. I know that Mikal is behind me in the corn. But I'm almost at the trees now. I fling my body forward.

Then, I'm at the edge of the forest, barging my way inside. The fields give way to underbrush and huge trees. Branches tear at my arms and whip at my face, but I don't care. I spin sideways and locate the black oak tree. I race toward it.

I reach the tree within seconds. It's even darker inside the forest, nearly pitch black. I clutch the bark, clawing at it. I move around the tree's huge trunk, trying to locate whatever item I'm supposed to find.

But I don't see anything.

Mikal is still nearby, stomping around in the forest and cursing. He's lost me for the moment. If he finds me here, I'll use my knife on him.

I move farther behind the tree. I'm surprised to see that there's a natural hollow opening in the massive trunk. It leads into a narrow place where I can seek refuge. I struggle to fit inside it.

It's narrow and dark inside the tree, and I can barely move. It smells like moss. I gaze around. *David said there would be something crucial for me at this tree.* But there's nothing. Just the damp interior of an ancient oak tree.

Rain begins to spatter down on the ground outside, and I smell ozone. A storm has begun, rain coming down out of nowhere in a torrent of water. I tilt my head back, trying to get a look at the roof of my enclosure.

That's when I see it:

A tiny green glass sphere, dangling inside the tree on a piece of fishing wire, just inches above my head.

I have no idea what it is, but I feel a flood of relief. I grab the sphere and yank it down. It's only an inch in diameter. The traveling rebels must have hid this here for me.

There's a small, hard black object inside. The only way to get it out is to smash the glass. So I drop the sphere to the bottom of my enclosure. Then I grind it under my boot until I feel a pop. Although it's hard to move around inside the tree, I bend over and sneak a hand down, getting a face full of rain blown in by the wind.

I search the wood and dirt beneath me, sifting through broken pieces of glass, until I find the object that was trapped inside. I grab it and stand up.

It's a tiny radio transmitter and receiver. I put it against one of my ears. I hear a distant hissing sound. I move the miniature dial on the side with my fingers.

"Hello?" I ask.

I'm expecting to hear David's voice come out of it. But instead I hear another familiar voice yelling at me.

Gadya.

"Took you long enough!" the voice crackles from within the object.

"Gadya! Thank god! Where are you?" I slip the tiny transmitter into my right ear.

"I'm nearby. Hiding in a dried-out concrete cistern in some ruins. I escaped from my host family in the Hellgrounds six hours ago. David helped me do it."

"Same here!"

"We need to find each other."

"No kidding." I'm overcome with relief. "I'm so glad you're out here! Tell me what to do. How do I get to you?"

"First you gotta do something . . ."

"What?"

"You're not gonna like it."

"I haven't liked anything that's happened since we got back to the UNA!"

I hear Gadya laugh. Just being able to talk to her makes me feel better.

"Well, what happens next really sucks," Gadya says. "It's gross. You're gonna have to cut those tubes out of your neck."

"*What?*" My stomach flip-flops.

"You heard me."

"But the tubes are connected to my spine! If I do that, I'll screw myself up for life. How's that going to help me?"

"Those tubes don't connect to your spine. They just store and deliver drugs into your bloodstream. When the switch is flipped, it sends out radio signals that release doses of strong sedatives from the tubes into you. Then you pass out, pretty much. When the switch is thrown again, stimulants wake you up. It's a new device the UNA is testing to create compliant citizens."

"Why the hell is it in my neck?"

"Because it's closest to your brain. But cutting the tubes won't paralyze you or anything. It'll just release her hold on you." Gadya pauses. "You need to slice the tubes in two, horizontally with the knife. Then yank out the roots. The roots are just thin needles sticking into your veins. You won't even bleed that much, promise. Use the alcohol to disinfect it, and the towel to mop up the blood."

"I lost those things. I only have the knife."

"That's good enough. C'mon, hurry up. It won't hurt more than a bee sting."

"How do you know? Did they implant tubes in your neck too?" I'm assuming she's already cut hers out.

There's a pause. "I actually haven't done mine yet—"

"Gadya!" I hiss at her. "Don't tell me it's gonna hurt like a bee sting! It's going to be way worse! And you better get your tubes out fast. Aren't you afraid they'll use the switch and knock you out?"

"I stole the switch and smashed it," she tells me. "I know I need to cut the tubes, but for some reason it really freaks me out! David said it would be okay. I still can't believe he's alive."

I wonder if she knows what kind of physical state David is in right now. I doubt that she's seen him in person. I figure there will be time to tell her about it later if she doesn't already know.

"We both have to do this together," I say. I grab the knife and touch its serrated edge with a fingertip. "A crazy kid from the farm is looking for me. I'm worried he'll go back and tell his mom to use the switch."

Gadya sighs. "Fine. I'll do mine if you do yours."

I reach the knife up to the back of my neck. My hand is trembling a little bit. "I can't see too well. I'm inside a hollowed-out tree."

"Yeah, I can't see either. There are no mirrors in a cistern."

I sigh. "Count of three?"

"Sure."

I take a deep breath, and then grab both tubes with my left hand. If David is wrong, this could mean the end of my life and Gadya's too. I press the tip of the knife against the tubes with my right hand.

We begin the countdown.

Both of us gasp "Three!" at the same moment. The sound of the storm outside covers the noise.

I slice the knife upward hard and fast, severing the two plastic tubes at the same instant.

I'm immediately hit with a wave of cold nausea. I struggle to keep my balance, staggering against the inside of the tree. I feel warm liquid dribbling out onto my hands, like I've punctured a water balloon. It's a slimy mix of chemicals, saline solution, and blood.

"Alenna?" I hear Gadya's voice saying. She sounds woozy. "Did you do it?"

"Yes," I croak.

"And we're still alive."

"That's good." I feel sick.

"We should tear the roots out now, or they'll poison us," Gadya says.

I tug at the ends of the tubes. The whole world is spinning.

"They're not coming out," I say, my words thick and heavy.

"Try harder. I got one of mine out already."

I yank on the tubes again. The top end of one of them begins to give way. Then the other. Gritting my teeth, I pull as hard as I can. With a sickening, fleshy noise, the top sections of the severed tubes finally come loose in my hand. Soon, I get the bottom parts out as well. Then I slump against the tree, coughing.

"It's done," I say. I glance down at the bits of yellow medical tubing in my hand, disgusted.

"Same here," Gadya says.

"We better move," I say.

"Agreed. The faster the better."

I stand there in the darkness, inside the tree. The rain is coming down even harder outside now. The sick feeling is receding. I fling the plastic tubing down to the ground.

I pause. "You have to tell me where I'm going."

"Keep the radio in your ear, and I'll guide you toward me. The cistern is desolate, and it's a good hiding place for us to regroup."

I nod. "Great."

I step out from the tree and into the rain. I'm on the lookout for Mikal, but I don't see him.

The droplets are coming down hard. Within seconds, I'm drenched. I wipe water out of my eyes, pushing back wet strands of hair. "C'mon, Gadya," I say. "I'm ready. Which way?"

"You need to start running due north. There aren't any trails in this part of the forest. Make your own, through the trees. Eventually you'll come to a trail after about five miles."

"Five miles!"

"Yeah, for the Hellgrounds, that's close. This place is huge."

"Fine."

I take a deep breath, and then push off from the tree. I move as quickly as I can, using the few stars I can see through the clouds to head north, slipping and sliding between wet branches and massive tree trunks. Trying not to lose my balance on the slippery leaves underfoot.

Fifteen minutes pass.

Then another fifteen.

By now the rain has dried up, and I've left the fields near the farmhouse far behind me. I'm deep inside the forest.

It helps to have Gadya's voice in my ear. She just keeps prodding me to keep running, no matter what.

Finally, after nearly an hour has passed, and my legs are aching, I see a trail. "I think I'm here," I say.

"Finally," she mutters.

I pause on the trail, gasping for air. Old hatchet marks line the trees along the trail's edges.

I glance down and see that the dirt looks like it has been trampled by many feet. The noises of the forest are loud around me. I swat insects away from my face.

"Take a left," Gadya's voice says in my ear. "I'll meet you about three hundred yards down the trail, and then we'll hike down to the cistern."

"How far are we from it? I thought we were there."

"No, I've been hiking this whole time so I could meet you partway." I hear the smile in her voice. "I wanted to surprise you. The cistern is about another five miles away—"

"Seriously?" I burst out. I'm already exhausted, and my feet are blistered. I don't want to keep racing full throttle through this treacherous forest. "I thought it was closer than that!"

Gadya doesn't answer.

"Gadya?" I fiddle with the object in my ear. I only hear static, like I've lost the signal. "Gadya!" I call out again. If she disappears now, I'll be completely lost.

Then I glance up and see an object moving through the trees ahead. *A light, shining out from the darkness.* I crouch, hiding behind a fallen tree trunk covered with lichens at the edge of the trail. I don't know what this light is. It could be Gadya, or it could be a group of UNA police on the prowl.

"Gadya?" I whisper again, but there's no answer.

I peer out above the tree trunk. The light is moving closer, in my direction, yellow and warm. It looks like the glow from an oil lantern. I want to run, but I'm afraid of making noise.

The lantern grows closer. I hide back down behind the tree trunk, holding my breath. I feel my pulse racing. I smell the damp earth, and feel the wet tangles of underbrush against my skin.

Then I hear a voice call out.

"Alenna, it's me!" the voice exclaims, as clear as a bell.

I instantly stand up. "Gadya?"

I squint to see the figure beyond the lantern. Suddenly, the light shifts, as the person holding it hoists it up, illuminating herself.

"You look stressed out," Gadya remarks.

"No kidding! Where did you go?"

"Signal failed."

I rush forward toward her, scrambling up the trail. She heads in my direction just as rapidly.

I reach her and the two of us hug hard and tight. Then we part. She puts the lantern down on the ground. We stare at each other. She has bruises across her face and all over her arms, along with some fresh lacerations.

"We made it," I say. "I can't believe it! Are you okay?"

"Barely. But now I know why they call it the Hellgrounds. I got beaten and whipped a few times. Nothing I couldn't take."

I hug her again. I know she's putting on a brave face. She winces as I touch her, so I let her go.

"Sorry. Still healing," she says.

"Let me take a look." I pick up the lantern and hold it up to her. I see that some of her wounds are surprisingly deep. "We need to get those cleaned."

She shrugs off my concern. "I've been through worse." She gazes at me. "How about you? You okay?"

"I didn't get beaten, but I got attacked by this woman's crazy son named Mikal. He wanted to come with us. He didn't like hearing 'no' for an answer."

"Nobody ever does."

I take the earpiece out of my ear and slip it into my pocket. I don't need it right now. Gadya does the same. I hand the lantern back over to her.

We begin hiking up the trail toward the cistern.

"Who made this path?" I ask.

She shakes her head. "No clue."

We keep walking. The trail starts narrowing a bit more.

The whole time we talk about what we experienced when we were captives. We also make plans for what we're going to do next. I still don't tell her about what happened to David's body. I can tell that she doesn't know about his injuries—or what he's done to himself. I'm not sure why I don't tell her. Maybe I'm just not ready to talk about it yet.

I ask if she's seen Liam, but she hasn't.

"But we're going to rescue him tomorrow," she says. "David told me where he is. It's not far."

"Tomorrow? David told you that and not me?"

"Yeah. He said he didn't want to make you emotional, or make you do something rash."

"Great." I pause. "Sometimes I feel like David is just jerking us around."

"Oh, he is. There's no question about that. But we just have to hope he's doing it for the right reasons."

"So Liam is nearby?"

"According to David, he's at a UNA work camp for boys. I have the directions. We'll go there when it gets light."

My heart is racing faster. "Did David say if Liam is okay?"

Gadya shakes her head. "I don't think he knows."

As we hike, we pass a large granite rock with the mutated UNA logo painted on its surface in gold lines. Instead of an eye hovering over a globe, there are five eyes surrounding the globe. Lines connect the pupils of each eye to the globe.

I touch Gadya's arm. "I've seen that symbol before."

"Really?"

"Before I got sent here. I got called in front of someone named Minister Hiram. He was one of Minister Harka's body doubles, but he was really creepy and seemed to be running New Austin. He kept some sort of giant mutant inside a glass prison in his office. The emblem was in his office too. I'm not sure what it means."

"Me neither. But that sounds weird as hell. Let's just keep going."

I glance back as we walk. The rock quickly recedes into darkness.

"Soldiers are probably patrolling this area, now that we've escaped," Gadya says, urging me forward.

I walk quickly with her. I tell her everything about my experiences with Minister Hiram. Neither of us knows what to make of it. Time passes quickly. Finally, the path broadens until it becomes a wide swath of grass in the forest.

"We're almost there," Gadya says.

The trees start thinning out on one side of the trail. I don't understand why at first. Gadya moves over to them. I follow. The trees thin even more, until they disappear completely.

She holds up her lantern, and says, "Stop walking if you want to live."

I stop—right as I realize that we've approached the edge of a cliff. It was obscured by darkness and by the trees. I'm confused. We've been walking at ground level. *How can there be a cliff here?*

Before I can ask her about it, Gadya walks over to the edge. Then she hops down and disappears, along with her light.

"No—" I gasp, thinking she's just thrown herself over the edge of some deep precipice.

Then I hear her muffled voice drifting back up to me: "There's a ledge here. Be careful."

I inch my way forward.

And then I realize what I'm looking at. I'm not at the edge of a natural cliff, but instead, I'm at the lip of a huge crater dug into the earth. Like a gigantic, ancient bomb crater. Or something made by a fallen meteor. Gadya is standing on a wide ledge made from dirt and rock, about four feet below me, staring out into the abyss.

The giant pit sprawls out in front of us, at least half a mile across, and a hundred feet deep. At the bottom of it are some ruins.

"What is this place?" I ask, gazing down at the crater in awe and confusion. I sit down and scoot myself onto the ledge, my feet landing with a thud.

"I don't know what it was. Something the UNA bombed, probably. But the bottom has an old cistern in it. Or at least what's left of it. That's where David told me to go and hide. And that's where he told me to take you."

I nod. "We better get down there somehow."

Gadya looks at me. "Getting down there is easier than getting back up. It took me twenty minutes to hike my way out of it."

"So how do we get down?"

Gadya grins. "We slide." She points to my right. "Look."

I see a smooth section of dirt with minimal rubble. This will be our path down to the cistern.

"Ready?" she asks.

Before I can answer, she moves herself forward on her hands and feet, like a crab, and then pushes herself off. She slides down the smooth dirt on her butt, heading down toward the bottom of the crater.

I move over and follow, pushing myself off after her. I start moving quickly. The earth and rubble tear at my clothes. I hold out my hands for balance as I descend farther toward the cistern. Gadya isn't far ahead of me.

Finally, the ground levels out and I come to a stop in a cloud of dirt and dust. Gadya is nearby, already standing up and brushing herself off.

"Pretty crazy, huh," she says.

I nod, standing up and picking rubble off me.

I stare ahead. I see a large circular concrete building, half destroyed and turned into ruins, staring back.

"You sure this place is safe?" I ask.

"Yep. There's food and water inside. I've already checked it out. I got here earlier in the afternoon."

I follow her across the blighted landscape toward the building. It's large and ominous, but with Gadya at my side I do not feel afraid.

"I've got more oil for the lantern in there," Gadya says. "But we have to be careful about using it, in case anyone's looking for us here."

We keep walking until we reach the edge of the ruins. Gadya steps up onto the rocks. I follow her as she slips into a dark opening in the building.

Soon we are standing inside together. Gadya hangs the lantern on a hook on the concrete wall. The place is filthy. I gaze around at it. I see rat droppings in one corner, and spiderwebs and dust everywhere I look.

"I think I liked my bed back at the farmhouse more than this," I joke.

Gadya smiles. "We won't be here too long."

I nod. "Tomorrow we find Liam. We're still in the Hellgrounds, right?"

She nods. "This region is gigantic. We could walk for days and still be in it."

"I wish we could go find Liam right now," I tell her.

"Me too. But they lock the boys up at night. That's what I've heard."

"Are you still in contact with David?" I ask.

She shakes her head. "Only occasionally. It's too risky for him to broadcast a signal this far."

"What about Liam?" I ask. "You think he's okay?" I try to suppress my worry about him.

Gadya nods. "I hope so."

Then she turns and rummages around on the floor behind us. "Check this out," she says.

She starts pulling up a brick from the floor with a grunt, and then another. I don't know what she's doing until I realize that the bricks are concealing a dark space within.

"What's in the hiding spot?" I ask, moving over to help her. I start pulling bricks up with her.

Gadya glances at me and smiles. "Something that we need for tomorrow."

I lean in to take a closer look. I help her get a few more bricks out of the way before I can see what she's searching for. Then, in the hiding spot, I see the gleam of metal and I realize what's hidden inside here.

"Guns," I say, both slightly afraid and also relieved.

"Just two of them. And some bullets as well. I wish we had more. They were stowed here by rebels a year ago in case anyone ever needed them."

She takes one out of the hiding place and gives it to me. It's an automatic assault rifle. I feel its weight in my hands.

"These will definitely help," I say, sliding the safety back just to check it. I know that two girls and two guns aren't much compared to the army of soldiers that we'll face when we go after Liam at the work farm, but it's better than knives.

Gadya takes the other gun out. "They won't expect us to have these. Not after we fled the farms."

I nod. "How many bullets?"

"Six large boxes. Probably no more than five hundred total. We're going to have to be careful with our shots, and save our ammunition if we can."

"Easier said than done," I point out. "When I got snatched at the rebel cell, and then taken to the local minister, there were hundreds of armed soldiers."

"We better hope they're not guarding Liam as well—and that they don't know that we're coming. I don't plan on getting shot. I need to live so I can see the UNA get taken down. We've made it so far. We have to see it through to the end."

I nod, hoisting the gun up to my shoulder. I practice taking aim at a large black spider crawling down one of the walls. "I feel the exact same way. We're going to rescue Liam and then continue our mission," I say.

For once, I feel almost confident that things will work out. But I know that it's very dangerous to think like that. The UNA is like the wheel. Just when you expect things to go a certain way, they can take a dangerous turn.

I take the weapon down from my shoulder. "I can't wait for tomorrow," I tell her.

She grins. "Me neither. Feels like old times."

That night, we take turns keeping watch. Gadya goes first, sitting up to stare out into the darkness with her rifle, while I curl up on the rocks and dirt, and try to get some sleep. It's almost impossible. I'm too worried about Liam.

Halfway through the night, Gadya wakes me and we switch positions. I sit on a broken slab of concrete, watching and listening as I drink some water from a flask. Gadya goes over to the dirt and lies down. Within a minute, I hear her snoring.

I stare out in the darkness with the gun across my lap, searching for any signs of light. But I see nothing. It feels like we're the only people alive out here. I fight the urge to fall asleep myself. Both Gadya and I are exhausted, but our journey hasn't even really begun yet.

When the sky finally starts to lighten, as the sun prepares to rise, I go over and wake Gadya up. "It's time," I say, touching her shoulder gently. She nods groggily and sits up, wiping the sleep from her eyes.

"You ready?" she asks.

"Absolutely." I grin at her. "I was born ready," I joke.

She laughs.

I help her up. We gather the flasks and the guns. Our siege on the boys' farm, and our rescue of Liam, is about to begin.

12 THE RESCUE

It's another long journey on foot through the forest to find the farm where Liam is being held captive. It takes us about two hours.

The whole time I'm worried that we will be sighted. But this land is completely desolate, and the tall grasses and trees provide adequate shelter. Our guns are slung over our shoulders and we both carry flasks of water at our waists, next to our knives.

Gadya and I have been trained on Island Alpha to survive, so we maximize our ability to blend in with our surroundings. Occasionally, I think I hear the sound of people in the distance, or the rumbling of helicopters in the sky. Each time we stop and hide ourselves in the underbrush. But the noises never get close to us. If there are soldiers out there, they seem to have no clue about where we are headed.

Finally, Gadya pauses. "We're almost there."

"How do you know?"

"I just do. David told me."

"You better be right."

"I am."

We keep moving slowly.

Finally, we reach our destination.

I can see a huge farm in a massive field, just sitting there in the middle of the thick forest. We creep up to the edge of the grass on our hands and knees, and stare out at the buildings.

This farm is much larger than the one I was on. In fact, it doesn't really look like a farm. It looks more like some kind of strange high-tech laboratory, slapped down in the fields. Many of the buildings are made of glass and steel. It looks out of place here, incongruous among the farmlands.

"Are you sure this is the right place?" I ask Gadya.

"Yes," she tells me. "And if it's not, then we get the hell out of here and back into the forest."

"Good idea."

But in my heart I know that Liam is somewhere nearby. I can just feel it. I also trust that David has led us to the right place.

We lie there in the tall grass, peering out at the landscape sprawling in front of us.

There is no sign of Liam. At least not yet.

The main building is huge and cylindrical, surrounded by metal and chrome walkways. Large steel chimneys pump out white smoke. It reminds me of the specimen archive back on Island Alpha, except that this place is not deserted. I see men and women in lab coats moving around the property on concrete pathways.

"This place looks really weird," Gadya mutters into my ear.

"Yeah, I was thinking that too. It doesn't really look like a farm."

We both keep watching, trying to figure out exactly what we're staring at.

"Over there," I say suddenly, pointing as movement catches my eye. A girl is being dragged across the grass by two soldiers. She's wearing a white smock that looks like a medical gown.

"Where did she come from?" Gadya asks.

"Out of that opening," I say, pointing. There is a large circular hatch in the side of a small square building, connected by metal stairs to the main one. This building doesn't have any windows. A guard stands watch at the entryway, an assault rifle slung over his shoulder.

"I thought this was where the boys were being held?" I ask Gadya. "Maybe we really are at the wrong place?"

"I don't understand either. This is where David told me to take us."

We keep watching the girl.

The soldiers continue dragging her forward. Her hair has been cut short and ragged, as though someone has chopped it off or tried to shave it and failed at the task. Her face is badly sunburned and peeling.

She doesn't struggle, but even from here, I can see the defiance in her posture and in the way she refuses to bow her head to look at the ground.

The guards continue pulling her forward.

She tilts her head upright to look at the sun. I see the pain and frustration in her eyes.

And that's when I recognize this girl.

My stomach lurches.

"*Rika!*" I say in shock.

"No way," Gadya breathes, looking closer. "Where?"

I point at the girl with the ragged hair and sunburned face. "That's her!"

Gadya squints. "Are you sure?"

"Yes." I feel a sinking sensation in my stomach. I can see beyond her hair and poor physical condition to recognize the face of my close friend. "It's definitely her."

"You're right," Gadya says, after scrutinizing the girl for a moment more. She sounds shocked too. "Why is she even in the UNA? There's no way she passed the test to come here! No way!"

"Agreed."

Rika was one of our best friends in the village on Island Alpha. She was the cook for our entire camp, and is one of the sweetest and kindest girls I ever met. But I'm also thinking about how Rika secretly joined us on the trip into the gray zone those months ago. How Veidman asked her to be a spy for him. There's clearly more to her than appears on the surface—just as there is to almost everyone that I encountered on the wheel.

"There must be a reason," I say. "But it doesn't matter now. She's been caught. We have to help her."

I watch numbly as Rika is dragged toward a metal box sitting out in the sun. It has a row of small airholes in it but nothing more.

I realize that the guards are going to put her in there. I can feel Gadya shifting next to me. I know that both of us are wishing that we could use our guns right now. Just two bullets would take care of these soldiers. But of course that would give our position away.

Rika is led to the box.

One of the soldiers pauses and flings the lid open.

For a second I'm startled. There's another girl already in the box. Her face is smeared with blood and dirt. She raises an arm, crying out for someone to help her. But instead of helping, the second soldier just shoves Rika into the box with her, the two bodies tumbling together.

Rika tries to struggle against the soldiers but she's easily over-powered. The first soldier slams the lid of the box and locks it. Even from our distance I can hear Rika and the other girl hammering on the metal sides to get out.

"We have to do something," I murmur. I feel sick watching a friend get treated this badly. I know it must be well above a hundred and twenty degrees in the box, and the day is only going to get hotter.

"They're punishing her for something," Gadya says. "Good. At least that means there's some fight left in her. They haven't broken her spirit."

I can't believe that we came here to find Liam and found Rika instead. "Do you think David knows she's here?"

"Probably. He seems to know everything, although I don't know how."

"Maybe that's why he sent us here first. To rescue her."

Gadya nods.

David once risked his own life to save Rika's, on the icy lake back in the gray zone on Island Alpha. I doubt he'd let her remain captive in a place like this. We were probably always meant to rescue her.

"Do you think Liam's here?" I ask Gadya. "I mean, inside some-where."

"I hope so," she says, musing. "We could get Rika on the way out, after we get Liam. It'd be easier then because there'd be three of us."

I'm scouting the fortresslike buildings. "Getting Liam is going to be harder than it sounds. This place is swarming with soldiers. Look."

She follows my gaze. I see a group of about fifteen men with guns standing in formation at the edge of the main building, doing basic drills. They're jumping up and down in the heat as their captain barks at them.

"I don't understand what this place even is," I say. "I wish David had told us more."

"Same here. But that's David for you, isn't it?"

Abrupt movement catches my eye again. "Check it out," I say.

Gadya and I both watch as another formation of soldiers appears on the other side of the building. They are walking across the fields toward a large glass tunnel that leads into a laboratory.

It takes me a moment to realize that there is a person inside the formation. Someone that the soldiers are guarding with guns. My heart leaps. *Maybe it's Liam!* But then I realize that it's not. It's a larger, twisted figure.

"What the hell is that?" Gadya whispers into my ear as she watches, sounding both startled and horrified.

I keep watching too. As the soldiers grow closer, their captive becomes more visible. It's a boy, but one about seven feet tall, and horribly disfigured, with raw, red skin. "It's a mutant," I say. "Like the one I saw in Minister Hiram's building."

Then I catch a glimpse of the back of the mutant's neck and almost throw up. There are tubes running down it and into his spine. But unlike the ones that were implanted temporarily in me and Gadya, these are fused deeply into his flesh. He's some kind of machine-like cyborg. A mass of flesh, tubing, and electronics. He's wearing a gas mask, so I can't see his face.

"This must be a research facility," I say, exhaling shakily. "A laboratory. A place for them to do experiments on kids like us."

Gadya continues to eye the huge lumbering boy warily. "I'm not sure who we need to be more concerned with—the soldiers or the mutant."

175

"Either way, we have to get Liam and Rika out of here right away." I pause. "Even if we're outnumbered. I'm not sure what to do."

"We have the element of surprise."

"Is that really such a big advantage? There's probably about a hundred soldiers down there, and even more UNA officials and scientists in those buildings. Not to mention crazy mutant kids. Once we go down there, we're going to get slaughtered."

Gadya looks back at me. "What choice do we have?"

I sigh. "We don't have one."

We stare at each other. This might be the end for us. There is no way either of us is letting Liam and Rika rot in a place like this. Even if it means our lives. Besides, we can't hide out in the forest forever, or we'll eventually be caught. I wish David's voice would turn up and guide us, but that's not going to happen.

A few moments later, we race down the hillside headed toward the farm below. I know we don't have long until we're spotted. Both of us clutch our guns with our fingers on the triggers. We move low in the grass.

I see the metal hot box where Rika is being held captive to our left. There's no time to get her now, even if we wanted to. We keep rushing forward. No one has seen us yet.

We are approaching the laboratory, its glass and steel walls shimmering in the sun, when I suddenly hear alarms start to blare.

"We've been spotted!" I yell to Gadya. We must have triggered some kind of automatic perimeter defense system.

The soldiers start looking around, almost as if they're surprised.

Gadya and I duck down behind a stone wall low in the grass. It gives us shelter. We're not far from the buildings.

"What do we do now?" I whisper to her.

She raises her rifle. "We go get Liam."

I swallow hard.

Then I peer around the stone wall. Amazingly, the soldiers don't seem to have spotted us yet. They're looking around for whatever triggered the alarm.

"Let do this," I say.

But then I hear a loud buzzing noise in the sky. I whip back around behind the wall again.

I recognize the sound.

It's a feeler.

I haven't heard one since the specimen archive on the wheel was shut down, and they all fell to the earth, destroyed. I can't believe they now have feelers back home in the UNA, and are using them on their own people.

I stare up at the sky as a dark shape moves toward us. Unlike the soldiers, the feeler knows exactly where we are. It must be able to track our heat or motion. Or maybe it has zeroed in on us via satellite.

Gadya and I crouch there, frozen for a moment. If we run back into the trees, we might get hunted down anyway, but we'd also have a chance to escape.

But then what will happen to Liam and Rika?

I know that if we try to fight and reach our friends, we will probably be snatched by the feeler, or gunned down by the soldiers.

The feeler is getting closer. It descends out of the clouds now and I see it clearly. It looks different from the other kinds we've battled before.

There are no blades to slice at things, and no metal tentacles to snatch kids. Only guns mounted underneath it as it buzzes its way forward.

I feel Gadya's hand grab mine.

I squeeze her hand back.

If we were caught by soldiers, maybe we could surrender. But there's no way to surrender against the flying machine zooming its way in our direction. The soldiers are now following it, using it to track us to our hiding place behind the wall.

"It's time," I say. I know that we can't afford to wait any longer. "Let's do this for Liam!"

"For Liam!" Gadya agrees. We let go of each other's hands.

Then we roll sideways in opposite directions and burst out from behind the wall with our guns raised.

I start firing right away, blasting away at the wretched machine in the sky. It opens up its guns on us at the same instant. I roll sideways in the grass to avoid getting hit by the bullets plowing into the earth around me.

Gunfire tears up a path of mud and grass right next to me. I keep rolling. The machine passes overhead. I manage to get into position, and I squeeze off more shots at it. Sparks fly as my bullets clash against its metal frame.

"Go!" Gadya is yelling at me as she races forward.

The machine is circling around for a second try at us. And the guards are rapidly heading our way, also firing shots.

We no longer have the element of surprise. And we can't afford to get captured. David never said it would be like this. Our best option now seems to be retreating into the trees. But it's probably too late for that.

I fire off more shots at the machine in the sky. I see a piece of metal fly off it, and the machine veers sideways. That gives me a second to move.

I start running again. The metal box that Rika is trapped inside is just a few paces away from me now. I can shelter behind it. I also realize that because getting to Liam is too hard, I might as well save Rika and the other girl trapped inside.

I race over to the box and shoot at the lock, as I dodge bullets. The lock splinters in a spray of sparks. I yank the metal sheet upward, opening up the box.

Rika and the other girl stare back at me, dazed.

Loud gunfire behind me makes me turn quickly. Gadya has seen what I'm doing and she's holding the guards at bay. At least for the moment. I don't have long.

"Rika! It's me!" I yell at her, as Rika blinks against the light. She looks sick and confused.

"Alenna?" she says back, her voice a broken rasp. The other girl just huddles there, dirty and scared.

I grab Rika's arm and pull her out of the box. The other girl follows rapidly. All I hear are gunshots. My ears are ringing.

"I can't hold them off much longer!" Gadya yells at me. She's crouching behind another nearby stone wall. More soldiers are flooding out of the building and heading in our direction.

I turn and fire at them. They run for cover as my bullets spray wildly at them. Then I turn back to Rika. I huddle behind the metal box with Rika and the other girl.

Rika is coming back to life. "What are you doing here?" she asks me.

"Rescuing you!" I tell her. "Why are you even back in the UNA?"

"Long story," she says.

I raise my gun again and peer out from around the metal box. I take aim as a row of soldiers approaches. I start firing. I hit one in the leg and he goes down. Instantly, bullets rain all around us. I feel one whisk past my elbow and I yelp.

Gadya races back over to us. The machine in the sky never recovered from our bullets. It is lazily on its way toward crashing into the trees. But the guards keep on coming as the sirens wail.

"We need to leave right now," Rika says to me, her words tumbling out rapidly. "This place is a nightmare. You don't know what goes on here!"

"I saw the mutant. I have some idea."

Gadya reaches us. "To the trees!" she yells. "Run! There's too many of them!"

We start racing back toward the forest, firing off shots as we go. Rika and the other girl stumble along with us.

Then I hear a sharp cry of pain. The other girl stumbles and falls to her knees. I think that she has tripped. I reach back to help her up. But blood is coming out of her mouth and from her nose. I realize that she's been struck by one of the guard's bullets.

"She's been hit!" I yell.

Gadya tries to help her up too. "Come on!" Gadya screams at her. The girl tries to say something to us, but more blood comes up, spattering the grass.

Rika suddenly screams at us, in a voice thick with fear and horror, "No! Stay away from her body! You don't understand! Something terrible is about to happen!" Rika starts backing away herself.

I'm completely confused.

"We need to help her—" I begin to say, ducking my head as more bullets fly past. Gadya returns fire. For some reason, the soldiers stop firing at us.

But then I glance at the bleeding girl. She's shaking. I can't see where the bullet hit her. Maybe her head or her neck. Then she opens her mouth wider. I'm expecting that more blood will come out, or that she's going to throw up.

Instead, I see a thin, wiry metal tentacle emerge from her lips.

I'm so stunned I can barely move.

"What the hell is that?" Gadya yells in total shock. She grabs my arm. We both start backing away.

"Run!" Rika screams at us.

But I can't tear my eyes away. The girl continues to cough and gag, falling onto all fours, as some kind of mechanical creature pries its way out of her mouth.

The girl can't even get enough air into her lungs to scream. The mechanical creature looks like a miniature electronic spider. It slips from her mouth in a whirring frenzy of gears, and a pool of saliva and blood. It lands on the grass on its six spindly metal legs.

"Don't let it get near you!" Rika yells at me and Gadya, trying to pull us even farther away from the girl. The girl is still coughing and bleeding.

"What's going—" I begin.

"She's dying!" Rika cuts me off. "And if you don't run, you're going to be dying soon too!"

I gaze at the mechanical spiderlike creature. It remains stationary on the grass. I hear whirring and buzzing. I can't believe this came out from the girl's body. I just keep staring in numb horror. Then Gadya shoots it, and it gets blasted into tiny pieces.

"Let's go!" Gadya yells, pulling at my arm.

Gadya and I start racing back to the forest. But Rika just stands there.

"C'mon!" I yell back at her, stopping for a moment. "You said she was dying! What are you doing? You're going to get shot! We need to run right now!"

Rika is still watching the girl. The girl curls up on her side in a fetal position. Blood continues to seep from her nose and mouth.

181

I can only imagine that the metal creature tore up her internal organs when it exited her body.

"Yeah, c'mon, Rika!" Gadya screams at her.

"I can't go with you!" she yells back, her face contorted in frustration and anger. I've never seen her look like this before.

"Why not?" I yell back, pausing for a moment. The soldiers are continuing to make their way in our direction, although I'm surprised they're not shooting at us. I know that soon another of the flying machines will find us. "There's no time! Rika, what are you doing?"

Her answer devastates me:

"I have one of those things inside me, too," she says, looking like she wants to throw up. "It's to stop us girls from running away. Angelica—that was her name—must have set hers off accidentally, or maybe she got shot and that set it off."

"You have one of those machines in you?" Gadya asks, sounding horrified.

"Yes. They put them in all of us. If we leave the grounds of this farm, they get activated."

"Are you sure?" I ask Rika.

She nods. "I was awake when they surgically implanted it in my stomach."

Gadya looks sick. I feel the same way.

"Is Liam here?" I ask desperately, realizing that he could help fight this battle for us. And maybe he would know how to help Rika.

"I've only seen him once. He was being taken to a different work farm, that way." She points into the forest, to our left. I see a narrow trail. "That's where they take a lot of the boys to break their spirit before they experiment on them."

"Is there any way to get the machine out of you?" I ask her desperately.

She shakes her head. "No. It stays curled up until it gets a signal to activate. Then it claws its way out."

"We have to get you out of here," I murmur.

"There's no hope for me," Rika says. She doesn't sound stoic or brave. She just sounds resigned. She has already come to terms with her fate. "Save yourselves. And find Liam, too."

A bullet hits a granite rock near me, sending off little chunks of rock and making me startle. The soldiers have started shooting. We hide behind rocks.

"Rika——" I begin. But I don't know what to say. Angelica is dying now, her breath shallow as she bleeds out on the grass.

"Give me one of your guns," Rika says. "I'll head in the other direction and draw their fire while you two make a run for it. Liam will be in the fields, in chains and shackles, digging the foundation of a new building for them. Or at least that's what I've heard the UNA is using the boys to do right now."

I nod.

"Now get moving before it's too late!"

Gadya and I look at each other. I can't believe there's no way to save Rika. There has to be a way.

I toss Rika my gun. "You need this."

She catches it.

"We better go," Gadya says.

Rika nods. "Yes, go!"

I want to ask her so many questions. *How did she end up back here in the UNA? What happened to her along the way?* But there's no time for anything right now but taking action. I tell myself that maybe she'll survive. As long as she doesn't try to run, then that metal creature won't burst out of her. Perhaps the soldiers won't kill her.

"We'll come back for you," I tell her.

She shakes her head. "Don't. Find Liam. Keep fighting. My struggle is almost over. Yours is just beginning!"

Under a fresh hail of gunfire, Gadya and I start racing toward the trees, in the direction that Rika pointed. Only luck keeps us from being hit. I know it's just a matter of time before one of us takes a bullet.

Then Rika unleashes a torrent of firepower from her rifle. I glance back and see her standing there shooting at the uniformed guards. Bullets plow into them, sending some of them straight down to the grass. But more guards keep coming.

"We can't leave her like this!" I yell at Gadya, my heart aching.

"We don't have a choice!" she yells right back. "Keep running unless you want to die and never see Liam again!"

But I keep looking back at Rika as I run. Everything is going so fast. I can't strand a friend like her. Maybe there's a way to get that awful thing out of her stomach.

Rika is firing fast and hard at the guards, drawing them away from us just like she promised. And so far she hasn't been hit. But suddenly, two bullets find her at once, plunging straight into her abdomen.

Rika gasps.

Her arms jerk upward and she fires into the air, as the force of the bullets knocks her off her feet.

"No!" I scream, staggering in my tracks. "Rika!"

My mind goes blank.

She falls down to the grass, dropping the gun and clutching her stomach with both hands. Her face is contorted into an agonized mask of pain.

"Rika!" I scream again. Everything sounds muffled. My vision starts sparkling like I'm getting a head rush. I can't catch my breath.

Gadya clutches my arm and drags me forward. She's seen what has happened. "Don't look," she tells me firmly. "Keep moving."

But I can barely move. I feel numb. I look back anyway. Rika is sprawled out in the dirt as soldiers approach her, firing their assault rifles in a barrage.

She turns her head, and her eyes find mine. I see surprise in them. And a world of pain.

"Go," she mouths at me and Gadya.

"Rika . . . ," I say one last time.

She blinks, and then more bullets find her, cutting into her chest and neck.

Her head arches back as her body goes into a convulsion.

And then she is at peace.

The life has gone from her body.

I feel like I'm going to collapse onto the dirt. *Rika died trying to help save us.* There is probably more we could have done. In fact, if we hadn't turned up, she would still be alive—stuck in the box in the sun, but alive. We are directly responsible for her death.

"Come on!" Gadya screams into my ear. "Don't think about it now! Or we'll end up the same way!"

I'm trying not to cry.

"You're a warrior!" Gadya yells at me. "You've seen kids die before. Keep going no matter what!"

"But it's Rika!" I yell.

"I know! But if you or I got shot instead of her, she'd keep on going. You can't give up! You can't stop!"

Gadya is hurting just as much as I am—probably more. Rika

was one of her best friends. If Gadya can pull herself together, then so can I. There will be time to mourn later.

Together, Gadya and I rush forward and into the trees, plunging down the path leading to the boys' camp.

"She's dead," I say numbly as we run. I can hear the soldiers in pursuit. "Do you realize that?"

"Of course!" Gadya snaps. Her voice breaks suddenly and I realize that she's close to tears too. "They shot her like an animal. They didn't even care. How can they act that way? They're worse than drones on the wheel."

I have no answers. "We need to find Liam before the same thing happens to him."

"Agreed." She swipes at her eyes angrily.

Gadya and I keep running down the path, pursued by guards. We must go fast or soon the guards will find us, or more flying machines will be dispatched to gun us down. Over and over in my head I see images of Rika's pointless, violent death.

If it weren't for her, we would be the ones lying there dead in the grass. She didn't need to sacrifice herself like that. Just like David did at the specimen archive, she risked everything to help our cause. Now it's up to me and Gadya to not screw up. We need to find Liam.

I wonder if I will be called to make the same sacrifice that she made. *And if that happens, will I be ready? Will I be capable of giving my own life for our greater cause?*

Gadya and I continue to race down the winding path. The forest is thick and tangled here. It's nearly as wild as the wheel. Huge trees are everywhere, with vines hanging between them.

We finally come to a crossroads in the forest, where another path intersects with ours. We pause for a second for breath.

"Which way?" Gadya yells.

"Left," I yell back.

"Are you sure?"

"No! But we have to decide right now!" I'm running on pure instinct.

"Then left it is!"

I can faintly hear soldiers yelling to one another in the distance. They are probably fanning out in the forest to search for us. It won't be long until they track us down on this trail.

We make a sharp turn and run down the new path. It's narrower, and branches rip at my clothes. I knock the branches away. My boots crunch down on the leaves and twigs.

We only have one gun now. One gun and two knives. I don't even know how many bullets we have left, but it can't be very many. *How are we ever going to rescue Liam with such a limited supply of weapons?*

I keep running forward anyway. Even if I get killed, I want to see him one last time. That thought gives me strength and motivation as I barge through the forest with Gadya.

"C'mon!" I yell at her.

If we don't move faster, then we're going to lose our only opportunity for survival. We race through the forest, heading toward Liam.

13 LIAM

GADYA AND I EXPLODE out of the trees. The trail ends at a large series of steel-and-red-brick buildings. Another work camp. Rika was right. This is where the boys are being kept. I see lines of them in chains, plowing the fields with primitive machinery.

We have very little time before the soldiers find us. I clutch the two knives. Gadya holds the gun.

We blaze out of the forest and toward the prisoners. They all have shaved heads. But these are not the drones of Island Alpha. These are normal boys who have been captured and enslaved. I wonder who these boys are. This must be where the UNA started sending kids who failed the GPPT once the rebels took over Island Alpha. And somewhere—at least if my heart is correct—Liam is among them.

There are lots of guards somewhere in the forest behind us, but only a handful down here, watching these shackled prisoners. They have obviously already been alerted to our presence, because their guns are raised and they are turning around, looking for intruders.

They notice us as soon as Gadya lets out a war whoop and begins firing.

They fire back in our direction, but they are no match for Gadya's aim. She cuts them down as the bullets whip past us.

A guard's gun misfires and I run straight toward him, screaming like a crazy person. He seems shocked. My knives are out and my teeth are bared. I plunge a blade straight into his heart, and then yank it out with my full strength. He topples to the ground, gagging and choking for air.

I leave him for dead, without another thought. After what the UNA did to Rika, there can be no mercy.

Then I'm back up and running again, searching the prisoners for Liam. The boys are already trying to escape, but they're chained together, so it's difficult. A group of them makes a run for the forest. Another group surrounds an injured guard and begins kicking and beating him, trying to get his gun.

"Liam!" I start yelling, as I desperately stare at their faces. The boys here look the same—muscular, but exhausted and covered with dirt. "Liam, where are you?" I yell.

Gadya is calling out his name too.

I feel rising panic. He's not here. I search face after face. "Liam!" I keep screaming, as I run past the lines of boys with both of my knives out. "Liam Bernal!"

I hear gunshots behind us. I spin around. The guards from the farm where we found Rika have located us. They are firing at Gadya across the field, and she is firing back. We have to get out of here soon or we will be shot. I'm stunned it hasn't happened already.

A hand suddenly grabs my arm. I yank my arm back, ready to stab whoever touched me. But the hand doesn't belong to a guard. Instead, it belongs to a shackled boy with haunted green eyes. His face is scarred from old battle wounds. His body is stooped and nearly broken.

"I know who you're looking for," he says.

"Liam Bernal," I say, startled. "You know him?"

"Yes. He's here with us. He said people would come to find him, and that he'd lead a rebellion. No one believed him. We all thought he was crazy."

"Where is he now?" I ask urgently, staring into the boy's eyes.

"Inside," the boy says, gesturing to the huge building that looks like a laboratory, sitting behind us in the field. "They took him away to experiment on, just yesterday."

"Thank you," I tell the boy. I'm about to move on and find Gadya, when he grabs at me again. "Is this the start of the revolution? Was Liam right all along?"

"Yes!" I say. "This is the revolution. It starts today!"

Then I hear Gadya scream in frustration.

"Are you hit?" I yell over to her.

"Worse!" she yells back. She races over to me. "I'm almost out of bullets," she says softly. "Only ten or twenty left!"

I pass her one of the knives. "Use this."

She grabs it.

Right then, I hear the pop of automatic gunfire and feel a burning sensation in my left upper arm. I cry out in pain. I look down at my arm and see a red spot blooming on my shirt.

"I've been shot," I say dully.

"Let me look," Gadya says, sounding worried. She tears part of my shirt away.

My arm feels cold. I crouch on the ground. More gunfire sounds nearby. But the boys are now taking care of most of the guards, by attacking them viciously and encircling them with their chains.

Gadya quickly inspects my wound. "You'll be okay. It looks

like the bullet passed through the fleshy part of your arm and didn't hit bone. Try to flex your fingers."

I do what she says. My fingers move.

"Good," Gadya says. "Now try not to get hit again, and let's go find Liam!"

I stand up, clutching the knife in my right hand. My left arm hurts but I ignore the pain.

We rush over to another group of boys. Gadya uses the gun to shoot the shackles chaining them together. Some of these boys are in terrible shape—bruised and with broken bones. Others look relatively healthy.

We go from one group to another, freeing all of them. Guards keep firing at us. Many of the boys get hit.

But the boys here are clearly ready to fight. They know that this is their one chance at liberation. As a group we begin charging toward the building.

The boys fan out to make themselves harder to hit. Gadya is still shooting with her gun, although I know she probably only has a couple bullets left by now. I see a guard take a bullet in the throat and go down spinning.

Some guards start racing inside, like they're preparing to close up the front doors and bulwark themselves inside until reinforcements can get here.

I see a lanky boy fashion part of the long metal chain that once bound him into a whip. He lashes it out at the back of a retreating guard, striking him so hard that the guard instantly falls down to the grass, unconscious. The boy then stands over him, whipping the guard again and again with the chain. Gadya and I run past him. All that is on my mind is finding Liam in this place before it's too late.

The guards are trying to close the gates at the front of the building but they are overrun by an army of boys, along with me and Gadya.

I see one guard fall, and then another. Boys leap onto their bodies, punching and kicking them. They take guns away from the guards and use them to shoot their way into the building.

Everything has turned into chaos, but for once, chaos is on our side. Gadya and I keep moving. We get inside the building.

"He better be here!" Gadya yells out to me.

"He is. A boy told me!"

Alarms are ringing throughout the building. A scientist in a lab coat with a red logo on the breast pocket steps out in front of us. The logo is that strange reenvisioning of the UNA emblem—a globe surrounded by five eyes. The scientist is bleeding from a cut on his face. "Don't hurt me!" he says, as I raise my knife and Gadya aims the gun at him. Boys are rushing past on either side of him, pursuing the guards.

"Then help us!" I yell at him. "Or you're going to die like everyone else who works for the UNA."

"Coward!" Gadya spits at him. "No real scientist would work for these monsters. You're a traitor."

"No, please! I'll help you," he bleats as Gadya and I advance on him.

"Give me an excuse to pull this trigger," she hisses, pointing the barrel of the rifle right at his head.

"We're looking for someone," I tell the scientist. "Liam Bernal. He's a captive here. We need to find him. Can you take us to him?"

"Yes," the man begins, as he digs into his pocket to take something out.

It could be a weapon.

I lash out with the knife, slicing his arm like I'm filleting a fish. He cries out in pain.

"Keep your hands where we can see them!" Gadya screams at him.

The object clatters to the ground as the scientist nurses his bleeding arm. It's not a weapon. It's a digital reader.

"It has the list of inmates—I mean, boys on it," he says.

"Go on. Pick it up," I tell him.

He crouches down and picks it up with shaking hands. Blood is running freely onto his fingers. He starts scrolling through the digital reader as chaos reigns all around us. The noise is almost unbearable as boys whoop and holler. They attack the guards and begin tearing the place apart.

"Yes! Here he is," the scientist says. "Liam Bernal. He's a new arrival. I can take you to him."

I nod. "Do it fast."

We push and prod him along. He leads us down a narrow corridor. I can hear screams of guards and kids alike, as well as loud gunfire.

"Faster!" Gadya yells at the scientist, slamming the gun against the back of his head.

I think about the scientists on Island Alpha, including my own parents, who got snatched because they refused to work for the corrupt UNA. Yet this man wearing a lab coat clearly has no qualms about working for a government that chooses to enslave and experiment on its own people. I don't feel any pity for him. I only feel anger and disgust.

The scientist keeps walking and we follow, down endless hallways in this strange, ominous laboratory.

Boys rush past us. One of them is about to strike the scientist with his fist, but we stop him, telling him that the scientist is our prisoner. They listen to me and Gadya because we are the ones who rescued them. They probably think we know a lot more than we actually do.

The scientist finally reaches a door and pauses, breathing hard. He's starting to look pale from blood loss. "He's in here."

"Open the door," I say.

He hesitates for a moment.

"Do it!" Gadya adds, raising the gun. I'm pretty sure she's out of bullets, but the scientist doesn't know that.

The scientist taps a code into the door. Then he presses his thumb against a fingerprint reader. I hear a whirring sound and then the click of a lock being opened. My heart is in my throat. I don't know what condition Liam is going to be in.

The door starts to slide open.

Right then, the scientist swings around and slams a fist into Gadya's face. Gadya yells and stumbles, firing off a round into the ceiling. The sound is deafening. For a moment, I'm stunned. The scientist grapples with Gadya, trying to get the gun. He's taken her off guard, and she's having trouble recovering her balance.

I snap into action. I raise the knife in a fluid motion and slide it straight into the scientist's stomach. The blade goes in cleanly, right to the hilt.

The scientist yelps and falls back, as blood cascades out of him, down his white lab coat. Gadya gets her balance again and aims the gun at his chest.

He stares at us, eyes burning with fury. "You girls don't know what—"

"Sweet dreams," Gadya mutters as she pulls the trigger. The bullet blasts a hole in his chest and he staggers against the wall.

I lean down and wipe my knife clean on his white lab coat.

"That was my last bullet," Gadya mutters, pulling the trigger and hearing an empty click. "At least I didn't waste it."

Then Gadya and I turn and walk into the room where Liam is being held.

I'm not sure what I'm expecting. Maybe something weird and creepy, like when I found him encased in that fluid-filled pod in the specimen archive. Or something even worse. After seeing what happened to David, I realize anything is possible. Not that it would matter—I would love Liam no matter what the UNA has done to him.

What I don't expect is that Liam is sitting there on a hospital bed in a stark white room, staring right at the door. He has an IV line running directly into his right arm, dripping some mysterious clear fluid from a bag hanging on a pole. He's wearing jeans and a T-shirt.

"Liam!" I say, rushing over to him. I hug him as hard as I can. He looks fine. He hasn't been mutilated. "Thank god!" Gadya rushes over too.

But then I pull away from Liam. He's staring at me blankly. And he hasn't hugged me back.

"Liam, it's me!" I yell at him, confused and scared. This is the boy I love most in the world, and he doesn't even seem to recognize me.

He tries to form a word but his mouth barely moves. "Who . . . ," he begins.

Without thinking, I raise my knife and slash the IV line. Gadya comes around and starts pulling the IV needle out of his skin.

"Who . . . are . . . you . . . ," Liam begins again.

"They've done something to him," I say, feeling sick.

"I know." Gadya sounds just as worried as I am.

"Maybe it's just a sedative," I tell her, glancing down at the liquid now dripping onto the floor.

"Maybe."

Gadya and I help him off the table.

"Is it time . . . for my surgery?" he asks us. His eyes are closing, as though he's about to fall asleep.

"No," I tell him. "No surgery today. We're getting out of here."

Gadya and I get him standing on two legs. He seems like he's about to pass out, but he manages to stay upright.

"This way," I say, dragging him toward the door as Gadya helps me.

Guns continue to fire all around us, as bullets ping off the metal corridors.

Liam sways unsteadily at the doorway.

"Liam, we need to go fast," I tell him. Although he's clearly under the influence of a drug, some part of him seems to understand. We start navigating the hallways at a rapid pace.

I'm on his left and Gadya is on his right. We are rushing down the halls, trying to find a way out.

I hear more gunfire. And from outside, the sound of feelers in the air. Boys are using guns taken off dead guards to fire back at the feelers. For now they are keeping the remaining guards and the machines at bay, but eventually the buildings will be overrun by the UNA.

"We need to get out of here," I say, as Gadya and I hold on to Liam, dragging him along with us.

"And where do we go?" Gadya asks, as we keep moving.

My mind is racing. "There must be vehicles here somewhere. I mean, we're not back on Island Alpha. There are roads and cities nearby. The scientists and guards must have cars so they can get to and from work."

"Maybe it's a residential lockdown facility and they all live here," Gadya says.

"Maybe." I turn to Liam. "Do you know if there are any cars here? Any vehicles we can use to escape?"

He looks at me blankly. "Cars . . ."

"Liam's not gonna be any help to us yet," Gadya points out.

"I can see that."

I start looking around for any indication of a parking lot or carport. There has to be something.

A boy races past. I grab his arm. "Cars. Vehicles," I say in a rush. "Have you seen any?"

"No, but if I do, I'm gonna destroy them! We're going to burn this place to the ground!"

He shoves me aside as he keeps running.

"Thanks for nothing!" I yell after him.

But then another boy comes up behind us. This boy is lean with dark skin and a shaved head. His fingers and knuckles are bloody, as though he's just beaten someone up. "I heard what you said," he tells me and Gadya. "I think I can help."

"You know where the vehicles are?" I ask.

"This way. I've seen some in a hangar out back. Come with me."

We start following him as he darts down the hallway. Liam is coming back to life—or at least his body is. He starts moving faster and faster. We race along the hallway after the boy.

Finally we reach a metal doorway and he steps through it. "Be quick, or other kids are going to tear them to pieces," he says.

We step through the doorway after him.

I see the vehicles sitting there, gleaming and untouched. But they are not normal-looking cars. They are armor-plated trucks, with huge tires and thick glass.

Gadya and I rush over to the nearest one with Liam.

"Are there keys inside?" I ask.

The boy opens his hand. "No. But there are keys right here." He tosses them to me. I catch them.

"Want to come with us?" Gadya asks the boy.

Surprising me, the boy shakes his head. "I'm going to stay here. I have to get revenge on the people who tortured me." He pauses. "This is the start of the revolution, though, right?"

"You're the second person to ask me that," I tell him. "So yeah, I guess it is. We came back here from Island Alpha to take over the UNA."

The boy's eyes widen.

"Rip this place up for us," Gadya tells the boy. "Burn it to ashes and kill all the guards that you can."

The boy nods.

We hear crashing noises from somewhere in the laboratory and then a dull thump of an explosion. An instant later I feel the floor ripple. Someone is setting off grenades.

"You better hurry," the boy says.

I open the door of the truck, and I get into the driver's side. I put the keys in the ignition, and start the engine. The boy helps Gadya get Liam inside. Liam sits between us in the front, as Gadya climbs on board too and swings the door shut.

The boy reaches down and passes Gadya a gun through the open window. "I got this off a guard. Careful—it's loaded."

"Awesome," Gadya replies. "Thanks!" She discards the empty gun in the back and clutches the new one.

The boy darts back to join the melee.

"I assume you don't know how to drive this thing," Gadya says to me, as she rolls her window up.

"Neither do you," I point out. "And Liam's no use to us right now."

"Fine. Then you work on driving, and I'll do the shooting." She lowers her window a crack and sticks the muzzle of the gun out of it. "Let's get out of here!"

I put the truck in reverse and begin backing out of the garage. While it's true I don't know how to drive a vehicle like this, it seems pretty straightforward. Not much different from a car. I push the pedal down, and hear the engine roar.

"Faster!" Gadya yells.

It's easier to steer the vehicle than I expected. I glance over at Liam. His eyes are looking a little clearer.

I keep backing up, picking up speed.

"How do we open the garage door?" I ask. There is a large, fortified metal door blocking the garage off from the outside world.

"I don't know! The kid didn't say."

"Great," I reply, gritting my teeth. "We're going to have to drive right through it. Brace yourselves." But as we approach, going even faster, the door begins opening on its own. It must have an automatic sensor.

For a split second, I feel relief.

But then I see what's waiting outside, beyond the door.

There's a battle raging between the kids and the guards. There are people everywhere fighting, and the endless flash of gunfire.

I spin the wheel as we pass through the opening, tires squealing, so that we're facing forward. My wounded arm aches, but I ignore the pain.

"This isn't good," Gadya mutters, surveying the carnage.

I see several feelers in the sky, zooming down and firing at kids. I also see guards swarming out of the trees, with even more guns. Still, the boys are fighting with everything they have.

I press the pedal to the floor and we tear forward across the grassy field. We need to get out of here as fast as possible, and into the forest, where we can flee on foot.

Gadya begins shooting as we drive. She lowers her window even more and leans out with the gun, firing at guards as we pass them.

"Be careful!" I yell at her, afraid that she's going to get hit.

"I'm fine!" she calls back over the constant noise of gunfire. "Worry about yourself!"

A group of armed soldiers in full riot gear is headed our way. Our vehicle, and Gadya's gun, has attracted attention. I push the vehicle to go even faster. Liam is still out of it, his head lolling sideways.

The guards open up their guns on us and we're suddenly peppered with bullets. The windshield splinters but holds even under the heavy barrage. The glass must be bulletproof. Gadya screams and pulls away from the window. She hurries to close it as fast as she can.

"You okay?" I ask.

"Just got nicked," she says. It looks worse than a nick. Her arm is bleeding badly. She tears off part of her shirt and uses it as a makeshift tourniquet.

More bullets hit our vehicle. I keep driving, aiming at the forest beyond this battle.

Suddenly, a large explosion rocks the truck, and part of the ground opens up right in front of us. The windshield is pelted with debris.

I cry out in surprise and spin the wheel, trying to avoid the hole in the ground. The truck almost topples into it. I manage to avoid the pit at the last second.

"Grenades!" Gadya yells.

I gun the engine again, and we continue forward. I see the grenade launcher now, sitting on the shoulder of a soldier only a few hundred yards away. He's preparing to fire again. We are his target.

Gadya rolls down her window an inch.

"Gadya, no!" I tell her, worried that she'll get shot for a second time.

But she just puts the muzzle through the open part of the window and begins firing right at the soldier.

Gadya's bullets strike their target just as the soldier unleashes another rocket-propelled grenade at us.

He topples backward and the grenade shoots straight into the sky.

"Nice work," I tell her.

Then I take one hand off the wheel for a second to check on Liam. I find his hand and squeeze it. I need him to be okay, or else none of this will have been worth it.

But he doesn't squeeze my hand back. I feel sick with worry.

"Liam, are you okay?" I ask. I risk a glance at him. His eyes still look glazed. He must still be recovering. I turn back and put both hands on the wheel. I keep driving as fast as I can. Gadya closes her window. I hear a detonation as the grenade lands somewhere behind us in the fray of the battle.

Feelers zoom overhead, no doubt tracking us, and preparing to shoot. But there's nothing we can do about them. I just keep driving, headed toward the nearby forest and hoping that we can make it there before we all get killed.

14 THE PLAN

A MINUTE LATER, WE reach the edge of the clearing without being shot or blown up by a grenade. I keep driving straight into the forest, dodging trees without stopping. The vehicle shakes as we run over rocks and thick underbrush. Thin trees get snapped by the force of our momentum and the weight of the truck.

But I realize we can't keep going. The forest is getting too thick.

"Watch out!" Gadya yells at me, as I narrowly avoid a huge tree trunk.

We slam against another tree and the impact jars us sideways. I'm going to have to stop driving soon. There are larger trees ahead, and the armored vehicle can't handle the terrain. There's no way to continue.

I bring the vehicle to a juddering halt.

"We have to get out!" I yell.

Gadya is already swinging open her door. I grab the keys, and open mine.

"Help me with Liam," I tell her.

Together, we get him out of the car.

"You need a weapon," I tell him. He seems like a shell of

himself. He's still not recovering. I hand him my knife. He takes it and stares at it for a moment.

"Thanks . . . ," he mumbles. Then he looks at me blankly.

I realize that he doesn't know my name.

"I'm Alenna," I tell him, fighting back panic. "Don't you remember me?"

He looks at me. "No."

"I'm Gadya," Gadya says. "Ring any bells?"

He shakes his head, sounding dazed. "I've never seen . . . either of you before. . . ."

My heart sinks. He doesn't even remember who I am. I need Liam back. I need to make sure that whatever was done to him isn't permanent.

"Try to think hard," I tell him. "Try to clear your mind."

He just keeps staring at me. "Where am I?" he asks. It's worse than I thought.

"We better move," Gadya says.

I nod. "Can you run?" I ask Liam.

"I think so," he says.

"Then let's go." Together, we race alongside Gadya into the forest, leaving the vehicle and the battlefield behind. I was afraid that feelers or soldiers would travel after us, but they are completely occupied by the army of boys. The sounds of constant explosions and gunshots reach our ears. We head deeper into the forest, seeking protection.

We run for a long time, making our way through the brush.

We only stop moving when we can no longer hear the sounds of the battle anymore. We find a small clearing. All of us crouch down to the ground, breathing hard. Liam's eyes are starting to look a little clearer now.

I hug him tightly. "I'm so glad you're alive."

He hugs me back tentatively. "Same here."

"You still don't know who I am, do you?"

He shakes his head. "No. I mean you sort of look familiar. But beyond that, it's just a blank."

Gadya sees that I am on the brink of tears. "I'll give you two a moment alone," she says. "But remember, we have to keep moving soon."

She walks about twenty paces away and crouches there, keeping watch for us so that no one attacks.

"What do you remember?" I ask Liam.

"Some of it's coming back to me. I remember that we're fighting the UNA. And I remember that they were about to operate on me—" He breaks off.

"Yes?" I prompt. I reach out a hand and touch him again. His skin is pale and he feels sweaty.

"I feel pretty sick," he confesses. "I mean, my thoughts and memories are just a big jumble." He pauses. "I also feel like I'm going to throw up."

"Go for it," I tell him.

Liam stands up and walks over to the edge of the clearing. For a moment, I'm worried that one of those terrifying metal spiders will be inside him. But he just throws up normally into the underbrush. Then he wipes his mouth with the back of his hand and walks over.

"Feeling better?" I ask.

He nods.

"Keep throwing up if you need to," I tell him. "Get the drugs out of your system. Maybe that will help."

"She's right," Gadya calls out.

How's your memory feeling?" I ask Liam.

"Not good," he says, with a grimace. "Like it's filled with holes."

I work hard not to break down. It never crossed my mind that we would rescue Liam just to find out that he doesn't even remember me. I don't know what drugs he was given. I don't know how long they will take to wear off. I don't even know if they will ever wear off. That thought fills me with dread.

Liam rests on a rock as I rub his back. It feels so good to touch his skin after being away from him for so long. There is so little time for tenderness or physical contact. But it also feels strange to touch him, because I can tell that his muscles aren't relaxed. They are still tense and he is guarded. *He doesn't know who I am.*

"Did anyone try to implant you with anything?" I ask, just to be sure. "Like a metal spider-type thing?"

He looks confused. "Wait. That does sound familiar. You've seen those?"

"Yes," I tell him.

A look of recognition comes across his face. "They're called Mechanized Implanted Obedience Devices. Or MIODs for short. I don't have one in me. For some reason they only put them in girls, I think. But they threatened us with them. I remember that."

"They put tubes in my neck, and in Gadya's too. She's another friend of ours—remember her?"

He shakes his head.

I continue anyway. "They were trying to control us with drugs. They were trying to train us to work for the UNA or something. We cut the tubes out."

Liam nods. "I don't think they put anything in most boys because they just wanted to use us as slave labor, at least at first. I remember hearing that they put the MIODs in girls they think are high flight risks, or extremely violent."

"Why didn't they put one in me? Or Gadya?"

"They probably had bigger plans for you two. . . ." I can tell that his memories are rushing back now in a flood. "The MIODs are also a form of experimentation—they think they can use them in battle against other countries, to get inside people and take over entire armies that way. There were obviously worse things waiting for me. You saved me from some surgery today. You got there just in time."

"I know." I stare into his eyes. "So do you remember me now? Who I am to you?"

He looks back. I see a look of emptiness and sorrow. "I want to remember you. . . . I wish I did. But I don't. For some reason, things and events are easier to remember than people. It's like some kind of partial amnesia."

I nod, trying to stay calm. I know that if I freak out, that will only make things worse. I remember what it was like when I surfaced from the isolation tank back on Island Alpha, and couldn't remember my situation for a few minutes. It was terrifying. I realize Liam probably feels scared too, but is hiding it.

I take his hand. I tell myself that it's just taking longer than I expected for him to recover from the drugs he was given. But inside, I feel rattled. Shaken up. I need his support and love. *What happens if his memory doesn't come back?*

I'm suddenly overwhelmed by a horrible feeling. If his memory doesn't come back, will he still be in love with me? What if he likes someone else? If he can't remember everything that we shared together, then will he still care about me?

"I'm your girlfriend," I tell him, my voice breaking.

"I guessed you probably were," he says.

"I love you," I continue. "We've been together for months. We met on the wheel. I rescued you when you got frozen in the specimen archive——" I break off. "Is any of this making sense to you?"

He gazes back at me. "Sort of. I have bits and pieces of memories. It feels like a dream that I've half forgotten." He pats my hand. "I'm sure my memory will come back."

"Guys, this is taking too long," Gadya says. "Speed things up!"

I have a sudden idea. Before I can think about it, I move toward Liam.

Then I lean in and kiss him.

He is startled at first. Hesitant. He almost pulls back from me. But I press my lips firmly against his. I have to help him find his way back.

If nothing else will help him remember me and our feelings for each other, then maybe this will. I can't think of anything better to do.

We kiss for a moment and then our lips part. I lean back and look deep into his eyes.

And I see a flash of recognition.

"Alenna . . . ," he says. "Yes, I remember something——" He stops talking.

"Tell me."

His eyes suddenly clear, like a veil has been lifted. "I remember you! Oh my god, of course." He grabs me and we hug. I feel tears in my eyes. "How could I not?"

It feels like we've been reunited for a second time.

He lets go of me. "I'm so sorry! Do you forgive me? It's all coming back now . . . everything . . ." He looks overwhelmed.

"It's not your fault," I tell him. I'm filled with a degree of relief that makes me feel ecstatic. "I'm just glad you're back!"

He leans in and kisses me again. This time it's more passionate. It feels like Liam again, and not some stranger. I don't want the kiss to end.

"I shouldn't have worried about trying to protect you," he says, holding me tightly. "In the end, you were the one who helped me when I needed it."

"We help each other," I say. "That's how it's always been."

Gadya strolls over. She's been listening, but she hasn't said anything yet. "You remember me now, I hope?" she asks Liam. She looks at me. "Should I kiss him too?" I can tell that she's kidding. I smile.

"Of course I remember you," Liam says to her. "How could I have forgotten you, Gadya? It seems crazy. The memories are all back. Well, most of them."

"Good to hear it."

Gadya hands me her knife. I realize she doesn't need it now that she has the gun. We can still hear the distant sounds of the battle.

Gadya inspects her gunshot wound. It has stopped bleeding. I glance down at mine.

Liam notices. "You're hurt. Both of you."

"It's nothing," Gadya and I say at almost exactly the same time.

Liam smiles. "You guys are hard-core."

"You mentioned a surgery?" I ask him. "Do you know what it was for?"

He shakes his head. "No, but something bad. I helped lead a group of boys to try to escape a couple days ago. Then the guards took me, beat me up, and put me in that room. They hooked me up to the IV. After that everything becomes sort of blurry in my mind." He pauses. "They're doing things to kids. Making some kind of hybrid creatures by using drugs to mutate their DNA and turn them into monsters that will fight for the UNA."

"We saw a mutant on a farm near where we found you. A boy that was, like, seven feet tall and deformed," I tell him.

Gadya nods. "Genetic experiments."

I realize that Liam doesn't know yet that Rika is dead. There will be time to tell him about that later. I don't want to overwhelm him yet, and Gadya isn't saying anything about it either. Rika's death is still hard for me to process. I don't want it to be true.

I hear faint noises. Liam and Gadya hear them too. We all stop moving around and talking.

Liam gestures to our left. "Someone's out there," he whispers.

We draw closer together. Gadya swings the gun in the direction of the noise. I raise my knife.

A moment later I see a shadowy figure in the trees, moving closer. One of the guards must have followed us from the battlefield.

"Who's there?" I call out.

"Show yourself or get shot!" Gadya ads.

A second later a person steps out of the trees. He's carrying a gun, pointed right at us, and he has a feral look in his eyes. His face is swollen and bruised, but I recognize him right away.

Mikal.

"How did you find us?" I ask, startled.

"Friend of yours?" Gadya asks me warily.

"Yeah, do you know him?" Liam asks me, as Gadya keeps her gun aimed at Mikal.

"I tracked you . . . ," he says to me. His voice sounds thick from the beating I gave his face.

"All this way?" I sound as surprised as I feel.

He grins. It's lopsided, and it makes him look demented. Many of his teeth are cracked and broken from my blows. "I told you I'd be seeing you again. . . . I know this land. . . . I grew up here. . . . I can track anyone and anything."

"Mikal, you can't come with us," I tell him warily.

"I don't want to come with you anymore," he says, looking at me with tired, bloodshot eyes. "I just want to get revenge."

He cocks his gun and takes a step forward. I don't know where he got the gun from, but I assume he either took it from his mother's farmhouse or found one along the way.

"Turn around and get out of here," Gadya says, pointing the gun directly at his face, "or I will blow your brains out."

"Go back home," I tell him. "Back to your mom and your sisters."

"I can't do that, Alenna," he says. Even with his swollen lips I see a mocking smile. "I burned down the farmhouse and left my mom and sisters to cry in the ruins. I'm never going back there."

He has gone insane. I see his finger tighten on the trigger. I prepare to throw my blade at his chest. I know that Gadya is ready to fire.

Suddenly, Mikal stumbles backward with a loud shriek as Liam leaps forward. I don't understand what's happened at first. Then I realize that Liam has thrown a fistful of dirt right into his face.

"My eyes!" Mikal screams. "I can't see!" He starts pulling the trigger of his gun and I flinch, expecting a barrage of bullets, but the gun doesn't fire. It's either empty, or it's jammed.

Liam keeps rushing forward and tackles Mikal. He climbs on top of his body. Liam punches him in the head as hard as he can. Gadya and I rush over. I grab Mikal's gun and yank it out of his hand. Gadya starts kicking him in the ribs.

There can be little mercy for Mikal. He would have shot all of us if he could. He is too unstable to trust.

Liam stands up. "He's out cold. I hit him hard enough to crack his skull. He'll be out for a few hours. Maybe longer."

"We should kill him," Gadya says.

"No need," I say. "He's not gonna get too far with a cracked skull. He'll probably die out here anyway."

Gadya strolls over to him. Suddenly, without warning, she stamps on his ankle. I hear the bones crack. "Just in case," she says. "I don't want him tracking us again."

I want to throw up. I glance down at Mikal's shattered face and cracked skull. There was no need for this brutality. He forced it upon us. We drag his body into the bushes and leave it there.

"So what's the plan?" I say, swallowing hard, as we start walking again. I look at Liam.

"David gave me instructions," he says. "He contacted me before I got sent here." Liam looks from me to Gadya and back again. He exhales. "At this point, I guess we have to trust him, but you know I'm always skeptical when it comes to David. Telling the truth isn't his strong suit."

"Did you argue with him?" I ask, worried that friction between Liam and David will make it harder to achieve our goals. I know we don't have much time left.

"No. I just listened. I thought he was crazy at first, but he spelled everything out for me. And now I'm telling you. Whether it's true or not is for us to decide."

"So we have to detonate a bomb or something, right? Something back at the lab?" I ask.

"No. The device is on board a satellite, a mile above us."

"What do you mean?" Gadya asks. "Explain."

"It's complicated."

"Try us."

Liam stares at me and Gadya. "According to David, the UNA has nuclear warheads in space, small ones attached to satellites. They're hidden there, so that its enemies don't know about them. The scientists have figured out that if we detonate a handful of them at a certain exact time, then the resulting high-altitude electromagnetic pulse, known as an EMP, will wipe out all the UNA computers and technology. They call this thing a HANE. A 'high-altitude nuclear explosion.' The pulse will destroy all electronics and circuits."

"Nuclear weapons?" I ask, confused. "That can't be the answer."

"Yeah, won't that kill us?" Gadya asks.

Liam shakes his head. "Supposedly not if it's done right. The bombs are so high up, we won't be affected much by the radiation. But the pulse will fry anything electric, and all computer circuits. Cars will stop working, along with all the government computers and machinery. It will put the people on equal footing with the government."

"I've heard about electromagnetic pulses," I say. "They're supposed to be bad things, not good ones. How is any of this going to help us?"

"Because the people will have a chance to rise up. The government won't be able to control us. They'll be taken off guard. According to David, the rebel cells are ready to take action. We'll use primitive weapons to take back the country."

"Wait, wait," I say, trying to figure this out. "But how are we going to detonate these bombs? This sounds like a crazy plan, even for David. And who put him in charge of everything?"

"I don't know. And I agree that the plan sounds crazy. But he had a lot of details to back it up. There are five nuclear devices. The scientists figured out which ones we need to detonate. They will create the most evenly spread electromagnetic pulse so that the government is completely wiped out. But it will be localized to the UNA. Other nations won't be affected. The European Coalition will still be able to step in and help us."

"And we're supposed to detonate all five warheads? How?"

Liam shakes his head. "Just one. There are four other teams somewhere out here in the UNA with us. Made up of kids, and rebels and scientists. We just have to detonate one of the bombs, perfectly synchronized with the other teams at the exact same time, so the UNA doesn't have a chance to stop the explosions." He pauses. "And we don't have long. David told me we had to do it by four p.m. tomorrow. That gives us about twenty-four hours."

"What?" I ask, startled.

"Yeah, how the hell do we do that?" Gadya asks. "I mean, if the bomb is up on a satellite?"

"David said that you'd have a key?" Liam asks me. "And that he gave you instructions. An address that we need to get to?"

I pause. So do Liam and Gadya. "I have a key, but no address. David left it for me in an envelope." I take the key out from under my bra where I have been hiding it. "Look."

Liam and Gadya peer at the key.

"That doesn't look like the key to a detonation device," Gadya says, sounding puzzled.

"I know," I tell her. "I don't know what it's for."

Liam sighs. "So David gave us each part of the puzzle. Typical."

"I'm guessing that he didn't want to tell each of us everything in case one of us got caught," I say. "Then the whole plan would fall apart if they used truth serum on us."

"But what if you'd been shot back there?" Gadya asks me. "We wouldn't even know about the key. It would have gotten lost."

"Maybe there are more than five teams out here. There are probably some fail-safes," I tell her. "In case we don't make it."

Gadya nods.

I glance down at the key again. Then I hold it up close to my face. I've inspected it many times before. "It just looks like a normal key," I finally say. "Nothing more exotic than that."

"So David didn't give you an address?" Liam asks. "He lied?"

I shake my head. "Maybe he left the address with someone else and we need to find that person."

"Let's hope it's not Rika or we're going to end up just like her—" Gadya breaks off, remembering that Liam doesn't know what happened to her.

Liam glances over at Gadya. "Rika? Is she here with us?"

I take his hand. "We didn't want to tell you. But yes, she made it here and she fought bravely. If it weren't for her, we wouldn't have been able to get to you . . ."

My words trail off because I don't want to start crying, and I'm right on the verge.

Liam keeps looking at me. "So she's dead."

I nod.

Liam sighs. I can tell that he's upset. "Another pointless death. She never should have been sent here. She wasn't cut out for this stuff."

"That's what I said," Gadya adds. I can hear the quaver of emotion in her voice. "She should have stayed back on the island, where she was safe."

"How could you not tell me about her?" Liam says to me. He almost sounds mad.

"I didn't know how," I say. "There wasn't time."

Liam looks at me closely. "Is there anything else you're keeping from me?"

"No, of course not!"

Silence falls for a moment. There is nothing we can say or do to make her death feel any better. We carry the wound of her passing with us. I don't want to fight with Liam.

"Rika came here because she wanted to conquer the UNA," I finally tell him. "I don't know how she got here, but obviously someone thought it was a good idea. It was probably her. Despite calling herself a pacifist, she never shied away from a battle." I pause. "And look. If it wasn't for her, we'd be dead. She ended up being able to fight just as capably as anyone else. She saved our lives. She proved that she had every right to be here, just like you and me."

"Someone should have stopped her," Liam says.

"Remember when we hiked into the gray zone, back on the wheel?" Gadya asks him. "She came after us then to be a part of it. Nobody could stop her if she wanted to do something."

"Yeah, she was a fighter," I say. "No matter what she said, or what she looked like."

Liam finally nods. "I can't disagree," he admits. "I just wish she were still alive and with us right now. I was friends with her for a long time."

"Same here," I say. I try not to think about Rika's final moments. I choose to remember her as she was on the wheel—with her braided hair and freckles, and her sunny smile. That's how she will live on in my heart.

Afraid that I'm going to start crying again, I take out the piece of paper that the key was wrapped in to distract myself from the pain. I kept this paper with me the whole time. For some weird reason it was in my clothes at the farmhouse. No one took it from me.

"What is that?" Gadya asks.

"The key was inside this paper, in an envelope," I say softly. "But there was no message, at least that I could find."

"Let me take a look," Liam says. I hand it over to him and he scrutinizes it. Gadya leans in too. He turns it over and back again. Nothing.

He holds up the key. There are no numbers or letters on it. No information to identify it. It looks completely nondescript. The only reason I know that it holds any importance is the fact that David left it for me.

"Did you try to see if David wrote a secret message on the paper?" Gadya asks me. "Like invisible ink or something, so that no one could see it if you got captured?"

I shake my head. "I don't know."

"This sounds crazy, but remember science experiments in school when we were little kids?" Liam says. "You could make invisible ink with lemon juice or baking soda. Or maybe he used something that's only visible in ultraviolet light."

"If so, we're out of luck," I say.

He holds the paper up to his face. "I don't see anything."

"It could be heat sensitive," Gadya says. "The travelers used to do that kind of thing to send secret messages, and David was tight with them. The travelers would use langsat juice and write on leaves. It was invisible, but when it got heated, it would turn brown and you could read the letters."

"We don't have matches or a cigarette lighter," Liam points out.

"Mikal does," I say. I walk over to his body, followed by Liam and Gadya. I don't even want to touch Mikal. He's lying facedown, unconscious. I can see the outline of the lighter in his back pocket. I quickly reach in and extract it, and toss the lighter to Liam.

He catches it, flicks it, and then begins running it a few inches under the paper—so it heats the page up. Gadya and I help hold the paper flat and tight so it doesn't catch fire.

We all stare at it. I'm startled to see very faint brown letters beginning to emerge on the page.

"Look at that," Gadya murmurs.

We all crane in closer.

"It's an address," I say, as the words start appearing. "And then some."

Liam reads the note out loud: *"Get to Dr. Carl Urbancic, 700 Woodbourne Trail, New Dayton, New Ohio."*

Gadya holds up the key. "So it's a house key?"

"Maybe," I say. "Or perhaps it opens something inside the house." I pause. "How are we going to get from here to New Ohio by four p.m. tomorrow? It seems impossible. We're going to have to figure out a plan and then hurry."

"Have you ever been to New Ohio? Have you ever heard of Dr. Urbancic?" Gadya asks me and Liam.

I shake my head. "I've never even heard of New Dayton."

"There's a large military base there," Liam says. "I remember reading about it when we were stuck at Southern Arc. The base at New Dayton is a UNA stronghold."

"Great. And we're supposed to burst in there and do what exactly?" Gadya asks.

"Locate the device that detonates the weapon," I say. "Who knows what else. Maybe David will meet us at the location on the paper."

"It always comes back to David, doesn't it?" Liam says out of the blue.

I shrug. "It seems to."

"Do we even know why?" Liam asks.

"Supposedly he's been trained since he was twelve to fight for the rebels. And he's smart too. Almost scarily smart."

Liam doesn't say anything more about it. I wonder if he still harbors doubts about David. I'm guessing that he does. But he's going along with David's plan. Maybe David has proved himself enough to Liam. It's hard to tell.

I trust David, but I'm still puzzled that he is playing such a major role in the rebellion. We have deviated very far from the plan that the scientists made with us on the wheel. David has become such a vital part of everything, but he's only been off the wheel for two months. He must have been involved from the start. From the very early planning stages, and we were just kept in the dark. I can't think of another explanation, no matter what he or the scientists claim.

Gadya spits in the dirt as she shoulders her rifle. "Let's just get to New Dayton. If we keep standing around, this will become a suicide mission." She smiles a bit. "Not that we haven't been on some of those already—and survived."

I smile back, even though it's not funny. "Suicide missions are becoming our specialty."

Liam smiles too.

But the moment is short-lived. We need to get out of the forest and away from the Hellgrounds for good.

There's obviously no way to walk all the way to New Ohio. So we decide to find the nearest road and try to hijack a car.

It takes about half an hour of hiking north through the woods to finally reach a road. It's just a two-lane highway heading through the fields. There are no cars on it. I'm guessing this is the upper edge of the Hellgrounds.

We hide in the grass at the edge of the road for a moment, trying to figure out a plan.

"I guess someone's going to have to stand in the road," I say. "I'll do it. I'll pretend there's an emergency and try to flag someone down."

"No, let me do it," Liam says.

I shake my head. "It's better if it's a girl. Less threatening. You look like a warrior. They won't suspect me as quickly. And Gadya is drenched in blood. It will scare people off." I glance down. My own wound has stopped bleeding and is barely visible. It doesn't even hurt.

"I don't agree," Liam says. "I'll do it. Stop putting yourself in harm's way."

"Stop worrying about me."

Liam sighs, exasperated. "Do you want to end up like Rika? I can't let that happen to you."

I stare back at him. "I'm not Rika. I'm me. A warrior. Remember? And I'm going to do it."

Gadya nods. "I'll cover you."

"Fine," Liam says, relenting. "Just be careful. I'll come and take care of the driver once you get the car stopped."

So a few moments later, I'm standing on the road, waiting there alone.

There are still no cars.

Liam and Gadya are on either side of me now, hiding on opposite sides of the road. I glance back and forth at them. A car has to come along eventually.

I keep waiting. We only have until four p.m. tomorrow. What happens if we fail? I don't want to find out. We must stick to the deadline. If David said it was important, then I'm certain that it is.

Finally, I hear the noise of a vehicle in the distance. I listen closely. If it sounds like a UNA truck, then I'll rush back into the foliage and hide. But this approaching vehicle doesn't sound like a truck. It just sounds like a normal car. So I stand my ground in the center of the road.

The car comes into view. It's a typical, functionally designed gray sedan. Like the kind that Shawn and Kelley drove. I see the silhouette of a driver behind the wheel, but no one else is in the car.

I hold my arms out, signaling for the driver to stop. I'm nervous, but I know that Gadya is hiding with the gun pointed right at the driver. She will fire if the driver does anything suspicious. I also know that Liam is on the other side of the road, ready to leap out at any point.

The car slows down.

The driver has seen me.

It's a middle-aged man, peering at me through a pair of glasses, with a startled-but-curious expression on his face. He's balding and wearing a black suit. Probably about fifty years old. Obviously he did not expect to find anyone blocking his path.

I start waving my hands animatedly to get him to stop.

He continues watching me as he brings the car to a halt. I make sure to stay right in front of his vehicle, so he can't drive around me. I lower my arms only when the car comes to a complete stop.

The driver's-side window slides down. "Can I help you?" the man calls out cautiously.

"Yes!" I yell. "Get out of the car. Please!"

"Why?" the man asks, sounding puzzled.

I see Liam start sneaking out of the brush at the edge of the road.

"I need to ask you to move," the man says, sounding surprisingly polite. I almost feel bad about what's going to happen to him.

"Just get out of the car," I say. "We need your help."

"We?" he asks.

Right then, Liam springs forward and rushes up from behind. The driver hears him and tries to lock the car doors. But it's too late.

Liam yanks the driver's door open and pulls the driver out. The driver struggles for a moment, but Liam quickly overcomes him. The man sprawls onto the road. Liam leans in and turns off the car's engine and snatches the keys.

At the same time, Gadya stands up from the underbrush, in plain sight. The driver can see that she has her rifle pointed right at him.

He gets up slowly and brushes dirt off the knees of his suit pants. He straightens his glasses and stares at all of us.

"What's going on here?" he asks, sounding oddly resigned instead of angry like I expected.

"We have to take your car. We need it to get out of here."

"Are you running away from something?"

"No. We're running *toward* something," Liam says.

Gadya walks over to my side, wearing a fierce expression and still pointing the gun at the man's head.

"You don't need to do that," the man says. "Who are you three kids?"

"You don't want to know the answer to that," I tell him. "The less you know, the better."

"You're rebels, aren't you?" he asks. And then, unexpectedly, he smiles. It's like he's trying to suppress a laugh. "This might come as a shock to you, but you're welcome to take my car, wherever you want to go."

"Really?" Gadya asks.

"Sure. I've been waiting many years for the citizens to do something and take back our country. I was a college professor at a university once—at least until Minister Harka, the UNA, and this lunacy took over and the universities were shut down. I wish I could do more to fight back myself."

"You can," Liam says. "Just don't tell anyone that we were here. That's what we need from you. That and your car."

"What should I say happened?" the man asks. "People will want to know where my car is."

"Just say that someone carjacked you," I say. "Not us kids, but someone else. A crazy old man with a gun or something. Throw the scent off us, okay?"

He pauses for a second and then nods. "Deal." Then he hesitates again. "I just need to get my briefcase. Will you let me have it? It's in the back."

"I'll get it for you," Liam says, eyeing him. "Just to be cautious."

The man nods. "I understand."

Liam rummages in the car and comes back with a shiny black briefcase. He hands it to the man, who receives it gratefully.

"Don't open it until we're gone," Liam says. "If it turns out there's a gun inside, and you try to use it, understand that we'll have no choice but to kill you."

"Of course," the man says, clutching his briefcase. "But I can assure you there are no guns in here. Only boring papers about American history." He smiles again. "Please take good care of my car. I doubt I'll ever see it again, will I?"

"Probably not," I admit.

"Then make sure you kids put it to good use. Do some damage for me."

"Oh, we will," Gadya says.

The man steps over to the side of the road. "I suppose I'll be walking from here on out."

I nod, grateful and relieved at his inexplicably positive attitude. "Thank you for helping us."

"I didn't really have a choice," the man points out.

"We better get moving," Gadya says to me. "Who wants to drive?" She keeps her gun trained on him.

"Me," I say. I walk around and get into the driver's seat.

Liam gets into the back of the car. "Do you want these?" he calls out, holding up some old paperback books.

The man shakes his head. "You can keep them. The government would classify them as revolutionary materials anyway."

"Then we're probably helping you by stealing your car," Gadya tells him. "If you drive around with a bunch of books out in the open, you'll be arrested."

"True," the man says. "Although fortunately for us, there aren't many police on these back roads."

Gadya walks past him and around to the passenger side of the car. She gets inside. Only then does she lower her gun and flick the safety on. "Who knew stealing a car would be so easy?" she murmurs to me.

"Thanks," I call out to the man again through the open window, as I get ready to start the car and begin driving.

"My pleasure." He pauses, taking a little half step toward us. "There's only one last thing . . ."

"Yes?"

"I think you rebels might be interested in this——"

He snaps the locks off his black briefcase, facing the opening toward us.

For a split second, I think he's going to show us something helpful or interesting. He opens the briefcase wider, aiming it at the open car window.

Then a metal device explodes out of the briefcase and through the open window, right into the vehicle with us.

I scream in terror.

It's one of the MIODs. Like the kind that burst out of the girl's mouth right before Rika died.

It flies past my face and lands in Gadya's lap. She scrabbles at it and tries to throw it out her window, but it scampers into the back.

The three of us are screaming.

Liam gives out a yell as the machine tries to claw and burrow its way into the flesh of his leg. Its metal tentacles are like sharp knives. He manages to get if off his leg, but it crawls back around to the front before he can grab it again.

Gadya struggles to raise her gun in the close confines of the car. Out the window, I see the man in the suit just standing there, smiling with delight as he watches the carnage. I can't believe he has done this to us. He had me fooled.

Then the creature is clawing at my mouth, like it's trying to get inside my body. I scream and shove it away. But it's persistent. It scrabbles like a wild animal. I feel its metal tentacles on my lips and tongue.

I cough and gag, retching in horror and pain. I taste blood. The thing is slashing up my hands and tongue as I battle it.

"Help!" I manage to scream out.

"Move out of the way!" Gadya yells. "I'm trying to shoot it!" But there's nowhere for me to go in the car.

Liam lunges forward and manages to grab the MIOD with both hands, grimacing as it cuts into his flesh. Its blades are whirring and gnashing, in a mechanical frenzy. All of us are covered in blood. The machine seems possessed with energy.

"Shoot it!" I yell at Gadya. "Do it now!" Liam is holding the machine away from us. But Gadya can't get the gun up in time.

"Start driving!" she yells at me.

As Liam keeps wrestling with the machine, I get the car started and floor the accelerator. The tires squeal, and then, with a spray of dirt, we begin to move forward.

At the same moment, Liam lifts the MIOD up. It claws at him, like it's desperate to enter his mouth and burrow inside him. I see the look of complete revulsion on his face. It mirrors my own.

Summoning his strength, with a yell, Liam finally tosses the machine right out his window. I see it spark and hear it clatter as it flies onto the road and tumbles down the asphalt away from us.

I can barely breathe. I look down at my hands, which are covered in bleeding cuts. But we won the battle. The machine is out of the car.

I see the man in the suit standing in the road behind us, watching us. He's not smiling anymore. He looks startled. I'm shocked that he turned out to be on the UNA's side. I realize now why he was able to drive around with books out in the open. *Because he works for the government and nobody would dare to stop him.*

"Hit the brakes!" Gadya yells.

I trust her enough to do it. I instantly stop the car with a screech.

She leans out the window with the gun.

The man looks back at us. He sees the gun. He turns to run.

"Thanks for the car, you bastard!" Gadya calls out to him. And then she pumps two rounds right into his back. The man falls to the ground, crumpling into a heap. "We can start driving now," she tells me.

Feeling like I'm about to throw up, I push the pedal to the floor and we begin speeding away.

"Was that necessary?" I ask her, as she rolls up her window.

"I had to," Gadya says. "If we'd let him live, he would have told the police that we're out here. I didn't have a choice."

I nod.

"It was either him or us," Liam adds.

I glance at the rearview mirror, concerned that the MIOD will be chasing after us. But there's no sign of it. I doubt it could keep up with the car, anyway. We're now going sixty miles an hour, and still picking up speed. I don't want to go too fast, because I don't want to get pulled over. I know that if any police stop us, we will have to fight them to the death.

"Just shows you can't trust anyone in the UNA," Liam says, musing about the man whom Gadya just killed.

"Who do you think he was?" I ask.

"A top UNA scientist? A government agent?" Gadya says with a sigh. "It doesn't matter. He was so nice at first, but he was just a phony, trying to trick us."

We keep on driving.

I know now that our journey will be just as brutal as the one we undertook on the wheel. Maybe even more so, because of the guns. I stare straight ahead out the windshield as we drive toward New Dayton. There, we will find the address that David left for us, and detonate the nuclear device, before time runs out and we lose our one chance.

15 NEW DAYTON

WE PASS PLENTY OF other cars, including some police vehicles and armored personnel carriers. Yet nobody stops us. I can't believe it.

Each time we pass a police car my heart leaps into my throat. I know that we could be apprehended at any moment. But every time, the police car just passes us by. Sometimes I sneak glances at the officers inside. They are usually staring straight ahead with earpieces in, not even concerned with us. I don't understand why.

The roads are not as crowded as I once remembered. Maybe more people are staying at home these days, given the high degree of civil unrest.

We pass two bad accidents, with bodies lying in the road and people crying for help. No ambulances come to their rescue, and nobody stops to help them.

Perhaps because of the wars the UNA is fighting in other countries, it no longer has the resources to run ambulances and fire trucks for civilian purposes. There were lots of roadblocks and police in Texas, but maybe they knew that rebels would be landing there that night.

The UNA has presumably put all its money into wars and counterterrorism measures, and obviously no longer allocates much money toward policing everyday citizens to the degree it once did. I'm guessing that after we destroyed Island Alpha, the government shifted its priorities to catching us rebels.

Most of the time, Liam, Gadya, and I are quiet in the car. We want to stay focused so that we don't get surprised by anything. Liam has used a rag to wipe off the blood from the gray vinyl seats so that the car doesn't look suspicious to anyone who glances inside.

I'm also on the lookout for any roadblocks. Luckily, I don't see any, even as our two-lane road widens into a four-lane highway.

Our plan is to stay off the giant twelve-lane Megaways and try to take smaller roads whenever possible.

The police must be looking for us already. I'm stunned they haven't stopped our car. There must be a reason.

"Looks like we have a problem," I hear Gadya say, as she gestures to the dashboard.

I glance down. A light is on. The car needs more gas. I've been so transfixed by driving that I didn't notice how low we were getting.

"What do we do?" I ask. "We don't have any money."

Liam leans forward. "We get gas anyway."

I glance over at Gadya and then down at the rifle in her lap. "We rob someplace?" I ask. "That's a pretty big risk. It might be easier to just take another car."

"But there's no guarantee it will have enough gas in it for the journey."

I nod. "Fair enough. Then we do it."

I hear Gadya take the safety off the gun in eager anticipation.

"No shooting unless they shoot first," Liam says. "I don't want either of you getting hurt."

I stare up ahead at the road. We are nearing a service station and a row of other small shops. Most of the shops are closed down. Some of them are burned out, just empty black shells.

"I'm going to pull in here," I say to Liam and Gadya. I begin slowing and prepare to come off the road. I switch lanes and take the first exit, heading toward the gas station.

"They'll have cameras watching us," Gadya says.

"Everywhere has cameras," I reply.

I pull into the gas station and glide up to a pump. I bring the car to a stop. The gas station is almost deserted. Another gray sedan is pulling away in front of us. I see an old heavyset woman sitting inside the empty station behind a cash register. "Make it fast," I say.

Gadya glances at me. "Oh, I will."

Liam gets out of the car and opens the gas tank. He puts the nozzle in it.

Gadya swings out of the car with her rifle in her hand.

She strides toward the old woman in the gas station, ready for action.

I sit in the car, prepared to gun the engine and get us out of here once the car is full of gas and Liam and Gadya are back inside.

"Tell her to let us fill it up for free," I call out.

Gadya kicks open the door to the gas station and holds up the gun. I can see her through the glass. The old woman looks shocked and afraid. *Is this what the UNA is making us do? Attack and scare innocent people?* Citizens who have probably been brutalized and lied to by the government just like us. Or is this woman going to turn out to be like the man in the suit? Someone on the UNA's side. Someone who wants us dead.

It makes me feel sick, but right now there is no option other

229

than violence. The UNA is turning us into criminals. I don't know whether this woman at the gas station sees us as monsters or potential liberators. But after what happened with the man and the briefcase, we can't afford to trust anyone.

Gadya holds the rifle up and points it at the woman. Gadya starts yelling. I can't hear it; I can only see it. The woman presses some buttons on the register.

"It's working!" Liam calls out, as gas begins to flow. He starts filling our car, keeping a lookout for any signs of danger.

I continue watching Gadya.

The woman at the gas station isn't making any abrupt moves. She's just sitting there. She looks emotional, like she's about to cry. Gadya has lowered her gun a little so that it's not pointing directly at the woman. The two of them are talking.

"Almost done!" Liam calls out loudly.

Gadya glances our way.

He signals to her. Right then I hear the click as the gas stops pumping. We're ready to go again. Gadya is already rushing out of the station toward us. I keep expecting that the woman is going to unleash an alarm. But nothing happens. She just watches as Gadya hops back into the passenger side of the car and I gun the engine.

Within seconds, we are back on the road, and the gas station is receding in my rearview mirror.

"That woman is going to call the police on us," I say nervously. "She looked terrified."

Gadya turns to me, as she hides her gun on the floor of the car.

"She's not calling anyone. Her son got taken and sent to Island Alpha two years ago. That's what we were talking about in there. I told her we were rebels, trying to fight the UNA."

"What did she think about that?" I ask.

"She wished us good luck."

"Did you see any signs of government surveillance in there?" Liam asks. "Or anything else weird?"

Gadya shakes her head. "No. She told me there's a security system but no one has monitored it for the past few weeks. Apparently the UNA doesn't have the time for civilian robberies anymore. They only care about protecting the government, and hunting rebels. She thought we'd get away with it. And she promised not to tell anyone."

"Nice," Liam says.

"I hope she's telling the truth," I say.

"I think she was," Gadya replies. "She told me she keeps a dartboard with Minister Harka's face on it hidden in a closet at home."

We keep driving.

We don't sleep that night. There is no time for anything but travel. We just stay on the roads. Certain stretches now have very low speed limits. Our journey takes much longer than it should. I watch the sunrise through the windshield. Unlike when we arrived in New Texas, there are no soldiers on the roads, and no police.

We drive the rest of that morning. Finally, around noon, we reach the exit for New Dayton. I feel relieved. We have made it here in time.

A large metal sign saying WELCOME TO NEW DAYTON has been vandalized—tagged with unidentifiable marks of graffiti. The graffiti looks fresh. Before I got sent to the wheel, graffiti would have been cleaned up instantly, and the perpetrators thrown in jail for life. The presence of the graffiti is reassuring to me. It means that people are finally starting to take a stand.

I turn off the road and onto a smaller one. There are more cars here. The sky is an oppressive shade of dark gray. We continue to drive.

Suburban houses line the roadway. Most of them look like they're in decent shape. I wonder what it would have been like to grow up in one of these homes, instead of in a tower block and then an orphanage.

"Looks pretty nice," Gadya murmurs. "Who would have thought it?"

"Probably homes of government workers," Liam adds. "People who sold out. People in league with the UNA."

These could also be the homes of regular people. It's hard to tell. I don't sense a strong government presence here, at least not yet.

"How far are we?" I ask.

"Let me look," Liam says. He consults the map on the car's display screen. "Not far. Ten minutes."

"Do you think Dr. Urbancic—whoever he is—knows that we're coming?" Gadya asks, sounding oddly thoughtful.

"Anything's possible," I tell her. "But I hope not. Element of surprise, remember?"

Gadya smiles. "It's certainly worked for us before. At least some of the time."

After a few more minutes of driving on winding asphalt roads, we reach Woodbourne Trail. Moments later, at the bottom of a gentle curve, we find the house. The house number is visible in bronze on the side of the wooden mailbox.

A lot of the houses look the same here. This one is a large two-story brick home with a blue door and an awning covering a side patio. Ivy grows up one wall of the building. It's the kind of place that only rich people live in.

We drive past it and park several doors down, under the shade of a large tree. The neighborhood seems deserted. People are probably at work.

"I'll handle this one," Liam says, looking at me and Gadya. Any lingering sign of the chemicals have finally worn off completely during the drive, and he's back to his usual self. "Stay here in the car in case there's trouble. We might need to make a quick getaway."

I nod. I remain behind the wheel, and Gadya covers him with the gun through the partially open window.

Liam gets out of the car. He jogs across the street toward the house. When he reaches it, he pauses for a second. Then he raises his hand and presses the doorbell. He stands there waiting.

Gadya is next to me with her eye pressed to the sight of the rifle. I feel nervous. Anything could happen next. Seconds tick past.

Liam rings the doorbell again. But nobody answers. He looks back at us again and shrugs.

"Looks like Dr. Urbancic isn't in," Gadya says, relaxing her finger on the trigger a little bit.

Liam presses the doorbell again and knocks on the door a couple of times.

Still nothing.

"We're gonna have to break in and wait for him," Gadya says.

"Maybe," I tell her. "Give it one more second."

Liam hovers at the door for a moment longer. He's just about to jog back to the car when I see the door open slightly. Just a crack.

Liam hears it too. He spins back to the door. It starts swinging open. Gadya's finger tightens on the trigger again. The door keeps opening as Liam moves back, ready to fight whoever is in the house if he has to.

I catch a glimpse of an old man standing there at the door. He takes a shuffling step forward so that the sun catches his face. He has a thick salt-and-pepper beard, glasses, and he's wearing a blue bathrobe. He is bone-thin—nearly skeletal. He is also unarmed. Both his hands are empty. He says something to Liam, but I can't hear it. *This must be Dr. Urbancic.*

I see Liam start talking back to him. I can't hear what he's saying either.

Gadya's finger remains tight on the trigger, in case Dr. Urbancic makes any sudden moves. But he doesn't. He just looks in our direction slowly. Then back at Liam.

Liam gestures toward us, motioning for us to join him.

"It's safe," I say. "Let's go."

Gadya opens the car door, and I open mine a second later. She keeps her gun up and pointed at the doorway.

We dart across the road toward the house. I know that leaving the car here is a risk, but I'm hoping it will go unnoticed for now. It's partially hidden by the oak trees. And there are other cars parked on the street too, so it doesn't seem out of place. Gadya has her gun aimed at the man, and I have my knife in my hand.

We make it across the street and reach the doorway where Liam is waiting for us.

"You okay?" I ask him, just to make sure.

He nods. "Fine."

Dr. Urbancic has already stepped back inside his house. Liam quickly ushers us through the doorway and into the vestibule. Then he closes the door behind us and locks it.

We stand there for a second. The air inside is cool and clean.

The house is spacious, with green tile floors, wood-paneled walls, and plush black leather furniture. This is not a world that I am familiar with. I see Gadya looking around too.

"So the rebels have arrived," Dr. Urbancic says to us. His voice is thin and reedy. His thinning hair is disheveled. I'm guessing he's in his late sixties, or perhaps older. He looks at each of us in turn. "Not what I expected, but good enough."

"David Aberley sent us here," I say.

Dr. Urbancic nods. "I already know that." He motions for us to follow him. "Come down to the basement with me." He begins heading down a hallway. I notice that he's wearing ratty old comfortable slippers. "No need for guns in this house," he calls out behind him. "You can put that rifle away."

Liam and I exchange glances and then we follow. Gadya still holds her gun on him. We've been through way too much to trust anyone—especially someone we just met.

"This way," he calls out again, as we keep walking down a hallway. His house is large and lavish. To get a house like this in the UNA, you usually have to be working for the government, in some capacity or another. That thought doesn't exactly put me at ease.

We keep following him until we reach a steel door. He punches in a combination and it opens up. He looks back at us. "I told you to put down that gun," he says to Gadya, more firmly this time.

"Make me," Gadya says.

He chuckles dryly. "I wouldn't expect anything less from a rebel, I suppose. No matter. You won't be needing it either way."

He starts heading jauntily down the stairs. For an old man being held at gunpoint, he seems remarkably spry. The three of us follow him cautiously.

"Close the door behind you," he calls out.

Liam swings it shut.

As we get closer to the bottom of the stairs, I see that the basement is much less lavish than the house. It's large, but it's not finished, and it looks like a homemade machine workshop, combined with a science lab.

"This is where I spend most of my time these days." Dr. Urbancic says, gesturing around. "Come, have a seat."

A few minutes later, we're sitting around a folding card table in Dr. Urbancic's basement. Electrical equipment surrounds us, along with mysterious, half-constructed machines.

He sees me looking at everything and says, "My real job. Ways to defeat government technology. I always try to stay one step ahead."

"Are they weapons?" Liam asks.

"No. Communication devices. Designed to intercept satellite signals and then disrupt—"

"We don't have time for small talk," Gadya interrupts. "We're here because David gave us a key, and we're on a deadline."

"I don't know anything about that," Dr. Urbancic says.

I hold the key up for Dr. Urbancic to see. "We're here because we need your help. At four p.m. today, we're supposed to set off a controlled nuclear device in the atmosphere—" I begin.

Dr. Urbancic raises his hands. "Let me stop you right there," he says. "I'm afraid that whatever David might have told you— and no matter how deep my involvement with the rebels runs—I can't be involved in such business." He shakes his head in dismay. "A controlled nuclear explosion is madness."

"At least tell us what this key is for," I say.

"The key opens a box," Dr. Urbancic replies. "A box that

contains a device that sends a signal to a nuclear bomb hidden on a satellite."

I nod. "Okay. And from what we understand, the resulting electromagnetic pulse will bring a halt to the UNA's technological supremacy without irradiating us. Then we can have a chance at fighting them."

"Exactly," Gadya adds.

"No, no, think about what you're doing," Dr. Urbancic says to us, looking agitated. "You don't realize what a high-altitude nuclear blast might do to the planet."

"It could save everyone from tyranny," Liam says. "In hand-to-hand combat with primitive weapons, I'm betting the rebels would be more than a match for the UNA soldiers."

"A HANE could destroy the planet!" Dr. Urbancic says, slapping his hand down hard on the table. "You don't understand. You are children."

"We might be young, but we're not children," I tell him. "You don't know what we've seen or been through."

At the same time, his words strike fear in my heart. Could he be right? I trust David's calculations and knowledge, and the other rebels, but there's a chance that Dr. Urbancic knows more than they do. I don't want to die.

"I feel sorry that you came all this way," Dr. Urbancic says. "But this plan to detonate nuclear devices at high altitudes is not—and cannot—be the answer. The rebel scientists floated this by me once before, years ago, and I explained that it wouldn't work. It is a desperate plan. It's too risky."

"It's our only plan," I tell him.

"I can't believe David would resort to this," Dr. Urbancic says.

"How well do you know him?" I ask.

"I knew David's father," he replies. "David has a genius IQ— nearly off the charts. It's been that way since he was a little boy. His parents were radicals and they taught him revolutionary tactics and extreme ways of thinking. David is one of our true hopes for the future. I always thought he would grow up to be a great leader, and perhaps one of the few people who could take down the UNA, and replace its corrupt madness with something positive for humankind. That's why I'm so puzzled by his current plan."

"Maybe there's no other choice," Gadya points out.

Liam nods. "The UNA has staked everything on technological supremacy. This might be the only way to take them down. I don't even like David much, but I can't think of a better, faster solution."

Dr. Urbancic leans forward, pressing his fingertips together. "Do you know what will happen if this plan goes wrong? You will destroy the earth's atmosphere. The planet will begin to die. Any discussion about whether the UNA is wrong or not will be a moot point. There will be no more countries and no more governments. There will just be radiation poisoning on a massive scale, and the death of every living thing. Your plan is worse than anything the UNA has done so far." He pauses. "You must cease advocating for this plan. You must change directions, and find a new course. Your impulse to deconstruct the government is a good one, but this is not the right path."

"What do you propose?" I ask Dr. Urbancic.

"I propose that you wait. Look around. You can see that the UNA doesn't have the strength that it once had. Eventually, perhaps just in a year or two, it may well find itself getting challenged from within. Like every other corrupt empire before it, such as Rome or Nazi Germany or Stalinist Russia, it will ultimately fall as a victim of its own twisted agendas."

238

"We don't have a year or two," Liam says. "Think how many people will die before then. And the government is doing genetic experiments on kids and trying to create mutants."

"Think how many people will die if your plan goes awry," Dr. Urbancic counters. You must weigh the good of the few against the good of the many. Besides, if the UNA is destroyed, another country will come and take it over, and enslave the populace."

"That won't happen," Gadya says. "The rebels have a plan to work with the European Coalition."

"You trust them?" Dr. Urbancic asks. "I've often felt there are hidden agendas within some of the rebels' plans. . . ."

"Maybe," I tell him. "But the world is sick of the UNA. They view it like a global cancer."

"A cancer needs to be cut out. But your plan essentially involves killing the patient," Dr. Urbancic says.

"How do we know you're not in league with the government?" I ask. "You obviously work for them as a scientist, am I right? You could be saying this stuff now to stop us from taking action, but it might not be true."

He nods. "Indeed. It might not be true. Perhaps the plan will work, and the electromagnetic pulse will serve your purposes without excessive radiation or atmospheric contamination. But there is less than a fifty percent chance of that. I can assure you that I am not in league with the UNA—I have spent my years working for them, but spying for, and advising, the rebels."

"We need to talk about this in private," I tell him. "Just the three of us." Dr. Urbancic has certainly shaken my faith in David's plan a bit. And he's right—there's no point in bringing down the UNA if the cost is a nuclear holocaust.

On the other hand, I've doubted David so many times in the

past, and he's always turned out to be right. He might know more than this scientist does.

"There's nothing to talk about," Gadya says. "We proceed with the plan. There's no time. We have to prepare."

Liam and I look at her.

"Gadya, we need to talk," Liam says.

She shakes her head. "No. We stick to the plan no matter what. That's the only way."

"Why don't we talk to David?" Dr. Urbancic cuts in.

We fall silent for a second, in surprise.

"You can talk to him?" I ask.

He nods. "Over an encrypted satellite signal. But the connection doesn't always work."

"Why didn't you say something earlier?" Liam asks.

Dr. Urbancic looks at him. "You didn't ask." He gets up and wanders off to a corner of the basement and returns with a transmitter. It has a small video screen attached to it. He begins fiddling with it.

"Hurry up," Gadya says, impatient as always.

He ignores her. Finally, the box comes to life. Electrical, crackling noises emanate from it. He turns a few dials, searching for a signal. The ancient video screen flashes with static and rolling lines.

Then he leans forward and says, "David? It's me. Are you there?"

Only static greets him. He keeps turning the dial.

"David?" I call out. The others chime in. But there's no response.

Then I hear a faint, distorted voice.

I can't understand the words, but I know that this is David.

240

"Got him!" Dr. Urbancic says. He spins another dial until the volume increases and the signal gets crisper.

"Hello, Doctor. I read you," David's voice says, tinged with static.

I hear Gadya gasp. I don't understand for a second, until I realize that David's image has appeared on the screen. It's dimly lit, but his ravaged face is clear to see.

"What the hell happened to you . . . ," I hear Gadya breathe.

Liam doesn't say anything, but I know that he must be surprised too.

David's electronic eye stares out at us, and even on the low-quality video screen, I can see the scars on his face.

"David, I have the rebels here," Dr. Urbancic says. "Three of them. Alenna, Gadya, and Liam."

"Hey, everyone," David says to us.

"Hey," I say back.

Liam echoes my greeting as well.

"What's wrong with your face?" Gadya asks, leaning forward and squinting at the image. "And your eye? Are you okay?"

David smiles. His image is fading in and out. He's harder to see now, but we can still hear him. "War wounds. Don't worry about it." He pauses. "I wish I could be there myself, but I can't move very quickly anymore."

Dr. Urbancic turns to us. "We don't have long. We can't risk transmitting the signal for more than a minute or two, or it might be traced. It's encrypted, so they can't discern the content, but they might be able to track our location. So let's wrap this up fast, shall we?"

I nod.

Dr. Urbancic says into the microphone, "David, these kids have a key to nuclear device thirteen on satellite 9B. I recognize it. And they say that you've instructed them to detonate it by four p.m. today, as a means of creating an EMP? Is this true?"

"Yes."

"You realize I can't do that, correct? The risk is far too great. I put it at forty percent likelihood for success, not in our favor. You need to come up with another plan."

"I knew that you'd say that, Doctor," David's voice replies. His image reappears faintly on the screen. He's not smiling anymore. "That's exactly why I sent Alenna, Gadya, and Liam to you, instead of just asking you to do it."

"So far they've been unable to convince me to change my mind," Dr. Urbancic says. "Perhaps their mission was in vain?"

David shakes his head. "No." He looks past Dr. Urbancic. "You have the key, Alenna. You will tie Dr. Urbancic up—without hurting him—and you will then unlock the box that contains the trigger for the bomb. The box is sitting behind him on the bookshelf. It's black, and the size of a brick. Should be easy to spot. The device inside is simple to operate. It will send a signal up to the satellite. At four p.m. you will press the red button on it, which will begin the detonation process. Stay in the basement for shelter in case—"

"David, you can't be serious!" says Dr. Urbancic, interrupting him angrily. "Even if you trigger an electromagnetic pulse successfully, without dumping radiation onto our heads, think of everyone who will die—people in hospitals. People reliant on technology to live. You, yourself, David, might die."

"Do it," David says to us, ignoring him completely. "I'm in a safe zone. Do it before he runs off or tries to hide the box."

I've been through enough with David to know that I should trust him. It seems like Gadya feels the same way.

242

"Got it," Gadya says, swinging her rifle around. "I have my gun out."

Dr. Urbancic stands up. "David, this is a terrible mistake—"

"Shoot the transmitter," David's voice says. "Or else the UNA will be able to trace this signal. After you detonate the bomb, Dr. Urbancic will help you meet up with more rebels tomorrow, to begin the ground assault. Good luck. Now shoot!"

Gadya aims at the transmitter.

"No, please—" Dr. Urbancic begins.

But Gadya fires anyway.

The blast is devastatingly loud in the basement. The transmitter is blown off the table and against the wall. It falls into a broken heap of crumpled metal. My ears ring.

Dr. Urbancic looks at us. "I can't let you do this."

"You can't stop us," I tell him. "Everything David has told us so far has turned out to be true. If he thinks this is the only way to stop more deaths, then we need to take the risk—as crazy and awful as it sounds. I don't want to die or destroy the planet any more than you do. But if we don't take action, the UNA is going to accomplish those things anyway."

"Exactly," Gadya says, brandishing her rifle at the doctor. "Now move aside."

"I'm not afraid of your gun," he says.

And then, faster than I thought possible, he stands up and grabs the end of the weapon, yanking it forward as hard as he can. Gadya is caught off balance, and she struggles to keep her hands on the weapon. Liam and I move back, both afraid that she's going to accidentally shoot him.

"Get off me!" Gadya yells. "I don't want to hurt you!"

We only have a few seconds until something terrible happens.

I move around behind Dr. Urbancic with my knife raised. If I have to stab him, I will. *Just to make him let go of the gun.*

Liam steps in and punches him in the back of his head, absolving me of having to do anything. Dr. Urbancic falls straight to the concrete floor, unconscious.

We stand there for a moment.

Gadya is panting, holding her weapon.

"I tried not to hit him too hard," Liam says. "It sounds like we need him alive to give us directions to the rebel cells."

I feel slightly sick, like we've crossed some kind of ethical line. We are becoming just as bad as the violent UNA thugs that we're trying to remove from power.

"Let's tie him up," I say, scanning the room for anything we can use as rope. I don't see any rope, but I see some bales of coated electrical wire. I go over to them and start cutting off pieces with my knife. Liam joins me. Gadya crouches down and checks Dr. Urbancic's body.

"He'll be out for a while," she says. "But I think he'll wake up. Maybe with a concussion."

Liam nods.

"What about the things he said?" I ask. "Think he's right?"

"I don't know," Gadya replies. "What choice do we have? If we do nothing, then the UNA wins."

"Liam?" I ask.

He looks at me. "I don't know either. We've come this far. It's hard to tell what's right or wrong anymore."

I nod. "Either way, I guess we need to tie up the doctor."

A few minutes later, we have Dr. Urbancic sitting upright in an old wooden chair, with his arms and legs bound tightly with electrical wire. There is no way for him to escape. He remains unconscious, his head lolling down to his chest.

We walk over to the bookshelf. As David said, the black metal box is easy to find. I take it from the bookshelf and place it on the table.

We stand around it.

I take the key out and insert it into the lock. The key turns, and the box opens up. I pull back its lid.

Inside the box, on a velvet base, sits a silver, palm-size object, with a lone red circular button on it covered with a snap-down glass top. We all gaze at it for a moment.

Then I pick it up and flick the top open. It's hard to imagine that this button controls something so powerful and devastating. The UNA must really trust Dr. Urbancic to give him access to such a device. Either he's fooling them, or he's fooling us.

"Be careful with that," Gadya warns.

I flip the top back down, so that the piece of glass covers the button again.

There is something oddly alluring about the button. All this time, the UNA has used their technology to subjugate us and make us victims of their fascistic madness. The idea of shutting them down and getting revenge has great appeal.

I wonder if the other four teams will be able to detonate their devices at the same time. If even one team fails, then perhaps we won't get complete coverage of the electromagnetic pulse, and some UNA war machinery might be able to survive and conquer us. There's nothing we can do about the other rebels. We just have to make sure that we succeed.

We sit there waiting for four p.m., talking about what we'll do if our plan actually succeeds. The EMP should bring everything with electronic components to a halt. No more guns, planes, cars, feelers, computers, tanks, or satellites. It will be like what happened on Island Alpha when David broke the cooling core and everything suddenly stopped working. But this will be on a far bigger scale.

When four o'clock approaches, we stand around the button. Dr. Urbancic is still passed out, which is probably for the best. I've checked his breathing, and it's slow but steady. He will live.

"Ready?" I ask the others, watching an old digital clock hanging on the wall of the basement. It displays the time down to the nearest second.

"Which one of us is going to push it?" Gadya asks. She flicks back the glass top with feigned nonchalance.

"I will," I say. "I trust David." I pause. "And I'm not afraid."

"Me neither," she replies.

"Liam?" I ask, turning to him. "Any reservations?"

"No, but David better be right," he says. "Let's do this together. The three of us. That way, we can all take responsibility if something goes wrong. And if it goes right, we can share the victory."

"Deal," I say. I place my finger on one corner of the button. Liam puts a finger on the other corner, touching mine. I look at him and smile. Then Gadya puts a finger on top of ours. I know that this button either has the potential to help destroy the planet, or to bring down the government that has ruined so many lives.

Or maybe it will just do nothing.

There's no guarantee that Dr. Urbancic hasn't disabled it in some way as a fail-safe, so that no one could operate it except him.

We just keep watching the clock as it ticks inexorably toward four p.m. The seconds seem to speed up as we get closer.

"Are you sure this is the right decision?" Gadya suddenly says, startling me with her words.

246

"No, of course not," I tell her. "But it's the one that we're making. Right?" I look over at Liam.

He nods. "It's going to take something massive to disrupt the UNA. We need to take the risk."

"Are you having second thoughts?" I ask Gadya. Her question has unnerved me. Usually I can rely on her to be the most warlike and eager for action. I'm not sure what to make of her hesitation.

"I just want to be sure."

"There's no way to be certain," Liam tells her. "You know that."

I'm watching the clock. We only have a minute left. "Almost time," I say. "It has to be exactly four p.m., or we won't be synchronized with the other teams. Are we ready?"

"More than ready," Liam says.

"I'm ready too," Gadya agrees.

I nod. "Then here we go."

The clock rushes toward four p.m.

"It's time," Liam says, in the second before the clock hits four.

And then as one, we push the red button down with a loud click. The sound echoes off the walls of the basement. I can't believe that this is it. I expected it to be much more complicated. But I realize it's like pulling the trigger on a gun. One simple action can have massive consequences. I just hope we've made the right choice. I hold my breath, ready for whatever happens next.

16 THE BLAST

I REALIZE THAT I'M expecting something major to happen right away. That we'll hear explosions high up in the sky, or some kind of massive blast wave will hit us. But nothing happens. There's just total silence.

"Did it work?" Gadya asks, sounding as puzzled as I feel. She pushes the button down again and again.

"I can't tell," I reply. "Maybe not?"

"Listen," Liam says.

"What?" Then I think I hear something faint. Very distant and quiet. Like the muffled sound of rolling thunder. Barely audible. I can't tell if it's related to the button or not.

But the lights flicker and dim.

"This must be it," I hear Liam say. The noise is getting louder outside. He puts an arm around me. We hold on to each other tightly. Gadya grabs us too. I'm both terrified at what we've unleashed, and also relieved that the button worked.

The lights flicker and buzz again, suddenly flashing bright white, as though there has been a massive electrical surge. It's like a lightning strike. I see Gadya's startled face in the bright white light, and Liam's too.

The whole basement gets lit up for a millisecond. I hear the wires in the walls sizzling and hissing. The clock stops. And then I hear distant explosions rumbling away outside, making the earth shake.

Everything abruptly cuts out. All lights. All electricity. The house goes totally silent and dark. I smell smoke.

I steady myself in the darkness. I realize that we have deliberately plunged the entire country back into the dark ages—or at least back into the nineteenth century. And that's assuming it went as planned, and we're not going to die of radiation poisoning.

"I think we did it," I say nervously. I don't know what comes next.

"I hope so," Gadya replies.

It's so dark in the basement, I can barely see. "We should have set up candles or something."

"Let's get out of here and start fighting," Gadya responds.

"No," Liam says. "David told us to stay. It might not be safe out there yet."

"From what David said, the blast is so high up, it won't affect us like a regular nuclear bomb," I reply.

"That's if everything worked," Liam says. "We have to wait. Just to be careful." His hand finds mine in the darkness. I know he wants to take care of me. Liam on his own would already be out that door and trying to figure out his next move.

I'm about to tell him he doesn't have to worry about me anymore. That I've proven myself. That I'm his equal. But then the smell of smoke gets stronger, and I see an orange curl of flames licking at the edge of a wooden cabinet. The orange flames also illuminate a gust of smoke puffing down the stairs to the basement, coming from underneath the steel door.

249

"I think the house is on fire," I say, sounding surprisingly calm. "So I don't think staying is really an option."

Gadya is already moving toward the stairs.

Liam grabs my hand harder and says, "Let's go."

"Wait—" I say, suddenly remembering. "The doctor. We have to take him with us!"

We rush over to him. He's still unconscious from Liam's blow. And he's tied down with the electrical wiring.

"I'll carry him," Liam says. We quickly untie him in the dim light, the wire lacerating our fingers. Liam picks him up and slings the old man over his shoulders with a grunt. Then we head to the stairs.

Gadya and I race up the stairs in the darkness. Liam is a few steps behind with Dr. Urbancic. Our only light comes from the flames that are trying to devour us. We reach the steel door and Gadya tries to turn the doorknob.

She yanks her hand away. "It's hot!"

Liam puts Dr. Urbancic down on the stairs. He grabs the knob and tries to turn it too. The knob is not only hot, but it also won't budge. The door is locked. Dr. Urbancic must have locked us inside.

"We're trapped in here!" Gadya yells. She kicks at the door furiously, but nothing happens.

There's an electronic keypad by the door, but of course now it no longer works. Maybe Dr. Urbancic didn't lock us in here. Maybe the circuitry controlling the door just got melted, and our own actions ended up trapping us. But I'm sure there's a way to circumvent it and get this door open. There has to be.

I lean down to Dr. Urbancic. "Wake up!" I scream at him. His eyes stay closed. "Wake up and tell us how to get out of here!" I yell again, slapping him hard across the face. He remains completely unconscious.

"He won't wake up!" I yell to the others.

"Move back," Liam tells me and Gadya.

Gadya and I step out of the way as Liam rears back and slams his body against the unforgiving metal door. The door rattles, but it doesn't open.

He hits the door again with his shoulder, nearly slipping and falling down the stairs. But he catches himself on the railing just in time. He's breathing hard. He rubs his shoulder from the blow.

"We can't get out, can we?" Gadya says flatly.

I feel a rising sensation of panic. The basement is filling with smoke faster than I thought possible. There are no windows and there's no other way to escape. It's just a large, solid concrete box under the earth. A box that could very well become our grave. We need to get through this door somehow, before we pass out and die from smoke inhalation.

"I need more room," Liam says to us, gearing up to try again. He takes a deep breath.

Gadya and I move farther down the stairs, dragging Dr. Urbancic's body with us.

"Be careful," I tell Liam between coughs, as he gets ready to assault the door one more time. Both Gadya and I are using our T-shirts to cover our mouths and noses as we try to keep Dr. Urbancic's body from slipping down the stairs.

Liam races up the stairs toward the door and slams against it with all his force.

This time, the door gives way.

The metal itself doesn't yield, but the hinges are torn out of the doorframe, sheared and broken. The door clatters open wildly as a wave of heat and smoke explodes into the basement, making all of us nearly fall back down the stairs.

I feel the heat singeing my eyebrows and hair. The smoke fills my lungs. I'm coughing and gagging.

"Come on!" I try to yell, moving forward up the stairs. I know that we don't have long. We have to get out of this house.

Liam turns back and grabs at me and Gadya. Both of us grab Dr. Urbancic's body and we stagger out of the basement together.

I take a lungful of air when we get into the living room, but instantly start coughing even harder. The air here is filled with acrid smoke. Two of the walls are on fire, and so is the ceiling. The EMP must have sent such a large surge through the electrical system that it caused sparks, which set the home alight.

The decorative curtains on the windows are burning. So is a large bookcase filled with books.

"Run! C'mon!" Liam yells as he pulls all of us along.

We head down the hall and straight for the vestibule and the front door. I feel like I can't breathe. My vision is going fuzzy and my head feels heavy. We reach the vestibule and I'm afraid that I'm going to pass out.

Then we hit the front door, and Liam yanks it open. We burst out, coughing and choking. My lungs are burning for air. I feel like my chest is on fire. I fall down onto the grass, trying to get my breath back. I hear Gadya throwing up somewhere nearby, in between angry curses.

Liam goes back and grabs Dr. Urbancic. He hauls his limp body out into the daylight. Dr. Urbancic is now making choking sounds like he's finally going to wake up. Either that, or he's about to die from inhaling so much smoke.

We drag him onto the grass and head away from the burning house, toward the sidewalk.

Three other houses nearby are already on fire. I see a handful of confused people out in their yards, and in the street. A few of them are wearing UNA uniforms. They're so preoccupied with what's happening to their homes that they don't notice us. At least not yet.

"To the car," I say. I know that the car won't start, not after the EMP, but at least it gives us a place to seek shelter for a moment.

We head toward it, Liam slinging Dr. Urbancic over his shoulder again. When we reach the car, Gadya opens the passenger door and gets inside. I get in the driver's seat. Liam takes Dr. Urbancic into the back.

"Try the engine," Gadya says to me. "Just in case."

I stick the key into the ignition and turn it. Nothing happens. The car is completely dead. Our plan seems to have worked. *But what do we do next?*

"I think Dr. Urbancic has a bad concussion," Liam says from the back. "Or worse. We can't take him with us. He's not going to be able to move fast enough to get out of here."

"Maybe we can leave him in the car," I say, thinking fast. "He'll be safe here. He can even claim he was the victim of a rebel attack if he wants to. Someone will find him and get him help. A neighbor or something. But we need to get that intel from him somehow."

Gadya nods.

Out the windshield I see another house ablaze. Its owner is trying to hose it down with water, but nothing is coming out of the hose. The electrical pump that brings water to the house must have been destroyed by the EMP. These fires will consume this entire neighborhood. No water, no fire trucks. Nothing. I wonder if it's like this across the entire UNA.

I realize that we have essentially turned the UNA into the wheel.

Gadya glances down at her rifle. "I bet the circuits are fried." She holds it out the window and pulls the trigger. Nothing happens. "It won't work."

"What about older guns?" I ask. "Like, really old ones."

She nods. "Maybe."

We hear frantic yelling sounds. I look out the windshield. Four armed UNA soldiers are heading down the street on foot. In the middle of them is a man in a suit.

"What's that about?" Gadya asks.

"Must be someone important," I say. "Looks like the soldiers are escorting him out of here."

I'm worried that the soldiers will see us, but they don't. We duck our heads down, trying to hide. They pass by our car, yelling for people to get out of the way. They have their guns drawn, but I'm guessing their guns don't work anymore, just like ours.

Once the soldiers have passed, Liam says, "We need to get moving."

We assess how many weapons we have. Only two knives, and the now-defunct gun. It's not much, but at least we are more prepared than the confused-looking UNA workers wandering the streets.

"We have to find the closest rebel cell," I say. "We have to start fighting."

I glance back at Dr. Urbancic. His eyes are fluttering open. He coughs and gags for a moment, wiping his mouth. Then he looks at Liam. "There was no need to hit me like that."

"You didn't give me another option."

Dr. Urbancic looks at us. Then he sees the flames out the window. "So you pressed the button," he says. "Didn't you?"

"Yes," I tell him.

"You don't realize what you've done," he says sadly. "One day, you will."

"Quit lecturing us and give us some help," Gadya snarls at him.

He glares back at her. His eyes look a bit bleary, but his voice and thoughts are clear. "David told me that I would be taking you to the closest major rebel cell in the center of New Chicago. That's five hours from here by car. I thought I would drive you. That's why I let you into my house. I had no idea that David had other plans for us."

"Where in New Chicago is the rebel cell exactly?" I ask.

Dr. Urbancic slips a hand into his pocket and takes out a slip of paper and a crumpled map. On the paper is typed an address. "Here. I have been saving this for the right moment." He hands the paper and the map over to Liam. "But you must find your own way. Use the map. You are supposed to meet up with the rebels tomorrow, incite the citizens, and help lead the revolution in taking over New Chicago from the government. I suppose the rebels must have an arsenal of weapons that still function after the EMP. Perhaps coated with lead. But that is just speculation. David obviously didn't tell me what their real agenda was."

Liam passes me the piece of paper. "We'll travel by foot," he says. "I've made journeys as long as that on the wheel."

"Do you want to come with us?" I ask Dr. Urbancic.

He shakes his head. "No. I will stay. It's best nobody knows my involvement in all of this. Besides, I'm too old to risk traveling." He glances at Liam. "Just leave me here." He gazes out the window. "I will watch my house burn to the ground, thanks to you."

"Fine, whatever," Gadya says. "You wouldn't even have that nice house if you didn't work for the government, like a traitor."

"Gadya, he's helping us," I point out. "He obviously doesn't work for them. Not really, right?"

Dr. Urbancic nods. "True. Like I said, I have spent many years being a double agent and trying to help you rebels. But now you are on your own. You must find your own way to New Chicago and fight your own battles there. The war ahead is not for old people like me. It is for the young."

"Is there any vehicle that can take us there?" I ask him.

He shakes his head again. "The EMP will have destroyed most electronic circuitry. Perhaps older-model cars might work, but good luck finding one of those. Your friend is right—traveling by foot is your only option." He shuts his eyes. "And I'm quite content to remain behind." He opens his eyes again. I see a sudden, unexpected glimmer of liveliness in them. "I can play the role of the sad, innocent old man. I will be fine." He pauses, and takes something out of his pocket.

"What is that?" Gadya asks, suspicious.

He holds up a clear pouch containing a handful of capsules. "A very concentrated form of potassium cyanide. One of the strongest kinds known to mankind. It's in case things don't work out. I keep pills on me at all times. I don't plan on getting tortured. Not at my age." He puts the pouch on his knee. "Now get moving, before you cause me any more heartache."

He pauses for a moment, resting his fingers on the pouch.

Then he speaks again. "You should each take a pill to carry on you. Just in case you get caught. You know too much now."

I feel sick. But I know that he is right.

Liam picks up the pouch and holds it up. Each capsule is small. It's hard to believe something this tiny could be so deadly.

"Let's do it," I say.

Liam opens the pouch and hands me and Gadya a capsule, and keeps one for himself. I put mine in my jacket pocket, deep in the bottom because I don't want it to fall out. Then Liam hands the pouch back to Dr. Urbancic. It still has two capsules in it. The doctor slips it into his pocket.

"You better hurry," he says.

"He's right," Liam says. "We need to go. Now." He opens his door.

The three of us get out of the car and close the doors behind us. "Which way?" Gadya asks.

"That way," I say, pointing to our left. "I don't want to meet up with those soldiers."

"We need to get off the roads," Liam says. "Cut through the yards as much as we can. Try to stay out of sight."

We hear an explosion in the distance. Probably the result of more fires. This area is going to be turned into a wasteland pretty soon. Houses are burning all around us. Everything looks apocalyptic and surreal. I didn't know the revolution would look like this. I'm scared about what we've put into motion, but I also feel the thrill of battle in my heart. This is the start of the UNA's destruction.

"What are we waiting for?" I say. I grab Liam's hand, and the three of us start running toward the grass.

I only glance back at the car once. Through the windows, I can see Dr. Urbancic sitting there calmly, just waiting to be found by someone. I know that he disagreed with what we did. But I also know that we can trust him not to tell anyone about us. I believed him when he said he'd take a cyanide capsule rather than submit to being tortured. We are safe, at least from him.

But now we must find a way to get to New Chicago and begin the battle in earnest. There will be no more guns. Only knives and fists. Maybe even bows and arrows. We will take our skills from the island to the city streets and unite with the angry citizens. We will only rest when we have won and the UNA is history.

We keep running across the grass and between the houses, leaping over low fences. The few people we encounter seem stunned by the sudden power outage and the resulting fires. They are too preoccupied with trying to save their homes to deal with us. Others are trying in vain to get their cars started.

I can tell that they are scared that nothing is working. Perhaps they think the UNA is under attack from another nation. Or maybe they know that this is the work of rebels.

We just keep moving. I hear more explosions in the distance. Black plumes of smoke rise up from the horizon. I smell smoke. I glance up at the sky. There's no sign of the nuclear blast, but I know that a dangerous radiation field is far above us in the atmosphere. I just hope that David is right and that it doesn't affect us.

I keep running. Electrical wires have exploded, and they dangle uselessly between poles. Some of the wires lie on the ground. There is no more electricity in them. They are burned out from the EMP. A few of the poles have been knocked sideways from the pulse.

"Faster!" Gadya yells as we run.

We're heading to a grove of trees at the edge of the housing development. I'm hoping that here we can find shelter for a moment and figure out our next move without getting spotted by anyone.

I glance back and see more people coming out of their homes. They look dazed, gazing at the destruction in horror. Most of these people are middle-aged. Probably UNA bureaucrats or scientists. None of them look like they're going to give us any trouble.

"C'mon!" Gadya says again.

We race across the lawns toward the trees, away from the burning houses. The battle to take back our nation has finally begun.

I feel a mix of nervousness, excitement, and complete terror. It's up to us from here on out. I know that we can succeed. But I also know that a difficult journey lies ahead of us. No matter what happens, I am ready for it. Or at least that's what I tell myself as I keep running next to Liam and Gadya.

17 THE ROAD TO NEW CHICAGO

WHEN WE REACH THE trees, we stop to catch our breath. I stare back at the sprawling array of houses. At least half of them are burning. The residents are running around everywhere. I now see the occasional group of UNA soldiers.

"I wish my gun worked," Gadya says. "I could take those people out one by one." She's clutching her weapon, even though it's useless.

Liam is consulting the map. "It's a three- or four-day hike to New Chicago. Longer than I thought."

"That far?" I ask. "Really?"

Liam nods. "And that's if we move fast."

"How are we going to manage four days of traveling?" Gadya asks. "By then the city will be in total chaos. And we'll probably get picked up along the way. We need a vehicle."

"There aren't any," I tell her. "That's kind of the point."

She sighs.

"What about bikes?" I suddenly ask. "That would help get us there faster. I don't mean motorbikes but regular ones. Like mountain bikes."

Liam thinks for a moment. "It would force us to stay on the

260

road, or on paths. But it would cut the travel time down to just a day or two at the most. We'd be close to the schedule."

"Then let's find some bikes!" Gadya says. "That's a risk I'm willing to take."

"Same here." I scan the houses. "There's got be some in this neighborhood."

"Let's check the garages," Liam says.

We burst back out of the trees and run to the nearest house. There's so much chaos going on around us that it's easy to smash a window and get into the garage. But the first house yields nothing.

It takes us fifteen minutes and eight different houses until we've found three suitable bikes. On our journey, we cycle past our abandoned car. I glance inside to check on Dr. Urbancic but he's no longer there. I'm startled for a moment, but then realize that maybe a neighbor came and rescued him. There's no time to worry about it now.

I lean forward on my bike, an old green twelve-gear Schwinn with wide tires. It's a relic of the pre-UNA years. It's been years since I've ridden a bicycle, not since before Minister Harka came to power, but I remember how to ride. Liam does too. Gadya is struggling a bit, but getting the hang of it.

We cycle out of the suburban development and up the main road. It's deserted here.

We stand there at the edge of the road with our bikes for a moment. No sirens wail. No trucks make noise. Everything is quiet except for continuing distant explosions. The electronic world as we knew it has been destroyed. The sky is empty of airplanes and helicopters. I realize if any were up there when the blast occurred, they probably crashed straight down to the ground, killing all the occupants.

"Let's do this," I say, beginning to pedal my bike up the road. Gadya and Liam follow.

Soon we are riding together on the desolate road, side by side. We ride fast, our heads down against the breeze. We pass parked cars. Most of them are empty, but sometimes the occupants are there, wandering confused by the side of the road.

A few people yell out to us as we fly past them. They sound scared and angry. We make sure to avoid them. I'm guessing that they want to steal our bikes.

"You!" a man's voice bellows right behind me. I startle as I glance around and see that he's run out from the side of the road. He's wearing a black UNA policeman's uniform.

Gadya swerves her bike to avoid him.

"Stop!" the man screams.

"Get away from us!" I yell.

"Or else!" Gadya adds.

Liam glances back and watches the man closely, ready to stop and attack him if need be.

The man tries to run after us, but he can't catch up. I see him take a pistol out of his pocket and aim it at my head.

I scream and jam on the hand brakes, almost falling onto the road as I try to avoid the impending bullet. I'm acting purely on instinct.

But then I realize that his gun doesn't work because of the EMP. He just keeps pulling the trigger. I can hear the faint click. *If his gun worked, I would be dead by now.* He curses in frustration and flings the weapon after us. It skitters on the pavement.

I turn to face forward again and start cycling, as we leave him behind. I hear his angry cries continue as we speed away.

"Get back here!" he's screaming, as though we're going to turn around and obey him. "I need those bikes!"

"Yeah, good luck with that," Gadya mutters, turning around and giving him the finger as a parting gift.

Soon we are racing down the road at about twenty miles an hour, and the man with the gun is just a memory. We're not wearing any helmets. I'm careful to look at the road in front of me, so I can avoid potholes. I don't want to wreck and get injured out here.

I'm also hoping we won't encounter any roadblocks. On either side of the road is extremely thick grass—nearly impossible to ride through with these bikes. We just have to hope that luck will be on our side.

Liam cycles up next to me. "You doing okay?" he asks.

"Yeah. Great. How about you?"

He laughs. "I'm not great, but I'm okay."

"Did you think our return would be like this?" I ask him. "The three of us riding bikes down the middle of the road to New Chicago, with no electricity. And no one else helping us?"

Liam keeps grinning. "No. But it's pretty much been impossible to predict anything since we left the wheel."

"True."

Gadya overhears us. "I didn't expect this either," she says. "It's not what I hoped for! Where are all the other rebels? I thought we'd run into more of them."

"Me too," I tell her. "They must already be on their way to New Chicago, and to other cities."

"We just have to keep biking," Liam says. "The faster we get there, the better."

"I'm guessing David still has some tricks up his sleeve," I say. I look up at the sky. "We didn't die yet. So David was right and Dr. Urbancic was wrong, at least in the short term. That's a good sign."

"David was right, but he could have helped us more already," Liam says. "He likes to play games. I know that he's smart, but I'm guessing he's not as smart as he thinks he is. People rarely are."

"He risked his life," I point out, annoyed that Liam is still questioning his motives. "We all thought he was dead. I don't think he was playing any games then. And you saw what happened to him. He lost an eye. And some fingers. He's made way more sacrifices than any of us have."

"Not more than Rika," Liam says, after a moment's thought. "I just don't want any more surprises. Not for any of us. I just want to win the battle that we came here to fight."

"Same here," I tell him. Our eyes lock. We are equally resolute.

"Winning is our only option," Gadya seconds. "After everything we've done, there's no way I'm going to let the UNA get the better of us. And for once, we might actually have the upper hand."

For the next several hours we ride on the bikes up a network of roads. We start to pass more people. At one point we see another man on a bike, and we pull off onto a side road so that he doesn't spot us. We can't risk being seen by anyone who can catch up to us.

The sun is setting. None of the bikes have lights on them, and even if they did, the lights probably wouldn't work. Night is going to be pitch dark, except for the stars and moon. *Just like it was on the wheel.*

I estimate that we only have about another half hour of light. Then we will have to pull over for the night. It's too risky to ride in the dark. We will sleep in the trees by the road, or try to find an abandoned building to take refuge in. Then, in the morning, we will continue our journey.

My legs are tired and my hands ache from gripping the handlebars. The bicycle seat is also digging into me uncomfortably.

I'm already looking forward to a rest, when I hear Gadya ask, "Do you see that?" There's a note of caution in her voice that instantly makes me worried.

"What?" I call back. She's riding nearby, to my left.

Liam cycles closer to me. We draw inward, trying to protect ourselves from whatever's out there.

"In the trees," Gadya says, pointing to the forest at the side of the road. "I saw something move."

I look, but I don't see anything. At least not yet. Neither does Liam.

"Let's keep riding," he says.

But right then I see a flash of light in the forest. In the dusk, I can see men with torches moving around. They're stepping out of the woods and onto the road, about a hundred yards ahead of us.

I slowly come to a stop, hoping that we haven't been spotted. Liam and Gadya bring their bikes to a halt too. We race to the side of the road and hide. I peer out through the underbrush.

What I'm looking at doesn't make sense at first. It's a large group of UNA soldiers—about forty of them—many holding lit torches. At the center of the group, some of the men are carrying a huge object, like a box. I try to get a glimpse of it. It's large, and made of glass.

Then I see that there is a mutant inside the glass box. The creature is humanoid, but large, with scaly silver skin.

"What the hell is that?" Gadya breathes.

Liam squints, trying to get a better view.

The soldiers are carrying and escorting this strange, trapped creature across the road. There's too many men to risk attacking.

I see that most of them are carrying knives and truncheons.

"It's a mutant," Liam says.

I nod. "Like the kind Minister Hiram had locked up in his office. He said they don't breathe. That they're some advanced form of life."

"'Some sick and twisted form of life' is more like it," Gadya says.

"They must be creating these mutants for some purpose," Liam adds. He turns to Gadya. "Give me your gun. I want to look through the scope."

She gives it to him. He puts his eye up to the viewfinder.

"What do you see?" I ask.

He's silent for a moment, scanning the glass container. "I'm not sure. It looks part human, and part . . . something else. The result of genetic experiments."

"Why are they doing things like this?" Gadya asks.

"For war. It's always about war," I tell her. "They're fighting the Europeans and Asians. Maybe they plan on unleashing these mutants on them." I'm already thinking that the perfect soldier is probably one who doesn't need to breathe, or eat, or even think—just like Minister Hiram said. "It's another form of drone. One that's worse than what we encountered on the wheel."

Liam nods and hands the gun back to Gadya. "I'm glad it's locked up. If it's designed for fighting purposes, then we don't want it on the loose with us."

I watch as the large group of soldiers makes it across the road and back into the forest. Their noises subside into the darkening gloom. We wait in the underbrush for several minutes, until we can't hear them anymore. Finally, we decide it's safe to start moving again.

266

We only travel another twenty minutes or so up the road until dusk starts to give way to night.

Then we pull off the road and into the forest. I find myself thinking of David. I remember my first day on the wheel, when he suggested that we climb up into a tree for shelter.

I had no idea back then that David knew so much about what was going on. I thought he was innocent and naïve, just like me. I didn't know he was already a hardened rebel. He fooled me. But I am not naïve anymore. The wheel has changed both of us. It made me grow up faster than I thought possible. I would be a totally different person if I'd never gotten sent to Island Alpha. And so would David.

I look around me. There are no trees large enough to bear our weight. The trees here are tall, but thin and leafy. So we decide to make a small encampment around the base of the largest tree we can find. We gather underbrush to hide behind.

Here, we are cloaked from view in case other UNA soldiers pass through this area.

"In eight hours it will be light again," Liam says. "We start moving again as soon as the sun comes up."

Liam sits down against the tree and I nestle against him. He puts his arm around me. I lean back into him. It feels so good to be with him. There has been no time recently for us to be together.

Gadya looks vaguely annoyed at me and Liam cuddling. I don't think she has feelings for Liam any longer, but I can tell that right now she's feeling left out.

"There's room for you too," I tell her, holding out my arm. "C'mon. Group hug."

She frowns. "I need to keep watch. I'm not going to start slacking off." She surveys the landscape around us.

"Fine," I tell her. "We'll trade off like usual tonight. You want first watch? I'll take second."

"I'll take third," Liam adds.

"Deal," Gadya says.

So we spend the night that way, shifting roles so that one of us is always awake.

The noises of the forest at nighttime are loud around us. I'm not bothered by them anymore. I used to be afraid of the dark, and the forest, and of insects and animals. But after the wheel, this forest in the UNA seems tame.

I curl up against Liam's body, as Gadya keeps watch nearby. But my eyes remain open.

"It's okay to sleep," he tells me.

"I know," I reply, looking up at him. "It's okay for you to sleep too."

He grins. "I'll sleep if you do."

"I don't feel tired. I mean, I do. But I don't think I can sleep."

"I know what you mean."

He leans down and kisses me. I kiss him back. I wish so much that we could be together, and not in a war zone. One day soon this will all be over, and we will either be dead or the UNA will be vanquished.

I pull back from Liam. I'm aware that we have to gather our strength now, before the real battle begins. In New Chicago, the showdown between the rebel forces and the UNA will take place tomorrow. And similar battles will be waged in cities all across the nation. We will find out then if everything has been worth it.

I shut my eyes. I think of the battles that we've fought. Of the ones we have won, and the ones we have lost.

Memories of Rika come flooding back. I can picture her face

so well. Her kind eyes and her smile. I can hear the sound of her voice too. And even taste the food that she cooked for us. I can't believe that she is gone. Along with so many other close friends.

I open my eyes again.

"Do you ever wonder if we wouldn't have been better off just staying on the island?" I ask.

Liam shakes his head. "No. We would have died there."

"Eventually, sure," I say. "But right now we'd probably be back in our village. You and I would just be hanging out together. Rika would be alive. We'd be eating stew around the fire pit."

"Maybe," Liam says. "But everything looks better in hindsight. Don't forget how the drones used to attack us all the time."

I nod. "True. But sometimes it's nice to pretend that things might have been okay."

Liam kisses me on the top of my head. "I know. But this is where our fate has taken us. We were meant to fight. That's our purpose."

"So you realize that I'm a warrior too? You're not going to keep trying to protect me, or anyone else? I just want you to look out for yourself when the fighting starts. I almost lost you back at that research lab in the Hellgrounds."

He nods. "Sure, I'll look out for myself. But no promises. You know how I feel about you. I'm always going to be looking out for you first."

I'm not sure whether to feel annoyed at him, or relieved. Maybe both. I lean back against him again.

I vow that we will conquer the fascists controlling the UNA and win. Our friends will not have died in vain, and we will not have suffered so much for nothing. I want our pain to be worth the sacrifice.

18 THE CITY AT NIGHT

BY THE LATE AFTERNOON of the next day, we reach the suburban outskirts of New Chicago. We've successfully navigated the roads leading into the city with our bikes. We were spotted and chased multiple times, but each time, we managed to avoid our pursuers. Without guns, or any obvious way to communicate with one another, the UNA soldiers seem like they don't know what to do.

Luckily, no one has recognized me as Alenna, or Liam or Gadya either. In this blighted landscape, we are just random kids riding around on bikes. The people who see us have no idea that we have returned here from Island Alpha, or done so much to attack the UNA.

The roads are more congested as we get closer to the city. Some people have camped out on the side of the highways, or have slept in their cars, which are stuck on the road. For the first time on our journey, we're forced to slow down and walk our bikes among civilians. Our dirty, angry faces keep most of them from talking to us.

"I'll give you ten thousand dollars for that bike," a woman calls out to me loudly.

270

I flash her the blade of my knife and glare at her. "It's not for sale!"

She falls silent.

Liam walks in the lead. His large figure discourages people from trying to steal our bikes. Gadya and I also carry knives, and her gun is slung around her back.

I know that we look half-crazed, grubby, and fierce. These random citizens of the UNA look scared and soft compared to us. But of course, I understand why. They never experienced the trial by fire of the wheel.

We walk through a group of people. I feel their wary eyes on us. Their whole lives have been ripped away from them unexpectedly. Children are crying. Some people are praying. Other people are cursing the government.

The sky is a strange hue of greenish yellow. It has been that way since the atomic bomb blast. There's no way to know if we're being dosed with radiation or not. I wonder if the change to the sky's color is permanent.

I hear a sudden commotion to our left. The three of us pause. A man's voice cries out in agony, like he's being tortured. It's a primal wail.

I don't want to stop and help him—or anyone—but at the same time it's hard to ignore such a cry of suffering.

"Let's check it out," Gadya says, voicing my thoughts.

"Be careful," Liam murmurs to me, as we follow Gadya toward the source of the noise.

When we get there, we see that a crowd has gathered around two men. One is wearing the black uniform of a UNA soldier. He is missing an eye. The wound is fresh. Blood and gore are running down his face. This must be the man who was screaming.

The other man is just dressed in jeans and a red flannel shirt, with his sleeves rolled up. He's rugged and muscular. They are circling each other, like two fighters in a ring.

"Get him!" a voice yells out.

"Make him pay!"

I realize that the crowd is shouting to the man in the flannel shirt. They are on his side, egging him on against the soldier.

The UNA soldier lunges forward with a fist, but the other man dodges the blow easily.

"Not so tough without your gun, are you?" he says, with a grin. "Next, I'll take your other eye. Leave you for dead in the ditch."

"You will have to answer for your insubordination!" the soldier says to him angrily, holding up his fists to his face like a boxer. "Assaulting an officer of the United Northern Alliance is punishable by death—"

As he says the final word, the other man strikes out with a fist and catches the soldier in the jaw. The soldier is knocked backward, and stumbles to the ground, dazed.

"Insulting me is punishable by getting your ass whipped," the man says. "Without your guns and technology, you don't have any power."

Gadya turns to me. "I like where this is headed," she says cheerfully.

But I don't. It just makes me feel queasy.

Gadya turns back to the fight. "Give him hell!" she calls out. Other voices in the crowd encourage the man as he advances on the soldier.

"I'll make sure you get arrested," the soldier says, spitting out blood. "I'll make sure your family gets arrested too!" He's looking around for someone to come and rescue him. A UNA convoy truck, or a helicopter. But all of those things are gone now.

The crowd is laughing and jeering at him. I wonder how many lives this soldier is responsible for ruining. How many parents he killed. How many children he orphaned. How many normal citizens he got locked up. I think about all my friends who died fighting men like this one. I also think about my dad, who would still be alive were it not for the UNA.

So I do nothing to intervene. I just watch. This man made his own decision to join the UNA. Now he must pay the price. He has already lost an eye. I'm sure much more is next.

The man in the flannel shirt advances on him again. The soldier gets up, ready to fight. But he's no match for the other man.

The man runs straight at him and slams the soldier's bloody face with a barrage of fists. The soldier is knocked to the ground again. The man stands over him and begins stomping his chest with his feet. I hear the crack of ribs breaking. The crowd rushes to join in. Soon, I can't see the soldier anymore because of the torrent of violent blows. They keep kicking him.

"This revolution is going to be easier than I thought," Gadya says.

I hear the soldier scream in agony as the crowd continues to brutalize him. They keep punching and kicking him in a blood-thirsty frenzy.

"We should keep moving," Liam says softly.

"Why?" Gadya asks. "These are my kind of people."

"They're getting out of control," I say. "Things could turn bad for us."

Liam nods. "They might come after our bikes next—and we won't be able to stop them. There's too many of them. We need to get past them while they're occupied."

So we keep walking our bikes as fast as we can, putting distance between ourselves and the group of people attacking the soldier.

We're stuck in the crowd, which seems to be endless. It's just a massive exodus of people from the suburbs heading into the city. There's no way to escape from them. I'm not even sure why they're traveling in this direction. Probably to help join the revolt against the government. Or maybe they think the city still has electricity.

These are the very people we need to enlist to help us in taking apart the UNA. Still, I'm uneasy. I don't even know how many of these people are normal, and how many work for the UNA and are just hiding that fact out of self-preservation. There's no way to know.

It's then that a rumbling sound comes from the distance. For a moment, I think it's some kind of blast wave. I stop my bike. So do Liam and Gadya.

I get jostled by the crowd. Some people keep moving, pushing roughly past us. They have all heard the sound, and they are talking and murmuring among themselves.

The sound gets louder.

"What the hell is that?" Gadya asks.

"I don't know," I tell her.

Liam cocks his head to listen. "Something's headed our way. Some kind of vehicle."

"But everything should be disabled by now," Gadya says. "Our entire plan is based on that!"

"Shhh," I tell her, trying to listen.

The sound increases in volume again. It almost sounds like a feeler, but larger. Then I see something come into view above the trees to our right.

"Look!" a voice screams.

"A helicopter!" someone else yells.

Gadya curses. "How did it survive the EMP?" she asks. "If David screwed up, I'm going to kill him!"

The helicopter approaches rapidly. We stand there with the crowd, trying to blend in. Some people start running for the trees, but most remain on the road, looking up. Without any guns, there is no way to take this helicopter out of the sky. And if it has guns, it's going to be able to kill a lot of people.

The sound of the helicopter gets louder. As it nears, I see why it probably survived the EMP. The entire thing, except for the glass windshield, is coated with thick metal plates. Probably made out of lead, to block the radiation. *Was the UNA prepared for this? Did they know about our plan?* My heart sinks. If they were prepared, then we did all of this for nothing.

But then a voice blares out from loudspeakers mounted on the bottom of the helicopter. "Alenna!" the voice calls out, sounding inexplicably elated. "Gadya! And Liam too! We found you!"

The crowd looks confused, but I feel a surge of joy. This is not some random UNA helicopter. This craft belongs to the rebels. I know this, because I recognize the voice, even through the noise of the rotors and the distortion of the speakers.

"It's Cass," I say.

"What? For real?" Gadya asks. "Are you sure?"

"It's her all right," Liam says. "I'd know that voice anywhere."

"But she failed the test to come here!"

"So did Rika," I point out. "There must have been a second wave of rebels sent over here or something. Or maybe she stowed away on a plane. With Cass, anything is possible, right?"

The helicopter turns in the sky as it buzzes the crowd.

"I see you guys!" Cass's voice calls out. "I'm here to give you a ride into the city! It's time to start fighting!"

The crowd is starting to scream happily and surge all around us. They can tell this isn't a UNA helicopter. They are not going to be shot at. But the crowd still poses a problem for us. Everyone wants to get on board the helicopter.

Liam voices my concern: "If that helicopter lands, then it's going to be mobbed by the crowd. They'll never let it take off again, even if they mean well."

"So what do we do?" I ask.

Liam stares up at the sky. "It's not up to us. It's up to Cass and whoever's piloting the helicopter."

The helicopter has gone overhead and is preparing to turn back around and fly over our heads again. It's then that I see a tangle of ropes and wooden beams get shoved out the open doorway.

For a second, I'm afraid they'll fly up and get caught in the blades of the helicopter, but then I see that there's a weight on the bottom of them. The ropes and beams fall down beneath the helicopter, swaying. It's a rope ladder.

"Well, I guess Cass solved the problem for us," I say with a sigh. "I don't think she has any plans of landing the helicopter."

At the same time, like she's reading my thoughts, I hear Cass blare over the loudspeakers, "You can do this, guys! C'mon!"

The helicopter gets lower. Other members of the crowd start to realize what's going on, and they want to get on board too.

I put down my bicycle and hold out my knife. "Keep your distance!" I scream. People start backing away from me. "We're rebels from Island Alpha! This is part of a plan. We need to get on this helicopter."

"You're from Island Alpha?" a voice calls out, sounding startled. "But nobody comes back from there."

"She's telling the truth," Liam bellows. "We need to get to

New Chicago as fast as possible. Don't get in our way. We're all on the same side."

"How do we know you don't work for the government?" a man asks Liam, sounding angry.

"Do I look like I work for the government?" Gadya sneers, showing off her prominent tattoos. "Get real!"

"You can have our bikes," Liam tells the people. Both he and Gadya have dropped theirs as well. "But if you come near us, we will kill you."

Cass helps guide the helicopter above us and it hovers there. "Climb on board!" she says. "Hurry!"

I don't need much encouraging. The ladder is closest to me, so I grab at it. But I'm not tall enough to reach it. Liam manages to leap and get it. All around us, the wary crowd is watching. I'm not sure if they want to hurt us, or if they're just surprised at what's happening.

The helicopter lowers itself a bit more and Liam hands me the ladder. "You first!" he yells at me over the noise.

I grab the ladder and feel the rope in my hands. I start scrambling up, using the wooden beams to support my feet. Gadya grabs the ladder too and starts coming up after me. Liam brings up the rear, flashing a glare at anyone who looks like they might want to hitch a ride with us.

The wind lashes at me as I keep climbing up the swaying ladder. I glance up and see Cass looking down at me from inside the helicopter. She's smiling broadly. She looks just like I remember her. "C'mon, girl!" she calls out jubilantly.

I don't know how she found us. But then I remember that Cass is an expert at technology. She learned it from her rebel cell before she got sent to the wheel. So maybe she had some way of tracking us. Or maybe she just knew we would be on this road because it's the fastest route to New Chicago.

I keep climbing, hand over hand, relieved and excited to see her and the other rebels. I know that Cass is a fierce warrior— just like me, Gadya, and Liam. With her on our side, there is even more of a chance that we will succeed.

I reach the top of the ladder. It's swaying a lot now in the wind. I glance down and see that Gadya is struggling to hang on. Liam is trying to help her.

Cass sticks her hands out. "Grab on to me," she says. Leather bracelets cover the scars on her wrists.

"I'm trying," I tell her.

With one hand I cling to the rope, but with my other, I take her hand in mine. I clutch on to her as hard as I can, and she does the same. She starts pulling me into the helicopter using all of her strength. Within seconds, I'm inside, sprawled on the metal floor.

I lie there for a moment, catching my breath. Then I clamber onto my knees to help the others.

I turn around, and with Cass's help, bring Gadya inside as well. She holds on to me to keep her balance.

Liam is the last one to get into the helicopter. People try to get on the ladder, but Liam kicks them off. Unlike me and Gadya, he then gracefully manages to climb inside without losing his balance. He automatically pivots and starts bringing up the ladder behind him.

I see people down below jumping for it again, trying to grab it and get pulled up after us. But we can't let them do that, because we can't risk letting a spy or government worker on board.

A man finally manages to take hold of the lowest rung of the ladder before Liam can swing it out of his grasp.

The man is swearing and yelling incoherently. I grab on to the top of the ladder with Liam and we both pull at it. For a second, the man hangs there, zooming across the landscape, about twenty feet off the ground.

Then Liam yanks the ladder hard, and the man gets startled. He loses his grip and plummets down to the ground below.

"Let's go," Cass says to the pilot. I can't see his face. He's wearing a helmet with a visor. He nods and we begin flying away.

Out the open door I can see the throngs of people below still watching us. The man who fell off the ladder is already back on his feet, shaking his hands at us and cursing.

Soon we are moving away from the road and over the trees, headed toward the heart of the battleground.

19 FLIGHT

CASS AND I HUG as the helicopter keeps moving. She pulls back from me and looks at all of us. "You guys are in better shape than I expected."

"Thanks," I tell her.

"How'd you make it back to the UNA?" Gadya asks.

"Second wave," Cass tells her. "You guys were the first wave. I passed the test on my second try and got flown out here yesterday, two weeks after you guys. My arm is feeling better with every day that goes by. There's going to be a third and fourth wave too. The travelers are all coming over here to help keep order. They're going to use their skills to rebuild the country and make sure the citizens don't get out of control."

"So the helicopter wasn't affected by the EMP?" Liam asks.

"The rebels in the UNA and the scientists managed to protect some technology from the pulse. The government didn't. That means we now have the upper hand."

Out the window, the ground is rushing past. The helicopter tilts sideways. I grab on to a metal railing near the door. Liam puts his arm around me.

"Rika's dead," I tell Cass.

She looks surprised. "I thought maybe she'd be okay," Cass says. Her eyes look sad. "Alun is dead too."

"Alun?" I ask, startled. "Are you sure?"

She nods somberly.

I feel sick to my stomach.

"They never should have sent Alun back here," Liam says. "He was missing an eye. That means he has no depth perception. It wasn't safe for him to fight anyone."

"He wanted to come. We couldn't stop him." Cass pauses. "I wish I could have. But he passed the test too. I don't know how."

"What about Emma?" I ask Cass, suddenly worried about her too.

"She's fine. Still back on Island Alpha."

All of us are silent for a moment. The noise of the helicopter is overwhelming.

I shut my eyes. I can picture Alun's wide face, with his black eye patch, and I can hear his jubilant voice. I can see his shaved head and the caps he always wore to keep it warm. He was instrumental in helping us survive on the wheel, and bring it under control. It's so hard to believe that he's no longer alive.

And David lives now in some strange in-between—part human and part machine. He is never far from my thoughts. I wish I could talk to him right now. I only hope that I will see him again soon.

I find my voice. "We need to let their deaths give us motivation to keep fighting," I say. "They would never want us to stop."

"I second that," Cass says, nodding.

"So we're heading to New Chicago to fight, right?" Liam asks, as our helicopter continues heading north.

Cass nods. "We're landing where some of the other protected

machinery is located. There are several ground convoys and more helicopters that were shielded from the blast. A few trusted rebels were told about David's secret plan in advance, so they were able to shield the equipment. We're going to use the equipment to take control of the air and the streets. We're going to get the people to rise up—if it isn't happening already."

"How do you have more information than any of us, when we're supposed to be the heart of this rebellion?" Gadya asks her.

Cass smiles. "I just eavesdrop and spy on everyone. It's the easiest way to figure out what's really going on."

"Why didn't the scientists just tell us the real plan from the start?"

"They thought total secrecy would ensure its success. Looks like it worked."

"What about the rest of the UNA?" I ask her. "New Chicago is only one city."

Cass nods. "The same revolutions are apparently taking place simultaneously in four other major urban areas across the country—New Los Angeles, New Manhattan, New Dallas, and New Washington, DC. These are the power bases of the UNA. Rebel cells are orchestrating everything." Cass glances behind her. "And we have more guns. Bullets, too."

"Yeah, bullets are pretty helpful," Gadya says.

"Why those cities?" Liam asks Cass.

"The UNA has multiple headquarters, like a snake with many heads. They all work together. We have to take them all out at once." She pauses. "New Chicago is the most fortified. It's where the main leader is."

"The main leader?" I ask.

"Yes," Cass replies. "No one knows who he is."

"I met one of the UNA leaders, in New Dallas," I suddenly say. "He called himself Minister Hiram. He was one of Minister Harka's former body doubles. He seemed nearly insane. He was keeping a mutant locked up in his office."

"Yeah, what's up with these mutants we keep seeing?" Gadya asks.

Cass shakes her head. "We don't know their purpose, but we assume military. We're going to have to fight them."

I stare out the window again. We're moving fast. At this rate, we'll be in Chicago within an hour.

"The sky looks so weird," I say, suddenly realizing that I haven't seen the sun unobstructed by clouds since the nuclear blasts. Liam puts his arm around me.

I remember Dr. Urbancic's words. That there's a potential we doomed the planet by taking action.

"The sun will come back out," Cass says. "Might take a few weeks. Obviously the nuclear blasts disrupted the typical weather patterns." Cass sounds unconcerned. But of course she didn't hear the warnings that we did from Dr. Urbancic.

Liam rubs my back. "Don't worry," he says.

I suddenly smile. "I guess I shouldn't even think about the sun coming out yet. It won't matter if we're not around to see it."

"Exactly," Cass says. "First we fight and conquer the UNA, then we figure out what to do after that."

"You make it sound so easy," Gadya says. But she doesn't sound annoyed. In fact, she's grinning. "Let's hope it goes down that way."

"That part is up to us," I say in the ensuing silence.

Everyone nods.

"So how did you find us, anyway?" I ask Cass.

"Easy. Remember those pills we had to take to get on board the airships back at Southern Arc?"

"Sure," I say. "The antidote to the chemicals on the wheel. Meant to prevent the Suffering."

"Those are the ones. It turns out some of them had microscopic tracking devices inside them. Tiny microchips that attached themselves to the intestines of anyone who took one of the pills. The guards were instructed to only give those special tracking pills to certain people. Dr. Barrett told them which ones, before he went insane."

I feel ill. "There's a tracking device inside me?"

"Inside you, and me, and Liam. Anyone who had been singled out for some reason as potentially important or crucial in the battle ahead. Apparently your mom made sure that you and Liam got them, probably so she could keep an eye on you."

"So I've been tracked all this time? You always knew where I was?" I'm incredulous.

"The signal comes and goes. It's not perfect, but it's pretty accurate."

"Unbelievable," I say.

"How did it survive the nuclear blast?" Liam asks Cass.

"The scientists designed it to withstand the EMP. They knew what they were doing this whole time."

"They should never have bothered lying to us," Liam says. "Not to me, Alenna, and Gadya."

"Can I get the device out of me?" I ask.

"They biodegrade naturally," Cass says. "At least that's what I heard. Even if they don't, who cares?"

"So the pills were another secret."

"Sort of," Cass says. "I mean, they really do protect against the

UNA drugs. But ours just had a little something extra in them."

"So you located us using the pills?"

"The pilot did," Cass says, gesturing at the man flying our helicopter. "He knew the general vicinity that you were in, and then homed in on your signals. Each pill broadcasts a specific sixteen-digit code, so they knew who you were."

"I'm glad I don't have one in me," Gadya says proudly.

"You're lucky you stuck with Alenna and Liam, or you would have gotten lost," Cass points out.

"Can anyone else trace them?" Liam asks.

Cass shakes her head. "No. It's encrypted. And they don't emit a signal. They have to be scanned by radio waves to get picked up. You're totally safe."

"I still feel weird about it," I tell Cass.

She grins. "I felt the same way too. But now it makes me feel kind of safe. Even protected in a strange way."

It still makes me feel uneasy. I am now a number in a database. It makes me think of the metal creatures implanted into Rika and the other girl back at the laboratory. Or the tubes that the UNA implanted in my neck.

The pills also remind me of David and his transformation into some kind of cyborg. I don't want to end up the same way. But what if I don't have a choice? What if defeating the UNA demands such a transformation?

"We should have been told the truth about the pills," I say, sharing a glance with Liam.

"Does it matter now?" Cass asks. "You still would have taken it. I would have too. They wouldn't have let us come back to the wheel otherwise. We would have been stuck at Southern Arc."

I nod. What she's saying is true. I never would have refused the pill, because that would have meant not seeing Liam again. But that doesn't really make me feel any better about what is inside my body. I just stare out the window again, anticipating our arrival in New Chicago.

Within an hour, I see the New Chicago skyline emerging on the horizon. We're flying over rolling hills and trees right now, dotted with suburban houses. Some of the houses have burned down, but most are still standing.

I see people on the ground, watching us in stupefaction. They have no idea how this helicopter can still be in the air. Some of them wave at us.

We move over them rapidly. The countryside is giving way to more roads and more houses. There are no other aircraft of any kind in the air with us yet—no airplanes, no helicopters, and no feelers.

I finally see a group of trucks on the road. I think they're UNA vehicles for a moment, until I realize that it's a contingent of rebels. A large one, of at least ten trucks. There's probably a hundred people on board them. I'm relieved to see some sign of rebel activity.

We get closer to the city. All the skyscrapers are dark. The sun is setting already, and there is no electricity left to power them. At nighttime, the city is going to be a very scary place. But I am not afraid. The wheel has trained me well. I'm used to fighting in darkness, and in places without any human comforts.

The only bright light now comes from fires below us. Some of them rage out of control, but others are clearly coming from torches. I wonder how long it will take until the UNA spirals completely out of control.

"So we fight in the dark?" I ask. "Is that the plan?"

Cass shakes her head. "No. In the day. With nothing else lit up, this helicopter is way too easy a target. If there are any UNA weapons that survived the EMP somehow, we could get shot down. In the day we'll have a lot more visibility and it'll be safer. Rebel scouts are going door-to-door, trying to round up UNA soldiers to arrest them."

"Where are we going to spend the night?" Gadya asks her.

Cass points out the window. "See that building?"

She's pointing to the tallest skyscraper around. It's massive, nearly a hundred stories tall, with a large flat roof. It's made of gleaming black glass. I can see the helicopter's reflection in its smooth dark surface.

Gadya nods.

"There's a helipad on the top level. We're going to land there and spend the night inside the building."

"Is that safe?" I ask.

"The building has been evacuated," Cass tells me. "It was a hotel for the very top UNA government officials. They rushed everyone out right after the EMP and took them to another location. The hotel is empty—or at least that's what we've been told."

The helicopter keeps zooming through the night sky, heading toward the dark building. Then I see orange flares appear on the roof, outlining the square of the helipad.

"Who's down there?" Liam asks, scrutinizing the scene out the window.

"Rebels. They've already secured the top floors of the building for us. I'm telling you, it's safe."

In some ways, Cass's confidence is reassuring. But then again, she hasn't seen all the things that we have since being back in the

UNA. She never saw the Hellgrounds or met Miss Caroldean and Mikal. She didn't see Rika get killed. And she didn't have to press a button that might have meant the end of the world. Sometimes it's easy to be confident when you don't know all the facts.

"Don't worry," Cass says, seeing the expression on my face. "We're going to be fine."

"I hope so."

Liam squeezes my hand. "We'll be there soon," he says.

I keep looking out the window as we fly lower in the night sky, approaching our landing zone. I see figures down there in the dark, moving around at the edges of the helipad. Some of them clutch burning torches. They're helping wave our helicopter down and into position.

"How many rebels are there?" I ask Cass.

"At the hotel? Probably a hundred or so. But more are amassing. Soon there will be thousands."

"Are there more helicopters like this one?" Liam asks.

"Of course. A whole fleet. And some armored personnel carriers too. The rebels worked in secret to build ones that would be able to survive the EMP."

I nod. "Good."

Cass grins. "For once, we'll have the technology on our side. Let's see how the UNA bosses like it."

Gadya cracks her knuckles in expectation. "I can't wait."

"We hope we have it on our side," I tell them. "The UNA has a nasty habit of surprising us—or have you forgotten?"

Cass doesn't answer, but Gadya looks my way. "Alenna's right. We need to keep our guard up. They might have EMP-resistant vehicles or weapons somewhere too, as a precaution."

"If they do, I haven't seen them yet," Cass says. "I think they were too arrogant to ever think that someone would challenge them on their home turf. I doubt that they're prepared for it."

We fly even lower, reducing our speed.

I feel my whole body tense up, so I try to relax. I was ready for battle, but that will be postponed until tomorrow. I have to save my strength until then. I exhale shakily, looking forward to getting out of the air and back on solid ground—even if that ground is soon going to become a battlefield.

20 NEW CHICAGO

A FEW MINUTES LATER, the helicopter lands, guided down to the roof of the skyscraper by the men with orange flares.

Before the rotors stop turning, we already fling open the doors and step out onto the helipad. It's so loud, I can barely hear. The wind blasts my face, blowing back my hair. It's cold up here. I see about ten people standing outside, all with friendly faces, watching us.

A few of them step forward to help us away from the helicopter.

We are led away from the helipad and toward a small structure on the roof, with an open door. There's a concrete stairway beyond the doorway, leading down into the building.

Liam, Gadya, Cass, and I follow the people into the stairway and out of the wind.

More flares and torches line the passageway. All the power is off. The electric lights in the stairway are dead.

"This way," one of the rebels says.

We follow him quickly into the stairwell and down the stairs. He opens a metal door for us. We head through it.

It takes me a moment to get my bearings. I realize we've

stepped into the wide hallway of a luxurious hotel. Gas lanterns light it up for us. The white carpet is thick and plush. The ceiling is high. It smells good in here, and it's warm.

"This must be the penthouse level," Cass says, the glee evident in her voice. "Where the richest UNA ministers stayed." She turns to look at us, her dark eyes flashing in the light of the oil lamps. "And now it's ours."

"Yeah, I feel like we've already won the war," Gadya cracks.

We start walking down the hall.

"These rooms are where we'll sleep tonight," one of the rebels calls back to us. "I bet you guys haven't seen a place like this in months."

"I've never seen a place like this," I tell him.

We stop at the large doorway to a room, and the rebel opens it up. It's a giant suite, with floor-to-ceiling windows providing a panoramic view of the darkened city. The room is cavernous. There's a king-size bed in the center, along with a huge leather couch and tables and chairs.

Even in the dim light from the oil lamps, everything looks so clean and fresh. I see a bathroom off to the side, with a shower and a soaking tub, and marble floors. *So these are the kinds of rewards you get if you decide to work for the UNA.*

I think about my parents' tiny apartment where I grew up, and the orphanage, and the wooden shacks on the wheel. We have sacrificed so much, while these UNA bureaucrats have gotten fat and rich, as they worked to enslave and control their own population. I feel a mixture of anger and disgust.

"We'll take it," Liam jokes about the room.

I'm expecting that we'll have to share the room with a bunch of other rebels, or at least with Gadya and Cass.

But the rebel just nods. Another rebel hands Liam a spare oil lantern. "We'll come for you in the morning," the rebel says. "Before sunrise at six a.m."

"What happens after that?"

"We go down to street level. More rebels and troop transports will be waiting there. We chase down the local minister. We tear down the pictures and statues of Minister Harka. And we liberate the people. We go door-to-door if we have to. We make the people rise up, if they want to or not."

The rebel starts to leave, swinging the door shut.

"Sweet dreams," Gadya calls out from behind him.

Then the door closes, and Liam and I are standing there in the middle of this extravagant room.

"At least we get one night in a place like this before we have to fight," I say.

Liam puts the oil lantern on a glass coffee table and walks over to me. He wraps his arms around me, hugging me tight. I nestle into his shoulder.

"Do you think we're going to win?" I ask him. "And what happens if we do? Maybe that's the question we should be asking."

"The scientists and rebels have a plan," he says, stroking my hair. "Once the UNA is deposed, they're going to take control."

I turn away from him to stare out the window. "Take control of what? A country with no electricity and without an infrastructure? We could have riots on our hands if we don't act fast."

"You sound like Dr. Urbancic a little," Liam says. He sounds vaguely amused.

"You think this is funny?"

"No," he says. "But I don't think we need to worry about that stuff yet. We still have a huge battle to fight and win."

"True."

"And the European Coalition will come and help."

"They'll take this country over."

"Maybe. Then we'll fight them."

I sigh, and move away from him and sit down on the bed. It's soft and comfortable. I'm not used to a bed like this. My body is aching all over. Liam can sense my discomfort.

"You okay?"

"Fine. Just a bit sore."

He comes over and sits down next to me and massages my shoulders. I stare at the city out the massive window, transfixed. Tomorrow this will become our battleground. But right now it seems peaceful.

"How many more of us are going to die?" I ask. The question rises out of me all of a sudden. I wasn't planning on asking it.

"No one else. Not if I can help it." Liam's strong hands continue to massage me, tenderly plying my flesh. I lean back against him.

"Can it really be this easy?" I ask. I feel like all my worries are tumbling out at once.

"Easy?"

"I just keep thinking that it's weird there isn't any resistance. There's no sign of any UNA soldiers."

"Maybe they're hiding. Or maybe they're trying to get sleep, like we should be doing."

"It just feels wrong to me. And what is our role in all of this? I feel like a cog in a machine. Did they just need us to get to Dr. Urbancic and detonate the bomb at the right time? Anyone could have done that."

"But they can trust us. They can't trust just anyone. I think that's why they value us so much. Trust is the one thing that has to be earned over time. You, me, and Gadya are never going to betray the rebel cause. The scientists know that—including your mom. They sent us because they could trust us to not screw up."

"I hope you're right."

"Are you thinking that something bad is going to happen? Tell me if you are. I learned on the wheel to always trust my instincts."

"I don't know. I guess I'm thinking there are probably some surprises left for us."

Liam nods. "I agree. But as long as we stick together, there's nothing that we can't do."

I suddenly feel like I'm about to cry. I've been holding back the flood of emotions for so long that I can barely take it anymore.

"I'm so sad about Rika," I tell Liam, shutting my eyes. My voice breaks. "And Alun, too. They didn't deserve to die. They died for nothing."

"No," Liam says, stroking my hair. "They died for this moment. So that we could get here and continue the battle for them."

"I hope it turns out to be worth it." I open my eyes again and wipe tears away with the back of my sleeve. "I want to feel like we're important. Like we're going to win."

"That part is up to us." Liam turns to face me. "We have to fight in their names." He pauses. "I lost so many good friends. I mean, before you got to the wheel. Other hunters that the drones killed when we were on different missions. I remember all their faces and names. Every single one. They're not really dead to me. At least they don't feel dead."

I nod. "I know what you're saying. But Rika and Alun should be here right now. So should David."

Liam nods. "There's hope for David. Maybe you'll see him again."

I lie down on the bed. Liam lies next to me and wraps his strong arms around me. "We need to get some sleep," I say. "While we still can."

The night passes quickly. Soon the sky is lightening. I can see it through the huge windows in our room when Liam wakes me up.

"It's time," he says.

I push the covers off me, get out of the bed, and slip my boots on.

Right then, a knock comes at the door. Liam walks over and opens it. Gadya and Cass are standing there. They are prepared for battle. Both of them are clutching lead-plated guns, and there are knives in their waistbands. "You guys ready?" Gadya asks.

"As ready as I'll ever be," I tell her.

"Good," Cass says. "We're heading downstairs right now to join the ground assault. It's seventy floors, so we gotta go fast."

"We can't take the helicopter from the roof?" Liam asks.

"It's already gone. C'mon."

Liam and I follow Gadya and Cass out of the room. We walk down the luxurious corridor toward the door that leads to the stairs.

"We need guns," I tell Cass.

She nods. "The rebels have them for you."

We reach the door that leads to the stairs and she opens it. Inside the stairwell I see two rebels, both of them armed.

"Where do we get guns?" Liam asks them.

"Ten floors down. We've set up a supply center there. We've got guns and knives, and anything else you might need. But you better hurry."

We move past them quickly and start going down the stairs. Our boots make loud noises that echo against the concrete walls.

We finally reach a door labeled FLOOR 60 and we pause.

"In here?" Liam asks.

Cass nods.

We go through the door.

Opposite the stairway is a hotel room. The door is propped open. Inside, the room has been turned into a weapons repository. I see rebels sitting in there, with a bunch of guns. Some are lead-plated machine guns that survived the EMP. Others are ancient-looking rifles that also survived the EMP because they had no electronic components.

Cass leads us to the doorway of the room. Rebels hand me and Liam lead-plated machine guns.

"Can I have two of them?" Liam asks.

The rebel shakes his head. "We need enough to go around. But you can have this." He tosses Liam a small, old silver pistol. It looks like something from a hundred years ago.

"Thanks." Liam sticks it into the back of his belt, where it gets hidden by his jacket.

Meanwhile, I clutch my machine gun. It's heavy. "Any secret to using this?" I ask the rebels.

"Just point it and fire," one of them says. "But it has a sharp recoil, so be careful."

"Put it against your shoulder," another rebel advises.

"We better go," Cass says.

We head out of the room and back across the hall, then into the stairway.

"Only sixty more flights," Gadya says. "Let's do it!"

Liam and I look at each other. And then we follow Gadya and Cass.

It takes about twenty minutes for us to get down to the bottom of the stairs, and into the massive lobby of the hotel.

Again, I'm struck by the deranged opulence. Everything is marble and glass. It looks palatial, with gleaming chandeliers overhead. I see large display screens everywhere, but all of them are black—destroyed by the pulse.

Outside, the sun is starting to rise.

I see crowds of people in the streets. These are the everyday citizens whom we saw earlier flooding the roads into the city. Now they have arrived. Some of them are clutching homemade banners. Everyone is congregating here, with the rebels trying to organize the chaos. The citizens of the UNA are taking this opportunity to fight back against the government.

We walk through the lobby and out the front doors of the hotel. Rebels stand positioned with guns along the wide street.

I finally hear the sound of vehicles. In the distance, I see two large trucks with lead-plated cabs heading our way. I also see another helicopter in the sky, way in the distance.

All of these vehicles belong to the rebels.

As we walk down the steps at the front of the hotel and toward the street, I hear the trucks broadcasting a message over loudspeakers. I struggle to hear it, and then I make out the words:

"The government of the United Northern Alliance has been overthrown by the rebel forces. You are safe! The power is currently down, but we will work to restore it. We will also try to hand out food and water shortly, if we have the resources, so please be patient. The UNA is finished. The people have retaken this country."

The words are greeted by cheers.

The voice continues speaking: "If you see any former UNA

soldiers or workers, you have the power to arrest and detain them. And if you are or were an employee of the UNA, you must officially surrender to us and join our side, or you will be arrested and punished. This new nation will be founded on trust and transparency. But if you claim to join our side and are later discovered to be spying, you will be put on public trial. This rebellion is taking place across the entire nation. From the tip of Canada to the southernmost part of Mexico."

"There might not be a battle for us to fight," Gadya says, looking around.

"I know." It seems as though everyone is on the same side. "What about finding the local minister and deposing him?" I ask. "The guy who runs this city?"

"Apparently some rebels went looking for him this morning, but they can't find him," Gadya says. "At least that's what Cass told me."

Cass nods. "It's true. He supposedly fled."

I think about Minister Hiram in his strange domain. I can't imagine him surrendering without a fight, or disappearing either. But maybe the minister who runs New Chicago is different.

I know that we have intervened just in time. With the government creating genetic mutants, and putting those MIODs inside kids, they were toppling into complete madness.

"Is there any news from the other cities?" Liam asks.

"Communications are pretty jammed up right now thanks to the EMP," Cass replies. "But from what we've heard, the other cities are similar to New Chicago. The UNA leaders are fleeing and the people are taking to the streets. It's what we hoped for all this time."

The helicopter flies closer overhead. I can hear it now. The crowd cheers.

298

"If the ministers and their men have fled into the forest, or to other cities, they'll be hunted down," Cass continues. "Once the travelers get here, there will be no way for them to hide."

I nod. I hope that they've fled. But I'm still uncertain about what's going to happen next.

Then I hear a strange noise. It's different from the sound of the helicopter—it's an unusual rumbling sound.

I look around for the source, but I don't see it.

"Do you hear that?" I ask.

Liam is already listening.

"Something's wrong," he says. Gadya pauses too. The bulk of the crowd is still moving around and cheering.

But then an object emerges in the sky. It's huge, plated with sheets of lead. I can't tell if it's a manned aircraft, or a gigantic feeler. On the bottom is the five-eyed new UNA logo.

It's shaped like an airplane, with a visible bomb bay underneath it, and racks of machine guns mounted under the wings. But it hovers as though it's a helicopter.

"Oh my god," Gadya says, raising her gun.

The crowd starts screaming in fear as they see it hover above the city. It grows closer to our street.

"Let's get back inside!" Cass yells.

But I'm transfixed by this strange aircraft.

As I watch, the bomb doors open, and I see black objects tumbling out of them.

Liam grabs my arm. "Let's go!" He says.

We all start moving back into the hotel.

And then the guns on the aircraft open up. At first I think they're going to fire at the people, but instead they fire directly at the approaching helicopter.

The helicopter is struck by a barrage of bullets. The bombardment is so fierce that the helicopter's blade is hit and destroyed almost instantly. The helicopter veers sideways and starts falling out of the sky.

Bullets continue to hit it precisely, as though the aircraft has locked on to it with some kind of tracking system.

"No!" Gadya yells, as the helicopter plunges downward.

It strikes the side of a skyscraper and bursts into flames. The crowd starts running, as bits of burning metal and glass rain down on them.

Then the aircraft turns its guns on the crowd, as it slowly moves forward down the street. Bullets rain down like hail. I see people get hit and fall face-first, dead.

We race up the stone steps and to the front doors of the hotel. When I look back, I see the strange black objects continuing to fall from the bomb bay doors.

I assume that they're bombs, but none of them are exploding yet.

Liam raises his gun and tries to fire at the aircraft, but it's too high up for him to hit. Gadya fires off some rounds too.

And then we reach the glass doors of the hotel and plunge back inside.

Citizens and rebels are racing around everywhere.

I'm stunned. But in my heart I knew that something bad would happen. Nothing is ever easy. The UNA somehow predicted our plans.

"What do we do now?" Gadya is yelling.

Cass looks shocked.

Liam grabs me. "Are you okay?"

I nod. "Yes."

Outside, more gunfire blasts the street, blowing out windows.

"I saw bombs—or something—falling from the plane."

"Me too. We better get deeper into the hotel."

"It has a basement," Cass says. "We can take shelter there if we need to."

But right then, I see something out the window, and I have a horrific realization. The plane was not dropping bombs on us after all. It was dropping something else entirely.

I can't even find the words. I just gesture out the windows for Liam and the others to look.

Cass yelps in surprise. I realize that unlike me, Gadya, and Liam, she hasn't seen these things before.

They are the small electronic spiders. The things called MIODs. Like the kind that burst out of Rika's friend.

"How did they survive the EMP?" Gadya asks.

"They must have been kept underground in some sort of lead-lined container," I say. And now hundreds—maybe thousands—of them are being dropped from the aircraft.

For a moment, we watch from the hotel lobby as the small metal creatures explode down the street, leaping onto people.

The rebels open up their guns, blasting at them. But more keep coming. The MIODs go for people's faces, trying to get inside their mouths and burrow their way into their bodies.

"We have to go and help!" I yell.

I start moving forward, and Liam does too, right at my side.

Gadya raises her gun. "Let's go!"

The four of us rush toward the hotel doors, ready to fight.

But two armed rebels step into our path.

"You can't go back out there," one of them says. "We've locked the doors. The doors and windows of this building are all bulletproof. That's why we chose it. We're safe in here."

"But what about the people in the street?" I yell. Outside it's becoming a brutal battle between the machines and the humans. On top of everything, the airship continues to fire down at the rebels with an endless barrage of bullets. "We're the rebels. We're supposed to be organizing everything! We can't abandon them!"

"We need to fight!" Gadya yells at the rebel, raising her gun.

"It's too risky to open these doors. You could put all of us in danger."

"Too bad!" Cass says.

Liam eyes the rebels. "Let us out," he says softly. "If we die, then at least we die fighting, and not hiding."

The two rebels look at each other. "Fine. But don't expect that we'll let you back in."

I nod. "That's a deal."

The rebels unlock the doors for a moment and Liam, Gadya, Cass, and I rush out of the hotel. The doors are instantly bolted behind us. There is no way to turn back now.

We raise our guns. In front of us is a sea of destruction. The MIODs are attacking the throngs of people. The rebels are firing back. Bullets destroy the MIODs, but there are just too many of them.

"Here they come!" Liam says, as a wave of MIODs rushes in our direction.

I aim and start firing. Like the rebel warned me, the gun has a huge kick. I almost lose control of it for a second as it rams against my shoulder. Then I manage to wrestle it back.

The four of us fire at as many of the MIODs as we can. They are hard to hit, but when we do hit them, they are blasted into little pieces.

302

"Take that!" Gadya screams as she unleashes a nonstop onslaught of bullets, spraying a row of MIODs. They disintegrate, spraying the roiling crowds with debris.

"Duck!" Liam suddenly yells at me.

I do what he says as bullets fire past our heads.

The aircraft is strafing us. We have to move.

As a group we rush down the steps at the hotel entrance and out to the street. Here we have less of a vantage point, but we are safer from the airship's guns because we are moving in the crowd.

"My gun's jammed!" Cass yells. She keeps pulling the trigger but nothing is happening.

Liam yanks out his spare pistol and tosses it to her.

"Thanks!" she calls back.

We keep moving forward.

I remember what it was like when the MIOD tried to get inside my mouth in the car. I'm not going to let any of those things come near me. I shoot sparingly but with precise aim. So does Liam.

We blast the MIODs into bits, working as a team.

I hear more noises in the sky and fear the worst.

But when I look up, I see another rebel helicopter up there. It's approaching the aircraft that hovers in the sky.

The aircraft begins to turn, but the helicopter is moving too fast.

For some reason the rebel helicopter isn't firing. It's just zooming through the air at top speed, right at the aircraft.

Then I understand what's going to happen.

It's a suicide mission.

The helicopter is going to fly directly into the aircraft.

The aircraft tries to pull back, but its size makes it unwieldy. MIODs keep falling from it, but it stops firing.

And then, a second later, the helicopter collides with it. There's a flash of white light, and a massive orange explosion.

I can't even see the helicopter anymore. It has just disappeared. But the aircraft has a huge burning, smoking hole in it. More explosions start happening as the aircraft begins to list sideways and disintegrate. It's going to crash.

I realize that whoever was piloting the helicopter just sacrificed their own life for all of us fighting down below.

Then an MIOD rushes toward me. I've been distracted. I raise my gun. But it's too late. I can't get it up in time. There's no room to fire.

Then there's a burst of light and the machine suddenly flies sideways, in pieces. I realize that Liam has shot it.

"Thanks," I say, exhaling shakily. For once I'm glad that Liam is looking out for me and protecting me, so I don't get killed. But I'm not going to admit that to him.

Then we hear the noise of destruction overhead as the huge aircraft sails into some nearby buildings and detonates. I crouch down. The ground shakes. The noise is unbearable for a moment, but then it quiets down. The UNA aircraft has been destroyed.

A cheer rises up from the remaining rebels and everyone else in the streets. The MIODs are still attacking them, but the tide is turning.

Liam, Gadya, Cass, and I keep shooting.

"We're gonna win!" Gadya yells.

"I hope so," I call back.

Another MIOD gets near us, and I blast it into a million pieces. There are bodies lying on the street. Some are wounded and some are dead. Once we've defeated these machines, then we're going to have to help all of these fallen fighters. I'm hoping this is the last battle I will ever have to fight.

I keep firing. We move forward, farther down the city street. The MIODs keep attacking, but the bullets keep them at bay. Now that the aircraft has been destroyed, their numbers are limited. We will be able to take them out, one by one.

I feel terrified but optimistic.

And that's when I see the first mutant, at the end of the street, heading straight in our direction.

21 MUTATIONS

"WHAT THE HELL IS that?" Gadya asks, as we stare at the huge, lumbering creature. Other people in the crowd have seen it too, and they've started firing in its direction. But for some reason, the bullets don't seem to hit it. Or if they do, they don't seem to cause it any pain. It just keeps moving.

The creature looks like the thing I saw in Minister Hiram's office, and the thing we saw out in the forest. But what it is—or why it's here—I have no idea. I fear that we are about to find out.

Then a familiar voice crackles out. It's loud enough to cut through the noises of the crowd. It's coming from all the government speakers lining the street. I thought they would be totally dead, but somehow they are functioning. Maybe they run on a protected power system, in case of emergencies.

"All rebels will be put to the death," the voice says through the speaker.

"It sounds like Minister Hiram," I say to Liam.

"And Minister Harka," Gadya points out.

All of us are confused. We stand there with the crowd of people and rebels. The mutant stands still too. Nobody is firing right now. All the MIODs have been destroyed, or have skittered off down side streets. Everyone wants to hear what the voice says.

"This is a temporary disruption, not a rebellion. The UNA is still in control of this nation, and this city. Put down your weapons. Or else you will be killed."

"He's bluffing. Whoever it is," Cass says.

"It's probably the minister who controls the city. The main one," I say. "You think he's still here?"

"Maybe," Liam replies. "But it could be remotely broadcast."

"If you do not surrender, then an army will be unleashed," the voice continues. "One that cannot be defeated. One that has a very different genetic code from yours. An army that does not need air, or sleep, or food. That is unaffected by radiation. It thirsts only for your death. It is the ultimate result of our genetic experiments. A perfect creature with eternal life."

"Great," Gadya mutters.

I raise my gun. There is no way we're going to surrender. In fact, more New Chicago residents are taking to the crowded streets. They are preparing to join the battle.

"These mutants are an unstoppable army. They are the future of the UNA. You are the past . . . unless you work with us, in harmony."

I remember all too well what happened when we surrendered to Meira on Island Alpha, right after the airships landed. There is no way I am going to make that mistake again.

Not a single person puts down their weapons. We all just stand there, waiting to hear if the voice says anything more.

"This is your last chance," it finally says. "And then your apocalypse begins."

"Go for it!" Gadya screams. She raises her weapon. We both aim at the mutant.

"Let's put this thing to sleep," I tell her. Other people in the crowd around us begin raising their old guns, knives, and home-made weapons as well and taking aim.

I hear the voice laugh. "You have done exactly what I thought you would. You have given me the perfect chance to test these mutants in a live environment." The voice pauses. "Today is your final day on earth. . . ."

With those words, we begin to fire.

The mutant rushes forward down the street.

It's only when it starts moving that I start to understand how fast it is. The bullets do nothing to stop it. Its rippling, bulging skin seems to absorb them, or perhaps repel them.

Even from a distance, I see that its face is contorted. Metal devices are locked on to its head. I wonder if it is being controlled without its knowledge, like a puppet made of flesh.

Everyone is screaming and yelling, as they continue to fire on the creature. It snarls and lashes out, trampling people and ripping them apart with its clawed hands.

And then I hear the sound of a stampede.

I turn and look as other, similar mutants emerge from the side streets. Some of them are as large and bulky as cars. They converge on the crowd, in a rabid frenzy of destruction.

I keep firing at them. I watch my bullets disappear into their nearly translucent flesh.

I'm suddenly reminded of the barrier on Island Alpha. The one we had to crawl through to get into the gray zone. It's like the skin of these creatures is coated with—or perhaps even made from—the same substance. Their flesh seems to slow everything down, like some sticky viscous fluid.

More mutants race into the streets. We are being overrun.

"We have to go back inside the hotel!" Cass yells.

There are now about thirty giant creatures on the street with us. Our weapons are useless against them for some reason. There are a couple thousand of us—a combination of citizens and rebels—but we are going to get massacred.

I see other people starting to flee. The crowd is going to disperse. We can't let the UNA win. But at the same time, we can't just get killed. Not after we've come so far.

"Cass is right!" I call out over the noise of the battle.

Liam nods. "Let's move."

We race back toward the hotel, turning every few seconds to fire behind us. We reach the steps and rush up them as a group to the doors.

Inside the hotel lobby, behind the foot-thick bulletproof glass, I can see the rebels standing there.

I reach the doors first, followed a second later by Liam. We slam our hands on the glass.

"Let us in!" I yell.

Gadya and Cass reach us.

"Hurry!" Cass screams at the rebels inside.

All of us are hammering on the glass. The rebels see us, but they don't make any move to open the door. I remember that they said they wouldn't let us back in, but this is an unexpected emergency.

My eyes lock with one of them. "Please!" I yell. He shakes his head.

I look behind me in fear and frustration. The mutants are overcoming the remaining humans. Soon they will spot us—if they haven't already.

Gadya steps back from the glass and raises her gun. "Watch out!" she yells at us. She backs up.

Then she begins shooting directly at the glass, from about six feet away.

It does nothing except put a few chips in the surface. Bullets ping past us as they ricochet off the glass. I duck.

"Be careful!" I yell.

Gadya stops firing.

The rebels are still watching us from inside. They are never going to open these doors.

"Alenna, look out!" Liam suddenly yells. I crouch down, sensing movement from behind me. Something passes over my head. I spin around.

One of the mutants has found us. If I hadn't ducked, a clawed arm would have grabbed me.

We back away from the mutant as a group. Gadya and Cass keep firing at it, but the mutant doesn't even seem to notice the bullets.

I stare at it closely.

It's some unholy combination of a human, an animal, and a monstrous cyborg. It's massive—at least ten feet tall. It's covered with muscles, but I also see electronic components that have been buried inside its pale, waxy flesh. It was once a person, but it has undergone a horrible transformation.

Its face is the most disturbing element. While it has two eyes, they no longer look fully human. Like a cat's eyes, each one has an additional protective gray eyelid that closes across it. And the eyes are very dark. Pitch black, with no whites. I can't see the irises.

The mutant opens its mouth. Its teeth are sharp and serrated, in tiny precise rows, like a shark's. I wonder what combination of DNA—or what drugs, chemicals and surgeries—produced this monster.

Its horrific appearance nearly mesmerizes me, but I break the spell. I aim my gun at its right eye and I fire.

But even its eye is protected. The bullet flicks off, deflected to one side. The protective gray lid has slammed down over the eye, covering it. It opens again, revealing that impenetrable blackness. The creature snorts like a horse, its awful gaze fixed on me.

Cass is now back at the doors, pounding on them for us to be let in.

Behind the mutant I can see others of its kind devastating the remaining people in the street. I'm so shocked that I can't even think straight.

The mutant moves forward.

I just let my gun hang down. There's no point wasting bullets.

Gadya is still firing, but Liam has stopped too.

Liam and I back away, edging closer to the hotel. I want us to run, but I don't want to turn my back on the mutant.

"Cass, c'mon!" I yell at her.

"Damn you!" Cass is busy screaming at the rebels in the hotel.

Time starts to slow down like molasses.

The mutant is still looking at me. Its mouth is hanging open. I can see its lolling, pitted pink tongue between its teeth.

Right then I have a sudden idea. I don't know whether it will work or not, but I have to try it.

The ultra-potent cyanide capsule from Dr. Urbancic.

These mutants have mechanical elements, but they are mostly biological, because they are based on human DNA. I doubt that the government expects us to have access to Dr. Urbancic's rare, premium-grade cyanide. Perhaps they did not prepare the mutants to withstand it.

The voice on the loudspeakers also said that these mutants

don't need food. Maybe the cyanide will both poison it and over-load its system. This mutant might be tough on the outside, but if I can get the cyanide capsule down its throat, maybe the cyanide will fry its internal organs. I have no idea if cyanide will even be toxic to this creature. Who knows how its biology works. But I'm going to guess that cyanide can't be good for it. My fingers fumble in my jacket pocket.

Gadya stops firing and glances over at me, just as I get the capsule out.

"No, wait—" she says, confused. For a second, she thinks I'm planning on ending my own life. But then she suddenly under-stands, as I raise my arm back. "Is that going to work?" she yells.

"I don't know!" I scream back.

"Do it!" Liam says, also realizing that I don't intend the capsule for myself, but for the mutant.

I fling the capsule straight into the mutant's gaping mouth.

It flies straight toward its target, glides over the surface of the mutant's tongue, and hits the back of its throat, where it disap-pears from view before the mutant can gag and spit it out.

As I watch, Gadya and Liam whip out their pills and pelt them into the creature's mouth. The mutant's mouth snaps shut, but it's too late. The mutant coughs and screeches, but it has ingested the capsules.

A split second later, the mutant lunges forward and goes into action. It lashes out at me with its long clawed arm. I fling myself to the concrete. Cass is rushing over now to help, but there's nothing she can do. If the cyanide doesn't work soon, there's probably no way we'll survive.

"Hey!" Liam screams at the mutant, firing at it again to dis-tract its attention from me. The mutant looks in his direction and begins to hiss and growl. It puts its head down low, like a feral dog, and begins moving toward him.

I see other mutants on the street heading our way too.

The mutant swings out at Liam, but Liam manages to roll out of the way at the last second. So far, the cyanide is doing nothing.

I race to Liam's side. Gadya and Cass start running over to us too.

The mutant is looking at us, and heading our way.

But then, it seems to catch a glimpse of Cass as she tries to dash past it, right behind Gadya.

The mutant pivots around, and snatches her up with a clawed hand.

Cass screams in pain as she fires her gun directly into its arm.

"Cass!" I yell, stopping in horror.

She keeps firing, but even at close range, the bullets do nothing to slow the creature's momentum.

It sinks its fangs into her chest and shoulder.

"No!" I scream, fumbling with my gun.

Liam runs forward and tries to grab her legs. I follow, right there with him. We manage to grab on to her feet. I can smell the stink of the mutant from here—an oily, sweaty chemical odor.

Blood is rushing down from Cass's body to the concrete.

The mutant whips its head sideways, digging its teeth even deeper into her chest. I lose my grip on her shoe. The mutant rears up, tearing at Cass's flesh. She screams once, loudly. Then she stops.

Gadya runs forward but slips on the blood and careens sideways, slamming down on the ground.

More mutants are headed our way. The street is filled with bodies of the rebels. And the regular civilians have fled.

This is it. This could be the end.

But then I notice something unusual. The mutant is moving less rapidly now. Its motions are spasmodic and strange. It flings Cass's body down to the street. Then it staggers sideways, jerking and twitching.

It takes me a second to realize that the cyanide must finally be having an effect on it. But it's too late for Cass.

I rush to her side as the mutant claws at its own throat and chest, staggering away from us with unholy cries.

"Cass, hang in there!" I yell, as I kneel down next to my friend.

She moves her head. But she can't speak. Blood is welling out of her mouth. I have flashbacks to Rika's death. And Veidman's death. "Please don't die," I tell her. "Stay awake."

"I'm so tired," she manages to whisper.

"I know. It's going to be okay. We'll get you out of here."

She stares back at me. Her eyes don't look frightened. They look oddly peaceful.

Blood is pumping out from the massive lacerations in her chest and arms.

Liam and Gadya are now at my side.

"Cass, c'mon," Gadya says. "You can pull through this."

"I'm going to pick her up, so we can get her help," Liam says.

But right then, Cass's eyes roll back in her head.

"Cass, no——" I gasp.

She opens her mouth to try to say something to us. I'm clutching her hand. And then her head falls sideways and she exhales.

I have heard this sound before.

Cass is dead.

I keep holding her hand. Gadya stands up. "Damn you!" she yells, firing her weapon at the remaining mutants. They slither and plod their way toward us. They are moving slower now that we have injured one of them.

The one that we poisoned has fallen onto its knees, choking and coughing up white foam. These mutants might be immune to bullets, but we've found a way to bring down one of them. Unfortunately, we have no more cyanide, and the other mutants keep advancing on us.

"We're going to die next," I say to Liam. I've accepted it. I let go of Cass's hand and grab on to him, and he puts his arm around me.

"We're not going to die. We need to run," he says. But for once, even in *his* voice, I hear little hope. These mutants can catch up to us. We won't be able to get away from them.

Then I hear a noise. I glance up, expecting the worst. But instead, I see the door to the hotel opening.

"Come on!" a voice calls to us from inside. "Hurry up!"

"Gadya!" I yell. "Look!" She turns around and sees the open door. Liam and I stand up. The three of us all run toward the hotel as fast as we can.

I glance back at Cass's body. There is no way to bring her body with us. Her journey is over.

I reach the open door and barge inside, along with Liam and Gadya.

I don't feel sad about Cass's death right now—I feel angry.

Two rebels bolt the door behind us, and two more approach us.

I can no longer control my rage.

I take my gun and rush at the nearest rebel. I slam him in the face with my weapon. He goes flying down to the marble floor. His head bounces on it.

"Cass died because of you!" I yell. Liam grabs me from behind, trying to calm me down. But it doesn't work. I wrench myself out of his grasp.

Gadya understands how I feel. She takes her gun and points it at one of the other rebels. "Why didn't you let us inside earlier?" she asks. "It took our friend getting killed before you'd open the door? Huh?"

"Stop," Liam is saying. "We're on the same side."

"Are we?" I snap at him, my anger boiling over. The rebel that I hit is now getting up, rubbing his jaw. "They're the reason that Cass is dead!"

I suddenly hear the sound of heels on the marble. A woman has just entered the huge lobby, coming down from a staircase.

I'm startled to see that it's Dr. Vargas-Ruiz.

"I instructed them to let you in," she says, her voice cutting through the din. "They didn't do it because your friend died. They would have let all of you die. They must protect as many of their men as possible, especially after the massacre."

I look at her. "I don't understand what's going on anymore. What are we doing? Whose voice did we hear out there on the loudspeakers? How come we didn't know about these mutants? We walked right into a death trap!"

Liam is staring at her too. We're all trying to figure the situation out.

Dr. Vargas-Ruiz walks over to Liam, Gadya, and me. "Lower your guns."

I reluctantly do what she says.

"We've discovered who is running the UNA now." She pauses. "You might already know this—or have suspected it. But the leaders in charge of the UNA are Minister Harka's former body doubles. His look-alikes. They are the ones who ousted him several years ago. They were able to keep up the deception that he was still alive until they could take full power. They managed to completely take over the government and rename themselves. They are the ones who now run things, from five different cities."

I'm nodding. "I've met one of them. Minister Hiram."

She nods. "Yes." Then she continues speaking. "The body doubles continued the genetic experiments begun by Minister Harka and took them to new levels he never dreamed of. Those creatures out there were once normal teenagers, but they have been given drugs and have undergone surgical modifications. To become monsters."

"What do we do?" Gadya asks.

"Is the body double who controls New Chicago still in the city?" I ask.

Dr. Vargas-Ruiz nods. "Yes. Minister Harvan. He was so confident he would win this battle, he didn't actually leave. He's in another skyscraper, not far from here. It's heavily fortified." She turns away. "Come with me. I'll tell you more as we go."

"Where are we going?" Liam asks.

"David is here on the penthouse level. I'll take you to him."

"*David?*" I stare at her retreating figure. "For real?"

"Yes. Follow me. We have to be quick."

Liam, Gadya, and I exchange looks. I can't believe that David has made the journey here, or that he's in this hotel with us. We walk after Dr. Vargas-Ruiz across the marble floor.

The rebel that I hit with my gun eyes me warily, but he doesn't say anything. I'm still furious and heartbroken about what happened to Cass. It didn't need to be that way. The rebels could have let us inside. *If people are still as heartless as they were under the UNA, then nothing will ever really change.* I wonder if

David could have intervened to prevent Cass's death. Does he even know that it happened? He and Cass were friends. I keep following Dr. Vargas-Ruiz, with a heavy heart.

We head toward the stairway. David is waiting for us, seventy flights up, and I have some questions for him.

22 _THE TOP FLOOR

THIRTY MINUTES LATER WE reach the top floor of the
building. My mind is fading in and out. I can barely feel my legs. I
keep thinking over and over about Cass.

Dr. Vargas-Ruiz leads us out of the stairway, back into the luxurious hallway. I glance out a huge window and see the streets
beneath us. Even from here I can see the bodies and all the carnage. The mutants are still roaming below us.

"Is it like this everywhere?" I ask. "I mean, in the other cities?

Dr. Vargas-Ruiz nods. "Worse."

"How can it be worse?"

"In New Washington and New Los Angeles there are almost
no survivors."

"What about the next wave? When the travelers get here?"
Liam asks.

"They're still coming, but now we know what we're up against.
This is going to be a tougher battle than we thought."

"So we were the guinea pigs?" I ask her. "We were supposed
to sacrifice our lives so you guys could figure out what kinds of
secret weapons the UNA possessed?"

Dr. Vargas-Ruiz shakes her head. "No. You are soldiers. Rebels, just like me. And just like the ones who will come after us. In war, nothing can be predicted. We had no more idea of what to expect than you did. I thought our plan of creating the EMP might destroy enough UNA technology to bring us victory." She pauses. "But it didn't turn out that way. At least not yet."

"So there's still hope?" I ask. "Did David know about the mutants?"

She nods. "David will explain everything. Come with me to the penthouse conference room."

Gadya looks at me. "David better have a great trick up his sleeve to get us out of here."

"I hope he does," I tell her.

We continue to follow Dr. Vargas-Ruiz. She leads us to a giant opening with two huge doors.

"Guns," she says, holding out her hand to receive our weapons. "For security reasons."

I shake my head. There is no way I'm giving up my gun after what happened outside.

"You have to, or I can't let you into the room," Dr. Vargas-Ruiz says. Liam and I pause.

Gadya suddenly steps forward, gun raised, and kicks open the door to the penthouse conference room.

"Wait!" Dr. Vargas-Ruiz calls out furiously.

But it's too late. We barge inside the room right after her. The room is massive and bright, with three glass walls, which make it an excellent vantage point to watch the streets below. It is completely empty of furniture.

I instantly stop moving and stagger backward. Liam grabs me.

David is standing there in the center of the room, facing the door. Since I last saw him, he has undergone additional transformations. His body is larger and bulkier, and his stomach is swollen as though he is bloated with some sort of terminal disease. Metal braces help support his legs.

More wires come out of him, attached to a computer system resting on wheels next to him, like an old person's oxygen tank.

"Oh my god," Gadya says. The three of us stand there staring.

I can't even speak.

Because it's not only David's appearance that has shocked us.

It's the fact that he is not alone in the room.

Standing around him are five horrific and terrifying figures in black UNA military uniforms, their lapels draped with ribbons and medals.

These are Minister Harka's body doubles.

I recognize Minister Hiram instantly. The others look similar— malformed, with plastic faces, dyed-black hair, and deranged eyes.

"You were supposed to take their guns!" David snaps at Dr. Vargas-Ruiz.

"I couldn't get them in time." Dr. Vargas-Ruiz shuts and locks the door behind us. She remains in the room.

"What the hell is going on?" Liam says, raising his weapon.

David gives him a mock salute. "Welcome to your future."

For once, Gadya is too stunned to say anything.

I look from David to Dr. Vargas-Ruiz and back again. My finger finds the trigger of my weapon.

"I know this is not what you expected," David begins, taking a step toward me, dragging the computer system on wheels along with him.

"Don't move," I warn him. "Those mutants might be immune to my bullets, but I know you aren't. David, what are you doing?"

A few of the body doubles chuckle.

"I told you she was feisty," Minister Hiram says to another nearly identical-looking man in black.

Seeing all the body doubles here at once is surreal, and it makes me feel sick. There are essentially five Minister Harkas. It is as though they have multiplied in my absence from the UNA. We have done nothing to stop them. And David seems to be on their side. *So does Dr. Vargas-Ruiz.* I feel lost.

"Explain this to me," I say to David angrily.

He nods. "Sure. The scientists and I made a wrong prediction. Just a single one. We didn't realize how far along the UNA had come in developing the mutants as weapons of war." He pauses. "We really did think that we could win. But after today, we realize that it is no longer a possibility."

I feel like I'm going to throw up.

"What are you saying?" Liam asks him, his voice low and dangerous. "Have you gone crazy?"

Dr. Vargas-Ruiz steps past us and over to David's side. "He's saying that we've decided to negotiate a civilized surrender."

"A what?" I'm shocked.

"Civilized?" Gadya yells. "Is that what you call the massacre down there?"

David nods. "Those were necessary casualties. Collateral damage. We can't overcome the mutants," he says. "The other cities have been recaptured by the UNA."

"This can't be happening," Gadya says, sounding dazed.

"We're going to work together," David continues smoothly. "I've convinced Dr. Vargas-Ruiz and the others that it is for the best. The only other choice is death for all of us. In fact, the ministers want to help us—if we help them."

"You mean betray everything we stand for!" I say.

I'm stunned.

Liam, Gadya, and I all have our guns ready now.

I never believed that David would turn on us like this. "How could you do this to us? It doesn't make sense! When did your views change? You're supposed to be a rebel, not some fascistic UNA supporter!"

"My views never changed. The situation changed. I had to be flexible and change with it." He pauses. "What I learned was that the UNA is not so different from us. The ministers will do anything to keep their power. And we will try anything to take it away from them. We are like two equal but opposing forces. Yet if we put those forces together, then who knows what can be achieved? I don't want to die, or rot in a UNA jail cell. I want to have access to their technology and continue my research." He lifts a hand. "They are interested in the future of the human race. So am I."

"You've lost your way," I tell him. "You're not thinking straight anymore."

"Look. We did our best," David said. "We must be gracious in our defeat. The ministers could have killed us by now if they wanted to. Remember that."

I see Minister Hiram and two of the other body doubles nodding in the corner.

"We need you," Minister Hiram says to me, Liam, and Gadya. "To help bridge a gap between us and the populace. Come and work for us and David. We can restore the power, because we have hidden generators deep underground. We will rebuild everything, and turn a corner in the UNA, so that we can defend ourselves against the European Coalition. You will have every luxury that you desire—"

"Luxuries mean nothing to me," I spit.

"Me either," Gadya seconds.

"What if we say no?" Liam asks in the silence. "Then you kill us, right? That's how this works."

Minister Hiram shrugs. "Not necessarily."

I look at David. I stare into his remaining human eye. I wonder whether this is some kind of elaborate scheme to help us win against the UNA. For a moment, my heart leaps with hope. But I don't see that in his eye. I see something dark and resolute. It's like his physical change has created a mental change.

"David?" I ask.

"Yes?"

"Did you always know this would happen? Did you plan this all along?"

"No," he says. "How could I have known?"

"Because you know everything. More than anyone else. You always have."

"I think on my feet."

But for once, I'm not confused anymore. I have known him long enough. I see something behind his eye that lets me know he is lying. *He planned this. He knew it would end this way.* With him in a position of power. Working with the very people who destroyed the country, for his own personal gain. This is not some arbitrary decision on his part.

I now realize in horror that he only wanted to defeat the UNA so that he could take it over. He is power-mad.

He never wanted to kill these leaders.

He merely wanted to become one of them.

I raise my gun. "You're lying. You've always been an egomaniac and a monster. I was just foolish enough to believe in you, and help you."

"That's not true!"

I aim my gun at his chest. "Prove it."

"Come on," David says. "This is crazy. We're beyond violence now. Haven't we seen enough murder and killing?"

On either side of me, I see that Gadya and Liam have taken aim as well.

The ministers back away from David, taking out guns of their own. The guns are pointed at us.

David holds out his arms, beseechingly. "If you fire, then you die. We want your abilities on our side. You're smart. You're good fighters. We can use you. Think of your journey to this room as one big test. You've proved yourselves. Don't do anything stupid."

"You know what, David?" I ask.

"What?"

"Liam always said you were untrustworthy. I should have listened to him."

"Just put down the gun."

Everyone is watching us. I can feel the ministers' guns pointed at me. The only reason they aren't firing is because they know that if they do, I will fire on reflex and strike David. My finger is tight on the trigger.

"Think about everything we shared!" David says. "You don't have to do this, Alenna. Calm down and lower the gun, and we can talk about it. There are ways to make this work out for all of us."

"Why did you want me here so badly?" I ask him, my mind churning. "What was so important about us going to see Dr. Urbancic? You could have gotten anyone to do that. Why us? Why me?"

He stares back. "Because you're the only one who always

believed in me, Alenna." He lets the words sink in. "You're the only one who never lost faith in me, no matter what I did on Island Alpha. You helped everyone else to trust me. You never wavered. I knew I could count on you to set off that bomb, and to have blind faith in me."

His words strike me like blows.

He used me.

"There weren't five teams out there, setting off nuclear bombs," he continues. "Just one team. You guys. When you pressed that button, it detonated the entire network of nuclear bombs and unleashed the EMP. I just made everyone think differently. It was up to you all along."

"You played us for fools," I say, trying not to cry, from rage and sorrow.

"You bastard," Liam says to David. I half-expect Liam or Gadya to fire at him, but they don't. At least not yet. If any one of us shoots, we will probably all die in a hail of bullets.

"I knew that Alenna would make sure that button got pushed," David says. "Liam, I could have had you killed, but I was afraid that your death would distract her. She's the only reason that you're alive. Same goes for you, Gadya."

I keep the gun steady on David. I have been trained to be a warrior, but I never thought I would have to aim a gun at David. My hand starts shaking. It's slight, but David sees it.

"It's okay," he says. "You don't need to kill anyone now. Not ever again. The key to success is working together. We can build a new future, even if it's not the one you were thinking of when you came here."

"What are your plans?" I ask him, choking the words out. "Become some benevolent ruler? The ministers will never let that happen and you know it. The UNA will just continue onward, like it is."

"That's not true. We can change things from within. The ministers have seen how unhappy the people are, and they realize they nearly lost the battle for the country. They want to start over. We can create a fairer and better UNA. It won't be perfect, but we can slowly work to improve conditions for everyone—"

"Stop lying!" I yell at him. My hand starts shaking more. I know that he is lying. I know that I should shoot him. He betrayed me. He was never my friend. He only saw me as someone gullible that he could use as a pawn in his psychotic plans. But I still can't do it. I blink tears away. I know that if I lower the gun, or Liam and Gadya start shooting, one of the ministers will shoot me. My finger loosens on the trigger.

"We've suffered so much," David continues, in an oddly soothing voice. "Each one of us. We tried our best. It's not wrong to accept a deal with the ministers now. We can have actual lives again. Don't you want that? And who knows—maybe there's a chance for you and me to have a life together, Alenna. I've always liked you. I just need you to see things my way."

"David—" I begin angrily.

Then I see something. Hidden in his hand is a small object. I don't know what it is, or where it came from.

"Raise your hands," I yell, tightening my grip on the trigger again. I'm aiming right at his heart.

In that instant, David raises his hands. I see that he has a gun. It must have been hidden up the sleeve of his jacket. And now it's pointed at Liam. No matter what his plans are for me, he's going to shoot the boy I love. I can't let that happen.

Before I can think about it, I pull the trigger.

David fires too, shooting wildly as Liam leaps out of the way. David staggers back as my bullet hits him, but he stays on his feet. The gun falls from his hand.

There's a split second of silence after the gunshots.

David looks at me, stunned.

"You shot me!" he says, sounding angry and hurt. Surprisingly, the ministers keep standing there, watching us closely. They don't fire. And they do nothing to help David. Neither does Dr. Vargas-Ruiz. I shot to kill David, but somehow he is still alive.

"Why would you shoot me?" he asks, sounding stunned. "You weren't supposed to do that!"

"Because you pointed a gun at Liam!" I yell. "Because you were going to kill him, and probably Gadya too!" I know it to be true. They are disposable to him now. More blood is coming out of David's wound.

"But I'm not supposed to die," he says. "Your friends are. . . . Not me. . . ."

"No, they're not," I tell him. "None of us are." I feel so shaky, I can barely stand up. I grab on to Liam for support. Both of us are breathing hard, transfixed by David and the stone-faced ministers.

A trickle of blood starts coming down David's shirt, and he wheezes for air. He raises a hand to his chest. "This whole time I thought you liked me. I thought I could manipulate you." He sounds oddly thoughtful and quizzical. The anger is gone from his tone now. "I didn't think you'd do this to me." He stumbles backward, nearly getting caught on the wires surrounding him. "How can you not understand. We lost. . . . There's no point being . . . on the losing team." His breath is coming in gasps.

"I'd rather be true to myself than win," I tell him.

I'm still waiting for the ministers to open fire on us, but it doesn't happen. They just keep watching David with their nearly identical faces.

David continues looking at me. My hand is shaking but I don't lower my gun. "Didn't you care for me at all?" he asks. He takes another step back. More blood is soaking through his shirt. "I'm . . . surprised."

"It doesn't matter what I felt for you once," I tell him, revolted by his actions. "That's over now. I don't care about people who switch sides. Who play the system. Who use other people. You took any feelings I might have had for you and threw them away. You were willing to kill me. You just never thought I would be willing to kill you. Face it. You're the one who lost."

David is getting pale. He glances back at Dr. Vargas-Ruiz. She has backed away into a corner of the room, expecting a gun battle. "I told you to take their weapons. . . ." David murmurs. "Just in case." He looks at me. "Why did you choose Liam over me? I still don't understand . . ."

Then he abruptly collapses backward onto the floor, in a jarring tangle, slamming his head down hard.

Gadya grips my arm. We don't know what's going to happen next.

I look away from David and see that all five ministers have their guns pointed at us again. Perhaps we will not be getting out of this room alive. I just hope we can take some of the ministers down with us.

I hear faint coughing sounds from David. He is dying. *I have killed him. I can't believe it. I feel like I'm going to pass out.* Then his choking sounds become even louder and more agonized. I see blood flowing from his lips, followed by some kind of strange tentacle.

I gasp.

"It's a MIOD!" Gadya yells.

Indeed, a large metallic tentacle is clawing its way out of David's mouth. David's body seizes up as he goes into his final death throes. The MIOD begins emerging, prepared to attack us.

My hand is too unsteady to shoot. But Liam and Gadya both fire at once, exploding the metal creature into fragments.

Is this why David did it? Did the ministers implant him with one of these, as a means to control him and keep him in line? I don't understand. Rika had one of those in her, but she was still willing to sacrifice herself so that we could live. David has no excuse. He made his choices. And he had to live and die by them.

Then the entire building begins to shake.

Confused and scared, I grab out for Liam. The floor feels like it's moving. The ministers run to the windows to look out.

I hear the roar of engines out the window.

Dr. Vargas-Ruiz tries to make a dash for the doors, but Liam grabs her.

"You traitor!" he yells at her.

"No, wait—" she cries out. "The ministers made me do it. I have a family. My brother and his young children. They said they'd have them killed if I didn't go along with their plans. Please don't hurt me." But in her hand, I see a small, sharp silver knife appear. Liam doesn't see it yet.

"You're lying," he says to her.

"Liam, look out!" I yell.

Just in time, he lurches back, barely avoiding her blade.

Then gunshots ring out and she falls backward. Gadya stands there. She has shot Dr. Vargas-Ruiz twice in the stomach. Dr. Vargas-Ruiz retches and falls to the ground. She tries to crawl away on all fours, like an animal.

I rush over to her and yank her up by her hair as she screams.

"How could you do this to us? Was my mother in on this?" I yell. I snatch the knife away from her.

Her scared eyes find mine. "No . . . ," she moans. "And I was never a rebel scientist. I was an operative for the UNA . . . sent to control the rebels as best I could. . . . Matthieu Veidman was my son. . . . Please—" She clutches at my hands. "Please forgive me for what I did to all of you."

I let go of her hair and she falls facedown to the floor, in an ever-widening pool of blood.

That's when the gunfire starts in earnest. The ministers begin firing their weapons at us. I fling myself down and narrowly avoid getting hit.

Outside the windows I inexplicably see aircraft rising up.

We are doomed.

These must be UNA craft. Clearly, thanks to David's and Dr. Vargas-Ruiz's treachery, the ministers knew all about our plans.

"Duck!" Liam yells, sheltering me as the aircraft closest to us opens fire.

The thick glass windows explode under the massive barrage of supercharged antitank shells from the aircraft.

I slide onto the floor, trying to grab hold of Liam and Gadya.

I see one of the ministers get hit in the head with a piece of shrapnel, as a wave of flying glass blasts over him. He screams, staggers a few steps forward, disoriented, desperately trying to pick glass out of his eyes, and then tumbles out the broken window. His screams echo back to us as he plunges to his death seventy stories below.

The other ministers are firing at us, and out the windows as well.

"They're not UNA aircraft!" I scream, in a moment of sudden understanding.

Gadya looks at me as she fires back at the surviving ministers. "What?"

Liam has realized the same thing. "It's ships from the European Coalition!"

We race toward the doors and unlock them as bullets fly.

I tumble into the hallway with Liam and Gadya. Behind us, the airplanes from the European Coalition continue to shoot at the ministers in the room.

Liam slams the doors behind us.

Rebels race out into the hallway, guns drawn. For a moment I think they will shoot us.

"Stop!" I yell. "David and Dr. Vargas-Ruiz were traitors! We're on the same side!"

"The Europeans are here!" Liam says.

The rebels look confused.

"No more shooting!" I call out. "But we need to get out of this building right now! The ministers are in the conference room. Kill them!"

The rebels don't disagree with that. Some immediately head into the room with their guns raised. The whole building is shaking as bombs hit nearby. I'm worried that the European Coalition will start bombing the hotel before we can get out.

We all run down the hall together and back to the stairway, heading down to ground level. I can't even believe what has happened.

I feel sick, but I also feel jubilant. The ministers and the mutants will all be killed by the European aircraft. The mutants might be able to survive bullets, but I doubt they can survive missiles and bombs. I just hope the same thing is happening in the other cities.

We hammer down the stairs as a group, moving as quickly as possible. More rebels enter the stairway at different levels and join us, forming a throng. Finally, we all burst back out into the lobby.

Through the massive windows, I can already see the bodies of mutants littering the street, along with the bodies of so many fallen rebels and citizens. Bomb craters are everywhere.

We run across the marble floor to the doors. I fling them open, and we race outside.

I immediately look up.

The sky is filled with planes. In the distance I can see more explosions. The European Coalition is destroying the remains of the UNA.

I clutch Liam's hand.

Liam, Gadya, and I stand there on the steps outside the hotel for a moment. I look behind me. The entire top floor of the building is on fire. David and the ministers are history.

"We're free," I say.

"I hope it turns out that way," Gadya replies.

"It will," Liam says. "I just know it."

I shut my eyes. All I can see is David's face. I know that I did the right thing. I want to be on the winning side only if they are fighting for the right reasons. The UNA is evil. It deserves to be torn down.

David lost his way, or perhaps he was corrupt all along. I don't want to fight the European Coalition. I want them to help us. This country is going to need every bit of help it can get.

Citizens who were hiding in other buildings, or on side streets from the mutants, are rushing back to the main street. They are dazed and pale, wearing shocked expressions. Nobody can understand what's going on. People are too stunned from the carnage to be congratulating one another.

Planes continue to fly overhead, bearing the emblem of the European Coalition.

"We're going to have to rebuild everything," I say.

Gadya sighs. "I guess so."

"We did it on the wheel," I tell her. "We can do it again here."

"This is our home," Liam agrees. "We can make it anything we want it to be. What happens next is up to us."

For a moment, I'm seized with a burst of optimism. I hug Liam. The three of us are still alive. And the UNA has been defeated. No matter what happens next, we achieved our goal.

"We did it," I tell Liam and Gadya. "We should be happy."

Liam nods. "This is victory, even if it doesn't feel like it yet."

Gadya looks at me. "We killed the UNA."

More citizens are flooding the streets.

"Victory," I say, looking around. "We have to make it count. We have to make it worth it for Cass, Rika, Alun, and everyone else who didn't survive."

Liam and Gadya nod. We stand there together, watching the street for a moment.

Right then I see a figure approaching us out of the corner of my eye. He's swaddled in gray blankets.

I turn toward him as he nears us, thinking that it's a civilian survivor of the massacre, possibly injured and needing our help.

His face is hooded by a blanket. He is about twenty paces away before I realize that this is not an ordinary person. There is something unusual about his gait and posture.

Gadya and Liam notice it at the exact same moment.

"Stop walking," Liam calls out to the figure, raising his gun.

Then the figure throws off his blankets.

It's Minister Hiram.

Somehow he must have gotten out of the penthouse conference room. His face is burned and raw, but he is very much alive. And he is smiling at us.

Gadya and I raise our guns, as we call out warnings to everyone. "Look out!" I yell. "It's one of the ministers!"

Minister Hiram keeps walking as we begin peppering him with bullets. They tear into his clothes and flesh but he continues moving.

"I have a gift for you rebels," he cries out, raising his black-gloved hands above his head.

I remember him back in that creepy room in New Dallas. How he touched my shoulder, and I felt electrical shocks. I didn't know what to make of it then, and I still don't. But I sense that he possesses some final kind of weapon that he wants to unleash on us.

"Keep your distance!" I yell, as the three of us keep backing away from him. The bullets aren't slowing him.

And then he yanks off one of his gloves and flings it to the concrete. I see that his hand is missing. In its place is a steel prosthetic, with lead-coated robotic fingers. He pulls off the other glove, revealing the same. Both his hands have been hacked off and replaced, like a cyborg.

A bullet pings off one of his metal fingertips.

Everyone is yelling and screaming.

Liam manages to hit him in the neck with a round, and the minister drops down to one knee in the street. He keeps holding his metal hands above his head. And he keeps smiling.

"You will never win!" he calls out with his final breath, as he touches his metal hands together. "The UNA will live forever!"

Instantly there's a huge roar of sound, as the street buckles underneath us. I lose my balance and fall down. It's like an earthquake is beginning. The ground is shaking and it won't stop.

Minister Hiram collapses. His metal hands have clearly acted as a detonation switch. When he touched them together, it began a chain reaction of explosions under the city streets.

"They must have put bombs underground!" Liam calls out. Everyone is screaming. I see buildings shaking. The noise becomes a deafening roar. It's like the city is self-destructing.

"Run!" I cry out. We start racing away, trying to find safety. Huge openings appear in the street, like massive sinkholes. I see people falling down into them, to their deaths. Bits of debris start toppling from buildings, as windows explode from the vibrations.

I hear more explosions beneath my feet as we keep running. This is the end of New Chicago. The UNA would rather destroy the entire city than accept any form of defeat.

I should have expected something like this. But I really thought it was over, and that we had won.

"Watch out!" Gadya screams, as a huge chunk of stone lands nearby to our left. On our right, more of the street collapses. We run faster. I'm not even sure where we're headed. All around us is total chaos.

Buildings are beginning to disintegrate. I know that some of them are going to collapse and fall onto the streets. The bombs will tear this place apart.

Suddenly the noise of explosions gets louder. A large part of the cement road drops away in front of me. I stop just in time and crouch down to the ground. Liam and Gadya are next to me.

We're looking around, trying to find a safe path out of the devastation. The noise is almost unbearable.

"Which way do we go?" Gadya yells.

"I don't know!" I reply.

Liam stands up. "We just have to keep moving! Get away from the city center!"

Clouds of dust are roiling around us. My whole body is shaking as the street keeps moving. More explosions go off. We try to start running, but it's nearly impossible to dodge the falling parts of buildings, and the holes opening under our feet. I can hear the European Coalition aircraft thundering above us, but they can't help us down here.

We're heading up a side street when it finally happens. I step forward, just as a huge slab of concrete gives way.

I scream, and try to back up, but it's too late. The entire city is crumbling beneath us. I slam downward, gasping in pain, as I fall straight into the abyss.

"Liam!" I cry out.

And then I hit my head and everything goes black.

EPILOGUE

Two Years Later

TWO YEARS HAVE PASSED since the day when the European Coalition took control of the former UNA—and the day when the ministers' hidden bombs destroyed New Chicago. Since then, so much has happened. We are trying to get our lives back. Things are progressing, but they are far from perfect.

I survived my fall into the hole that day. Gadya fell with me, and she survived as well. Liam was able to climb down and bring us up one by one. We were both unconscious. Other rebels came and helped Gadya. But Liam carried me out of there himself, and to safety.

When the bombs finally ceased detonating, the city was mostly ruins. Tens of thousands of people died that day. It was the final strike by the UNA before they were consigned to history forever.

I broke both of my ankles in the fall. Although they have healed, I now walk with a slight limp. It's barely noticeable. Only on damp days do my bones ache, making me feel like an old person.

Gadya was less lucky. She cut her foot open on some of the

debris and the wound became infected. Her foot had to be amputated. But in typical fashion, this has done little to slow her down. The scientists made her a prosthetic, and she is able to get around nearly as fast as I can. Both of us know that these wounds are a small price to pay for what we were able to achieve on that day.

The United Northern Alliance was officially disbanded. Canada, the United States, and Mexico were immediately reinstated as independent democratic nations under the provisional and temporary guidance of the European Coalition—the peaceful consortium of European countries that helped save us from the UNA's tyranny.

The European Coalition worked with the rebels to help quickly restore electricity by rebuilding power stations and the electrical grid, as well as the infrastructure of the nation.

The travelers and the scientists returned from Island Alpha to assist in the rebuilding effort. The travelers put their ingenuity and skills to work to remake the nation.

Even Dr. Barrett slowly found his way back to something close to sanity. He was brought back from Island Alpha and spent several months in the hospital. He will never be the same man that he once was, but he seems to be at peace with himself. Occasionally I see him in the news, being hailed as a war hero.

I was reunited with my mother three months after the UNA fell, as well as with other surviving friends, including Emma. I was still recovering from my injuries. My mom and I vowed never to be separated again. We both know how close we came to not seeing each other alive. Some of my friends disappeared, never to be seen again. I assume they are dead. Markus is one of them. We searched for him for a long time before finally giving up hope.

The power was restored to most of the country not long after that. Electronic devices were imported from Europe to allow for communication and access to the Internet. Newspapers began printing again, and television stations slowly came back on the air, most of them running news twenty-four hours a day.

One of the cornerstones of the new United States is a complete freedom of information and transparency. A free press exists, and a multitude of voices are allowed to be heard, without fear of persecution.

Liam, Gadya, and I were appointed to a council of leaders, working to help oversee the reconstruction of several major cities, including New Chicago. My mom works for the government too, using her skills as a geneticist to try to help reverse what was done to the mutants. It turns out there were nearly a thousand of them. Many were hidden in labs in the Hellgrounds, awaiting battles that never came. We are trying to help them.

It took me a long time to get over what I did to David—and what he did to us. I had to learn to trust my instincts again. I hadn't recognized David for the sociopath that he was. I'd been distracted by his intelligence and all his plans and energy. I didn't see the truth until it was nearly too late.

The only thing David was right about was that the nuclear blasts did not completely destroy the planet. However, the blasts caused extensive damage to the upper atmosphere above the United States and also to the earth's ecosystems. Dr. Urbancic now works for the government too. He is trying to figure out ways to restore the atmosphere and minimize the damage.

The temperature seems to get warmer each month, and many species have been completely eradicated. Flooding has decimated certain regions of our continent.

Still, this is a much better fate than death and destruction at the hands of the UNA. Everyone is happy to have their freedom back. Some people don't even seem to remember what is was like to be free. They are rediscovering how it feels to not live under the yoke of the UNA.

Families are being reunited, people are finding their relatives, and all of the UNA's political prisoners have been released. Every single prison colony has been shut down. Other people are mourning the dead, and learning about the deaths of their own family members. There is both a collective sense of grieving and a sense of hope.

Trials for the UNA leaders and soldiers are still being held, even though all five of the ministers—the real leaders—are dead. Many former UNA employees tried to flee to other countries, but no one would give them asylum. They were sent back here to face justice. There are no death sentences, only life sentences in prisons. Everyone is tired of murder and butchery.

Some of the UNA leaders and soldiers are being sent to prison forever, to live out their days behind bars. But many of the UNA soldiers were given lesser terms, especially those who claimed that they'd been forced into their actions because the government had threatened their families. Everyone is eager to shake their memories of the past and put it behind them. It is a time of new beginnings.

There were some pro-UNA holdouts at first. Mostly former soldiers who attacked the citizens in the name of Minister Harka. But those attacks dissolved over time into sporadic acts of terrorism that ultimately faded away.

Still, there is a lingering sense of not knowing who to trust. People tend to be guarded with one another, at least when they first meet. Police sent over from the European Coalition make sure that people obey the laws. But these soldiers are fair and not like the nearly psychopathic UNA soldiers who once dragged me from my home as a little girl.

Liam and I continue on as a couple, working together each day and spending each night together. We made it through our odyssey together, and I love him more than ever. We plan to marry when I turn twenty-one. My mom has already given us her blessing. Gadya remains my best friend, and my closest confidante. I know how lucky I am to have both Liam and Gadya in my life.

I remain haunted by memories and bad dreams of everything that happened to us, but I know that with time, the bad dreams will fade. And if they don't, I am fine with that too. These traumas have become part of me and have made me who I am.

Sometimes at night I dream that I am back on the wheel. That I am in the village, sitting around the fire pit eating hoofer meat with Liam, Gadya, Rika, Markus, Sinxen, Veidman, Meira, and everyone else.

I don't mind dreams like these. The wheel is the place that forged me. I know that part of me will never really leave it. I know that Liam and Gadya feel the same way, although we rarely talk about it.

I usually just try to focus on the present. Even now, there is so much work to be done. It will probably take a decade before the nation is fully functional again. I imagine that I will spend my life working to make—and keep—our country free and safe. But I'm not sure what my own future holds beyond that. The possibilities are so different and huge compared to what I imagined only a few years ago, on the day when I took the GPPT.

I am in love, I have a best friend, I have my mother back, and